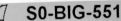

AWA UPSHOT

PRESENTS

E-RATIC

KAARE ANDREWS
Writer, Artist and Cover Artist

BRIAN REBER
Colorist

SAL CIPRIANO
Letterer

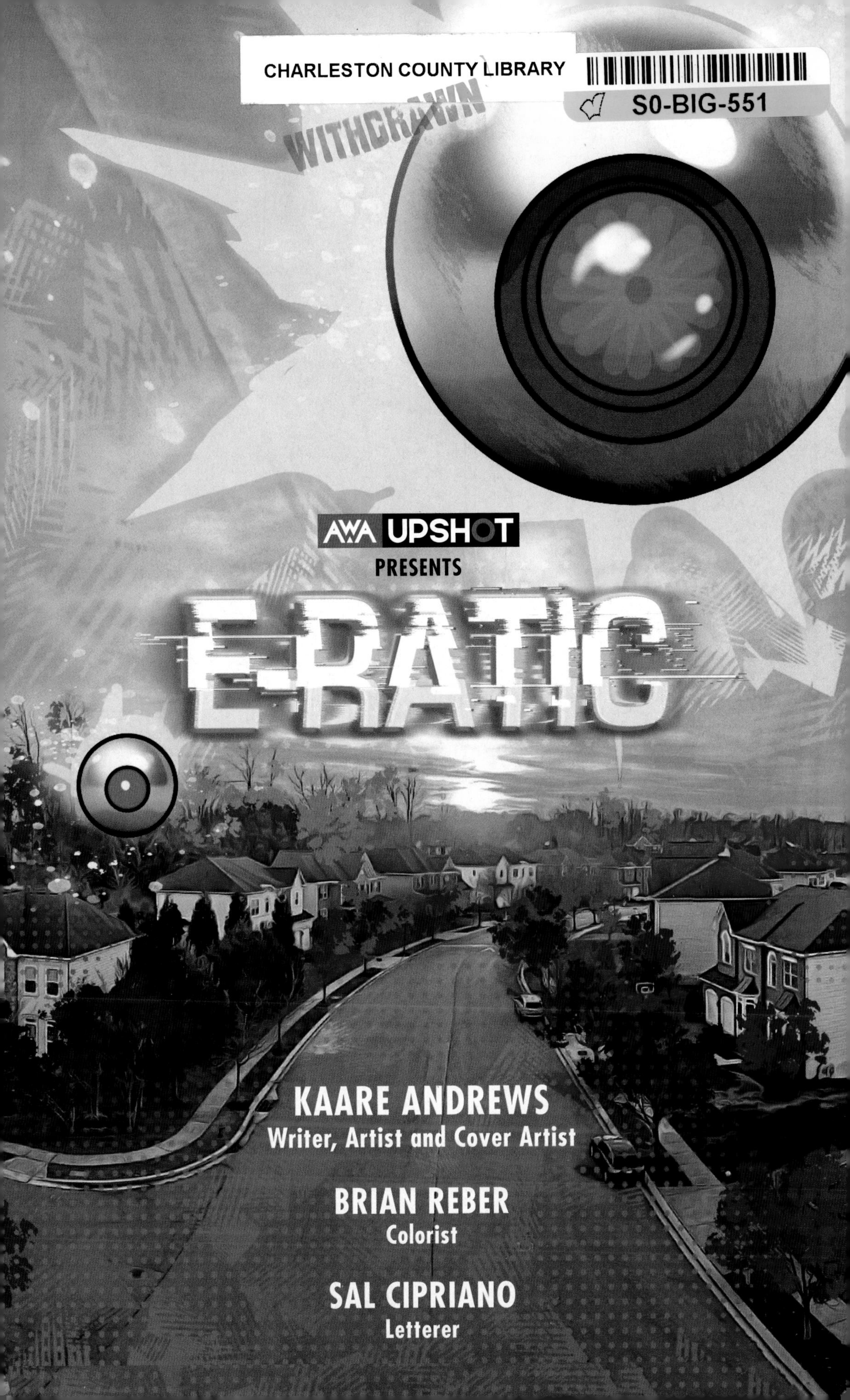

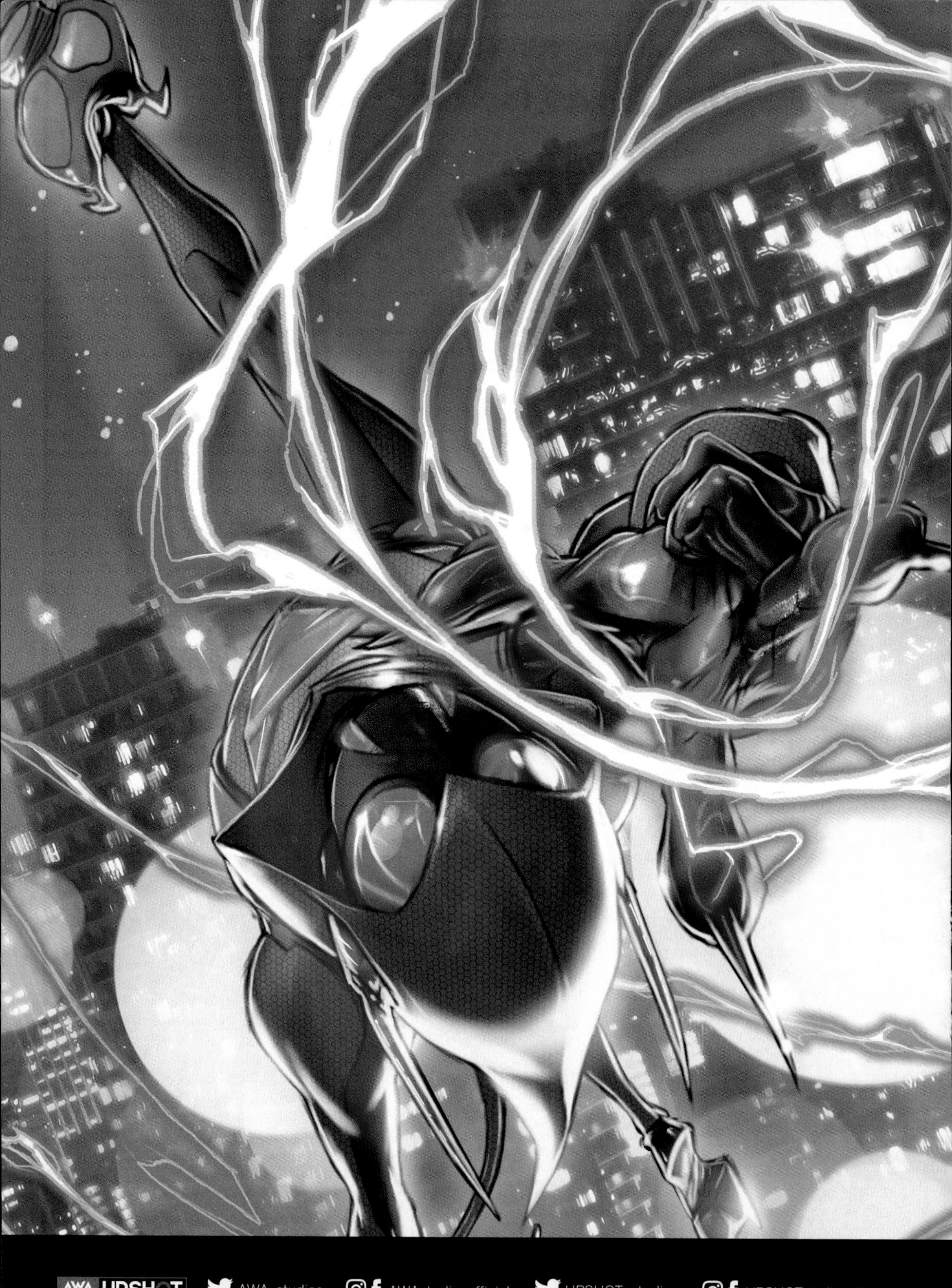

AWA UPSHOT AWA_studios AWAstudiosofficial UPSHOT_studios UPSHOTstudiosofficial

Axel Alonso Chief Creative Officer
Ariane Baya Accounting Associate
Chris Burns Production Editor
Thea Cheuk Assistant Editor
Stan Chou Art Director & Logo Designer
Michael Coast Senior Editor
Frank Fochetta Senior Consultant, Sales & Distribution
William Graves Managing Editor
Bill Jemas CEO & Publisher
Jackie Liu Digital Marketing Manager
Bosung Kim Graphic Designer
Allison Mase Project Manager
Dulce Montoya Associate Editor
Kevin Park Associate General Counsel
Harry Sweezey Finance Associate
Lisa Y. Wu Marketing Manager

E-RATIC VOL.1. June 2021. Published by Artists Writers & Artisans, Inc. Office of publication: 178 Columbus Avenue #237194 New York, NY 10023. **Printed in Canada.**

10 9 8 7 6 5 4 3 2 1

WHAT IF YOU HAD THE POWER TO DO THINGS NO ONE ELSE COULD?

WHAT IF THAT ULTIMATE POWER CAME WITH LIMITS?

WHAT IF YOU WERE FIFTEEN YEARS OLD AND HAD TEN MINUTES TO SAVE THE WORLD?

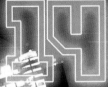

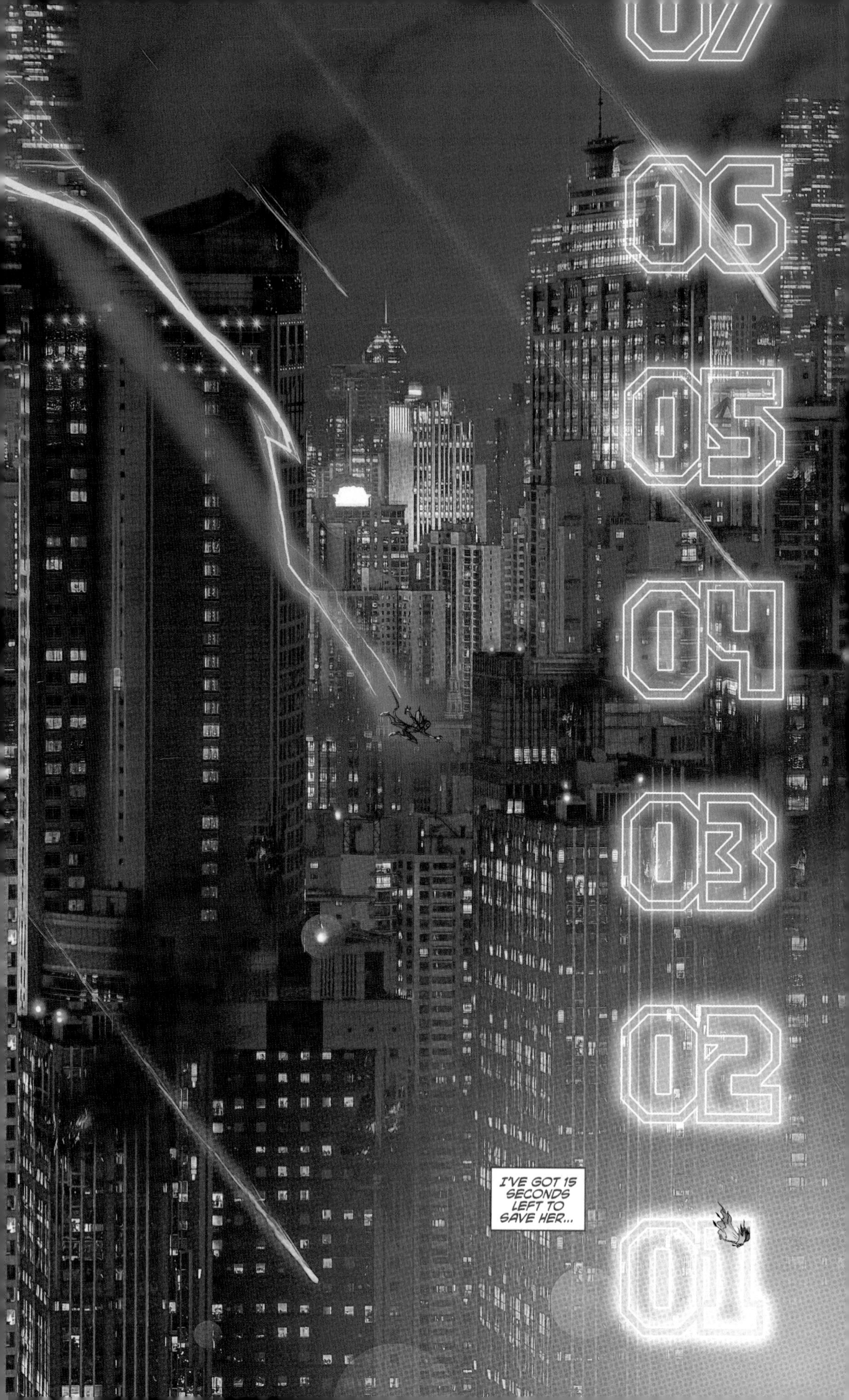
07
06
05
04
03
02
I'VE GOT 15 SECONDS LEFT TO SAVE HER...
01

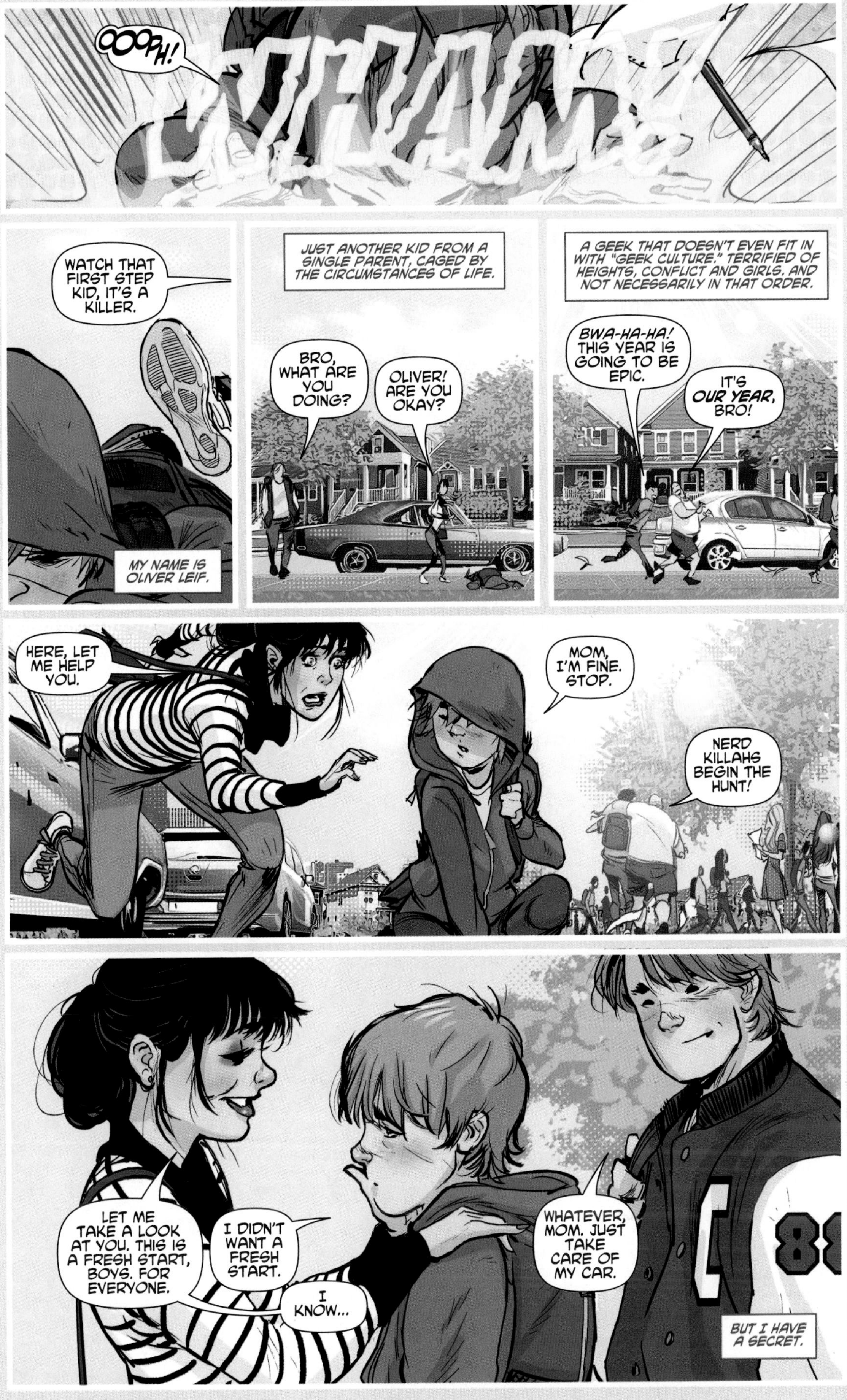
OOOPH!
WATCH THAT FIRST STEP KID, IT'S A KILLER.
MY NAME IS OLIVER LEIF.
JUST ANOTHER KID FROM A SINGLE PARENT, CAGED BY THE CIRCUMSTANCES OF LIFE.
BRO, WHAT ARE YOU DOING?
OLIVER! ARE YOU OKAY?
A GEEK THAT DOESN'T EVEN FIT IN WITH "GEEK CULTURE." TERRIFIED OF HEIGHTS, CONFLICT AND GIRLS. AND NOT NECESSARILY IN THAT ORDER.
BWA-HA-HA! THIS YEAR IS GOING TO BE EPIC.
IT'S OUR YEAR, BRO!
HERE, LET ME HELP YOU.
MOM, I'M FINE. STOP.
NERD KILLAHS BEGIN THE HUNT!
LET ME TAKE A LOOK AT YOU. THIS IS A FRESH START, BOYS. FOR EVERYONE.
I DIDN'T WANT A FRESH START.
I KNOW...
WHATEVER, MOM. JUST TAKE CARE OF MY CAR.
BUT I HAVE A SECRET.

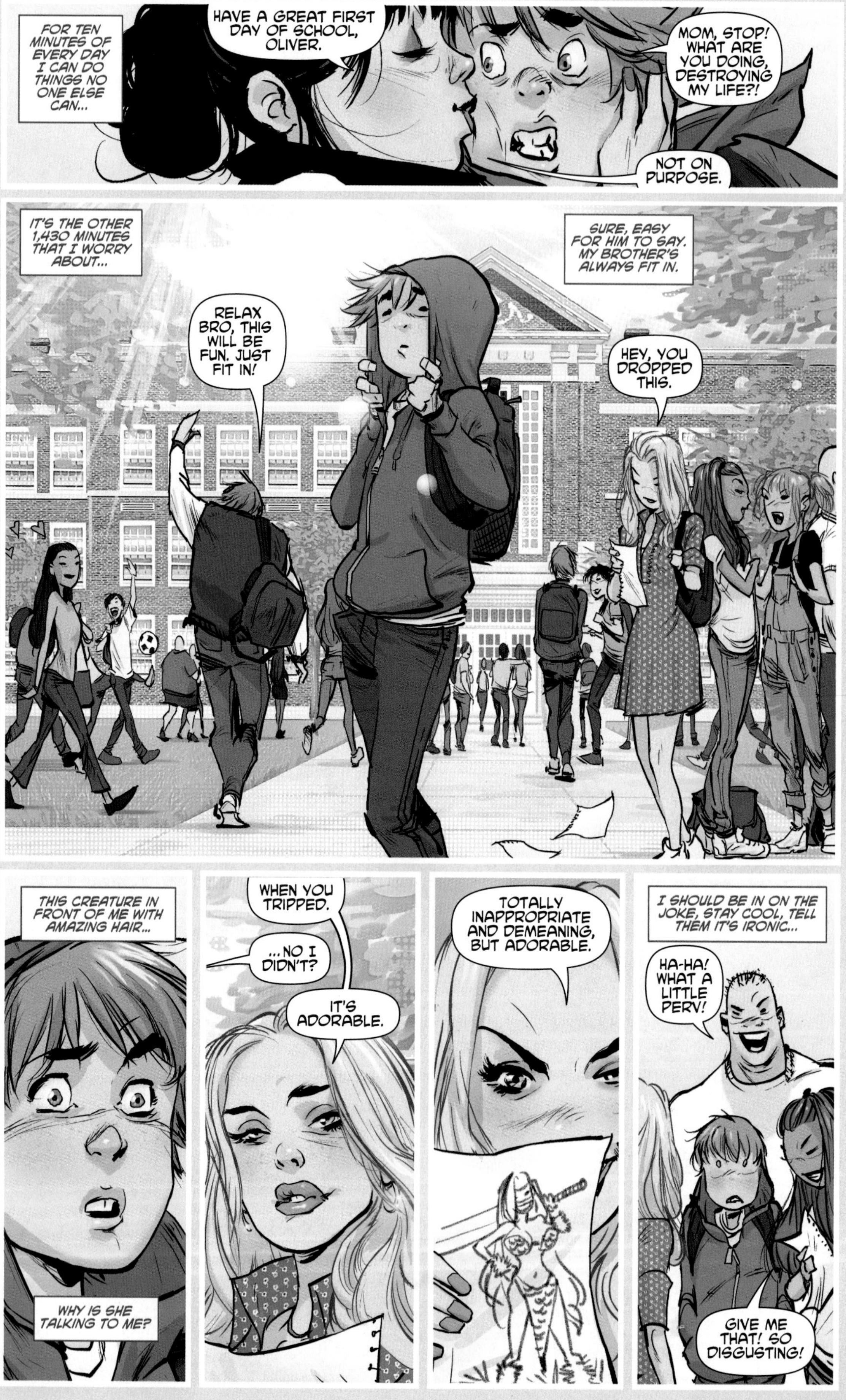
FOR TEN MINUTES OF EVERY DAY I CAN DO THINGS NO ONE ELSE CAN...
HAVE A GREAT FIRST DAY OF SCHOOL, OLIVER.
MOM, STOP! WHAT ARE YOU DOING, DESTROYING MY LIFE?!
NOT ON PURPOSE.
IT'S THE OTHER 1,430 MINUTES THAT I WORRY ABOUT...
SURE, EASY FOR HIM TO SAY. MY BROTHER'S ALWAYS FIT IN.
RELAX BRO, THIS WILL BE FUN. JUST FIT IN!
HEY, YOU DROPPED THIS.
THIS CREATURE IN FRONT OF ME WITH AMAZING HAIR...
WHY IS SHE TALKING TO ME?
WHEN YOU TRIPPED.
...NO I DIDN'T?
IT'S ADORABLE.
TOTALLY INAPPROPRIATE AND DEMEANING, BUT ADORABLE.
I SHOULD BE IN ON THE JOKE, STAY COOL, TELL THEM IT'S IRONIC...
HA-HA! WHAT A LITTLE PERV!
GIVE ME THAT! SO DISGUSTING!

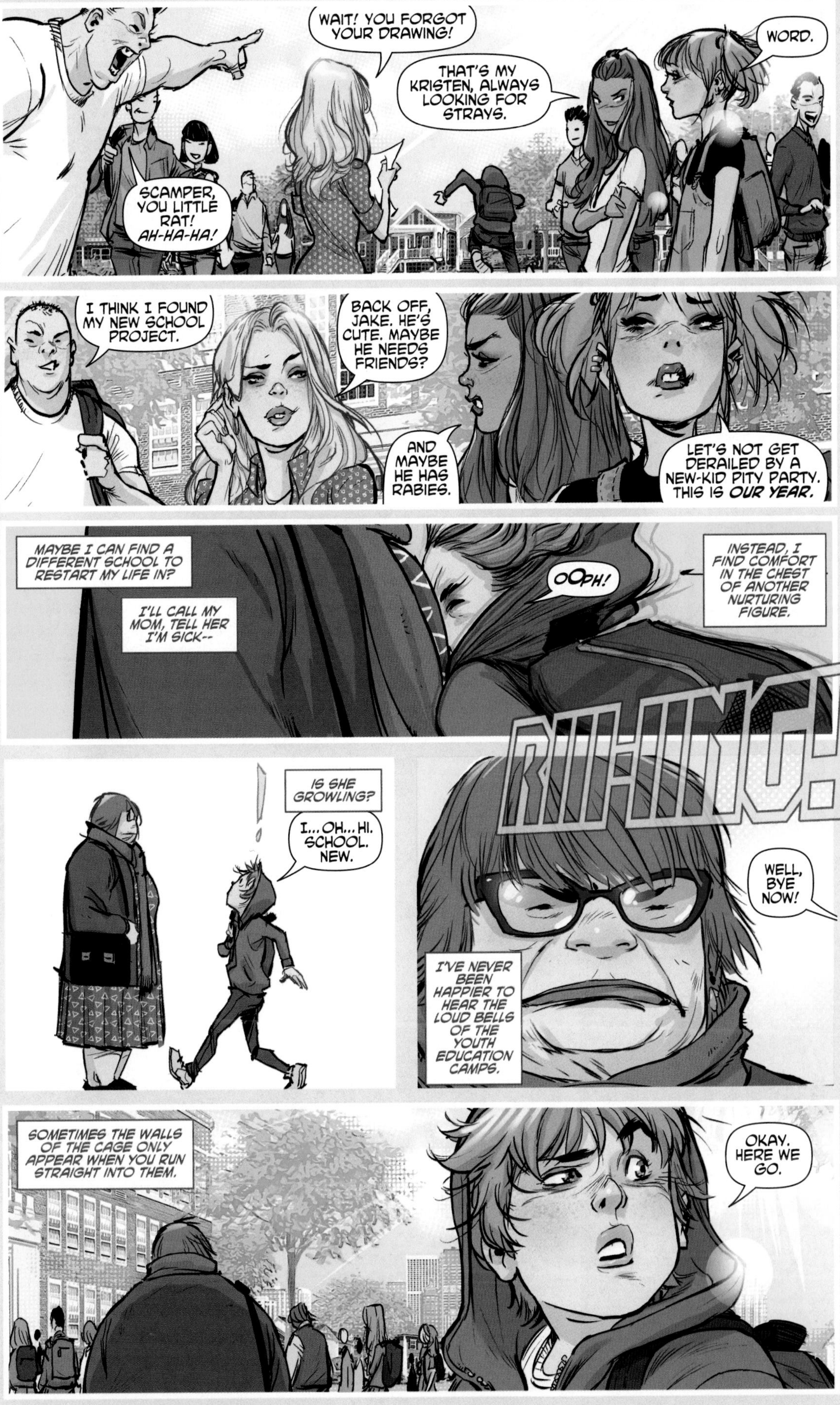
WAIT! YOU FORGOT YOUR DRAWING!
THAT'S MY KRISTEN, ALWAYS LOOKING FOR STRAYS.
WORD.
SCAMPER, YOU LITTLE RAT! AH-HA-HA!
I THINK I FOUND MY NEW SCHOOL PROJECT.
BACK OFF, JAKE. HE'S CUTE. MAYBE HE NEEDS FRIENDS?
AND MAYBE HE HAS RABIES.
LET'S NOT GET DERAILED BY A NEW-KID PITY PARTY. THIS IS OUR YEAR.
MAYBE I CAN FIND A DIFFERENT SCHOOL TO RESTART MY LIFE IN?
I'LL CALL MY MOM, TELL HER I'M SICK--
OOPH!
INSTEAD, I FIND COMFORT IN THE CHEST OF ANOTHER NURTURING FIGURE.
RIIIIING!!
!
IS SHE GROWLING?
I...OH...HI. SCHOOL. NEW.
WELL, BYE NOW!
I'VE NEVER BEEN HAPPIER TO HEAR THE LOUD BELLS OF THE YOUTH EDUCATION CAMPS.
SOMETIMES THE WALLS OF THE CAGE ONLY APPEAR WHEN YOU RUN STRAIGHT INTO THEM.
OKAY. HERE WE GO.

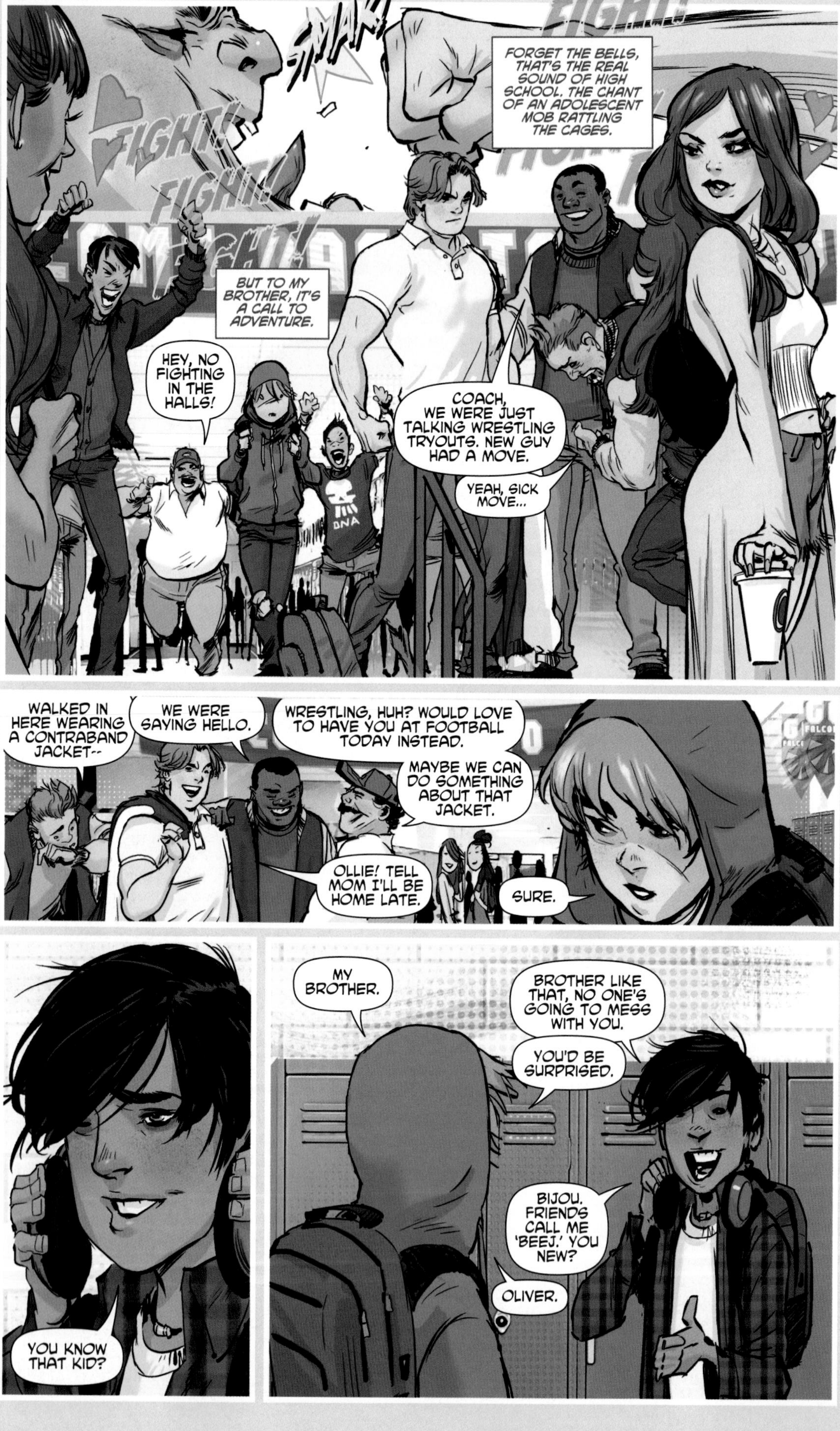
-SMAK!
FIGHT!
FORGET THE BELLS, THAT'S THE REAL SOUND OF HIGH SCHOOL. THE CHANT OF AN ADOLESCENT MOB RATTLING THE CAGES.
FIGHT!
FIGHT!
FIGHT!
BUT TO MY BROTHER, IT'S A CALL TO ADVENTURE.
HEY, NO FIGHTING IN THE HALLS!
COACH, WE WERE JUST TALKING WRESTLING TRYOUTS. NEW GUY HAD A MOVE.
YEAH, SICK MOVE...
WALKED IN HERE WEARING A CONTRABAND JACKET--
WE WERE SAYING HELLO.
WRESTLING, HUH? WOULD LOVE TO HAVE YOU AT FOOTBALL TODAY INSTEAD.
MAYBE WE CAN DO SOMETHING ABOUT THAT JACKET.
OLLIE! TELL MOM I'LL BE HOME LATE.
SURE.
YOU KNOW THAT KID?
MY BROTHER.
BROTHER LIKE THAT, NO ONE'S GOING TO MESS WITH YOU.
YOU'D BE SURPRISED.
BIJOU. FRIENDS CALL ME 'BEEJ.' YOU NEW?
OLIVER.

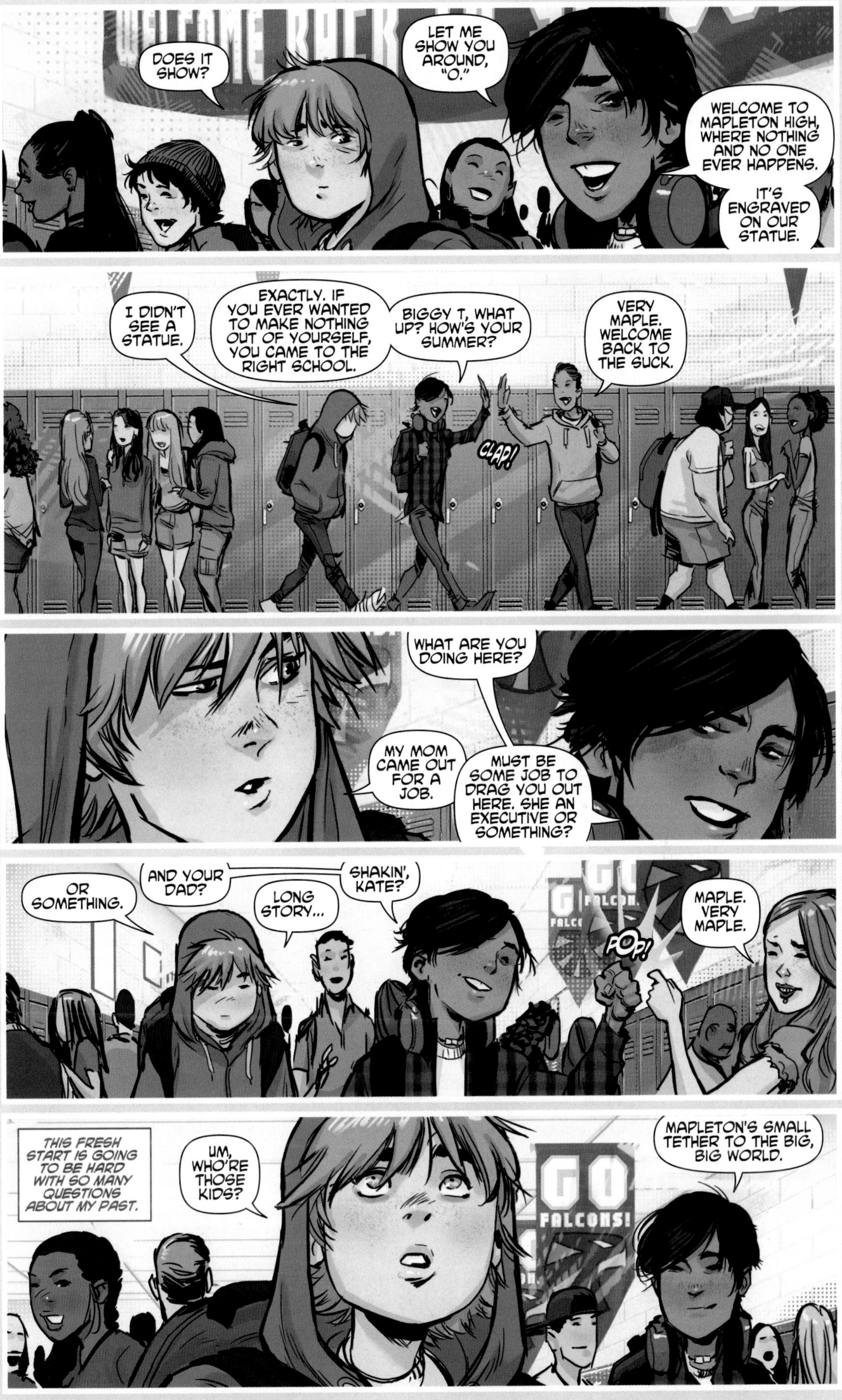
DOES IT SHOW?
LET ME SHOW YOU AROUND, "O."
WELCOME TO MAPLETON HIGH, WHERE NOTHING AND NO ONE EVER HAPPENS.
IT'S ENGRAVED ON OUR STATUE.
I DIDN'T SEE A STATUE.
EXACTLY. IF YOU EVER WANTED TO MAKE NOTHING OUT OF YOURSELF, YOU CAME TO THE RIGHT SCHOOL.
BIGGY T, WHAT UP? HOW'S YOUR SUMMER?
VERY MAPLE. WELCOME BACK TO THE SUCK.
CLAP!
WHAT ARE YOU DOING HERE?
MY MOM CAME OUT FOR A JOB.
MUST BE SOME JOB TO DRAG YOU OUT HERE. SHE AN EXECUTIVE OR SOMETHING?
OR SOMETHING.
AND YOUR DAD?
LONG STORY...
SHAKIN', KATE?
MAPLE. VERY MAPLE.
POP!
GO FALCONS!
THIS FRESH START IS GOING TO BE HARD WITH SO MANY QUESTIONS ABOUT MY PAST.
UM, WHO'RE THOSE KIDS?
MAPLETON'S SMALL TETHER TO THE BIG, BIG WORLD.
GO FALCONS!

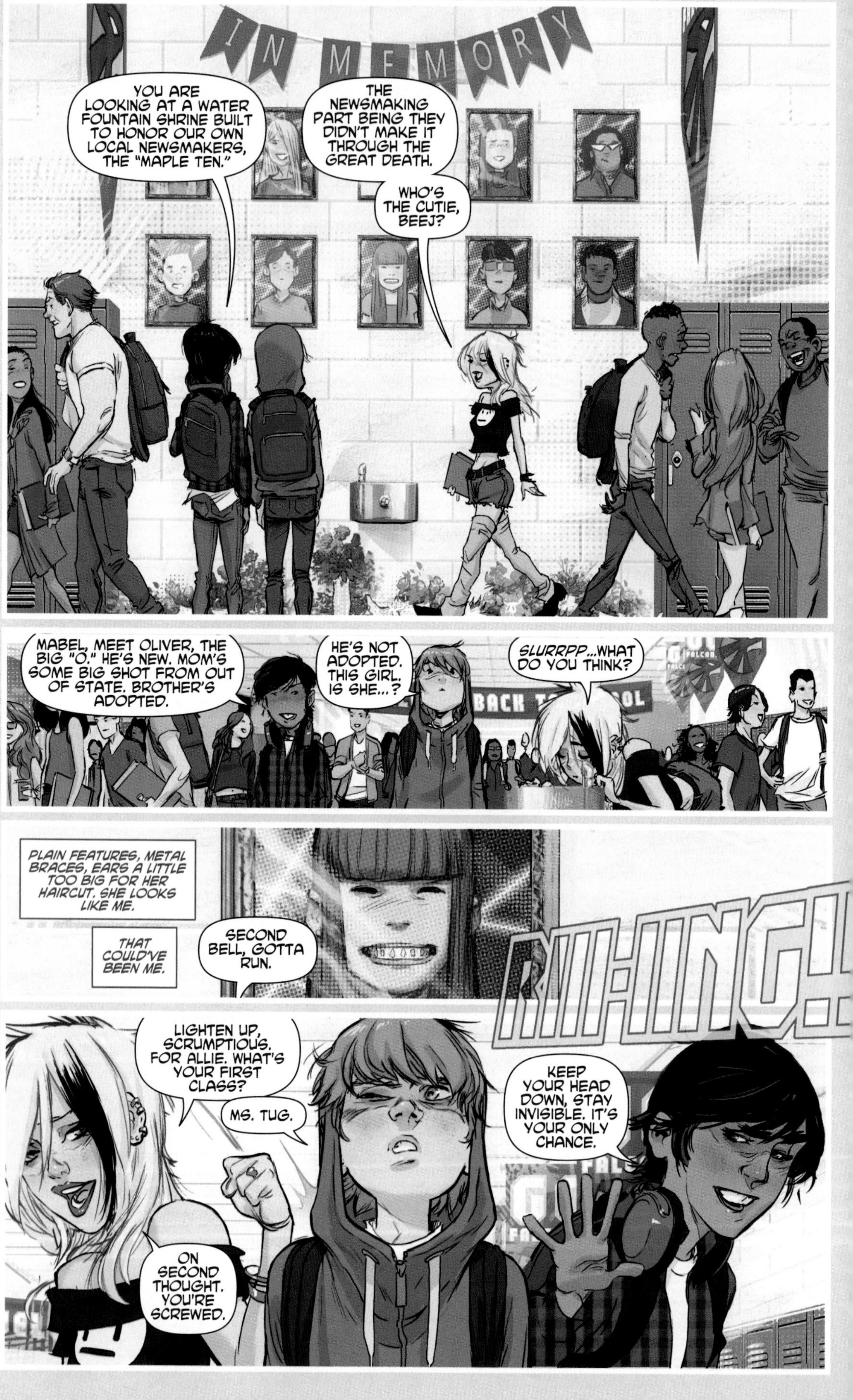
IN MEMORY
YOU ARE LOOKING AT A WATER FOUNTAIN SHRINE BUILT TO HONOR OUR OWN LOCAL NEWSMAKERS, THE "MAPLE TEN."
THE NEWSMAKING PART BEING THEY DIDN'T MAKE IT THROUGH THE GREAT DEATH.
WHO'S THE CUTIE, BEEJ?
MABEL, MEET OLIVER, THE BIG "O." HE'S NEW. MOM'S SOME BIG SHOT FROM OUT OF STATE. BROTHER'S ADOPTED.
HE'S NOT ADOPTED. THIS GIRL. IS SHE...?
SLURRPP...WHAT DO YOU THINK?
PLAIN FEATURES, METAL BRACES, EARS A LITTLE TOO BIG FOR HER HAIRCUT. SHE LOOKS LIKE ME.
THAT COULD'VE BEEN ME.
SECOND BELL, GOTTA RUN.
RRRIIING!!
LIGHTEN UP, SCRUMPTIOUS. FOR ALLIE. WHAT'S YOUR FIRST CLASS?
MS. TUG.
KEEP YOUR HEAD DOWN, STAY INVISIBLE. IT'S YOUR ONLY CHANCE.
ON SECOND THOUGHT. YOU'RE SCREWED.

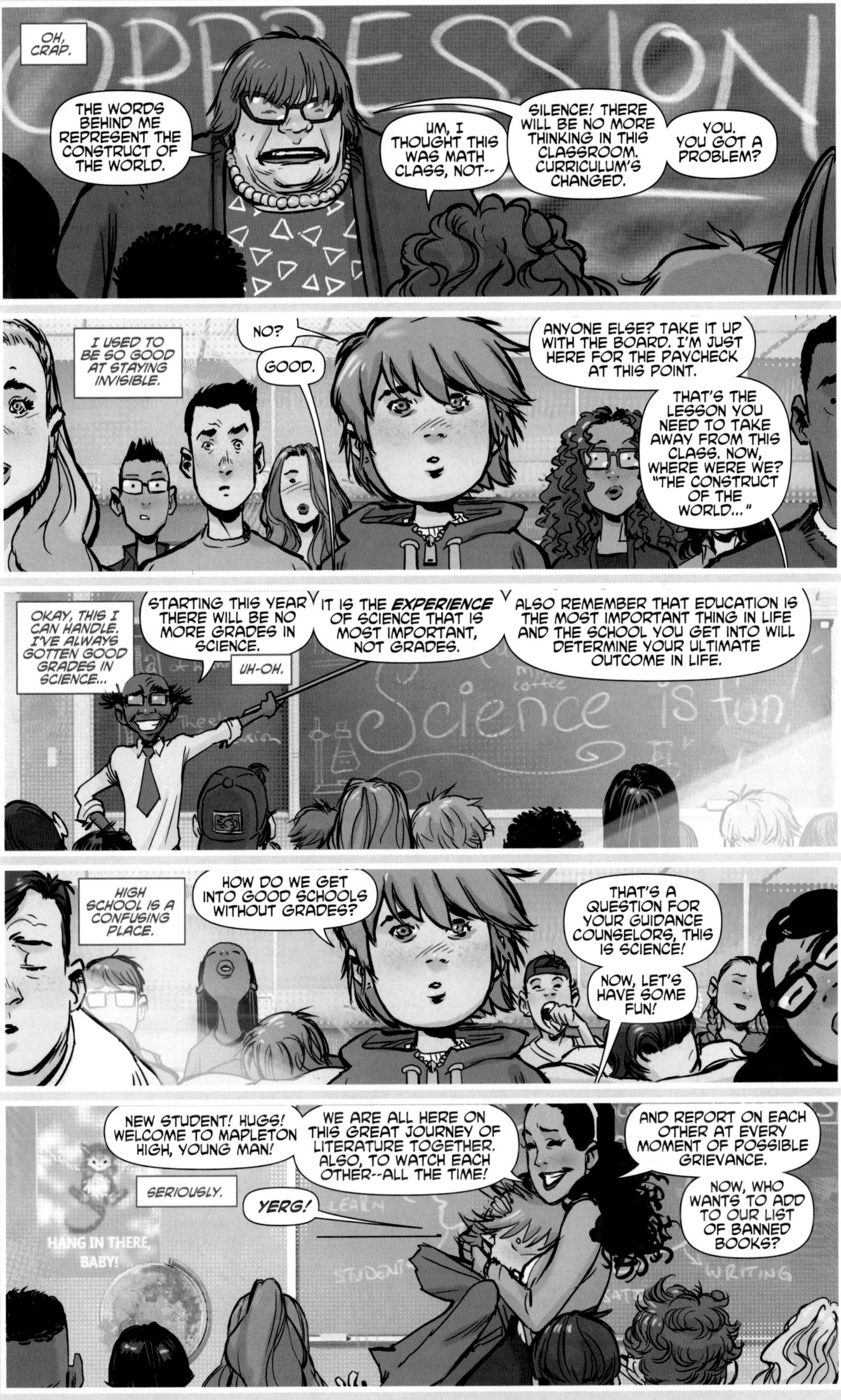
OH, CRAP.
THE WORDS BEHIND ME REPRESENT THE CONSTRUCT OF THE WORLD.
UM, I THOUGHT THIS WAS MATH CLASS, NOT--
SILENCE! THERE WILL BE NO MORE THINKING IN THIS CLASSROOM. CURRICULUM'S CHANGED.
YOU. YOU GOT A PROBLEM?
I USED TO BE SO GOOD AT STAYING INVISIBLE.
NO?
GOOD.
ANYONE ELSE? TAKE IT UP WITH THE BOARD. I'M JUST HERE FOR THE PAYCHECK AT THIS POINT.
THAT'S THE LESSON YOU NEED TO TAKE AWAY FROM THIS CLASS. NOW, WHERE WERE WE? "THE CONSTRUCT OF THE WORLD..."
OKAY, THIS I CAN HANDLE. I'VE ALWAYS GOTTEN GOOD GRADES IN SCIENCE...
STARTING THIS YEAR THERE WILL BE NO MORE GRADES IN SCIENCE.
UH-OH.
IT IS THE *EXPERIENCE* OF SCIENCE THAT IS MOST IMPORTANT, NOT GRADES.
ALSO REMEMBER THAT EDUCATION IS THE MOST IMPORTANT THING IN LIFE AND THE SCHOOL YOU GET INTO WILL DETERMINE YOUR ULTIMATE OUTCOME IN LIFE.
Science is fun!
HIGH SCHOOL IS A CONFUSING PLACE.
HOW DO WE GET INTO GOOD SCHOOLS WITHOUT GRADES?
THAT'S A QUESTION FOR YOUR GUIDANCE COUNSELORS, THIS IS SCIENCE!
NOW, LET'S HAVE SOME FUN!
NEW STUDENT! HUGS! WELCOME TO MAPLETON HIGH, YOUNG MAN!
SERIOUSLY.
WE ARE ALL HERE ON THIS GREAT JOURNEY OF LITERATURE TOGETHER. ALSO, TO WATCH EACH OTHER--ALL THE TIME!
YERG!
AND REPORT ON EACH OTHER AT EVERY MOMENT OF POSSIBLE GRIEVANCE.
NOW, WHO WANTS TO ADD TO OUR LIST OF BANNED BOOKS?
HANG IN THERE, BABY!

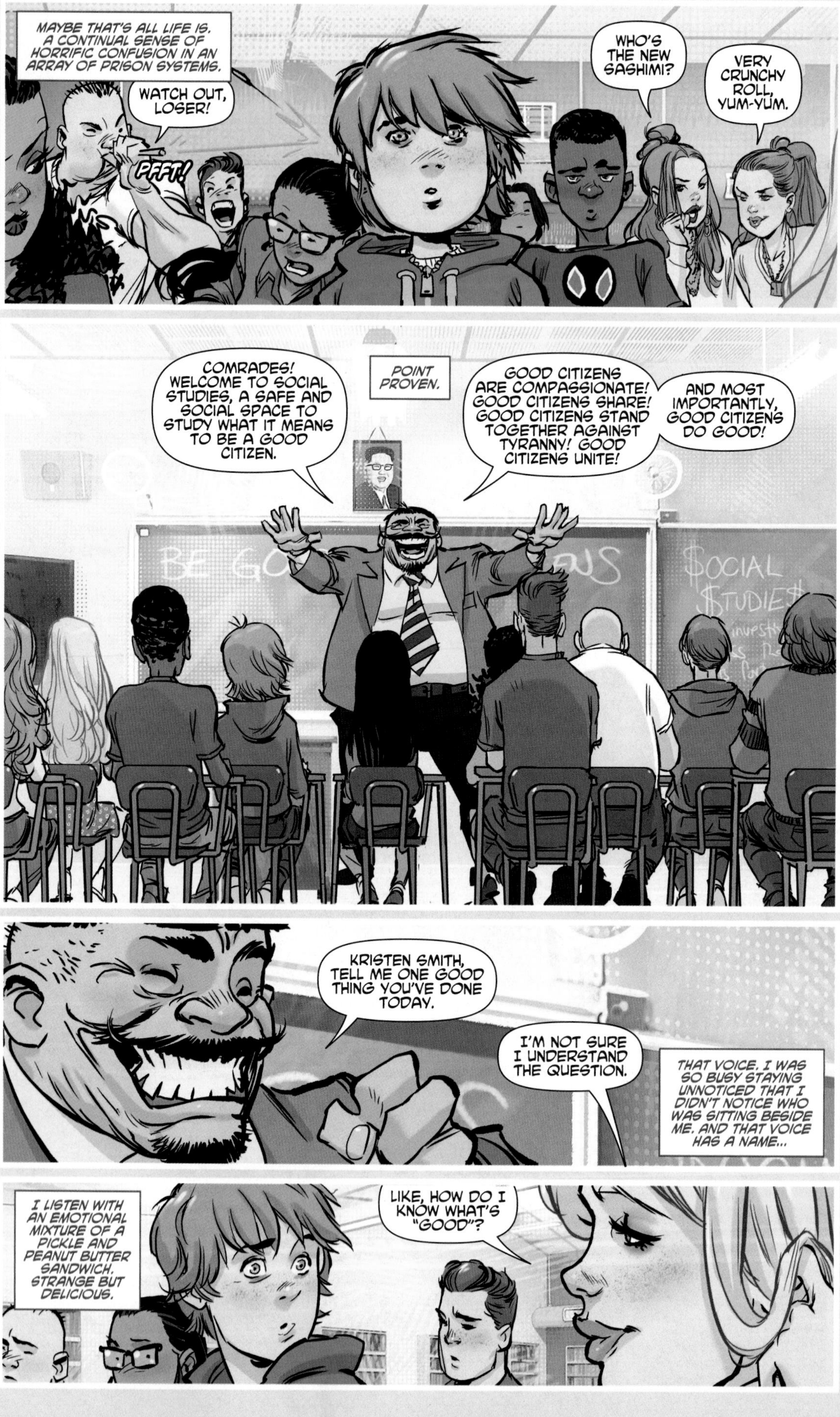
MAYBE THAT'S ALL LIFE IS. A CONTINUAL SENSE OF HORRIFIC CONFUSION IN AN ARRAY OF PRISON SYSTEMS.
WATCH OUT, LOSER!
PFFFT!
WHO'S THE NEW SASHIMI?
VERY CRUNCHY ROLL, YUM-YUM.
COMRADES! WELCOME TO SOCIAL STUDIES, A SAFE AND SOCIAL SPACE TO STUDY WHAT IT MEANS TO BE A GOOD CITIZEN.
POINT PROVEN.
GOOD CITIZENS ARE COMPASSIONATE! GOOD CITIZENS SHARE! GOOD CITIZENS STAND TOGETHER AGAINST TYRANNY! GOOD CITIZENS UNITE!
AND MOST IMPORTANTLY, GOOD CITIZENS DO GOOD!
SOCIAL STUDIES
KRISTEN SMITH, TELL ME ONE GOOD THING YOU'VE DONE TODAY.
I'M NOT SURE I UNDERSTAND THE QUESTION.
THAT VOICE. I WAS SO BUSY STAYING UNNOTICED THAT I DIDN'T NOTICE WHO WAS SITTING BESIDE ME. AND THAT VOICE HAS A NAME...
I LISTEN WITH AN EMOTIONAL MIXTURE OF A PICKLE AND PEANUT BUTTER SANDWICH. STRANGE BUT DELICIOUS.
LIKE, HOW DO I KNOW WHAT'S "GOOD"?

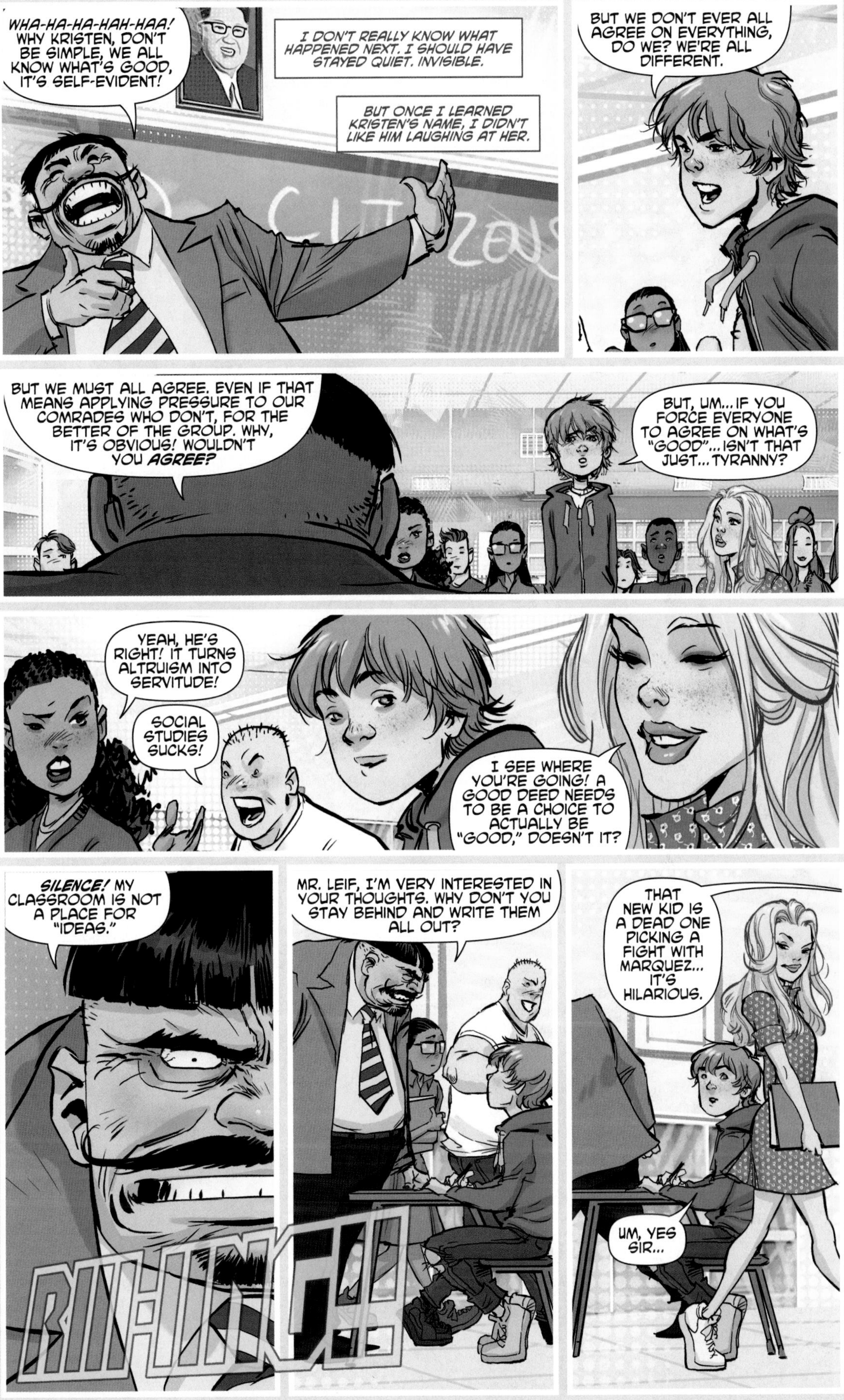
WHA-HA-HA-HAH-HAA! WHY KRISTEN, DON'T BE SIMPLE, WE ALL KNOW WHAT'S GOOD, IT'S SELF-EVIDENT!
I DON'T REALLY KNOW WHAT HAPPENED NEXT. I SHOULD HAVE STAYED QUIET. INVISIBLE.
BUT ONCE I LEARNED KRISTEN'S NAME, I DIDN'T LIKE HIM LAUGHING AT HER.
BUT WE DON'T EVER ALL AGREE ON EVERYTHING, DO WE? WE'RE ALL DIFFERENT.
BUT WE MUST ALL AGREE. EVEN IF THAT MEANS APPLYING PRESSURE TO OUR COMRADES WHO DON'T, FOR THE BETTER OF THE GROUP. WHY, IT'S OBVIOUS! WOULDN'T YOU AGREE?
BUT, UM... IF YOU FORCE EVERYONE TO AGREE ON WHAT'S "GOOD"... ISN'T THAT JUST... TYRANNY?
YEAH, HE'S RIGHT! IT TURNS ALTRUISM INTO SERVITUDE!
SOCIAL STUDIES SUCKS!
I SEE WHERE YOU'RE GOING! A GOOD DEED NEEDS TO BE A CHOICE TO ACTUALLY BE "GOOD," DOESN'T IT?
SILENCE! MY CLASSROOM IS NOT A PLACE FOR "IDEAS."
RIIIIING!!
MR. LEIF, I'M VERY INTERESTED IN YOUR THOUGHTS. WHY DON'T YOU STAY BEHIND AND WRITE THEM ALL OUT?
THAT NEW KID IS A DEAD ONE PICKING A FIGHT WITH MARQUEZ... IT'S HILARIOUS.
UM, YES SIR...

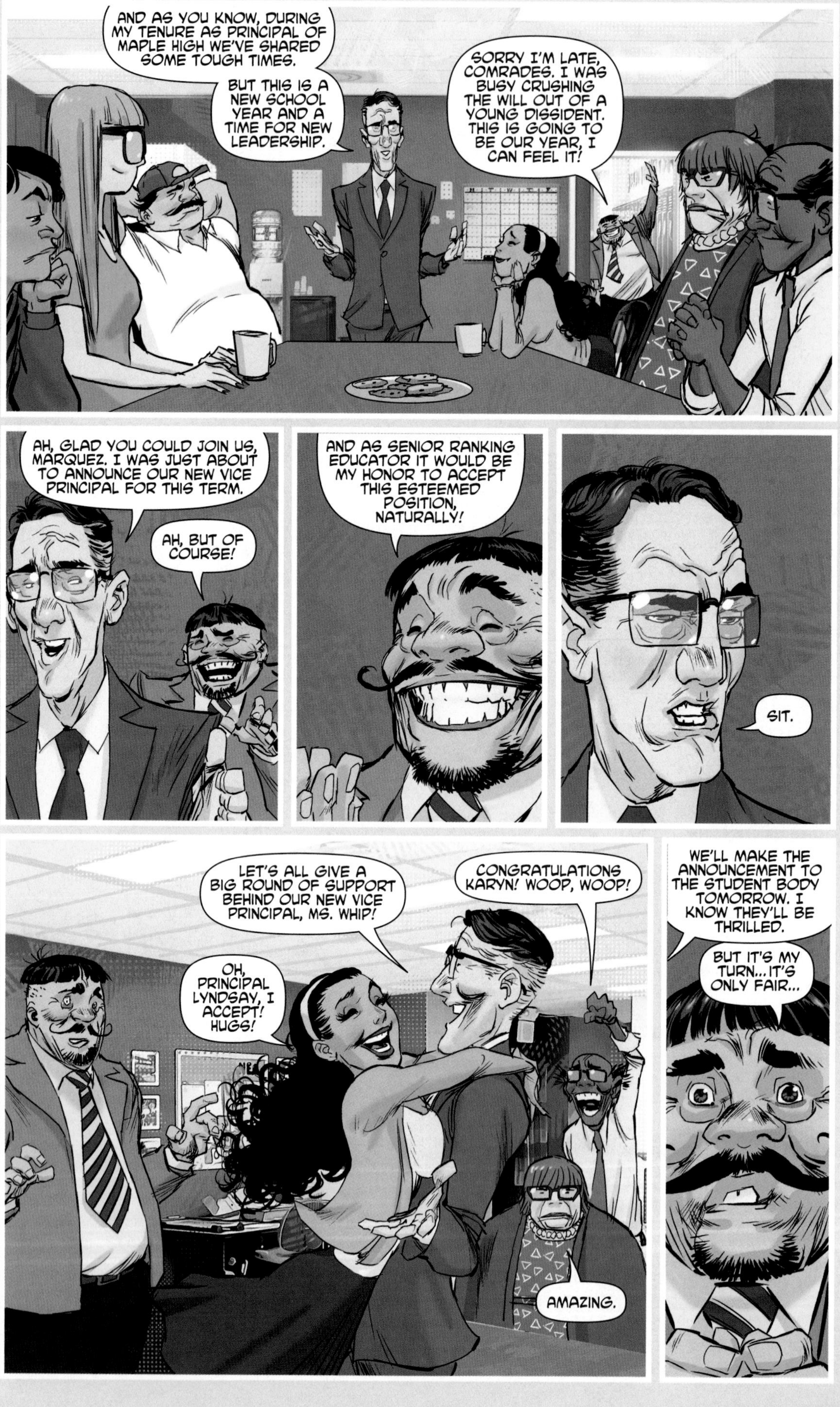
AND AS YOU KNOW, DURING MY TENURE AS PRINCIPAL OF MAPLE HIGH WE'VE SHARED SOME TOUGH TIMES.
BUT THIS IS A NEW SCHOOL YEAR AND A TIME FOR NEW LEADERSHIP.
SORRY I'M LATE, COMRADES. I WAS BUSY CRUSHING THE WILL OUT OF A YOUNG DISSIDENT. THIS IS GOING TO BE OUR YEAR, I CAN FEEL IT!
AH, GLAD YOU COULD JOIN US, MARQUEZ. I WAS JUST ABOUT TO ANNOUNCE OUR NEW VICE PRINCIPAL FOR THIS TERM.
AH, BUT OF COURSE!
AND AS SENIOR RANKING EDUCATOR IT WOULD BE MY HONOR TO ACCEPT THIS ESTEEMED POSITION, NATURALLY!
SIT.
LET'S ALL GIVE A BIG ROUND OF SUPPORT BEHIND OUR NEW VICE PRINCIPAL, MS. WHIP!
CONGRATULATIONS KARYN! WOOP, WOOP!
OH, PRINCIPAL LYNDSAY, I ACCEPT! HUGS!
AMAZING.
WE'LL MAKE THE ANNOUNCEMENT TO THE STUDENT BODY TOMORROW. I KNOW THEY'LL BE THRILLED.
BUT IT'S MY TURN...IT'S ONLY FAIR...

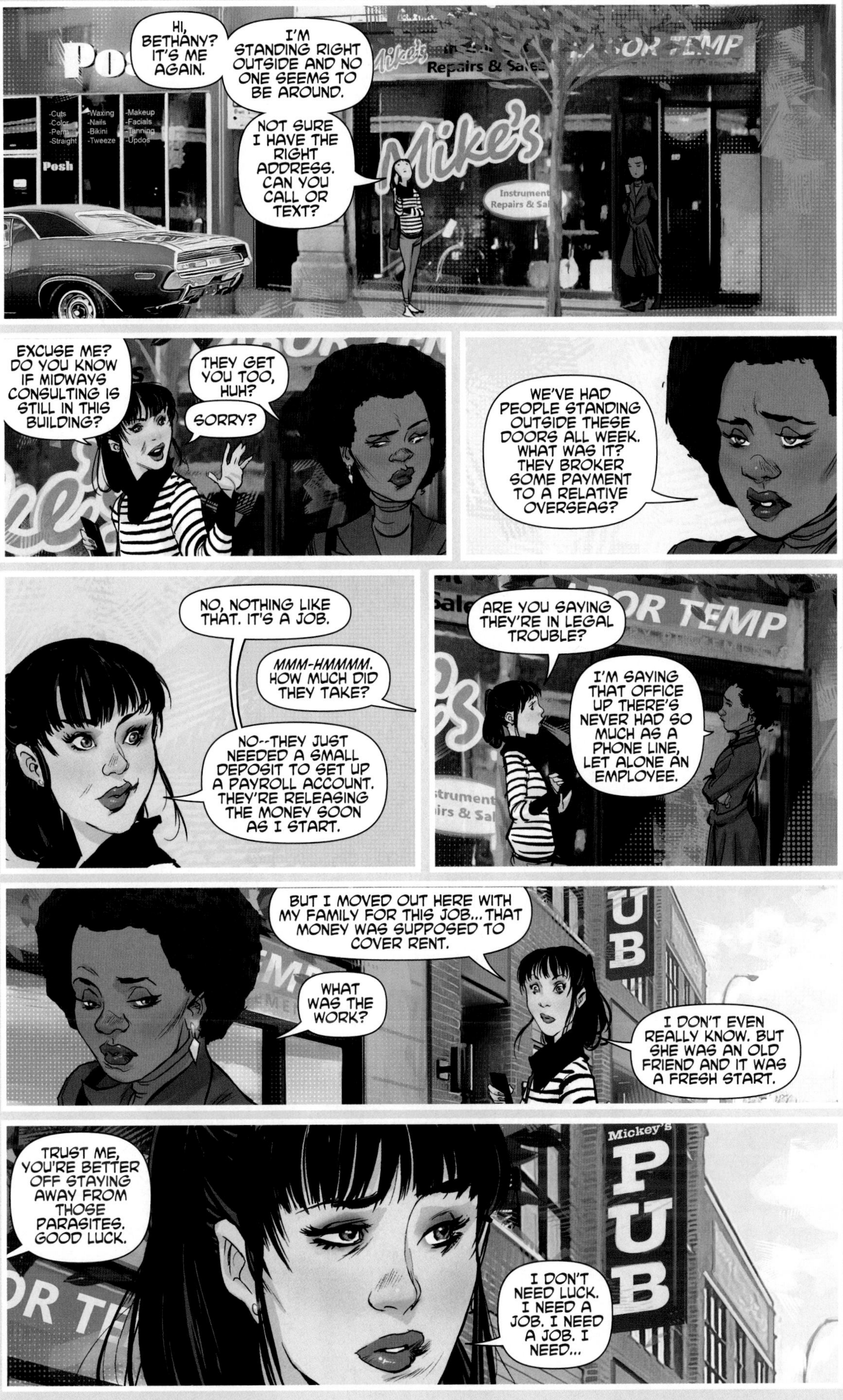
HI, BETHANY? IT'S ME AGAIN.
I'M STANDING RIGHT OUTSIDE AND NO ONE SEEMS TO BE AROUND.
NOT SURE I HAVE THE RIGHT ADDRESS. CAN YOU CALL OR TEXT?
Posh
-Cuts -Color -Perm -Straight
-Waxing -Nails -Bikini -Tweeze
-Makeup -Facials -Tanning -Updos
Mike's
Repairs & Sales
EXCUSE ME? DO YOU KNOW IF MIDWAYS CONSULTING IS STILL IN THIS BUILDING?
THEY GET YOU TOO, HUH?
SORRY?
WE'VE HAD PEOPLE STANDING OUTSIDE THESE DOORS ALL WEEK. WHAT WAS IT? THEY BROKER SOME PAYMENT TO A RELATIVE OVERSEAS?
NO, NOTHING LIKE THAT. IT'S A JOB.
MMM-HMMMM. HOW MUCH DID THEY TAKE?
NO--THEY JUST NEEDED A SMALL DEPOSIT TO SET UP A PAYROLL ACCOUNT. THEY'RE RELEASING THE MONEY SOON AS I START.
ARE YOU SAYING THEY'RE IN LEGAL TROUBLE?
I'M SAYING THAT OFFICE UP THERE'S NEVER HAD SO MUCH AS A PHONE LINE, LET ALONE AN EMPLOYEE.
BUT I MOVED OUT HERE WITH MY FAMILY FOR THIS JOB... THAT MONEY WAS SUPPOSED TO COVER RENT.
WHAT WAS THE WORK?
I DON'T EVEN REALLY KNOW. BUT SHE WAS AN OLD FRIEND AND IT WAS A FRESH START.
TRUST ME, YOU'RE BETTER OFF STAYING AWAY FROM THOSE PARASITES. GOOD LUCK.
Mickey's PUB
I DON'T NEED LUCK. I NEED A JOB. I NEED A JOB. I NEED...

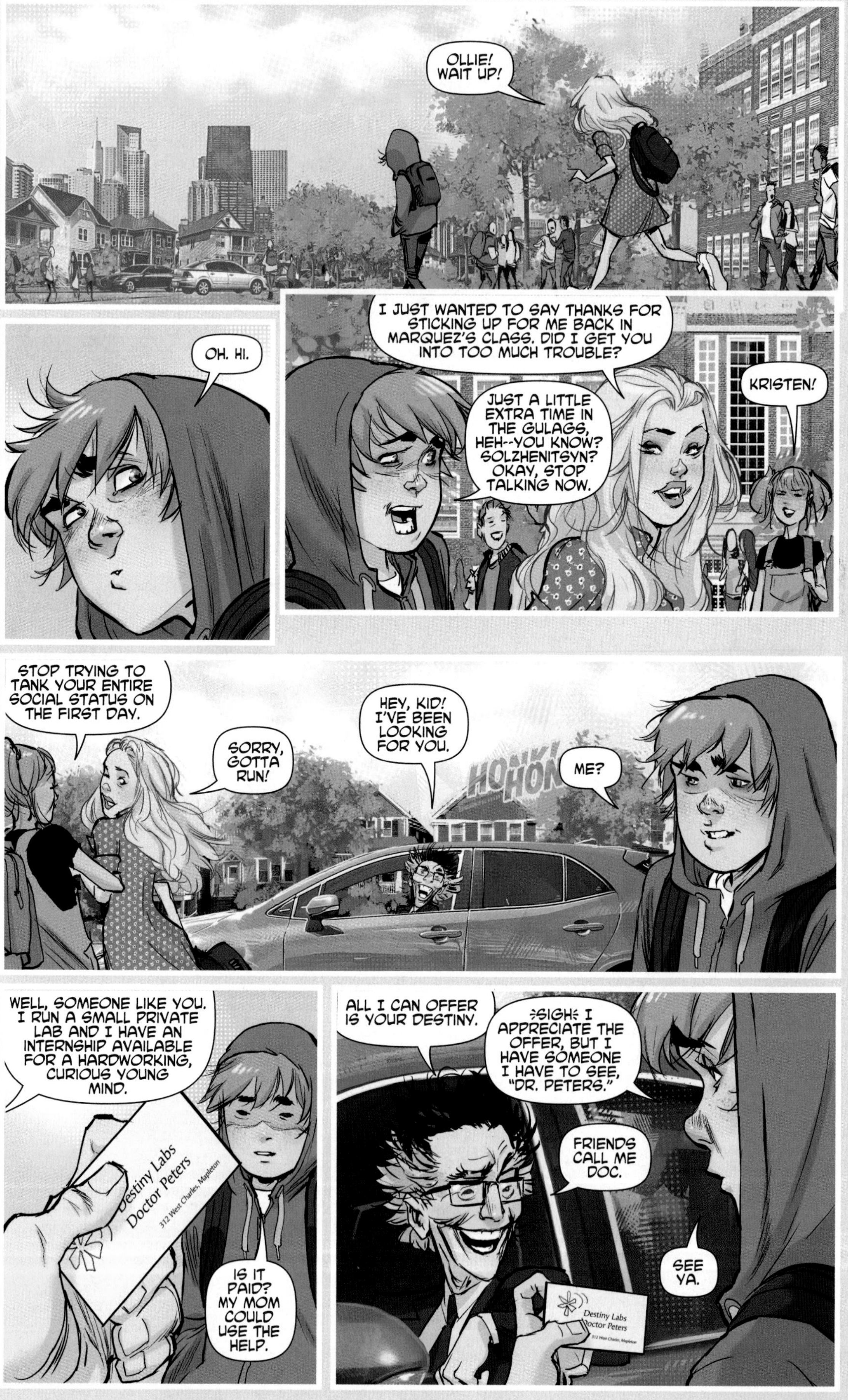
OLLIE! WAIT UP!
OH. HI.
I JUST WANTED TO SAY THANKS FOR STICKING UP FOR ME BACK IN MARQUEZ'S CLASS. DID I GET YOU INTO TOO MUCH TROUBLE?
JUST A LITTLE EXTRA TIME IN THE GULAGS, HEH--YOU KNOW? SOLZHENITSYN? OKAY, STOP TALKING NOW.
KRISTEN!
STOP TRYING TO TANK YOUR ENTIRE SOCIAL STATUS ON THE FIRST DAY.
SORRY, GOTTA RUN!
HEY, KID! I'VE BEEN LOOKING FOR YOU.
ME?
WELL, SOMEONE LIKE YOU. I RUN A SMALL PRIVATE LAB AND I HAVE AN INTERNSHIP AVAILABLE FOR A HARDWORKING, CURIOUS YOUNG MIND.
Destiny Labs
Doctor Peters
312 West Charles, Mapleton
IS IT PAID? MY MOM COULD USE THE HELP.
ALL I CAN OFFER IS YOUR DESTINY.
SIGH I APPRECIATE THE OFFER, BUT I HAVE SOMEONE I HAVE TO SEE, "DR. PETERS."
FRIENDS CALL ME DOC.
SEE YA.

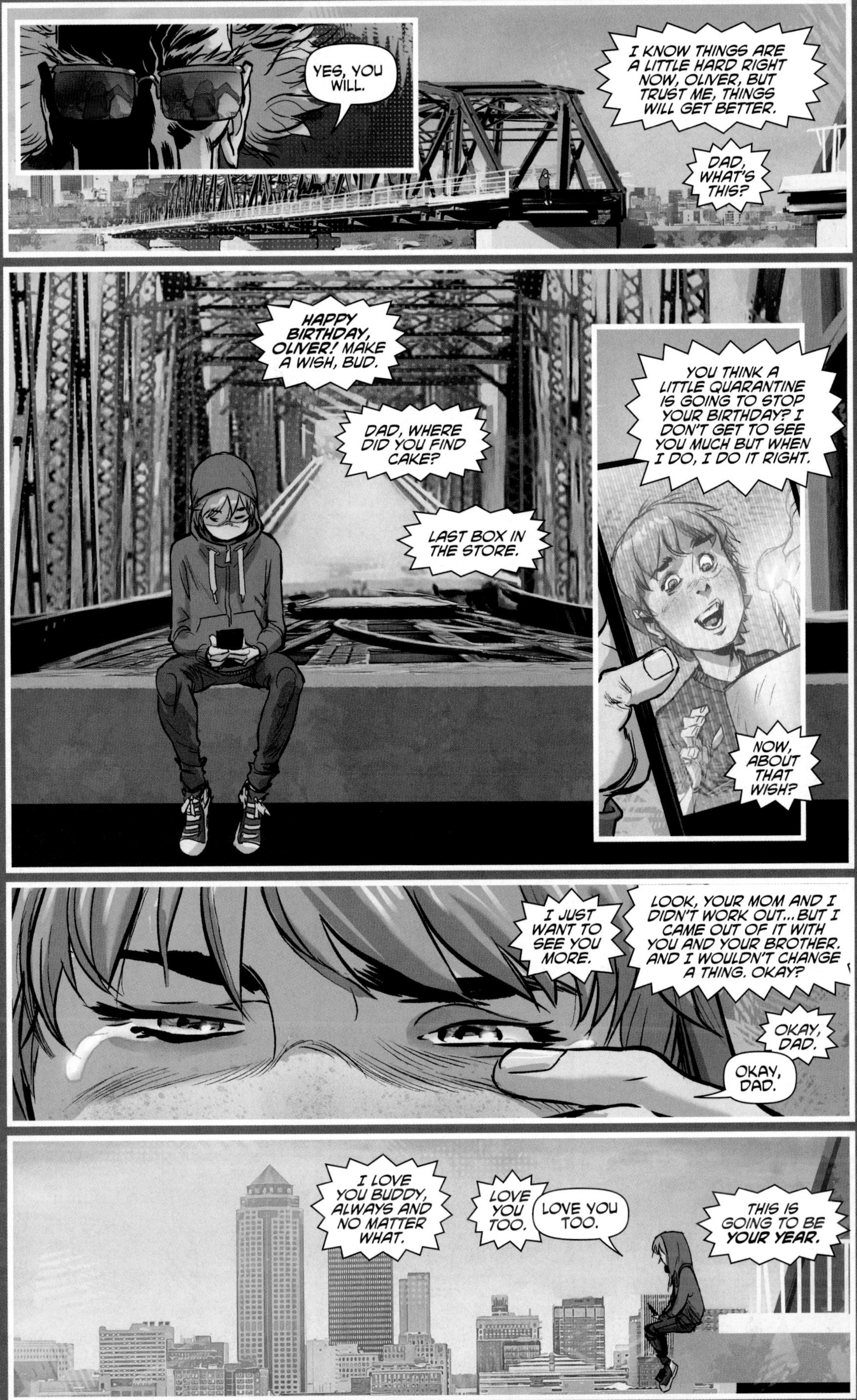
YES, YOU WILL.
I KNOW THINGS ARE A LITTLE HARD RIGHT NOW, OLIVER, BUT TRUST ME, THINGS WILL GET BETTER.
DAD, WHAT'S THIS?
HAPPY BIRTHDAY, OLIVER! MAKE A WISH, BUD.
DAD, WHERE DID YOU FIND CAKE?
LAST BOX IN THE STORE.
YOU THINK A LITTLE QUARANTINE IS GOING TO STOP YOUR BIRTHDAY? I DON'T GET TO SEE YOU MUCH BUT WHEN I DO, I DO IT RIGHT.
NOW, ABOUT THAT WISH?
I JUST WANT TO SEE YOU MORE.
LOOK, YOUR MOM AND I DIDN'T WORK OUT... BUT I CAME OUT OF IT WITH YOU AND YOUR BROTHER. AND I WOULDN'T CHANGE A THING. OKAY?
OKAY, DAD.
OKAY, DAD.
I LOVE YOU BUDDY, ALWAYS AND NO MATTER WHAT.
LOVE YOU TOO.
LOVE YOU TOO.
THIS IS GOING TO BE YOUR YEAR.

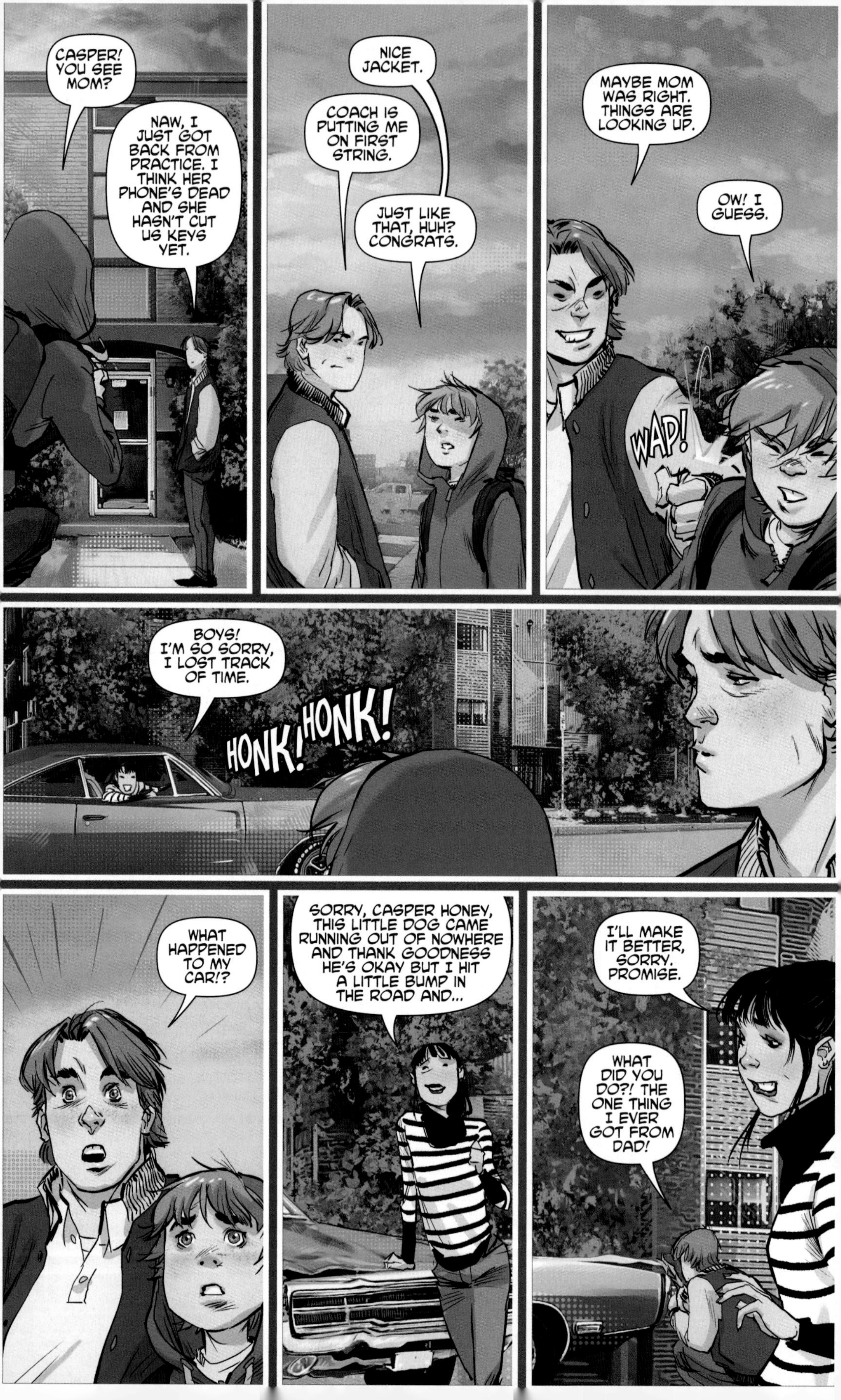
CASPER! YOU SEE MOM?
NAW, I JUST GOT BACK FROM PRACTICE. I THINK HER PHONE'S DEAD AND SHE HASN'T CUT US KEYS YET.
NICE JACKET.
COACH IS PUTTING ME ON FIRST STRING.
JUST LIKE THAT, HUH? CONGRATS.
MAYBE MOM WAS RIGHT. THINGS ARE LOOKING UP.
WAP!
OW! I GUESS.
BOYS! I'M SO SORRY, I LOST TRACK OF TIME.
HONK! HONK!
WHAT HAPPENED TO MY CAR!?
SORRY, CASPER HONEY, THIS LITTLE DOG CAME RUNNING OUT OF NOWHERE AND THANK GOODNESS HE'S OKAY BUT I HIT A LITTLE BUMP IN THE ROAD AND...
I'LL MAKE IT BETTER, SORRY. PROMISE.
WHAT DID YOU DO?! THE ONE THING I EVER GOT FROM DAD!

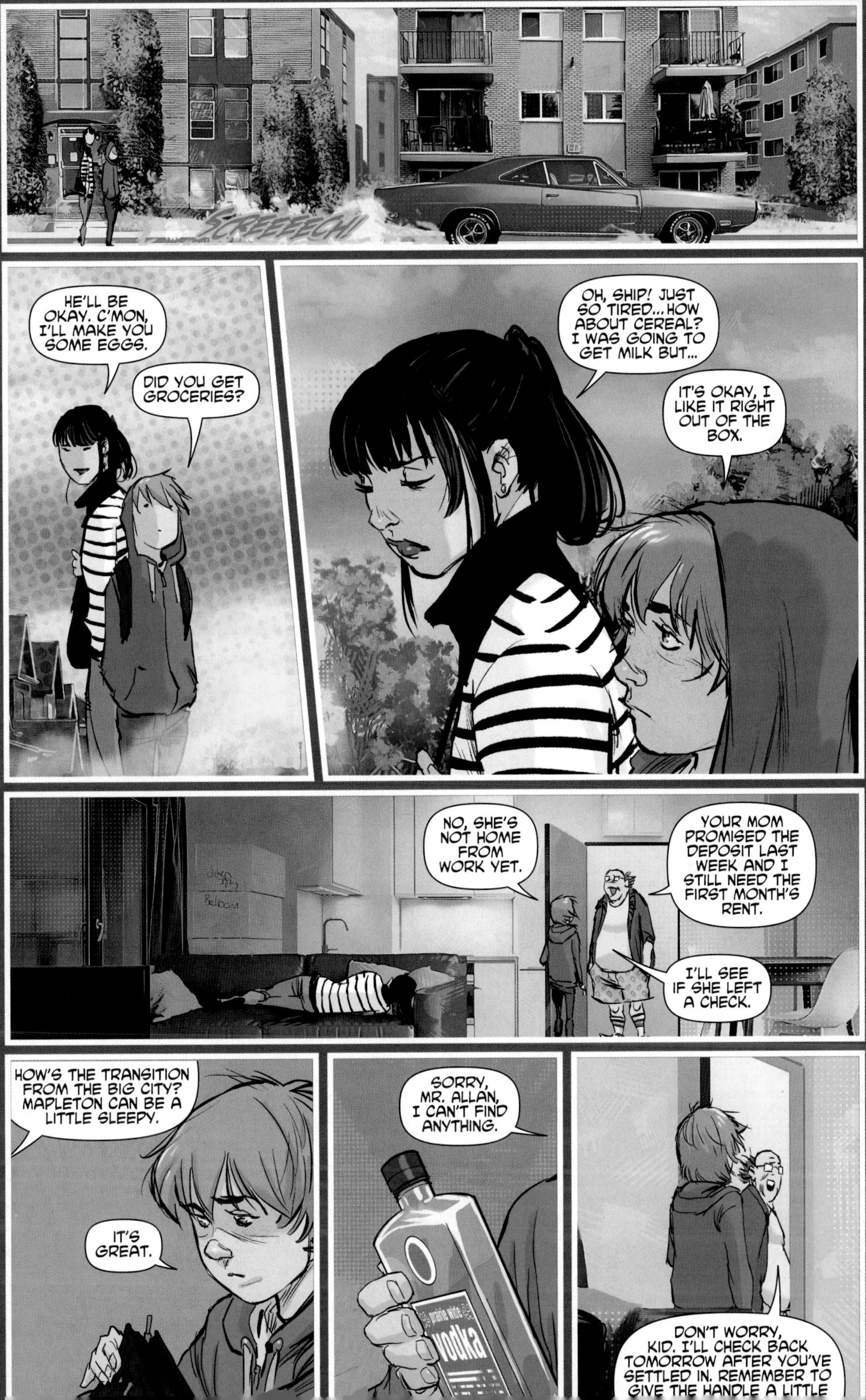
SCREEEEECH!
HE'LL BE OKAY. C'MON, I'LL MAKE YOU SOME EGGS.
DID YOU GET GROCERIES?
OH, SHIP! JUST SO TIRED... HOW ABOUT CEREAL? I WAS GOING TO GET MILK BUT...
IT'S OKAY, I LIKE IT RIGHT OUT OF THE BOX.
YOUR MOM PROMISED THE DEPOSIT LAST WEEK AND I STILL NEED THE FIRST MONTH'S RENT.
NO, SHE'S NOT HOME FROM WORK YET.
I'LL SEE IF SHE LEFT A CHECK.
HOW'S THE TRANSITION FROM THE BIG CITY? MAPLETON CAN BE A LITTLE SLEEPY.
IT'S GREAT.
SORRY, MR. ALLAN, I CAN'T FIND ANYTHING.
prairie wide vodka
DON'T WORRY, KID. I'LL CHECK BACK TOMORROW AFTER YOU'VE SETTLED IN. REMEMBER TO GIVE THE HANDLE A LITTLE

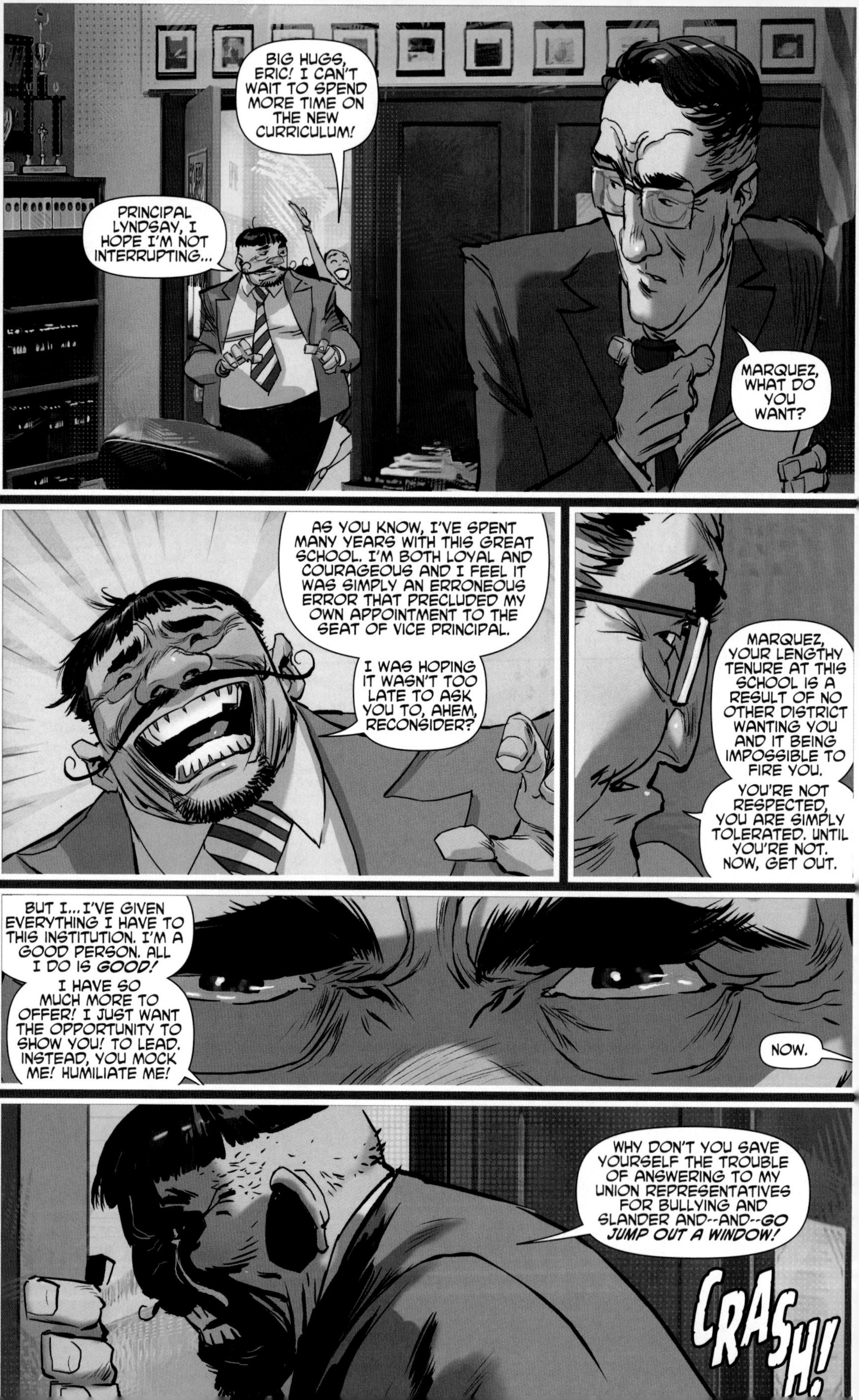
PRINCIPAL LYNDSAY, I HOPE I'M NOT INTERRUPTING...
BIG HUGS, ERIC! I CAN'T WAIT TO SPEND MORE TIME ON THE NEW CURRICULUM!
MARQUEZ, WHAT DO YOU WANT?
AS YOU KNOW, I'VE SPENT MANY YEARS WITH THIS GREAT SCHOOL. I'M BOTH LOYAL AND COURAGEOUS AND I FEEL IT WAS SIMPLY AN ERRONEOUS ERROR THAT PRECLUDED MY OWN APPOINTMENT TO THE SEAT OF VICE PRINCIPAL.
I WAS HOPING IT WASN'T TOO LATE TO ASK YOU TO, AHEM, RECONSIDER?
MARQUEZ, YOUR LENGTHY TENURE AT THIS SCHOOL IS A RESULT OF NO OTHER DISTRICT WANTING YOU AND IT BEING IMPOSSIBLE TO FIRE YOU.
YOU'RE NOT RESPECTED, YOU ARE SIMPLY TOLERATED. UNTIL YOU'RE NOT. NOW, GET OUT.
BUT I... I'VE GIVEN EVERYTHING I HAVE TO THIS INSTITUTION. I'M A GOOD PERSON. ALL I DO IS GOOD!
I HAVE SO MUCH MORE TO OFFER! I JUST WANT THE OPPORTUNITY TO SHOW YOU! TO LEAD. INSTEAD, YOU MOCK ME! HUMILIATE ME!
NOW.
WHY DON'T YOU SAVE YOURSELF THE TROUBLE OF ANSWERING TO MY UNION REPRESENTATIVES FOR BULLYING AND SLANDER AND--AND--GO JUMP OUT A WINDOW!
CRASH!

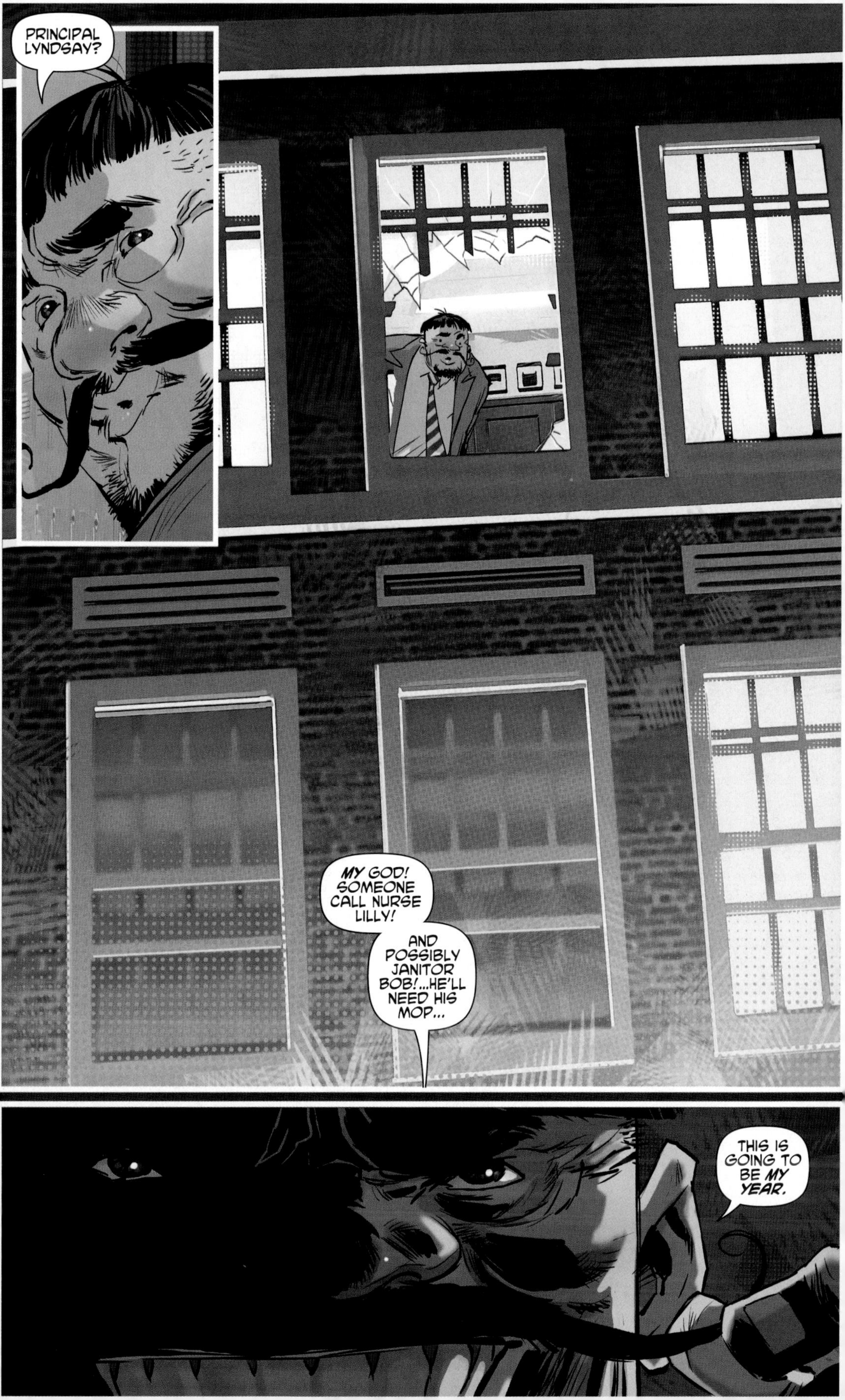
PRINCIPAL LYNDSAY?
MY GOD! SOMEONE CALL NURSE LILLY!
AND POSSIBLY JANITOR BOB!...HE'LL NEED HIS MOP...
THIS IS GOING TO BE MY YEAR.

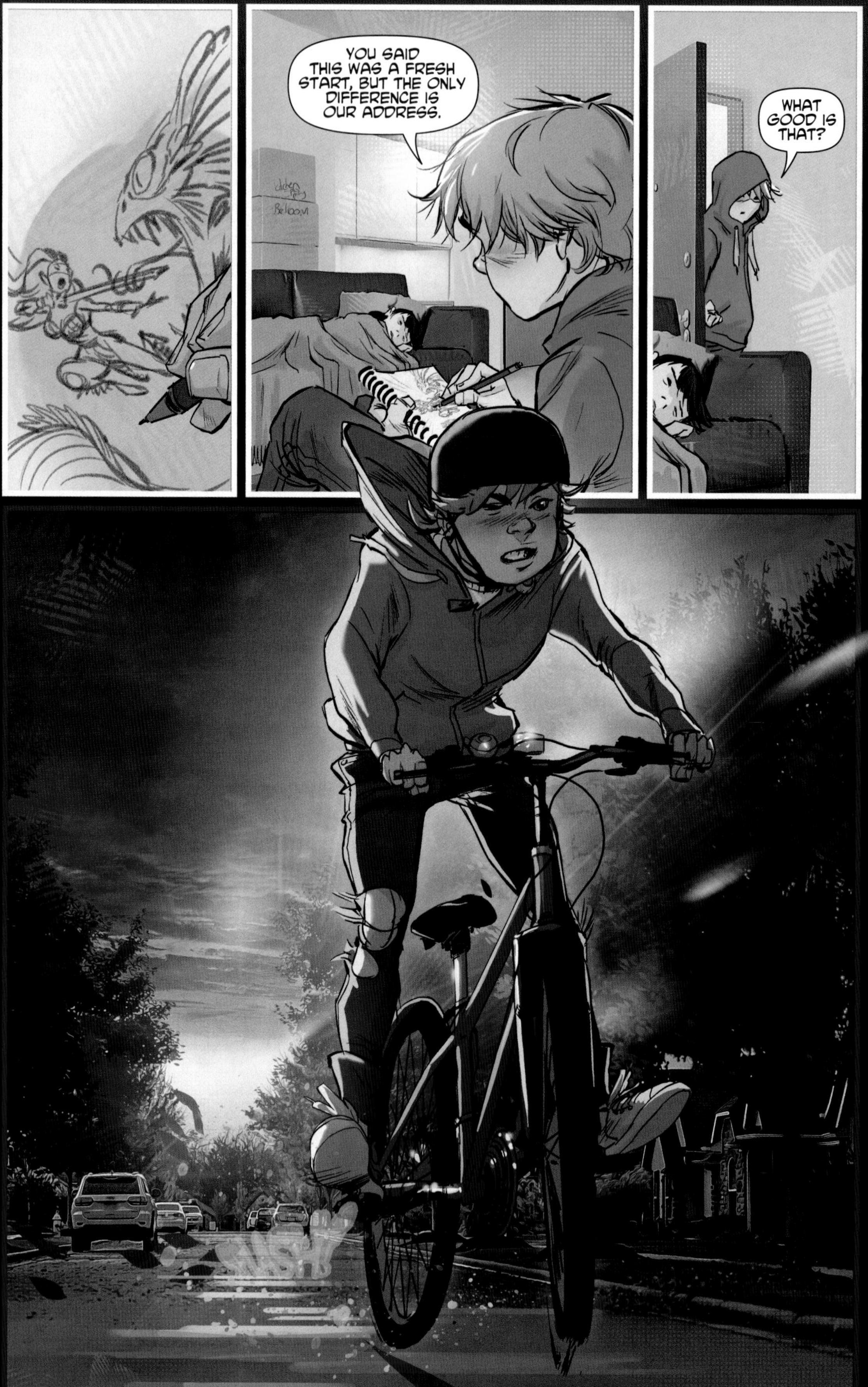

YOU SAID THIS WAS A FRESH START, BUT THE ONLY DIFFERENCE IS OUR ADDRESS.
WHAT GOOD IS THAT?

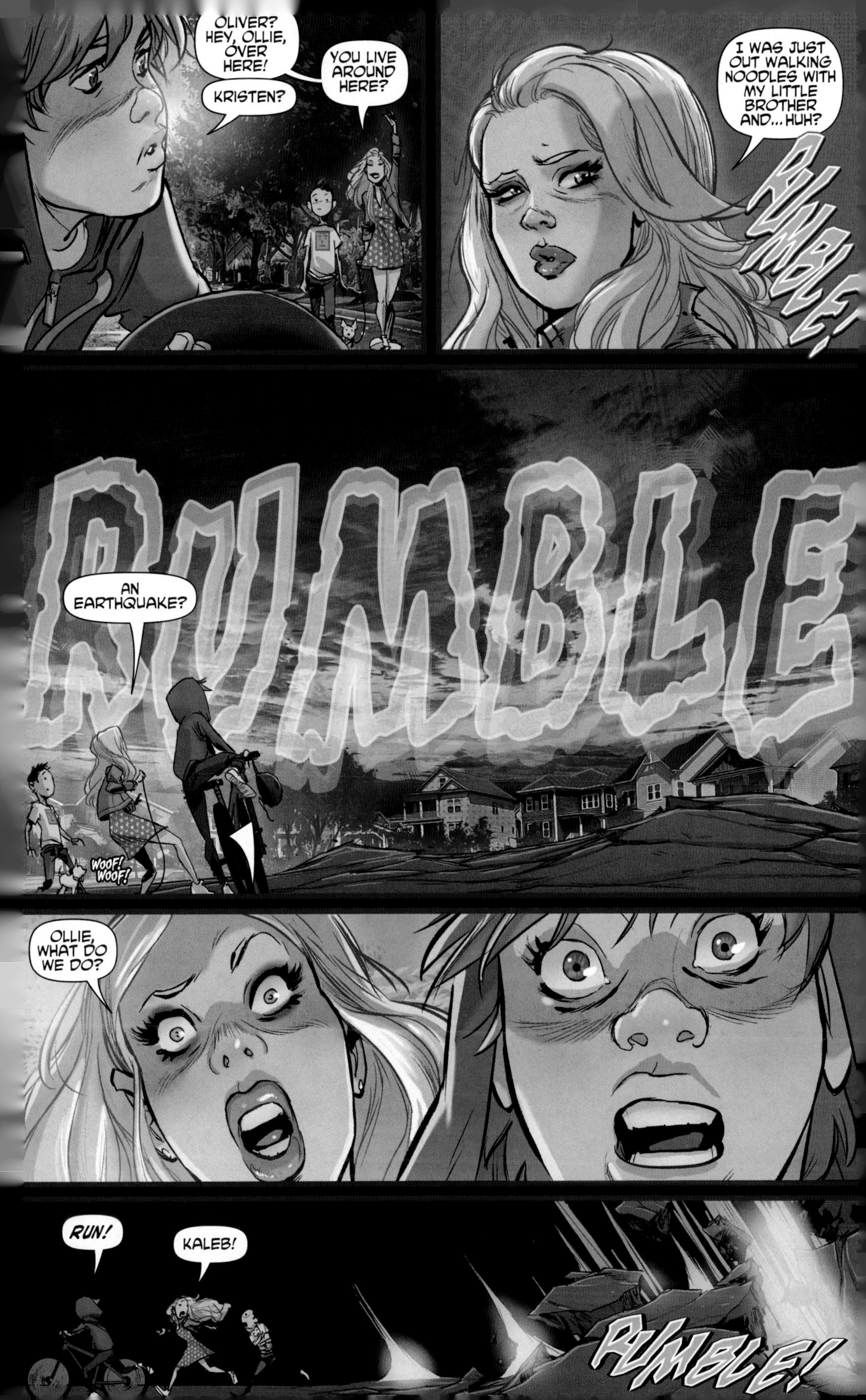

OLIVER? HEY, OLLIE, OVER HERE!
KRISTEN?
YOU LIVE AROUND HERE?
I WAS JUST OUT WALKING NOODLES WITH MY LITTLE BROTHER AND... HUH?
RUMBLE!
RUMBLE
AN EARTHQUAKE?
WOOF! WOOF!
OLLIE, WHAT DO WE DO?
RUN!
KALEB!
RUMBLE!

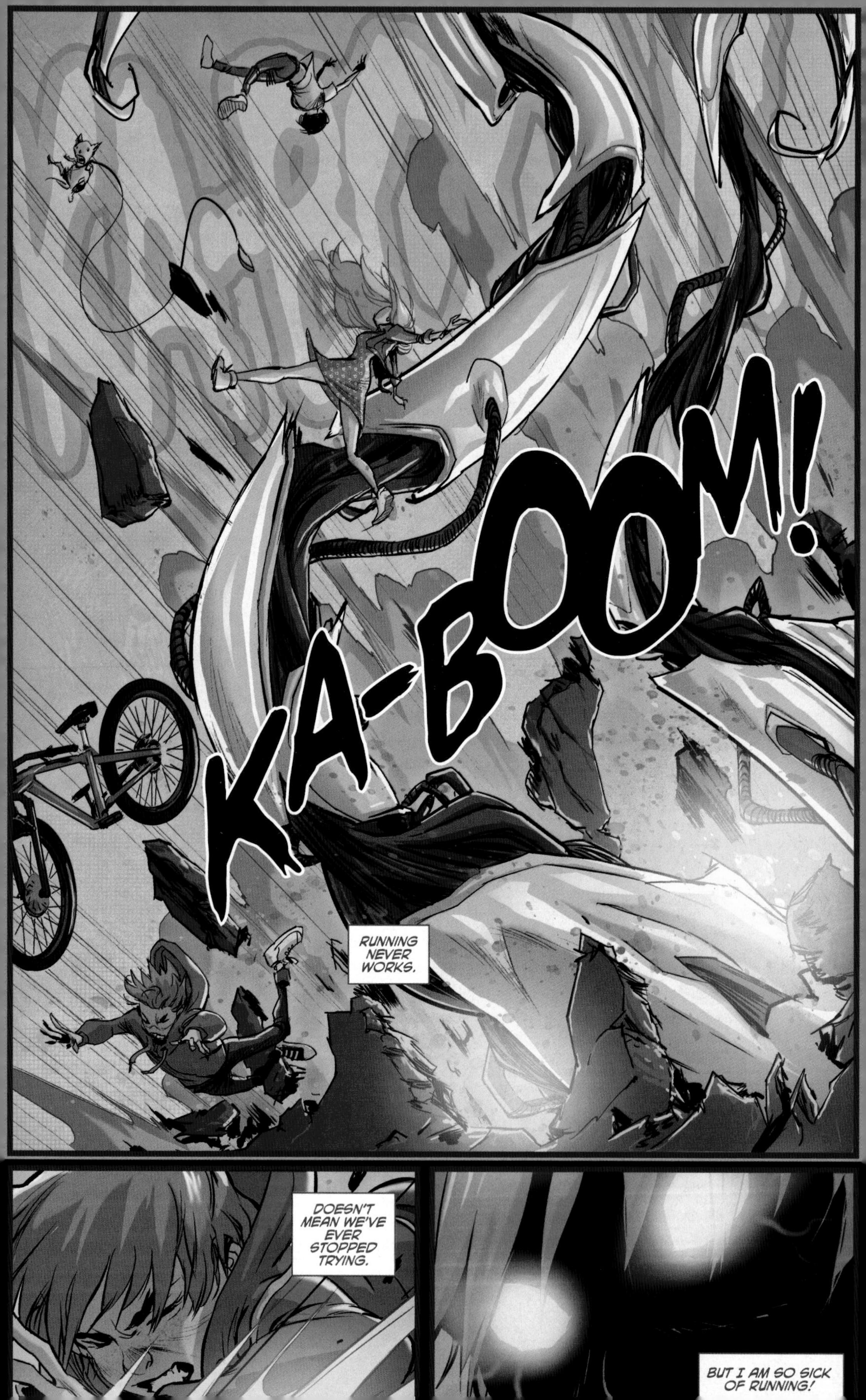
KA-BOOM!!
RUNNING NEVER WORKS.
DOESN'T MEAN WE'VE EVER STOPPED TRYING.
BUT I AM SO SICK OF RUNNING!

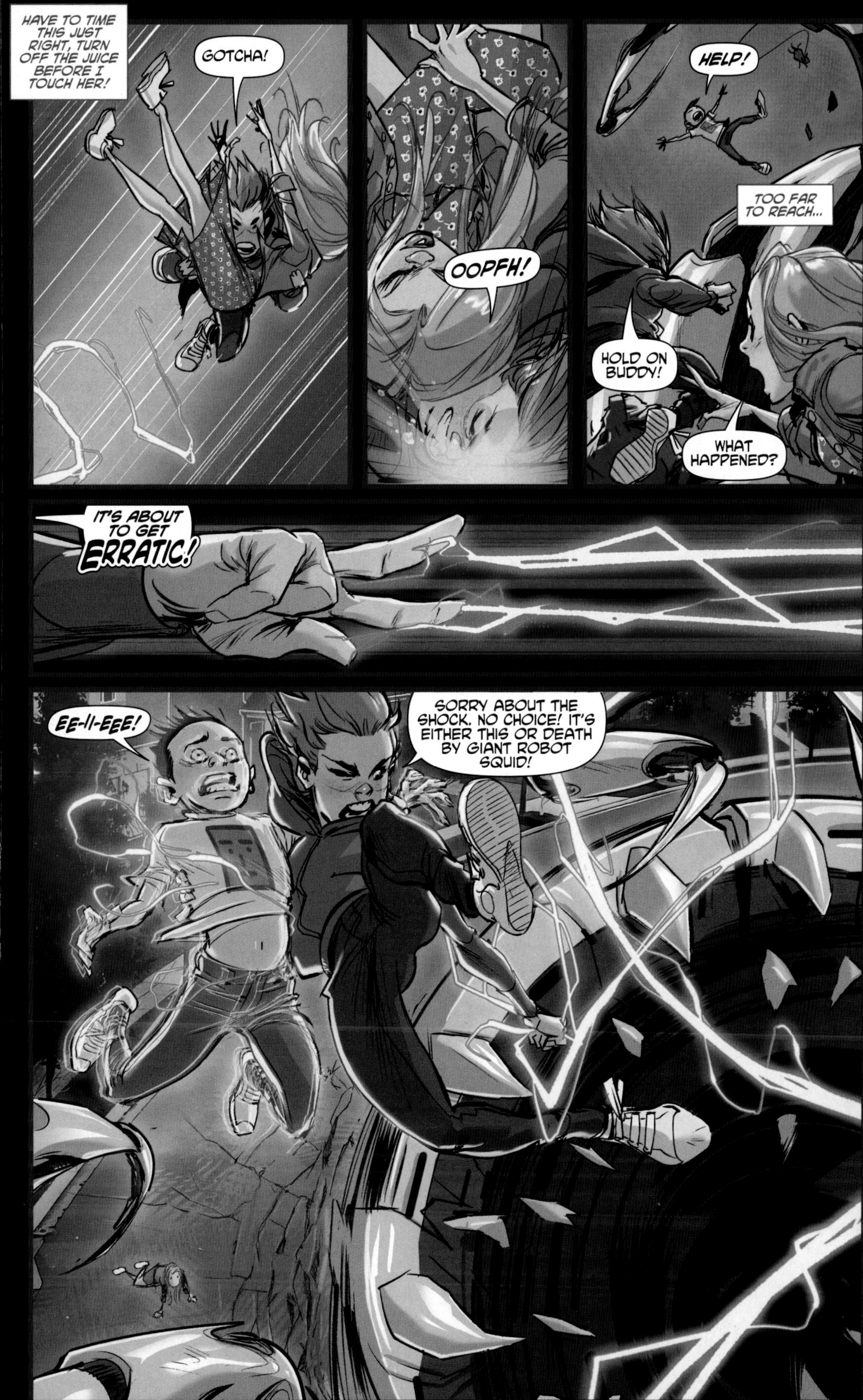
HAVE TO TIME THIS JUST RIGHT, TURN OFF THE JUICE BEFORE I TOUCH HER!
GOTCHA!
OOPFH!
HELP!
TOO FAR TO REACH...
HOLD ON BUDDY!
WHAT HAPPENED?
IT'S ABOUT TO GET ERRATIC!
EE-II-EEE!
SORRY ABOUT THE SHOCK. NO CHOICE! IT'S EITHER THIS OR DEATH BY GIANT ROBOT SQUID!

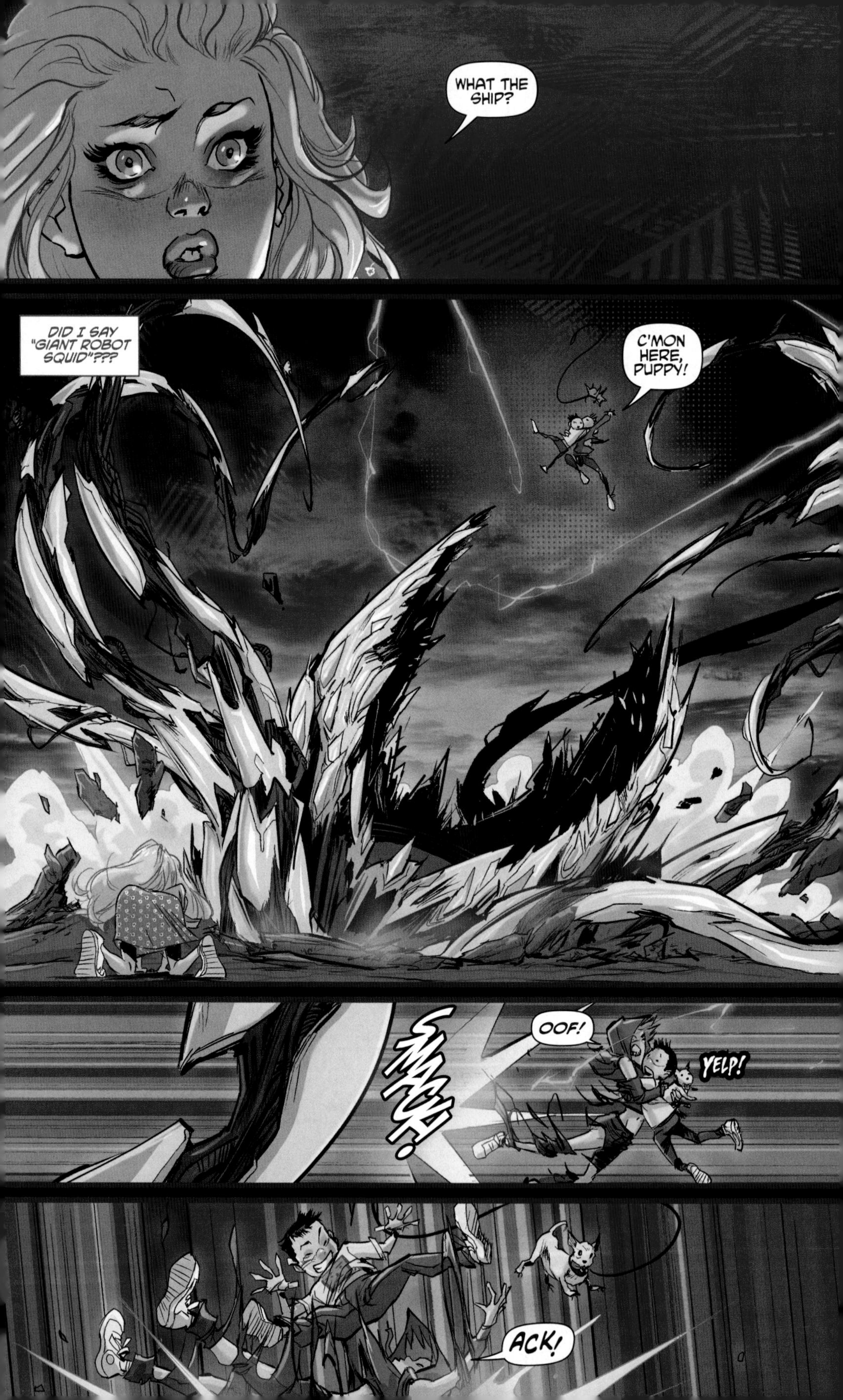
WHAT THE SHIP?
DID I SAY "GIANT ROBOT SQUID"???
C'MON HERE, PUPPY!
SMACK!
OOF!
YELP!
ACK!

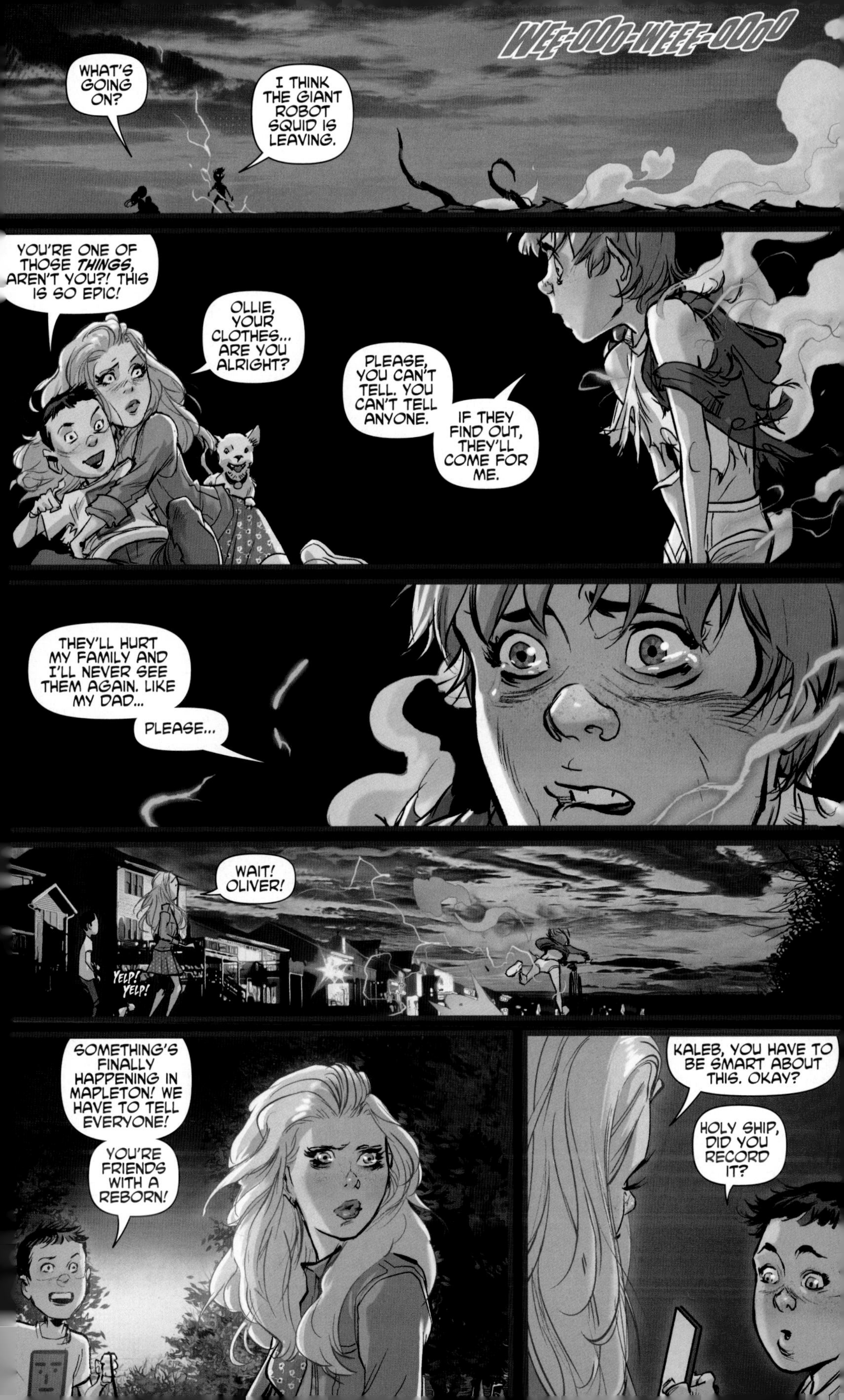
WEE-OOO-WEEE-OOOO
WHAT'S GOING ON?
I THINK THE GIANT ROBOT SQUID IS LEAVING.
YOU'RE ONE OF THOSE *THINGS*, AREN'T YOU?! THIS IS SO EPIC!
OLLIE, YOUR CLOTHES... ARE YOU ALRIGHT?
PLEASE, YOU CAN'T TELL. YOU CAN'T TELL ANYONE.
IF THEY FIND OUT, THEY'LL COME FOR ME.
THEY'LL HURT MY FAMILY AND I'LL NEVER SEE THEM AGAIN. LIKE MY DAD...
PLEASE...
WAIT! OLIVER!
YELP! YELP!
SOMETHING'S FINALLY HAPPENING IN MAPLETON! WE HAVE TO TELL EVERYONE!
YOU'RE FRIENDS WITH A REBORN!
KALEB, YOU HAVE TO BE SMART ABOUT THIS. OKAY?
HOLY SHIP, DID YOU RECORD IT?

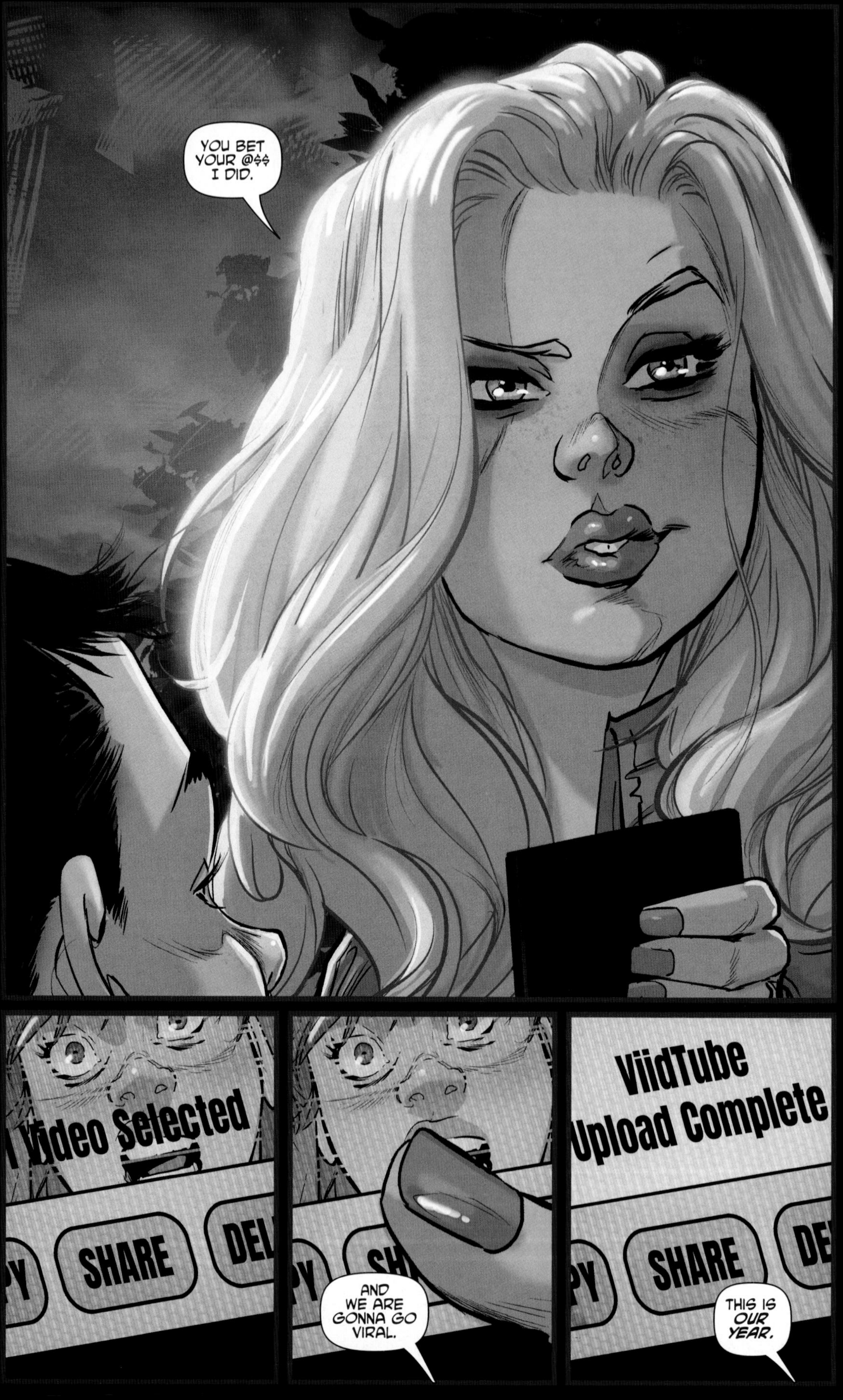
YOU BET YOUR @$$ I DID.
Video Selected
SHARE
ViidTube
Upload Complete
SHARE
AND WE ARE GONNA GO VIRAL.
THIS IS *OUR YEAR.*

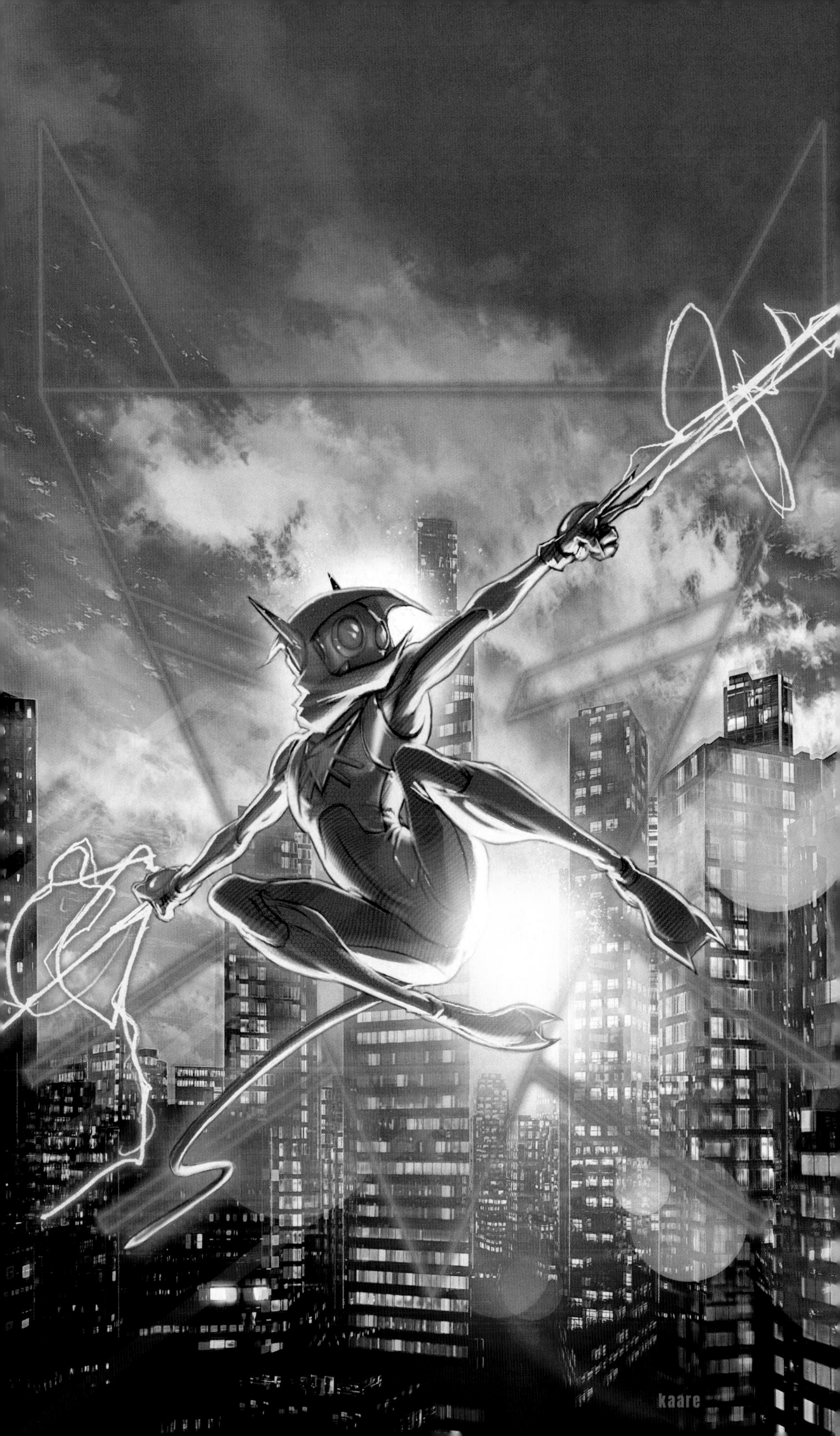
kaare

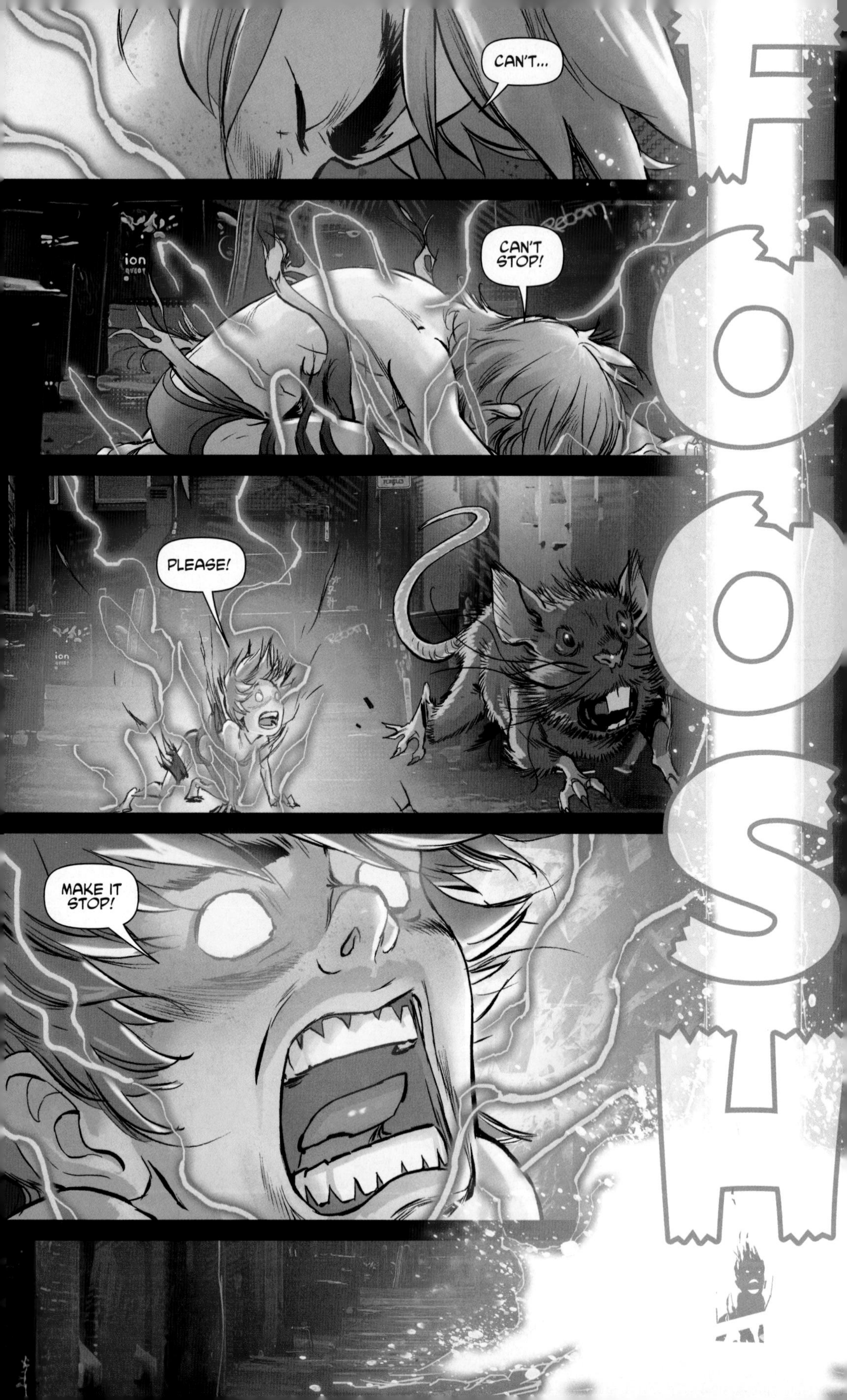
CAN'T...
CAN'T STOP!
PLEASE!
MAKE IT STOP!
FOOSH

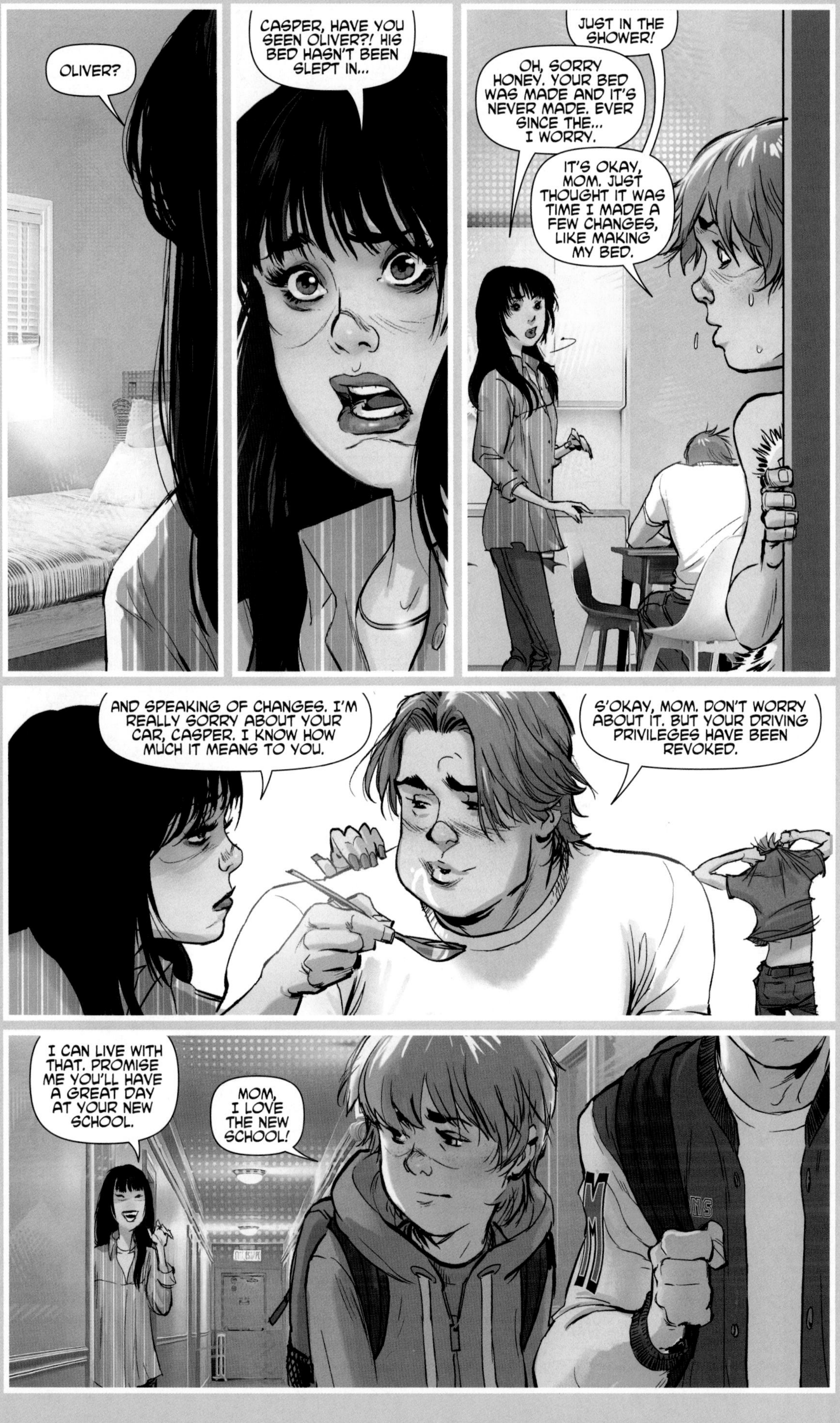
OLIVER?
CASPER, HAVE YOU SEEN OLIVER?! HIS BED HASN'T BEEN SLEPT IN...
JUST IN THE SHOWER!
OH, SORRY HONEY. YOUR BED WAS MADE AND IT'S NEVER MADE. EVER SINCE THE... I WORRY.
IT'S OKAY, MOM. JUST THOUGHT IT WAS TIME I MADE A FEW CHANGES, LIKE MAKING MY BED.
AND SPEAKING OF CHANGES. I'M REALLY SORRY ABOUT YOUR CAR, CASPER. I KNOW HOW MUCH IT MEANS TO YOU.
S'OKAY, MOM. DON'T WORRY ABOUT IT. BUT YOUR DRIVING PRIVILEGES HAVE BEEN REVOKED.
I CAN LIVE WITH THAT. PROMISE ME YOU'LL HAVE A GREAT DAY AT YOUR NEW SCHOOL.
MOM, I LOVE THE NEW SCHOOL!

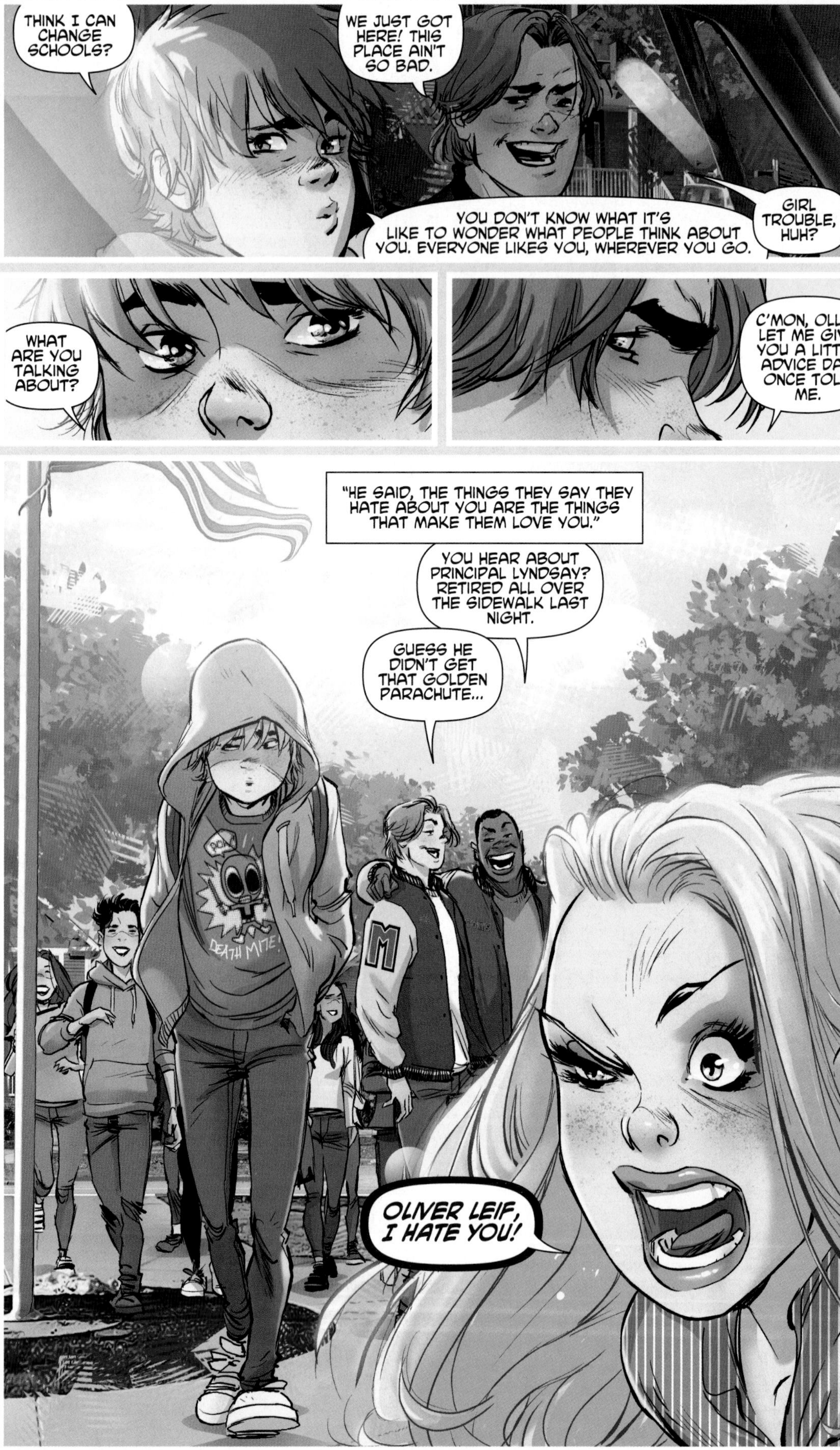
THINK I CAN CHANGE SCHOOLS?
WE JUST GOT HERE! THIS PLACE AIN'T SO BAD.
YOU DON'T KNOW WHAT IT'S LIKE TO WONDER WHAT PEOPLE THINK ABOUT YOU. EVERYONE LIKES YOU, WHEREVER YOU GO.
GIRL TROUBLE, HUH?
WHAT ARE YOU TALKING ABOUT?
C'MON, OLLIE. LET ME GIVE YOU A LITTLE ADVICE DAD ONCE TOLD ME.
"HE SAID, THE THINGS THEY SAY THEY HATE ABOUT YOU ARE THE THINGS THAT MAKE THEM LOVE YOU."
YOU HEAR ABOUT PRINCIPAL LYNDSAY? RETIRED ALL OVER THE SIDEWALK LAST NIGHT.
GUESS HE DIDN'T GET THAT GOLDEN PARACHUTE...
DEATH MITE!
OLIVER LEIF, I HATE YOU!

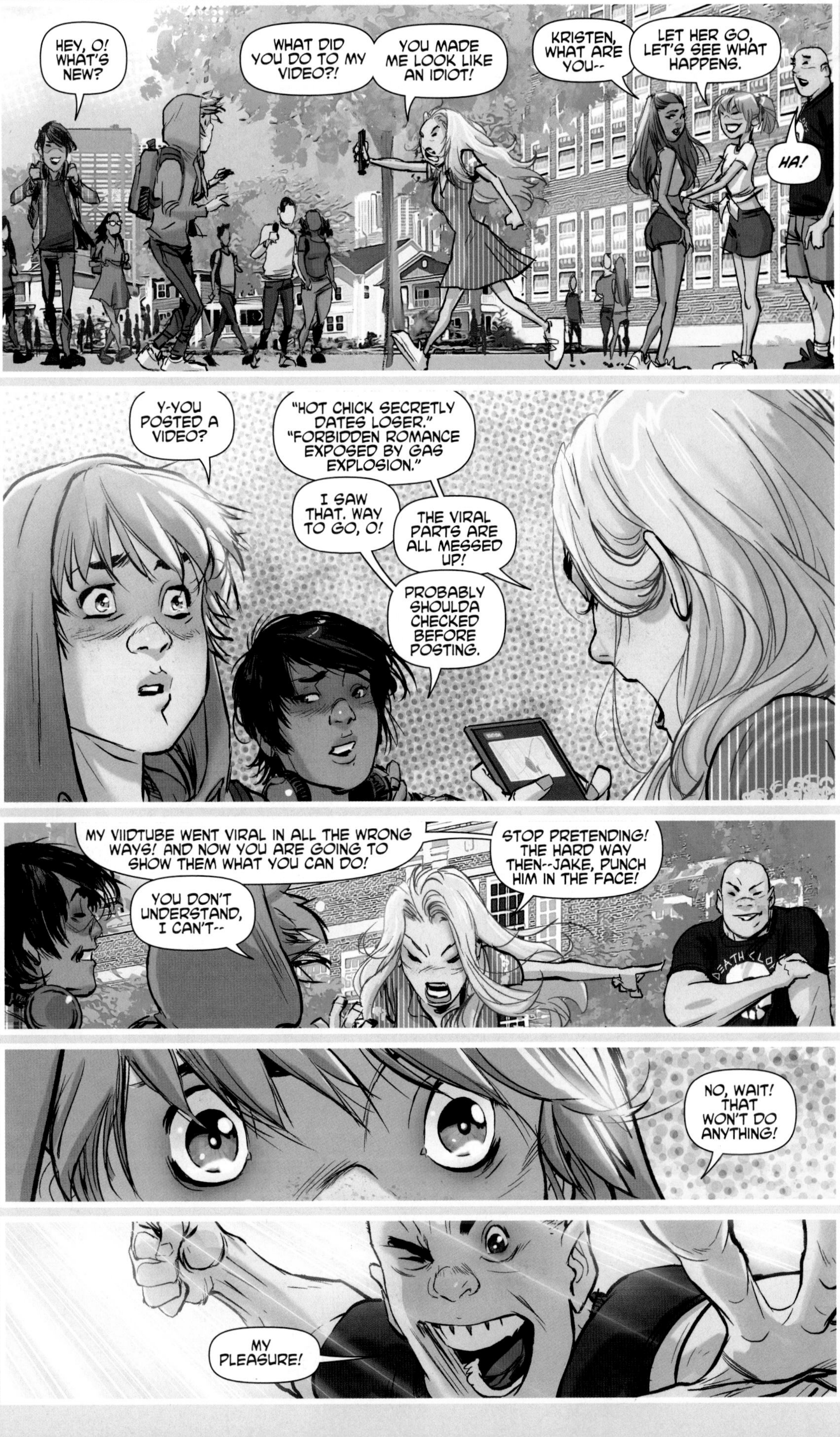
HEY, O! WHAT'S NEW?
WHAT DID YOU DO TO MY VIDEO?!
YOU MADE ME LOOK LIKE AN IDIOT!
KRISTEN, WHAT ARE YOU--
LET HER GO, LET'S SEE WHAT HAPPENS.
HA!
Y-YOU POSTED A VIDEO?
"HOT CHICK SECRETLY DATES LOSER." "FORBIDDEN ROMANCE EXPOSED BY GAS EXPLOSION."
I SAW THAT. WAY TO GO, O!
THE VIRAL PARTS ARE ALL MESSED UP!
PROBABLY SHOULDA CHECKED BEFORE POSTING.
MY VIIDTUBE WENT VIRAL IN ALL THE WRONG WAYS! AND NOW YOU ARE GOING TO SHOW THEM WHAT YOU CAN DO!
YOU DON'T UNDERSTAND, I CAN'T--
STOP PRETENDING! THE HARD WAY THEN--JAKE, PUNCH HIM IN THE FACE!
NO, WAIT! THAT WON'T DO ANYTHING!
MY PLEASURE!

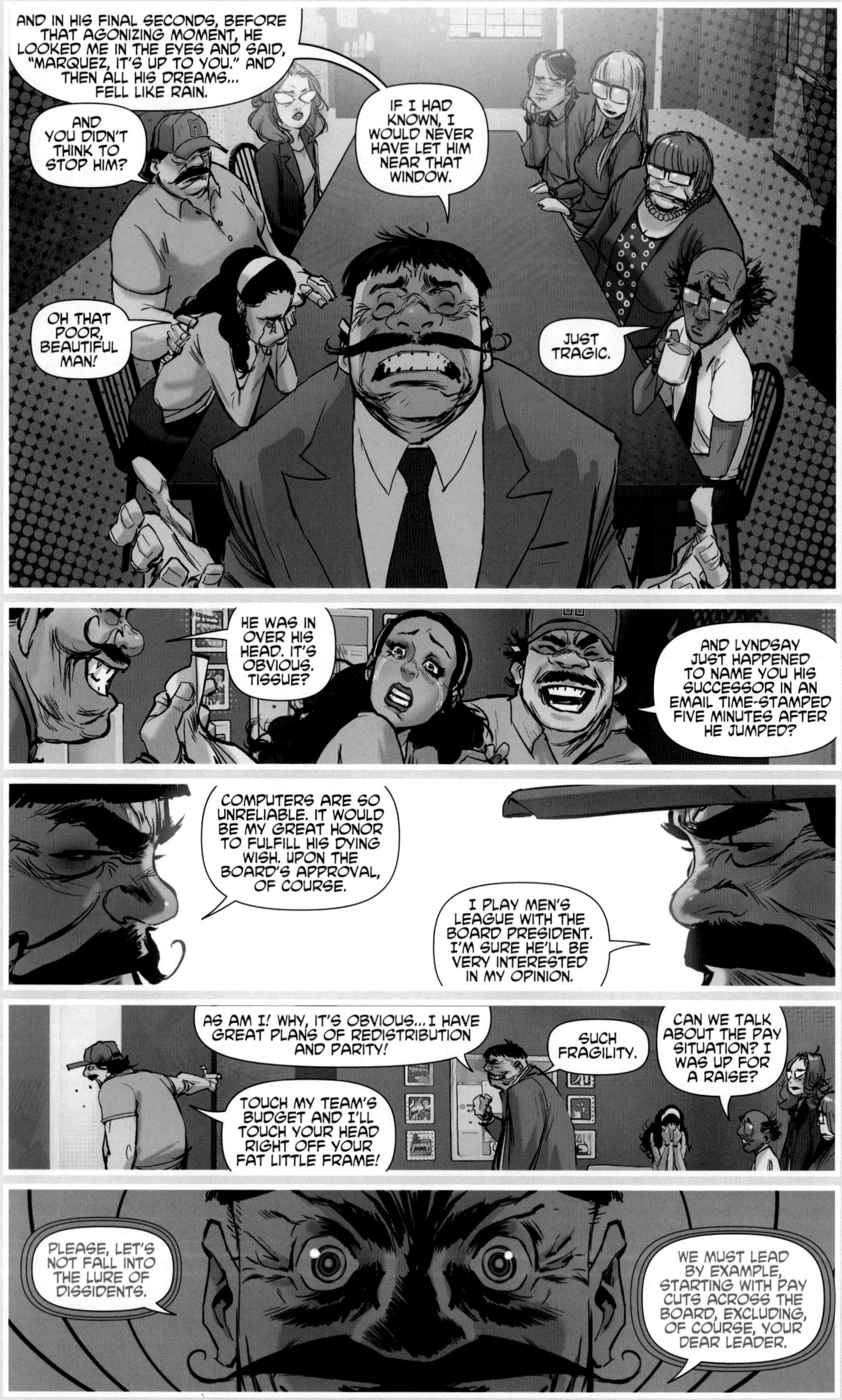
AND IN HIS FINAL SECONDS, BEFORE THAT AGONIZING MOMENT, HE LOOKED ME IN THE EYES AND SAID, "MARQUEZ, IT'S UP TO YOU." AND THEN ALL HIS DREAMS... FELL LIKE RAIN.
AND YOU DIDN'T THINK TO STOP HIM?
IF I HAD KNOWN, I WOULD NEVER HAVE LET HIM NEAR THAT WINDOW.
OH THAT POOR, BEAUTIFUL MAN!
JUST TRAGIC.
HE WAS IN OVER HIS HEAD. IT'S OBVIOUS. TISSUE?
AND LYNDSAY JUST HAPPENED TO NAME YOU HIS SUCCESSOR IN AN EMAIL TIME-STAMPED FIVE MINUTES AFTER HE JUMPED?
COMPUTERS ARE SO UNRELIABLE. IT WOULD BE MY GREAT HONOR TO FULFILL HIS DYING WISH. UPON THE BOARD'S APPROVAL, OF COURSE.
I PLAY MEN'S LEAGUE WITH THE BOARD PRESIDENT. I'M SURE HE'LL BE VERY INTERESTED IN MY OPINION.
AS AM I! WHY, IT'S OBVIOUS... I HAVE GREAT PLANS OF REDISTRIBUTION AND PARITY!
TOUCH MY TEAM'S BUDGET AND I'LL TOUCH YOUR HEAD RIGHT OFF YOUR FAT LITTLE FRAME!
SUCH FRAGILITY.
CAN WE TALK ABOUT THE PAY SITUATION? I WAS UP FOR A RAISE?
PLEASE, LET'S NOT FALL INTO THE LURE OF DISSIDENTS.
WE MUST LEAD BY EXAMPLE, STARTING WITH PAY CUTS ACROSS THE BOARD, EXCLUDING, OF COURSE, YOUR DEAR LEADER.

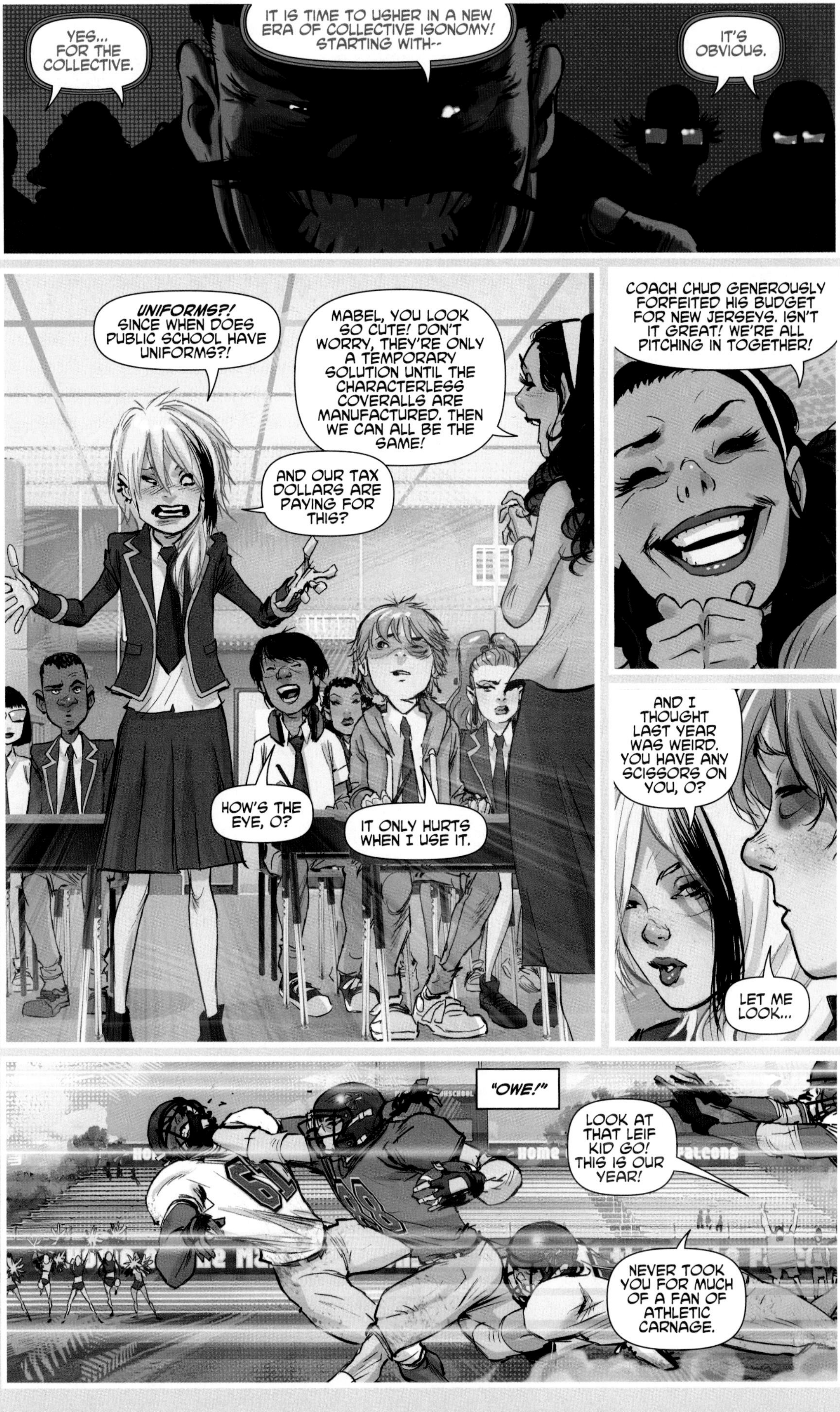

YES... FOR THE COLLECTIVE.
IT IS TIME TO USHER IN A NEW ERA OF COLLECTIVE ISONOMY! STARTING WITH--
IT'S OBVIOUS.
UNIFORMS?! SINCE WHEN DOES PUBLIC SCHOOL HAVE UNIFORMS?!
MABEL, YOU LOOK SO CUTE! DON'T WORRY, THEY'RE ONLY A TEMPORARY SOLUTION UNTIL THE CHARACTERLESS COVERALLS ARE MANUFACTURED. THEN WE CAN ALL BE THE SAME!
AND OUR TAX DOLLARS ARE PAYING FOR THIS?
HOW'S THE EYE, O?
IT ONLY HURTS WHEN I USE IT.
COACH CHUD GENEROUSLY FORFEITED HIS BUDGET FOR NEW JERSEYS. ISN'T IT GREAT! WE'RE ALL PITCHING IN TOGETHER!
AND I THOUGHT LAST YEAR WAS WEIRD. YOU HAVE ANY SCISSORS ON YOU, O?
LET ME LOOK...
"OWE!"
LOOK AT THAT LEIF KID GO! THIS IS OUR YEAR!
NEVER TOOK YOU FOR MUCH OF A FAN OF ATHLETIC CARNAGE.

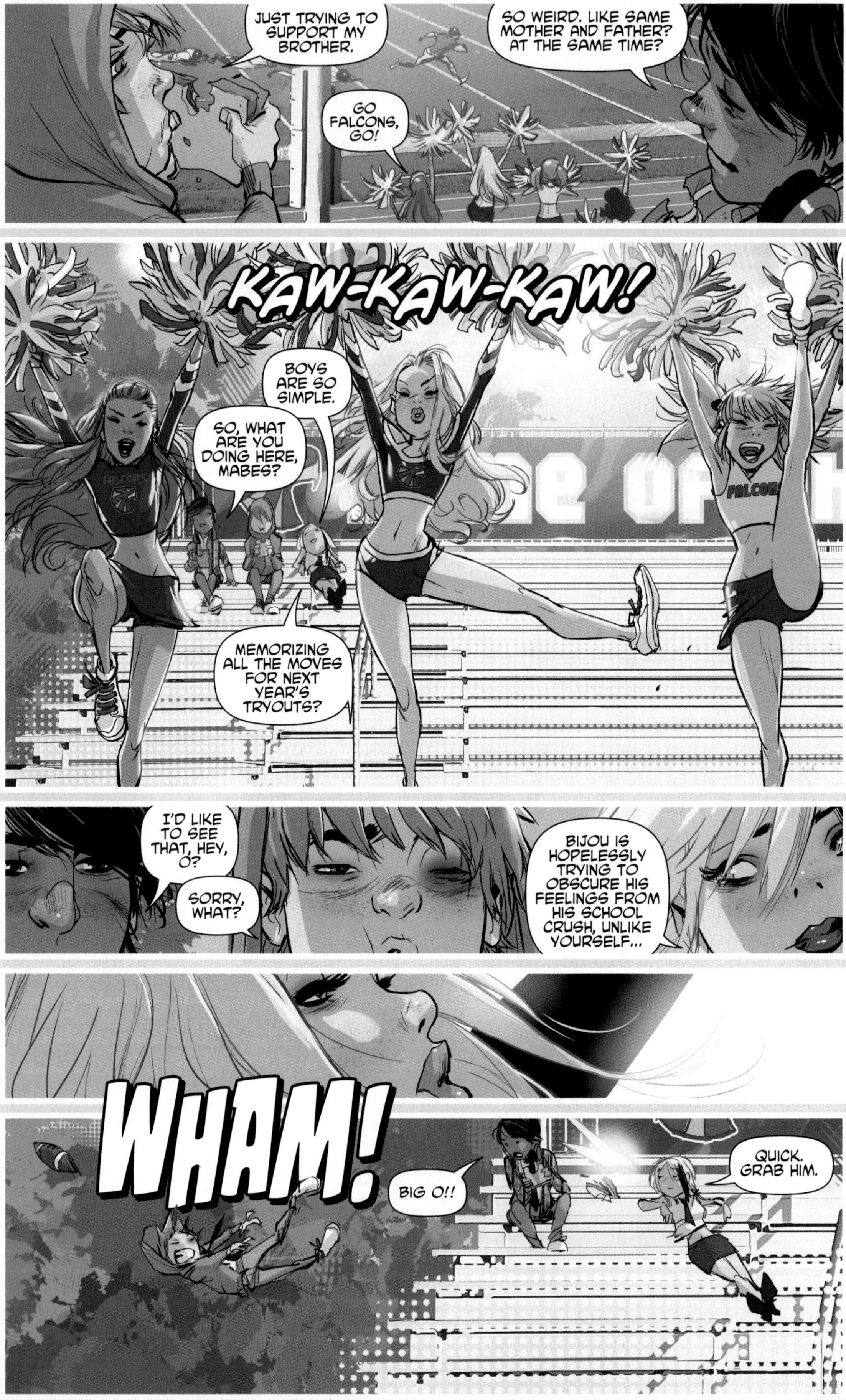

JUST TRYING TO SUPPORT MY BROTHER.
SO WEIRD. LIKE SAME MOTHER AND FATHER? AT THE SAME TIME?
GO FALCONS, GO!
KAW-KAW-KAW!
BOYS ARE SO SIMPLE.
SO, WHAT ARE YOU DOING HERE, MABES?
MEMORIZING ALL THE MOVES FOR NEXT YEAR'S TRYOUTS?
I'D LIKE TO SEE THAT, HEY, O?
SORRY, WHAT?
BIJOU IS HOPELESSLY TRYING TO OBSCURE HIS FEELINGS FROM HIS SCHOOL CRUSH, UNLIKE YOURSELF...
WHAM!
BIG O!!
QUICK. GRAB HIM.

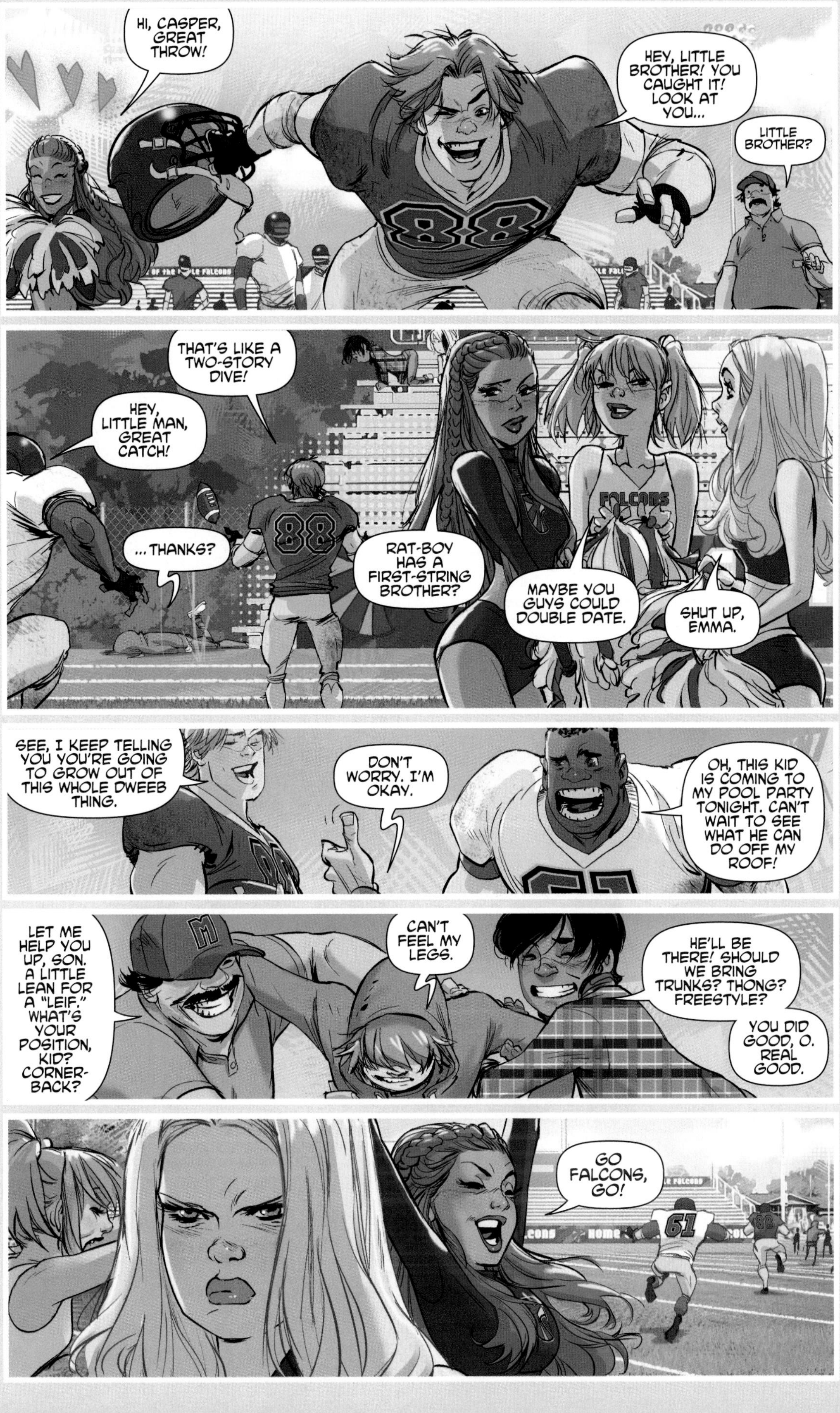
HI, CASPER, GREAT THROW!
HEY, LITTLE BROTHER! YOU CAUGHT IT! LOOK AT YOU...
LITTLE BROTHER?
THAT'S LIKE A TWO-STORY DIVE!
HEY, LITTLE MAN, GREAT CATCH!
...THANKS?
RAT-BOY HAS A FIRST-STRING BROTHER?
MAYBE YOU GUYS COULD DOUBLE DATE.
SHUT UP, EMMA.
FALCONS
SEE, I KEEP TELLING YOU YOU'RE GOING TO GROW OUT OF THIS WHOLE DWEEB THING.
DON'T WORRY. I'M OKAY.
OH, THIS KID IS COMING TO MY POOL PARTY TONIGHT. CAN'T WAIT TO SEE WHAT HE CAN DO OFF MY ROOF!
LET ME HELP YOU UP, SON. A LITTLE LEAN FOR A "LEIF." WHAT'S YOUR POSITION, KID? CORNER-BACK?
CAN'T FEEL MY LEGS.
HE'LL BE THERE! SHOULD WE BRING TRUNKS? THONG? FREESTYLE?
YOU DID GOOD, O. REAL GOOD.
GO FALCONS, GO!

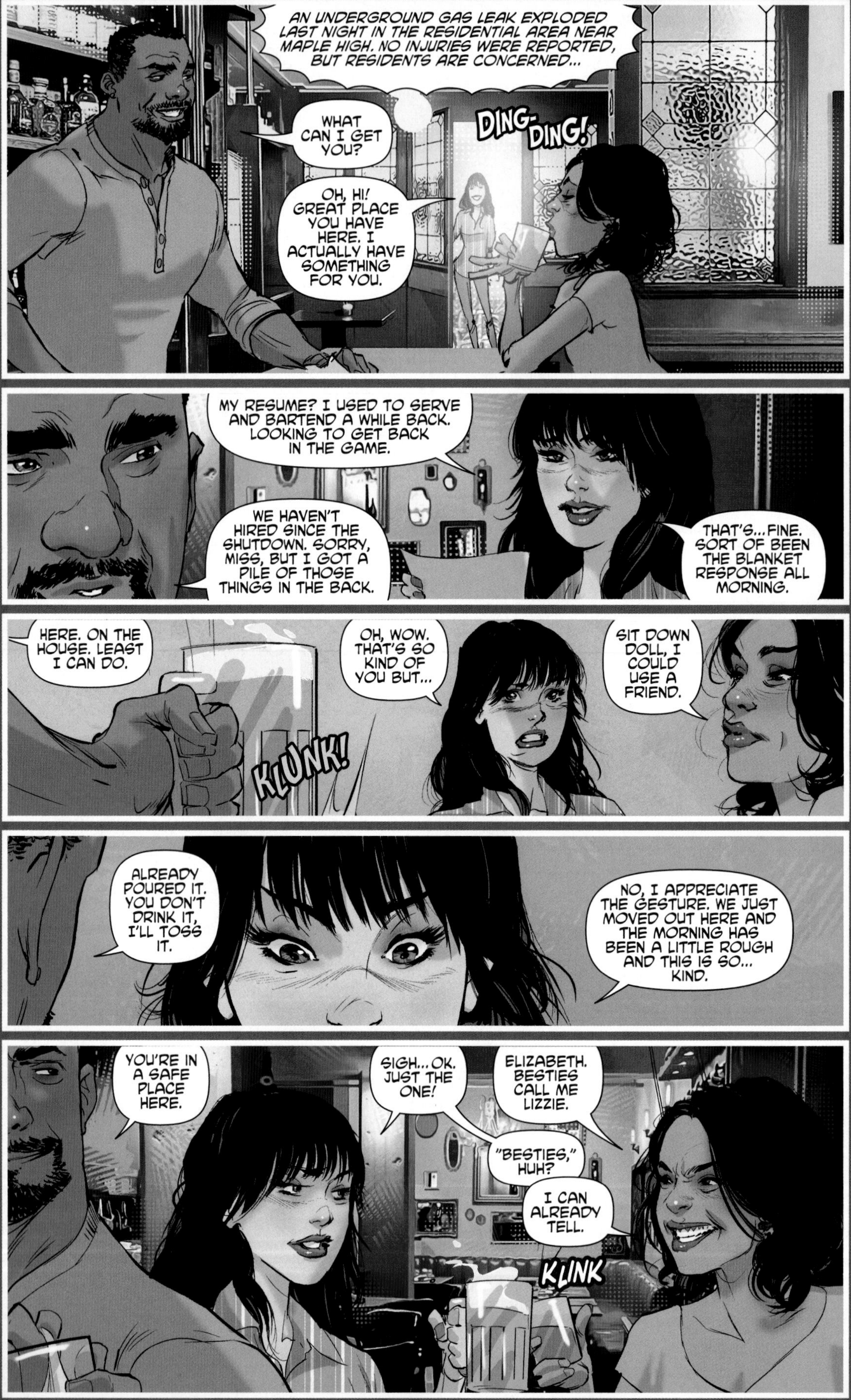
AN UNDERGROUND GAS LEAK EXPLODED LAST NIGHT IN THE RESIDENTIAL AREA NEAR MAPLE HIGH. NO INJURIES WERE REPORTED, BUT RESIDENTS ARE CONCERNED...
WHAT CAN I GET YOU?
DING-DING!
OH, HI! GREAT PLACE YOU HAVE HERE. I ACTUALLY HAVE SOMETHING FOR YOU.
MY RESUME? I USED TO SERVE AND BARTEND A WHILE BACK. LOOKING TO GET BACK IN THE GAME.
WE HAVEN'T HIRED SINCE THE SHUTDOWN. SORRY, MISS, BUT I GOT A PILE OF THOSE THINGS IN THE BACK.
THAT'S...FINE. SORT OF BEEN THE BLANKET RESPONSE ALL MORNING.
HERE. ON THE HOUSE. LEAST I CAN DO.
OH, WOW. THAT'S SO KIND OF YOU BUT...
SIT DOWN DOLL, I COULD USE A FRIEND.
KLUNK!
ALREADY POURED IT. YOU DON'T DRINK IT, I'LL TOSS IT.
NO, I APPRECIATE THE GESTURE. WE JUST MOVED OUT HERE AND THE MORNING HAS BEEN A LITTLE ROUGH AND THIS IS SO... KIND.
YOU'RE IN A SAFE PLACE HERE.
SIGH...OK. JUST THE ONE!
ELIZABETH. BESTIES CALL ME LIZZIE.
"BESTIES," HUH?
I CAN ALREADY TELL.
KLINK

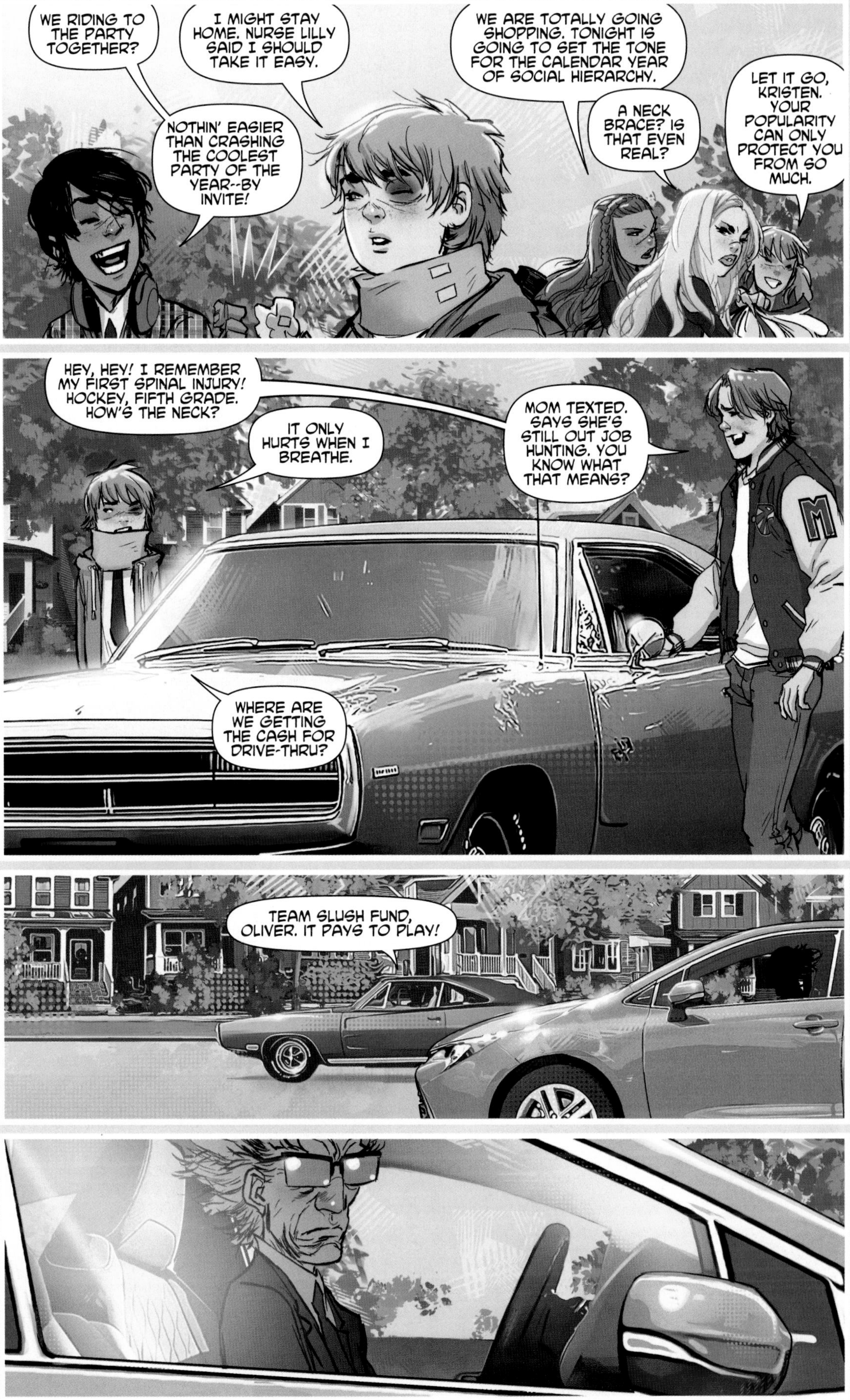
WE RIDING TO THE PARTY TOGETHER?
NOTHIN' EASIER THAN CRASHING THE COOLEST PARTY OF THE YEAR--BY INVITE!
I MIGHT STAY HOME. NURSE LILLY SAID I SHOULD TAKE IT EASY.
WE ARE TOTALLY GOING SHOPPING. TONIGHT IS GOING TO SET THE TONE FOR THE CALENDAR YEAR OF SOCIAL HIERARCHY.
A NECK BRACE? IS THAT EVEN REAL?
LET IT GO, KRISTEN. YOUR POPULARITY CAN ONLY PROTECT YOU FROM SO MUCH.
HEY, HEY! I REMEMBER MY FIRST SPINAL INJURY! HOCKEY, FIFTH GRADE. HOW'S THE NECK?
IT ONLY HURTS WHEN I BREATHE.
MOM TEXTED. SAYS SHE'S STILL OUT JOB HUNTING. YOU KNOW WHAT THAT MEANS?
WHERE ARE WE GETTING THE CASH FOR DRIVE-THRU?
TEAM SLUSH FUND, OLIVER. IT PAYS TO PLAY!

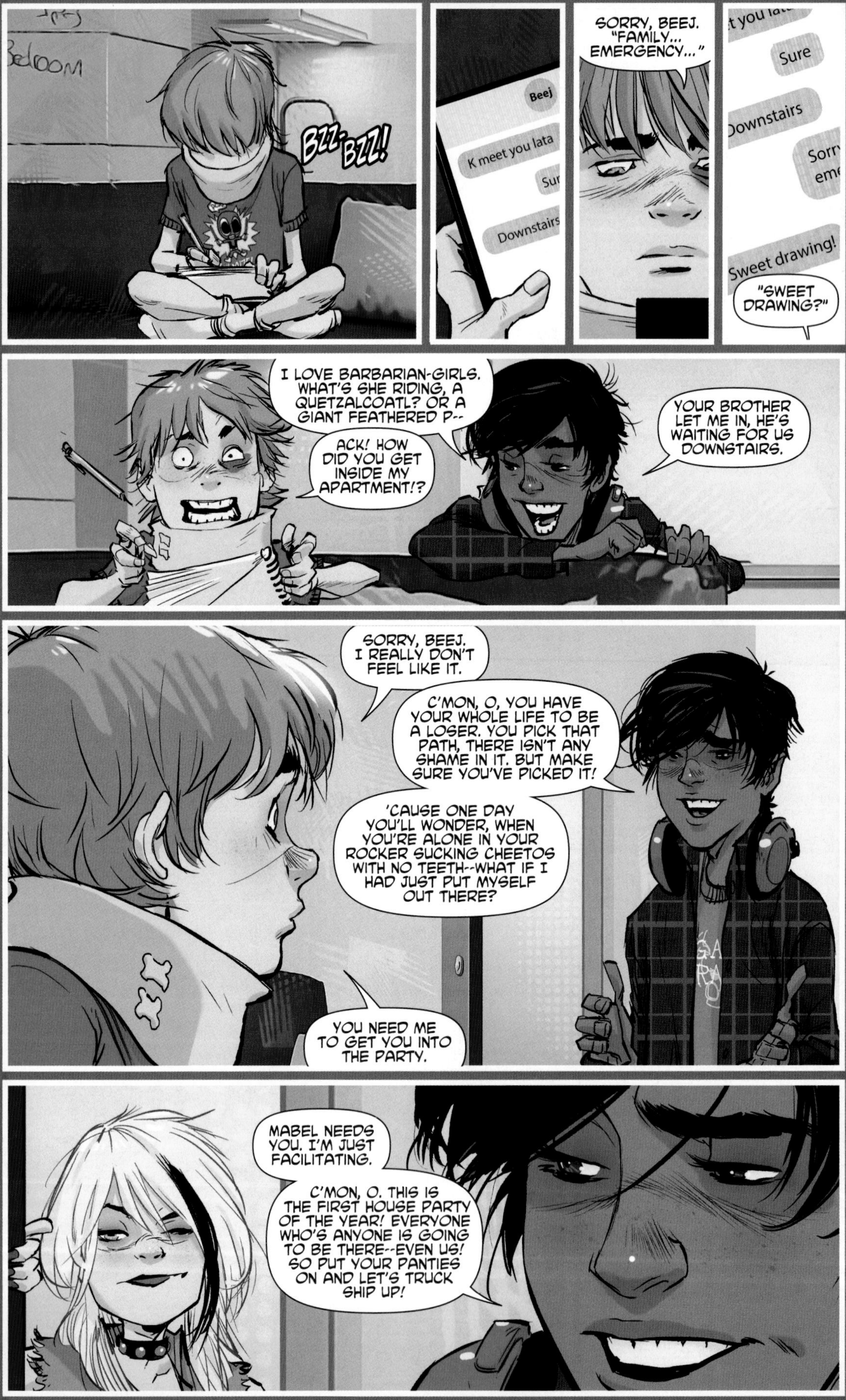
Bedroom
BZZ-BZZ!
Beej
K meet you lata
Sur
Downstairs
SORRY, BEEJ. "FAMILY... EMERGENCY..."
Sure
Downstairs
Sweet drawing!
"SWEET DRAWING?"
I LOVE BARBARIAN-GIRLS. WHAT'S SHE RIDING, A QUETZALCOATL? OR A GIANT FEATHERED P--
ACK! HOW DID YOU GET INSIDE MY APARTMENT!?
YOUR BROTHER LET ME IN, HE'S WAITING FOR US DOWNSTAIRS.
SORRY, BEEJ. I REALLY DON'T FEEL LIKE IT.
C'MON, O, YOU HAVE YOUR WHOLE LIFE TO BE A LOSER. YOU PICK THAT PATH, THERE ISN'T ANY SHAME IN IT. BUT MAKE SURE YOU'VE PICKED IT!
'CAUSE ONE DAY YOU'LL WONDER, WHEN YOU'RE ALONE IN YOUR ROCKER SUCKING CHEETOS WITH NO TEETH--WHAT IF I HAD JUST PUT MYSELF OUT THERE?
YOU NEED ME TO GET YOU INTO THE PARTY.
MABEL NEEDS YOU. I'M JUST FACILITATING.
C'MON, O. THIS IS THE FIRST HOUSE PARTY OF THE YEAR! EVERYONE WHO'S ANYONE IS GOING TO BE THERE--EVEN US! SO PUT YOUR PANTIES ON AND LET'S TRUCK SHIP UP!

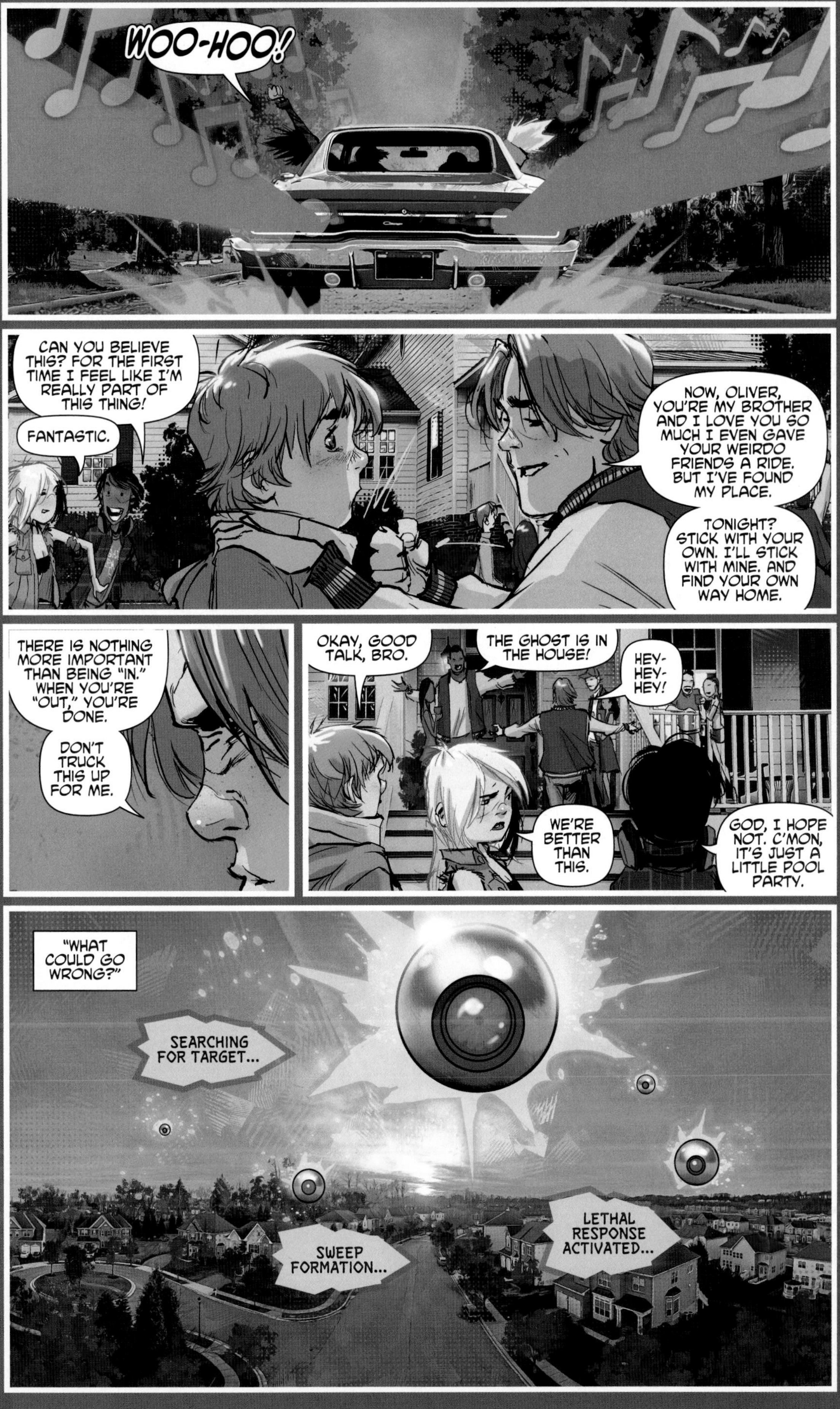
WOO-HOO!
CAN YOU BELIEVE THIS? FOR THE FIRST TIME I FEEL LIKE I'M REALLY PART OF THIS THING!
FANTASTIC.
NOW, OLIVER, YOU'RE MY BROTHER AND I LOVE YOU SO MUCH I EVEN GAVE YOUR WEIRDO FRIENDS A RIDE. BUT I'VE FOUND MY PLACE.
TONIGHT? STICK WITH YOUR OWN. I'LL STICK WITH MINE. AND FIND YOUR OWN WAY HOME.
THERE IS NOTHING MORE IMPORTANT THAN BEING "IN." WHEN YOU'RE "OUT," YOU'RE DONE.
DON'T TRUCK THIS UP FOR ME.
OKAY, GOOD TALK, BRO.
THE GHOST IS IN THE HOUSE!
HEY-HEY-HEY!
WE'RE BETTER THAN THIS.
GOD, I HOPE NOT. C'MON, IT'S JUST A LITTLE POOL PARTY.
"WHAT COULD GO WRONG?"
SEARCHING FOR TARGET...
SWEEP FORMATION...
LETHAL RESPONSE ACTIVATED...

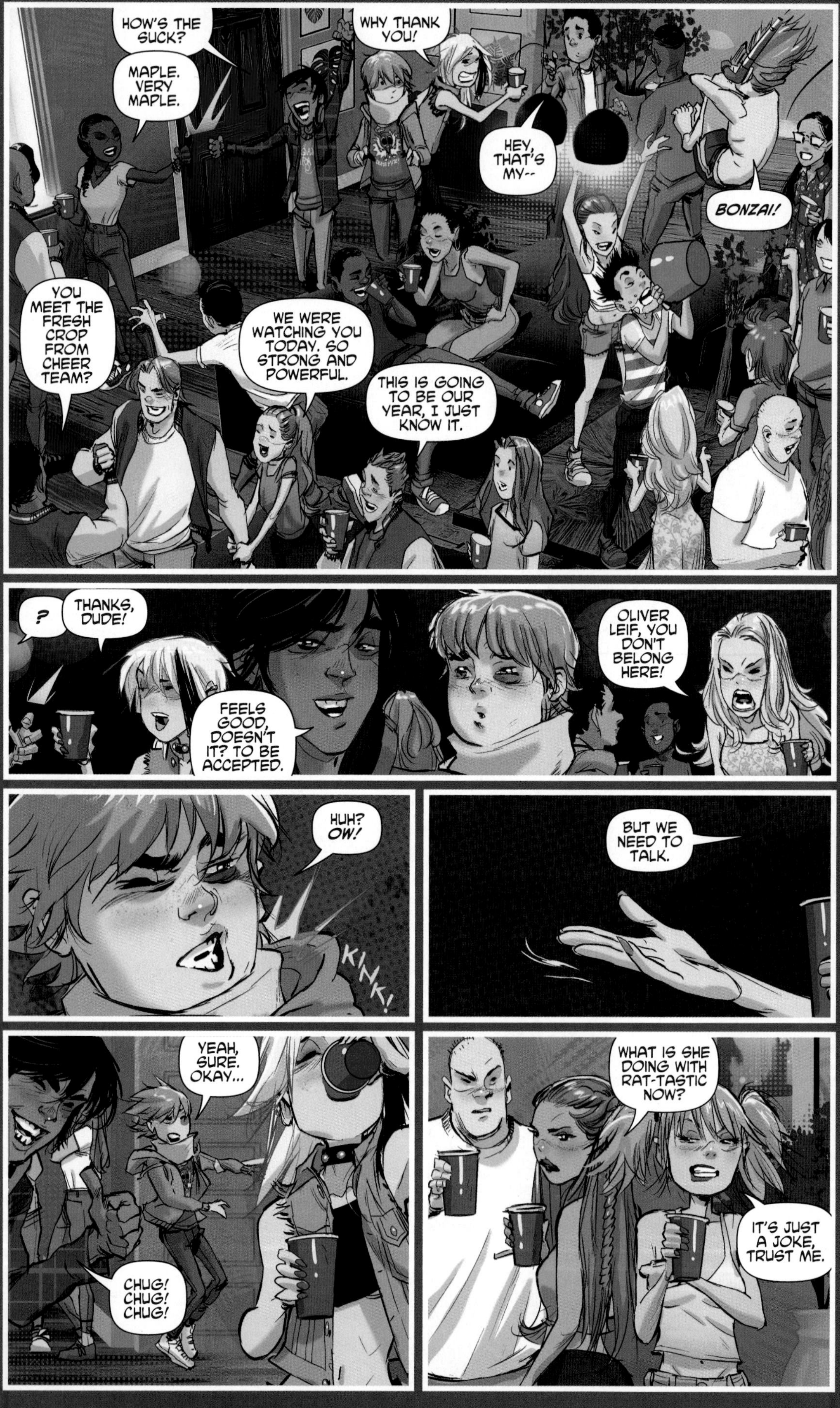
HOW'S THE SUCK?
MAPLE. VERY MAPLE.
WHY THANK YOU!
HEY, THAT'S MY--
BONZAI!
YOU MEET THE FRESH CROP FROM CHEER TEAM?
WE WERE WATCHING YOU TODAY. SO STRONG AND POWERFUL.
THIS IS GOING TO BE OUR YEAR, I JUST KNOW IT.
?
THANKS, DUDE!
FEELS GOOD, DOESN'T IT? TO BE ACCEPTED.
OLIVER LEIF, YOU DON'T BELONG HERE!
HUH? OW!
KINK!
BUT WE NEED TO TALK.
YEAH, SURE. OKAY...
CHUG! CHUG! CHUG!
WHAT IS SHE DOING WITH RAT-TASTIC NOW?
IT'S JUST A JOKE, TRUST ME.

WHAT IS THIS, SOME KIND OF JOKE?!

I KNOW WHAT I SAW! WHAT DID YOU DO TO MY VIDEO?!

MY LITTLE BROTHER AND I DIDN'T JUST HALLUCINATE FROM SOME GAS LEAK. TELL ME I'M NOT CRAZY. PLEASE...

THAT STUFF YOU SAW ME DO... IT'S ONLY TEN MINUTES AT A TIME.

ONCE I TURN IT ON, IT'S LIKE TRYING TO STOP A FIRE HOSE. AND THEN IT'S GONE. IT TAKES ME TWENTY-FOUR HOURS TO, I DON'T KNOW WHAT TO CALL IT... "RECHARGE"?

YOU'RE TELLING ME YOU HAVE ALL THE POWER OF THE WORLD'S CRAPPIEST CELL PHONE BATTERY?

SO, I'M NOT CRAZY.

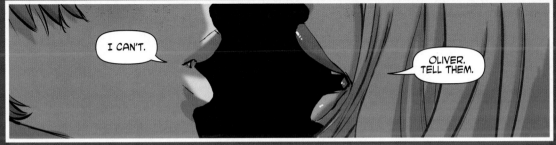

I DIDN'T SCREW WITH YOUR VIDEO. IT JUST GETS MESSED UP WHEN I DO MY THING. I'M NOT A SCIENTIST AND I DON'T KNOW WHY. IT JUST DOES.

YOU NEED TO TELL PEOPLE. THEY'RE ALL LAUGHING AT ME.

I CAN'T.

OLIVER. TELL THEM.

MY DAD... IT WAS MY FAULT.

IF PEOPLE KNEW WHAT I COULD DO, EVERYONE I CARE ABOUT WOULD BE IN DANGER... INCLUDING YOU.

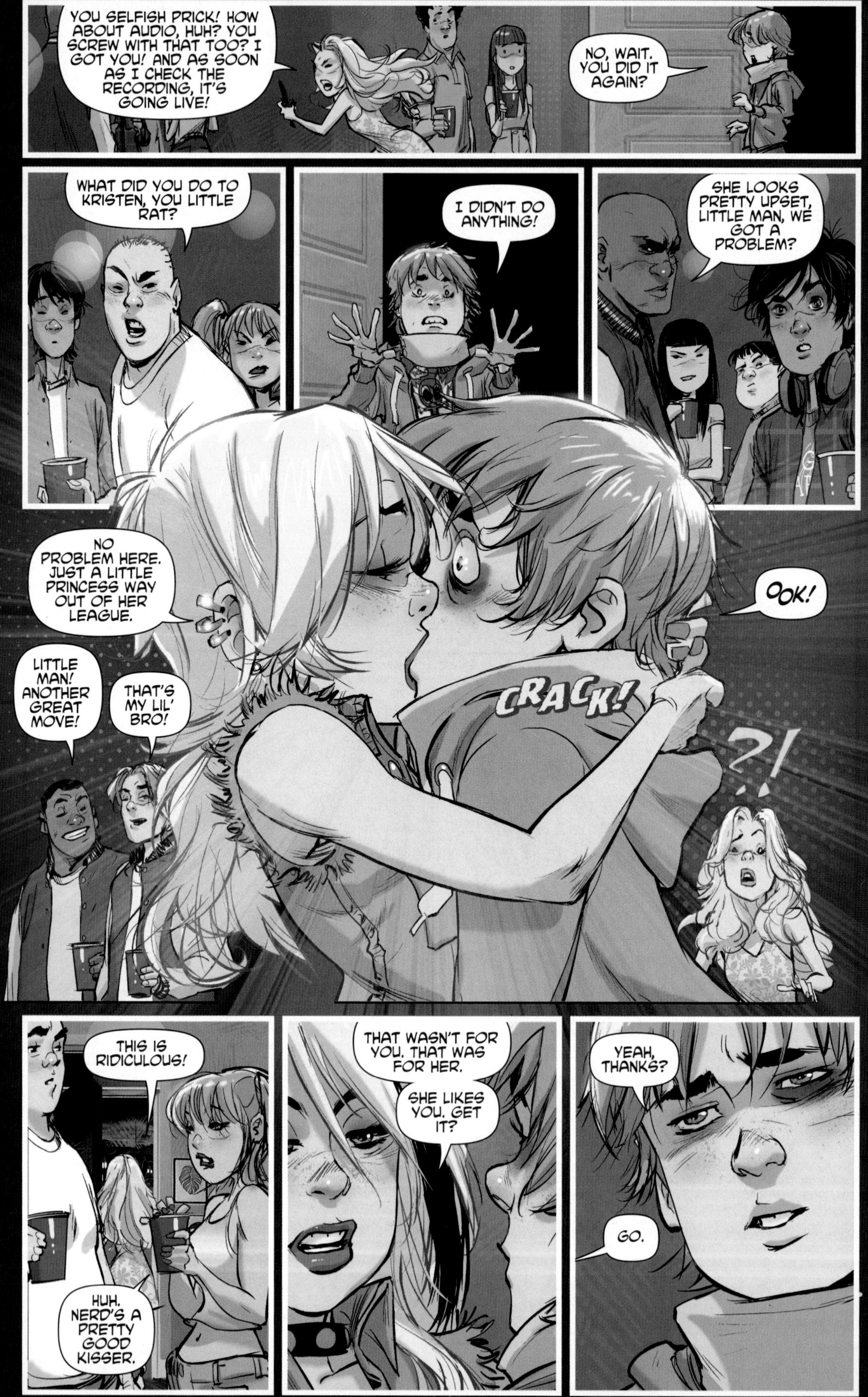
YOU SELFISH PRICK! HOW ABOUT AUDIO, HUH? YOU SCREW WITH THAT TOO? I GOT YOU! AND AS SOON AS I CHECK THE RECORDING, IT'S GOING LIVE!
NO, WAIT. YOU DID IT AGAIN?
WHAT DID YOU DO TO KRISTEN, YOU LITTLE RAT?
I DIDN'T DO ANYTHING!
SHE LOOKS PRETTY UPSET, LITTLE MAN, WE GOT A PROBLEM?
NO PROBLEM HERE. JUST A LITTLE PRINCESS WAY OUT OF HER LEAGUE.
OOK!
CRACK!
LITTLE MAN! ANOTHER GREAT MOVE!
THAT'S MY LIL' BRO!
?!
THIS IS RIDICULOUS!
HUH. NERD'S A PRETTY GOOD KISSER.
THAT WASN'T FOR YOU. THAT WAS FOR HER.
SHE LIKES YOU. GET IT?
YEAH, THANKS?
GO.

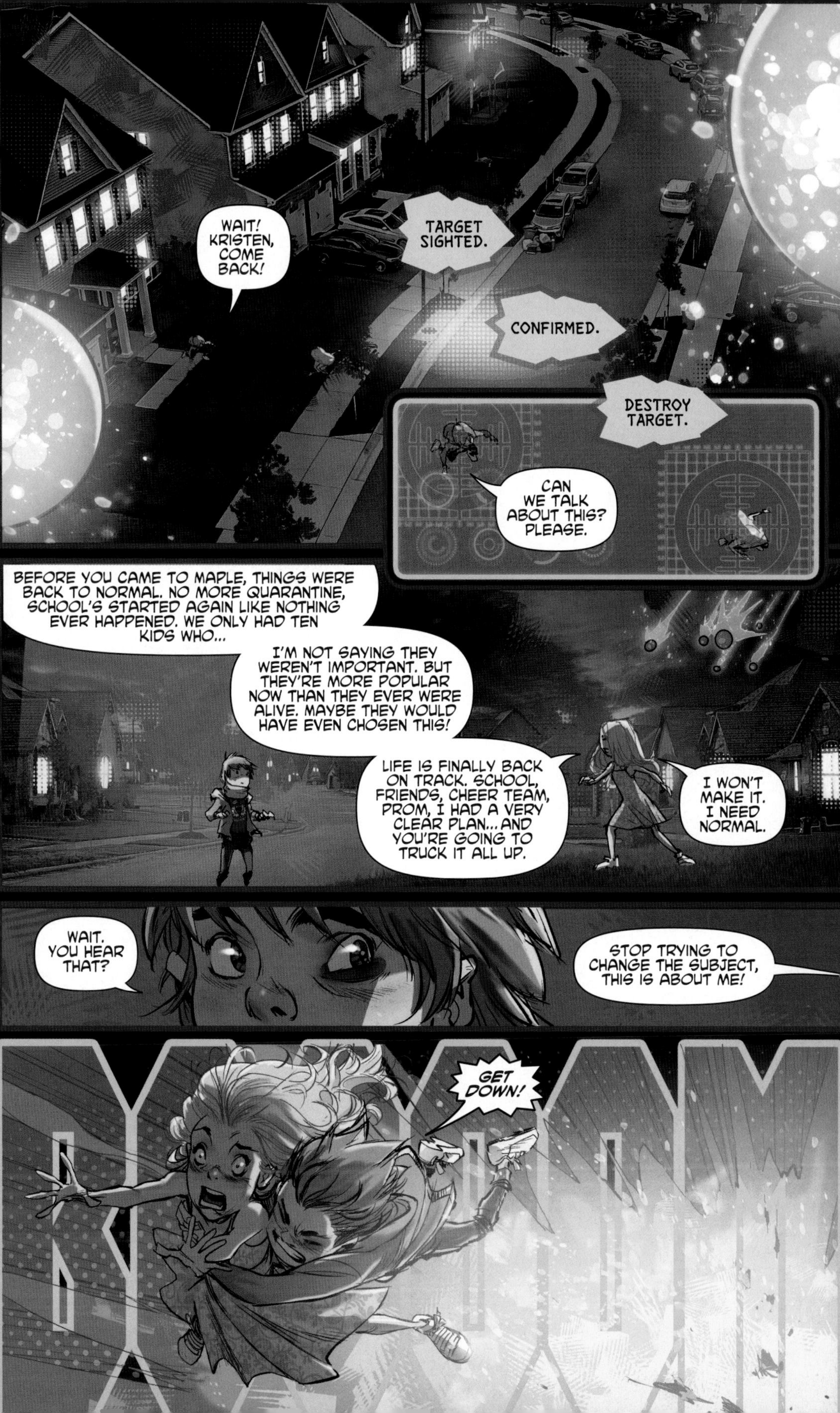

WAIT! KRISTEN, COME BACK!
TARGET SIGHTED.
CONFIRMED.
DESTROY TARGET.
CAN WE TALK ABOUT THIS? PLEASE.
BEFORE YOU CAME TO MAPLE, THINGS WERE BACK TO NORMAL. NO MORE QUARANTINE, SCHOOL'S STARTED AGAIN LIKE NOTHING EVER HAPPENED. WE ONLY HAD TEN KIDS WHO...
I'M NOT SAYING THEY WEREN'T IMPORTANT. BUT THEY'RE MORE POPULAR NOW THAN THEY EVER WERE ALIVE. MAYBE THEY WOULD HAVE EVEN CHOSEN THIS!
LIFE IS FINALLY BACK ON TRACK. SCHOOL, FRIENDS, CHEER TEAM, PROM, I HAD A VERY CLEAR PLAN... AND YOU'RE GOING TO TRUCK IT ALL UP.
I WON'T MAKE IT. I NEED NORMAL.
WAIT. YOU HEAR THAT?
STOP TRYING TO CHANGE THE SUBJECT, THIS IS ABOUT ME!
GET DOWN!

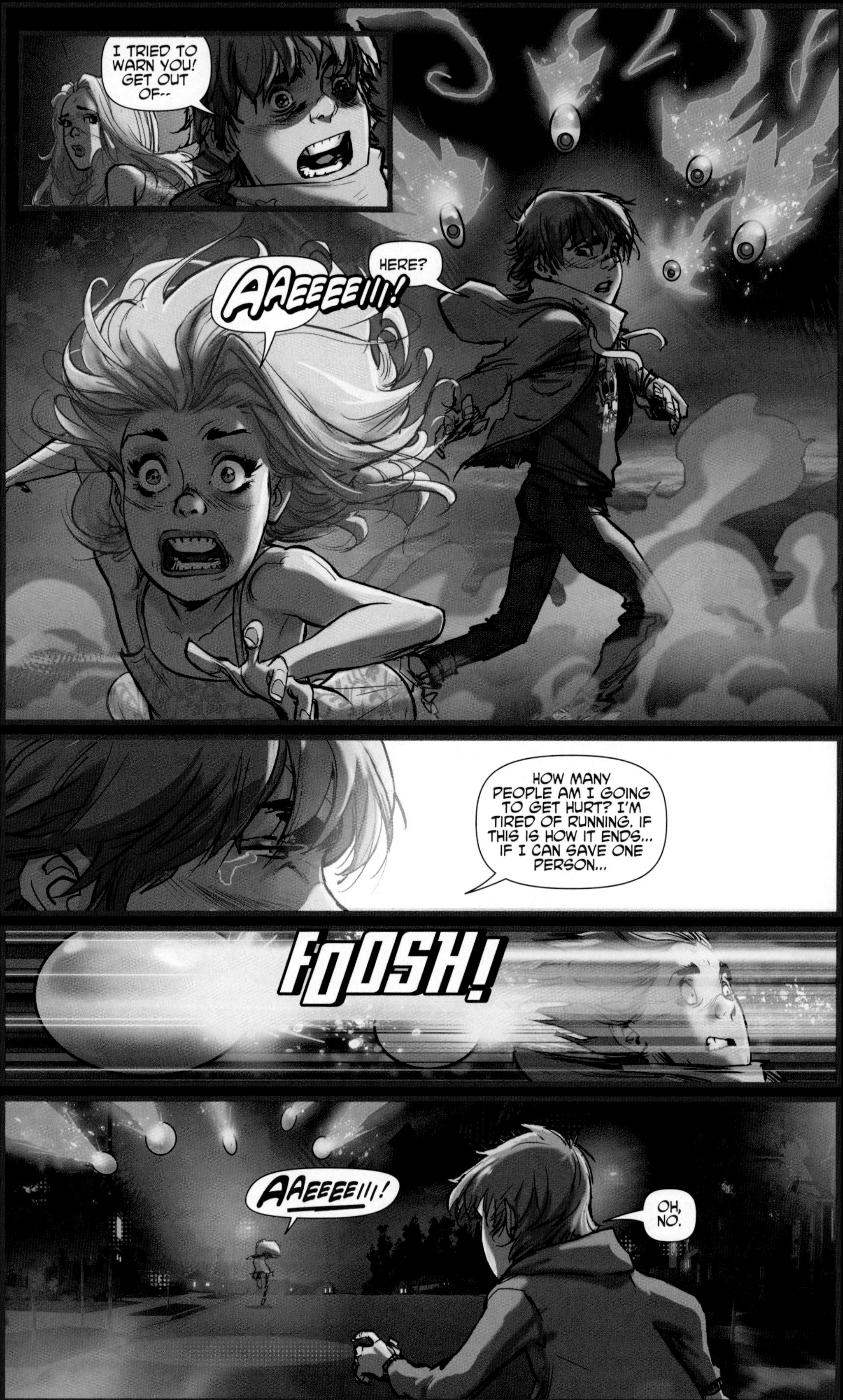
I TRIED TO WARN YOU! GET OUT OF--
HERE?
AAEEEEIII!
HOW MANY PEOPLE AM I GOING TO GET HURT? I'M TIRED OF RUNNING. IF THIS IS HOW IT ENDS... IF I CAN SAVE ONE PERSON...
FOOSH!
AAEEEEIII!
OH, NO.

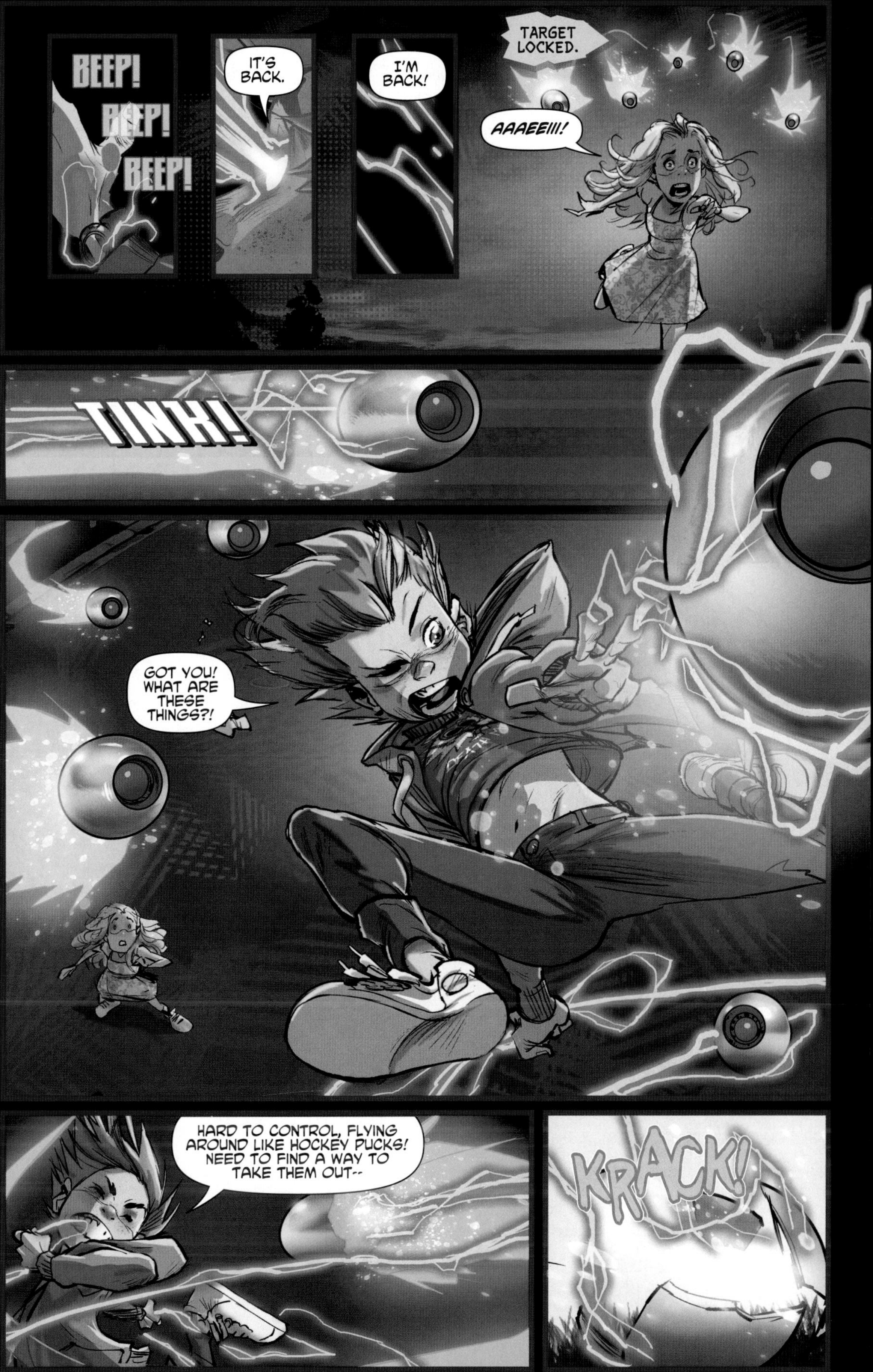
BEEP! BEEP! BEEP!
IT'S BACK.
I'M BACK!
TARGET LOCKED.
AAAEEIII!
TINK!
GOT YOU! WHAT ARE THESE THINGS?!
HARD TO CONTROL, FLYING AROUND LIKE HOCKEY PUCKS! NEED TO FIND A WAY TO TAKE THEM OUT--
KRACK!

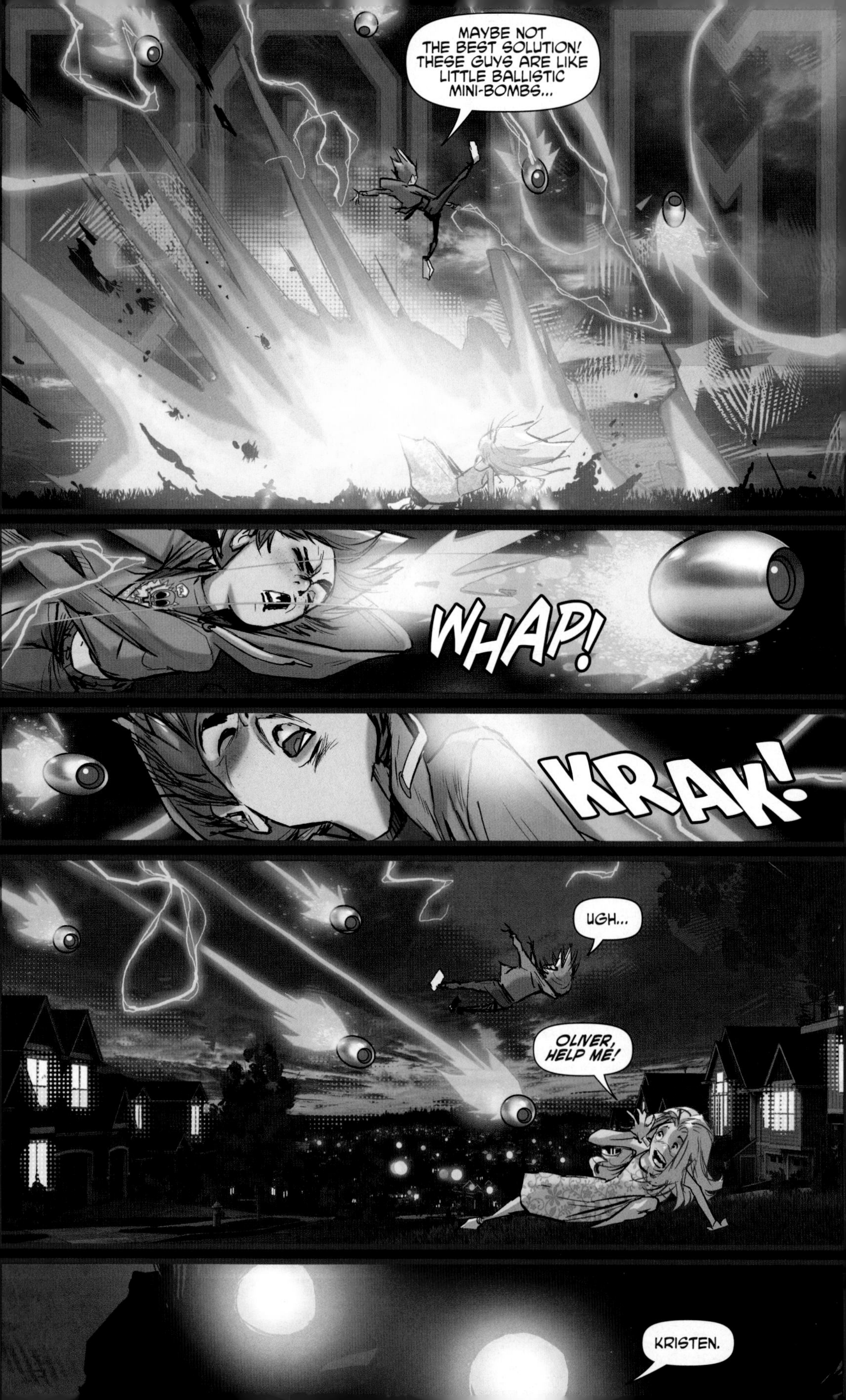
MAYBE NOT THE BEST SOLUTION! THESE GUYS ARE LIKE LITTLE BALLISTIC MINI-BOMBS...
WHAP!
KRAK!
UGH...
OLIVER, HELP ME!
KRISTEN.

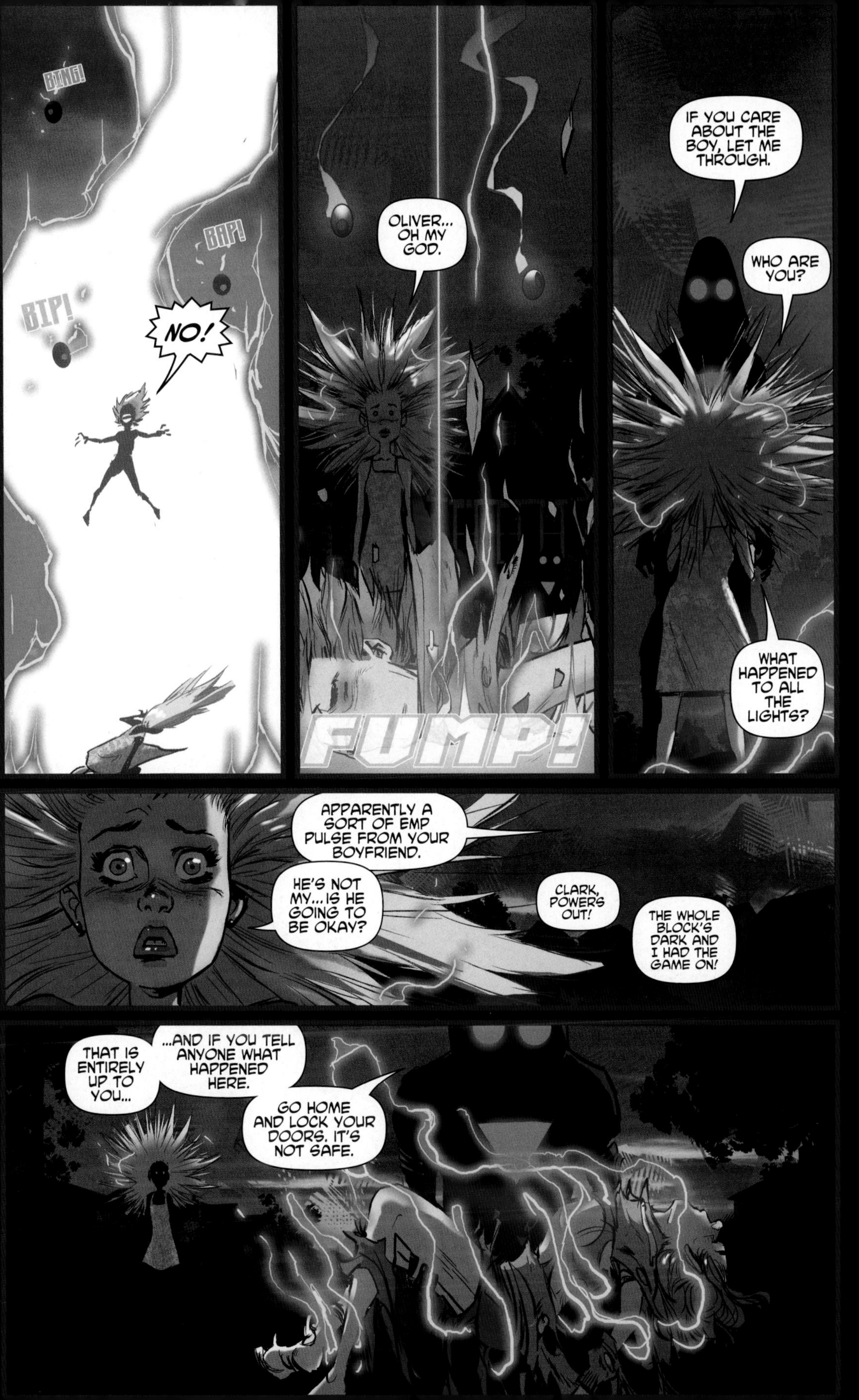
BING!
BAP!
BIP!
NO!
OLIVER... OH MY GOD.
FUMP!
IF YOU CARE ABOUT THE BOY, LET ME THROUGH.
WHO ARE YOU?
WHAT HAPPENED TO ALL THE LIGHTS?
APPARENTLY A SORT OF EMP PULSE FROM YOUR BOYFRIEND.
HE'S NOT MY... IS HE GOING TO BE OKAY?
CLARK, POWER'S OUT!
THE WHOLE BLOCK'S DARK AND I HAD THE GAME ON!
THAT IS ENTIRELY UP TO YOU...
...AND IF YOU TELL ANYONE WHAT HAPPENED HERE.
GO HOME AND LOCK YOUR DOORS. IT'S NOT SAFE.

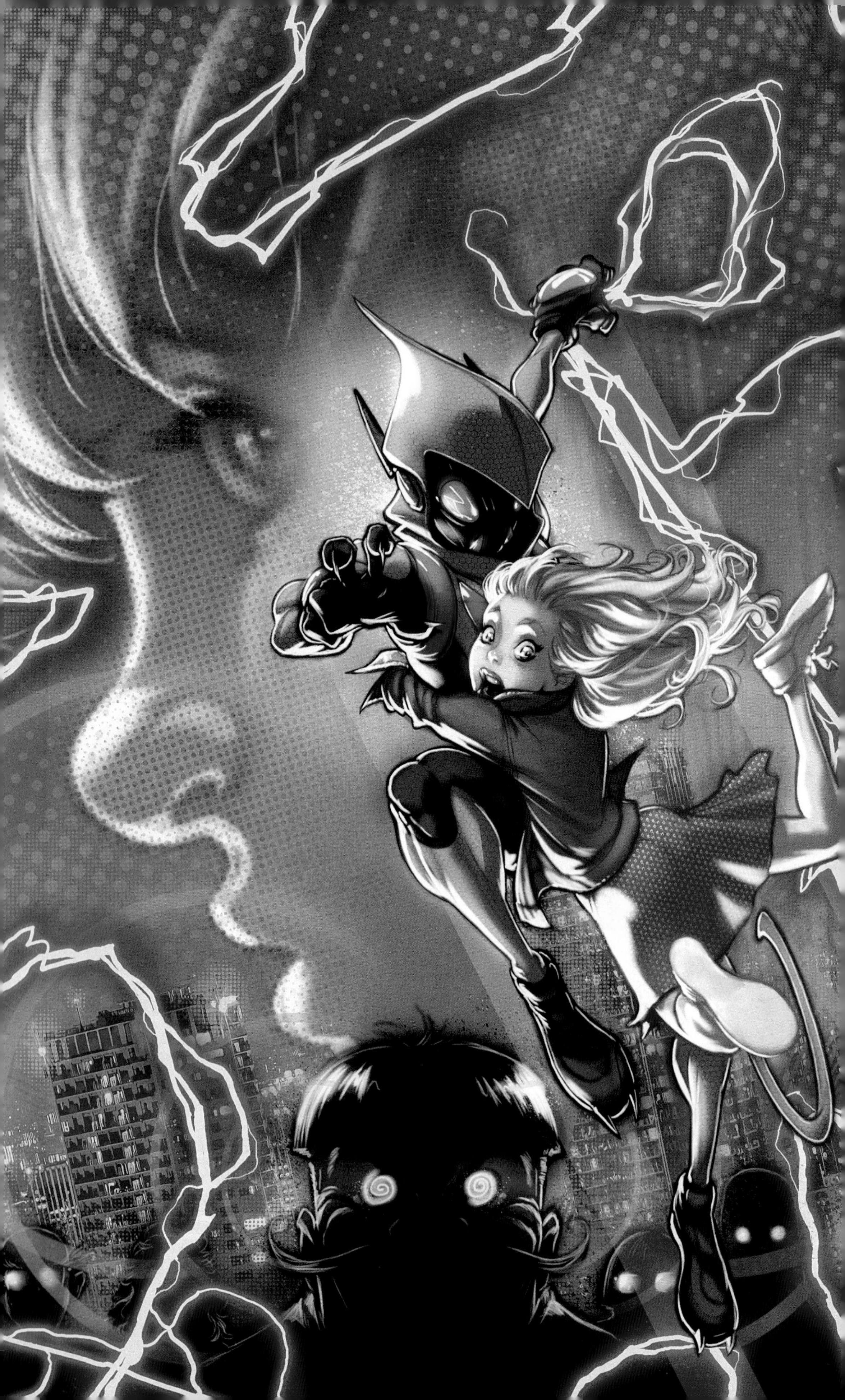

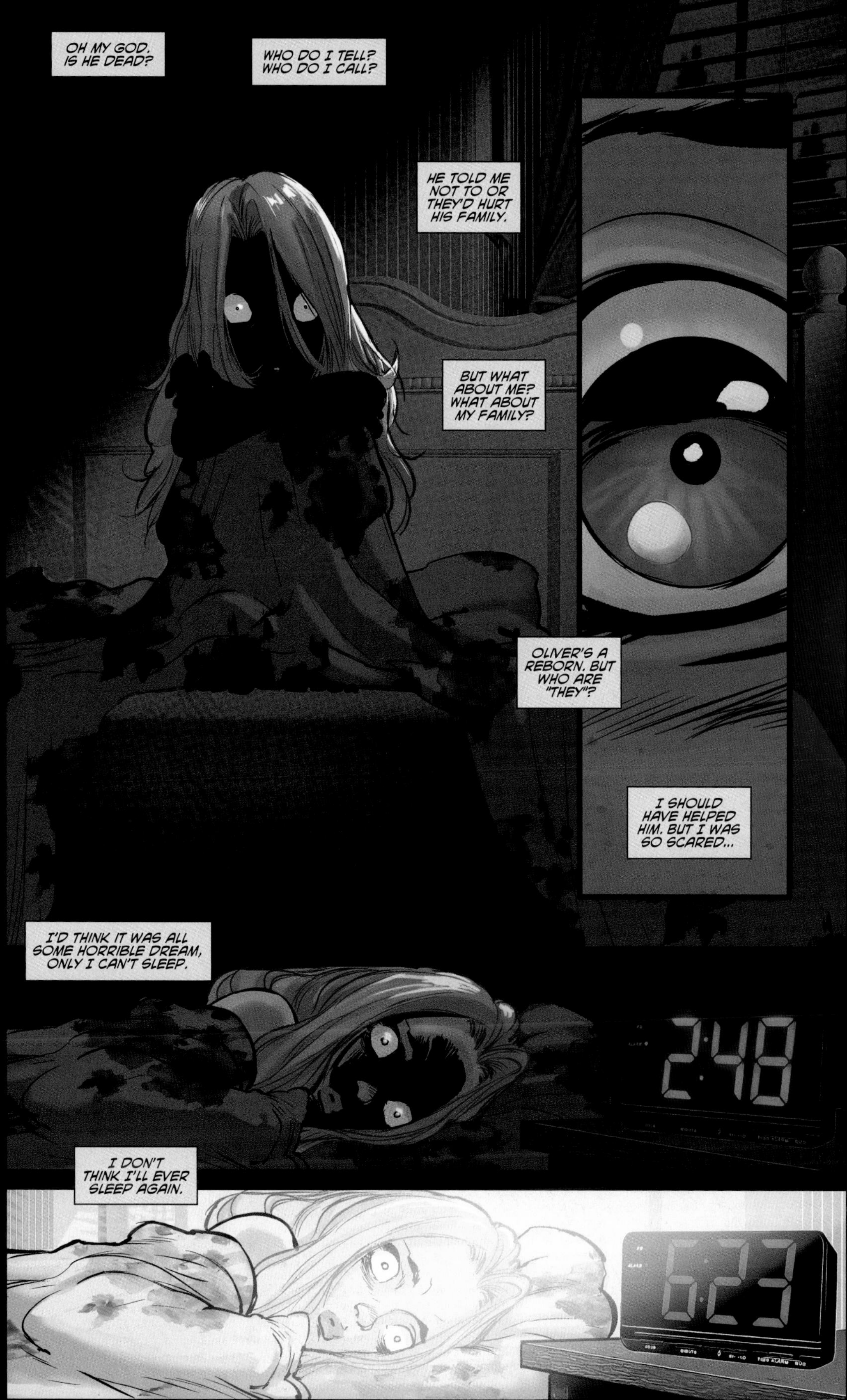
OH MY GOD. IS HE DEAD?
WHO DO I TELL? WHO DO I CALL?
HE TOLD ME NOT TO OR THEY'D HURT HIS FAMILY.
BUT WHAT ABOUT ME? WHAT ABOUT MY FAMILY?
OLIVER'S A REBORN. BUT WHO ARE "THEY"?
I SHOULD HAVE HELPED HIM. BUT I WAS SO SCARED...
I'D THINK IT WAS ALL SOME HORRIBLE DREAM, ONLY I CAN'T SLEEP.
2:48
I DON'T THINK I'LL EVER SLEEP AGAIN.
6:23

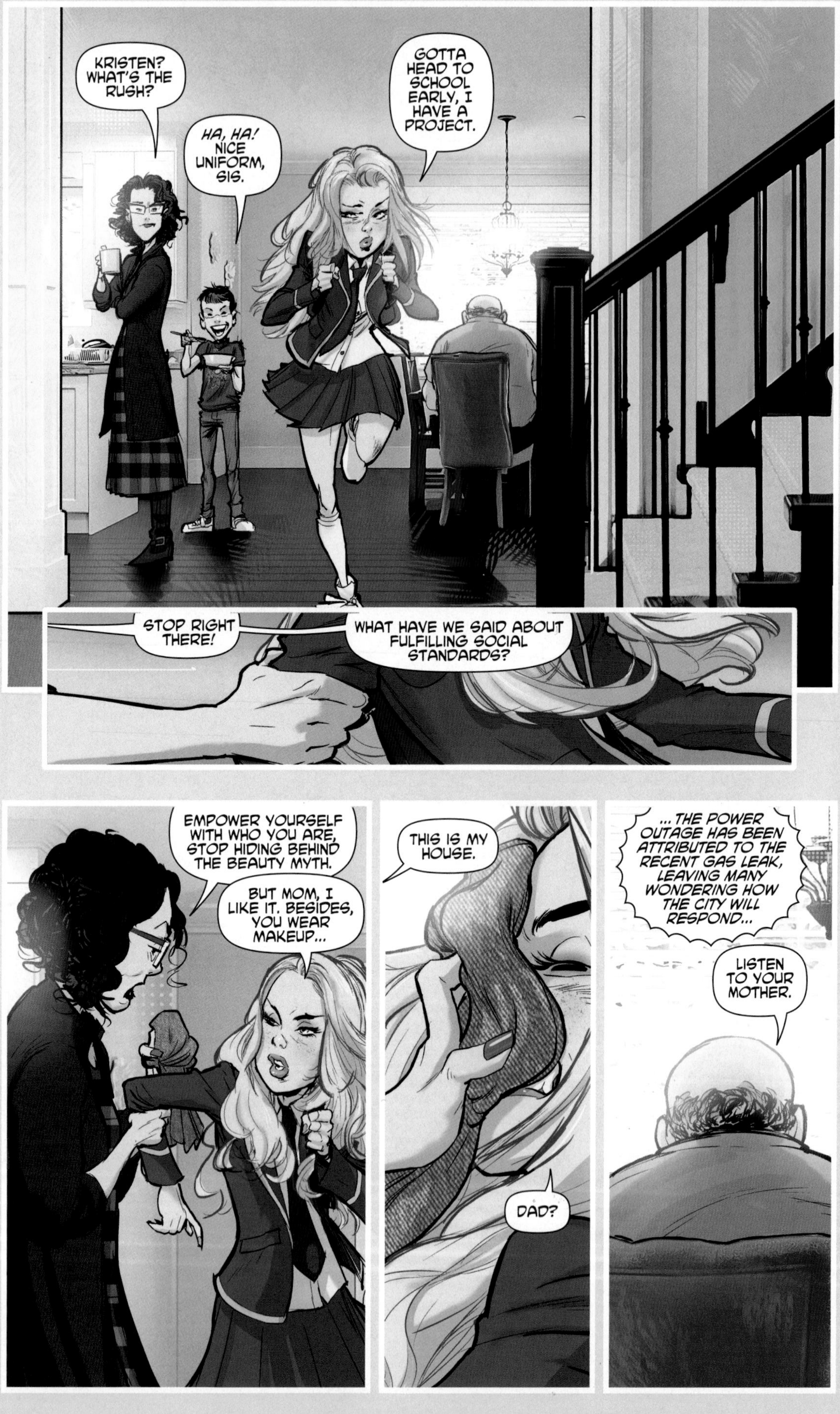
KRISTEN? WHAT'S THE RUSH?
HA, HA! NICE UNIFORM, SIS.
GOTTA HEAD TO SCHOOL EARLY, I HAVE A PROJECT.
STOP RIGHT THERE!
WHAT HAVE WE SAID ABOUT FULFILLING SOCIAL STANDARDS?
EMPOWER YOURSELF WITH WHO YOU ARE, STOP HIDING BEHIND THE BEAUTY MYTH.
BUT MOM, I LIKE IT. BESIDES, YOU WEAR MAKEUP...
THIS IS MY HOUSE.
DAD?
...THE POWER OUTAGE HAS BEEN ATTRIBUTED TO THE RECENT GAS LEAK, LEAVING MANY WONDERING HOW THE CITY WILL RESPOND...
LISTEN TO YOUR MOTHER.

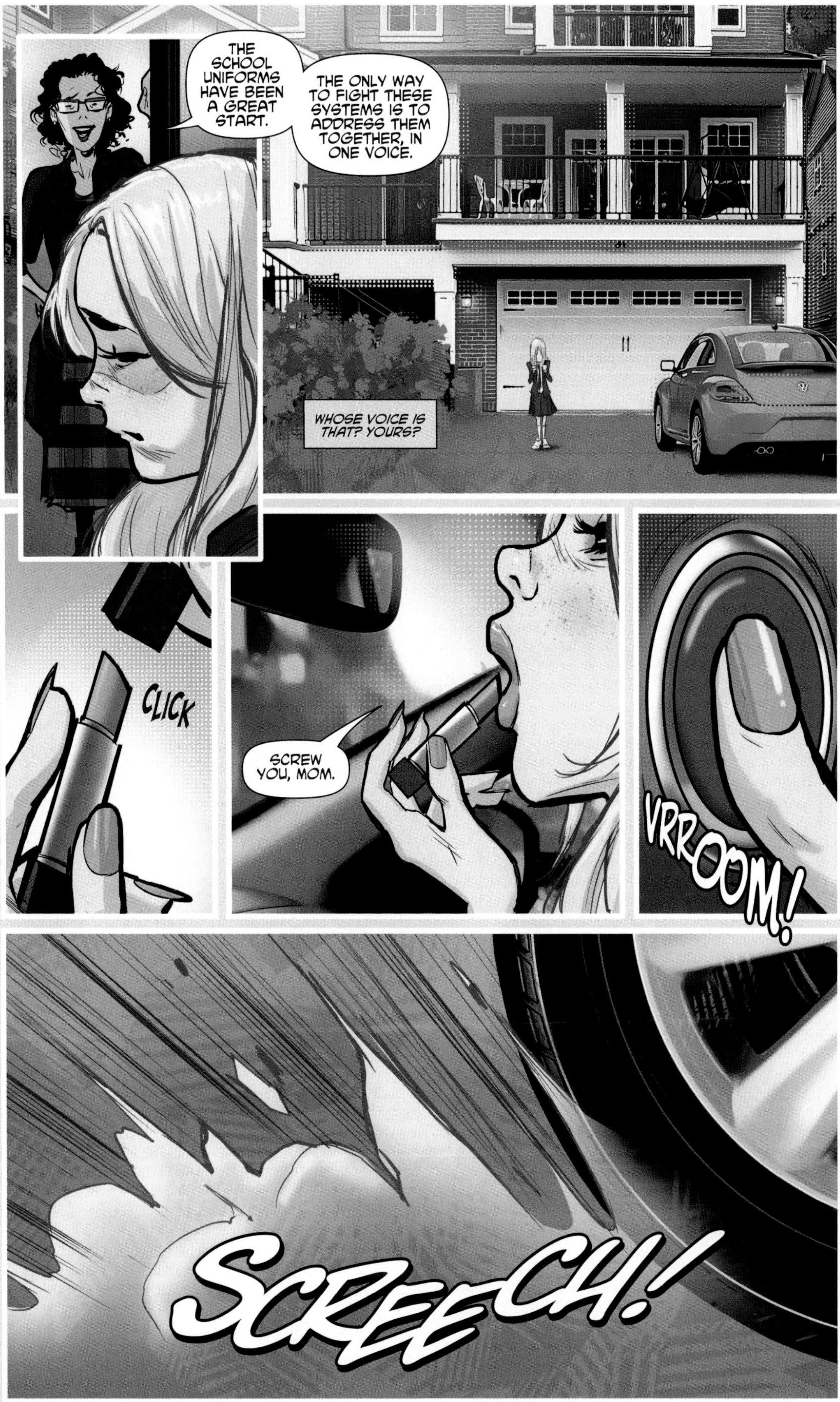
THE SCHOOL UNIFORMS HAVE BEEN A GREAT START.
THE ONLY WAY TO FIGHT THESE SYSTEMS IS TO ADDRESS THEM TOGETHER, IN ONE VOICE.
WHOSE VOICE IS THAT? YOURS?
CLICK
SCREW YOU, MOM.
VRROOM!
SCREECH!

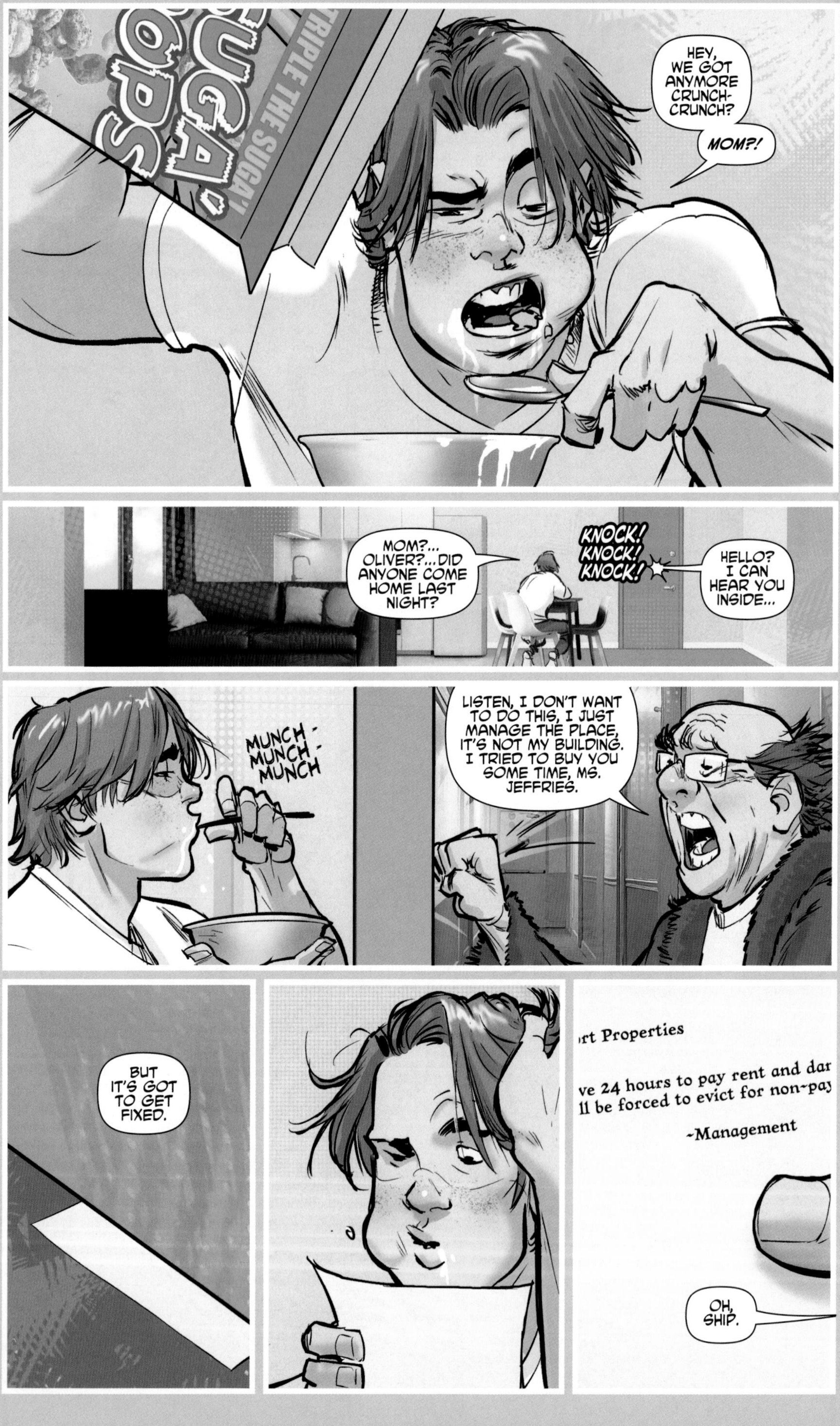
TRIPLE THE SUGA'!
SUGA' OPS
HEY, WE GOT ANYMORE CRUNCH-CRUNCH?
MOM?!
MOM?... OLIVER?...DID ANYONE COME HOME LAST NIGHT?
KNOCK! KNOCK! KNOCK!
HELLO? I CAN HEAR YOU INSIDE...
MUNCH-MUNCH-MUNCH
LISTEN, I DON'T WANT TO DO THIS, I JUST MANAGE THE PLACE, IT'S NOT MY BUILDING. I TRIED TO BUY YOU SOME TIME, MS. JEFFRIES.
BUT IT'S GOT TO GET FIXED.
rt Properties
ve 24 hours to pay rent and dar
ll be forced to evict for non-pay
~Management
OH, SHIP.

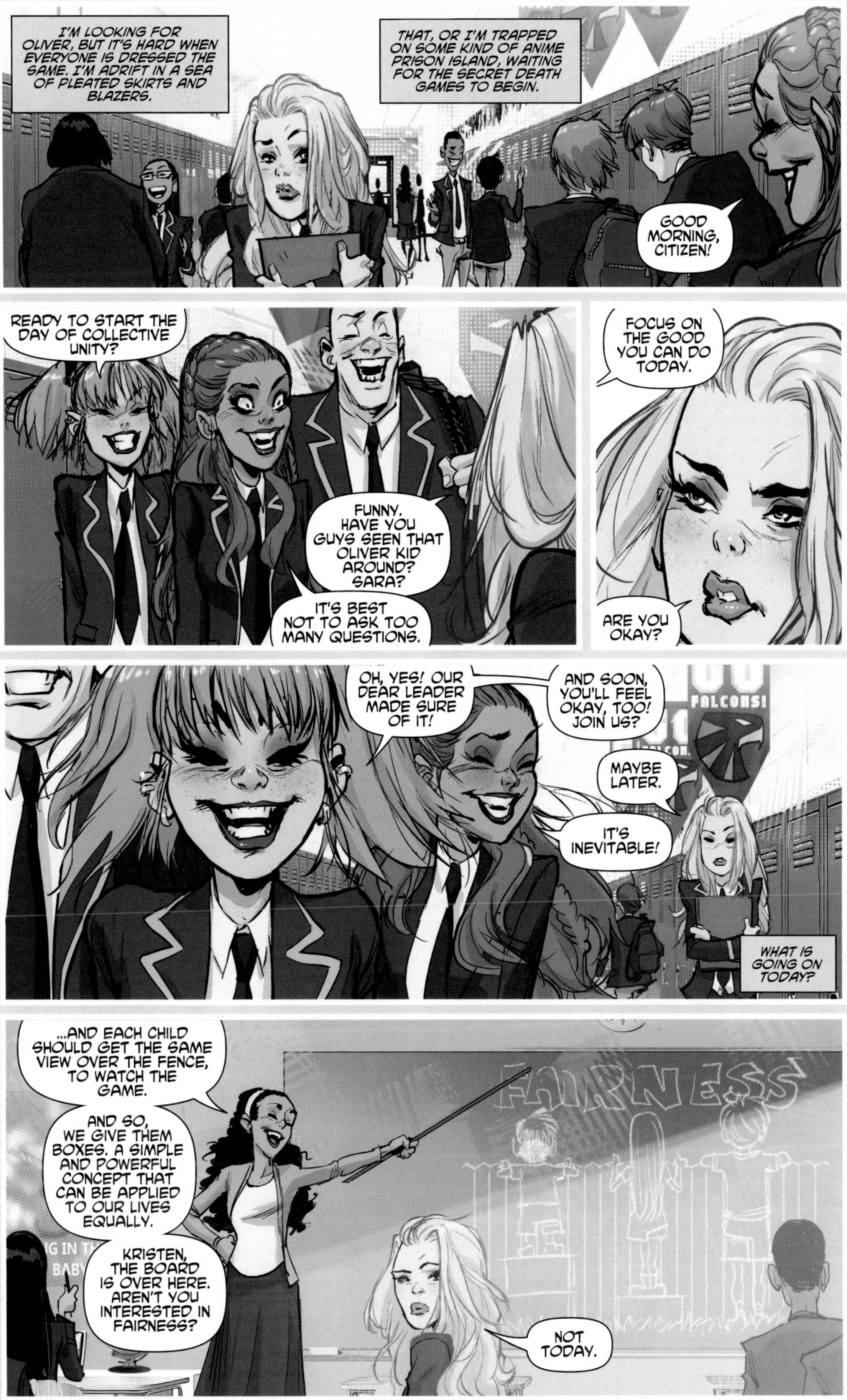
I'M LOOKING FOR OLIVER, BUT IT'S HARD WHEN EVERYONE IS DRESSED THE SAME. I'M ADRIFT IN A SEA OF PLEATED SKIRTS AND BLAZERS.
THAT, OR I'M TRAPPED ON SOME KIND OF ANIME PRISON ISLAND, WAITING FOR THE SECRET DEATH GAMES TO BEGIN.
GOOD MORNING, CITIZEN!
READY TO START THE DAY OF COLLECTIVE UNITY?
FUNNY. HAVE YOU GUYS SEEN THAT OLIVER KID AROUND? SARA?
IT'S BEST NOT TO ASK TOO MANY QUESTIONS.
FOCUS ON THE GOOD YOU CAN DO TODAY.
ARE YOU OKAY?
OH, YES! OUR DEAR LEADER MADE SURE OF IT!
AND SOON, YOU'LL FEEL OKAY, TOO! JOIN US?
FALCONS!
MAYBE LATER.
IT'S INEVITABLE!
WHAT IS GOING ON TODAY?
...AND EACH CHILD SHOULD GET THE SAME VIEW OVER THE FENCE, TO WATCH THE GAME.
FAIRNESS
AND SO, WE GIVE THEM BOXES. A SIMPLE AND POWERFUL CONCEPT THAT CAN BE APPLIED TO OUR LIVES EQUALLY.
KRISTEN, THE BOARD IS OVER HERE. AREN'T YOU INTERESTED IN FAIRNESS?
NOT TODAY.

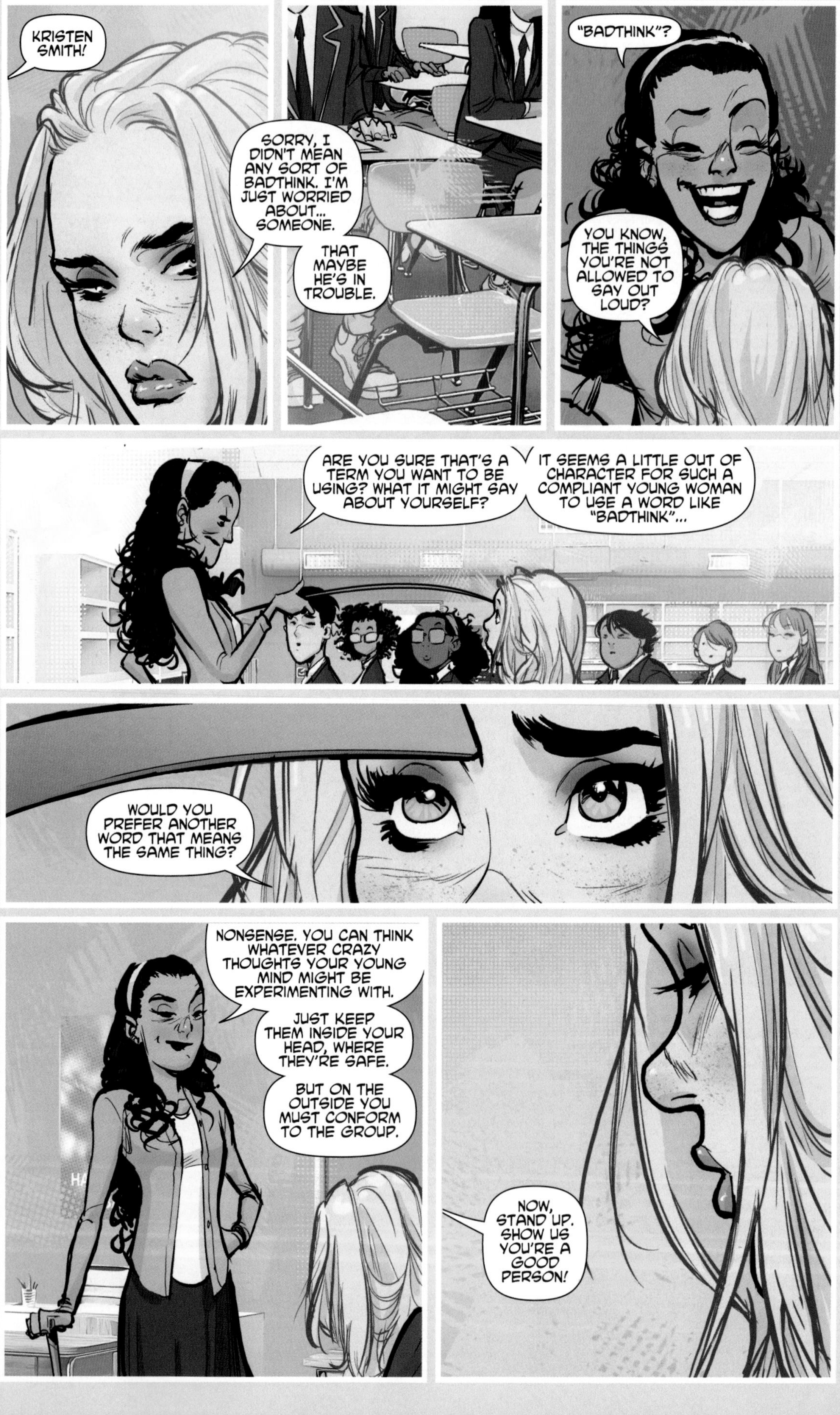
KRISTEN SMITH!
SORRY, I DIDN'T MEAN ANY SORT OF BADTHINK. I'M JUST WORRIED ABOUT... SOMEONE.
THAT MAYBE HE'S IN TROUBLE.
"BADTHINK"?
YOU KNOW, THE THINGS YOU'RE NOT ALLOWED TO SAY OUT LOUD?
ARE YOU SURE THAT'S A TERM YOU WANT TO BE USING? WHAT IT MIGHT SAY ABOUT YOURSELF?
IT SEEMS A LITTLE OUT OF CHARACTER FOR SUCH A COMPLIANT YOUNG WOMAN TO USE A WORD LIKE "BADTHINK"...
WOULD YOU PREFER ANOTHER WORD THAT MEANS THE SAME THING?
NONSENSE. YOU CAN THINK WHATEVER CRAZY THOUGHTS YOUR YOUNG MIND MIGHT BE EXPERIMENTING WITH.
JUST KEEP THEM INSIDE YOUR HEAD, WHERE THEY'RE SAFE.
BUT ON THE OUTSIDE YOU MUST CONFORM TO THE GROUP.
NOW, STAND UP. SHOW US YOU'RE A GOOD PERSON!

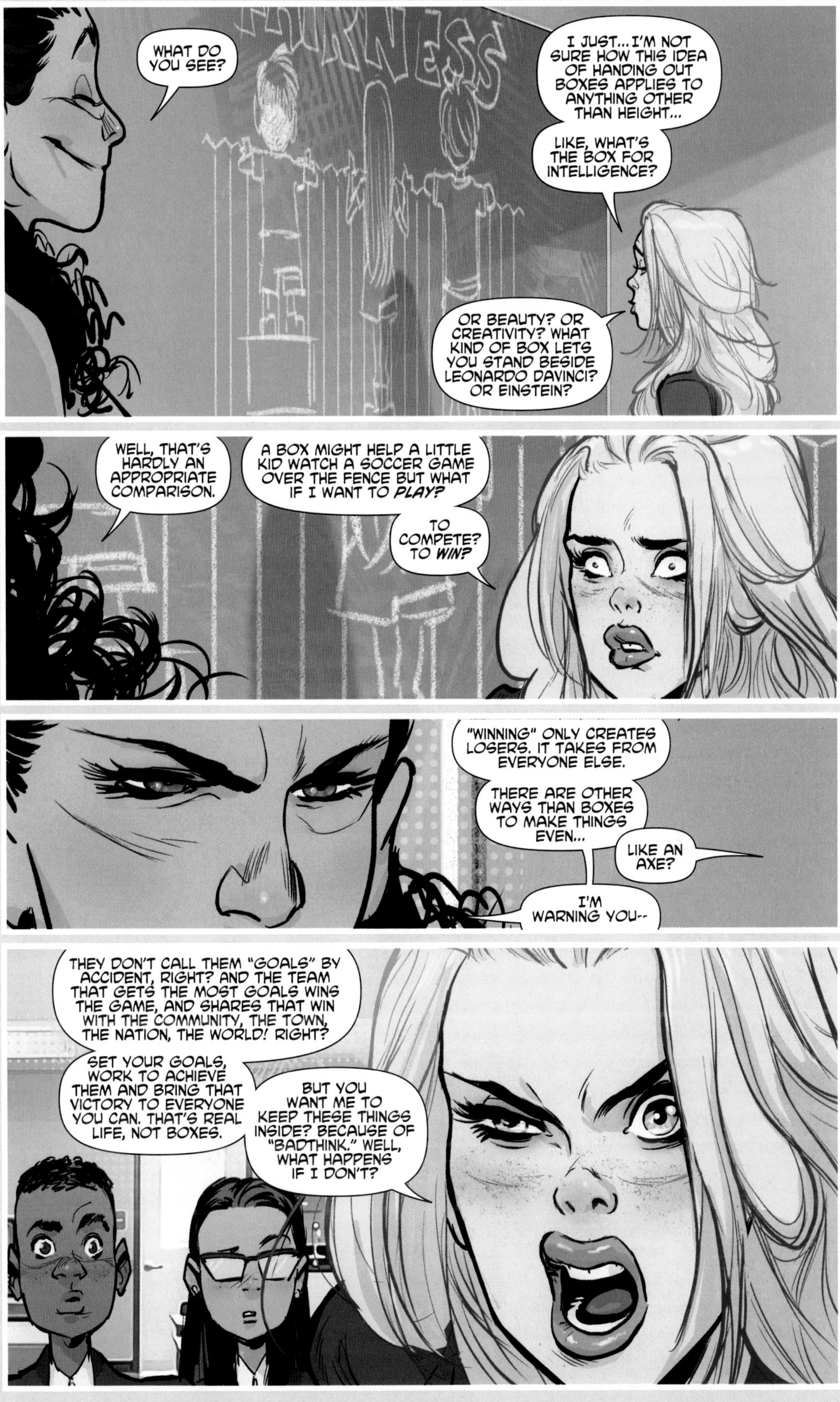
WHAT DO YOU SEE?
I JUST... I'M NOT SURE HOW THIS IDEA OF HANDING OUT BOXES APPLIES TO ANYTHING OTHER THAN HEIGHT...
LIKE, WHAT'S THE BOX FOR INTELLIGENCE?
OR BEAUTY? OR CREATIVITY? WHAT KIND OF BOX LETS YOU STAND BESIDE LEONARDO DAVINCI? OR EINSTEIN?
WELL, THAT'S HARDLY AN APPROPRIATE COMPARISON.
A BOX MIGHT HELP A LITTLE KID WATCH A SOCCER GAME OVER THE FENCE BUT WHAT IF I WANT TO *PLAY?*
TO COMPETE? TO *WIN?*
"WINNING" ONLY CREATES LOSERS. IT TAKES FROM EVERYONE ELSE.
THERE ARE OTHER WAYS THAN BOXES TO MAKE THINGS EVEN...
LIKE AN AXE?
I'M WARNING YOU--
THEY DON'T CALL THEM "GOALS" BY ACCIDENT, RIGHT? AND THE TEAM THAT GETS THE MOST GOALS WINS THE GAME, AND SHARES THAT WIN WITH THE COMMUNITY, THE TOWN, THE NATION, THE WORLD! RIGHT?
SET YOUR GOALS, WORK TO ACHIEVE THEM AND BRING THAT VICTORY TO EVERYONE YOU CAN. THAT'S REAL LIFE, NOT BOXES.
BUT YOU WANT ME TO KEEP THESE THINGS INSIDE? BECAUSE OF "BADTHINK." WELL, WHAT HAPPENS IF I DON'T?

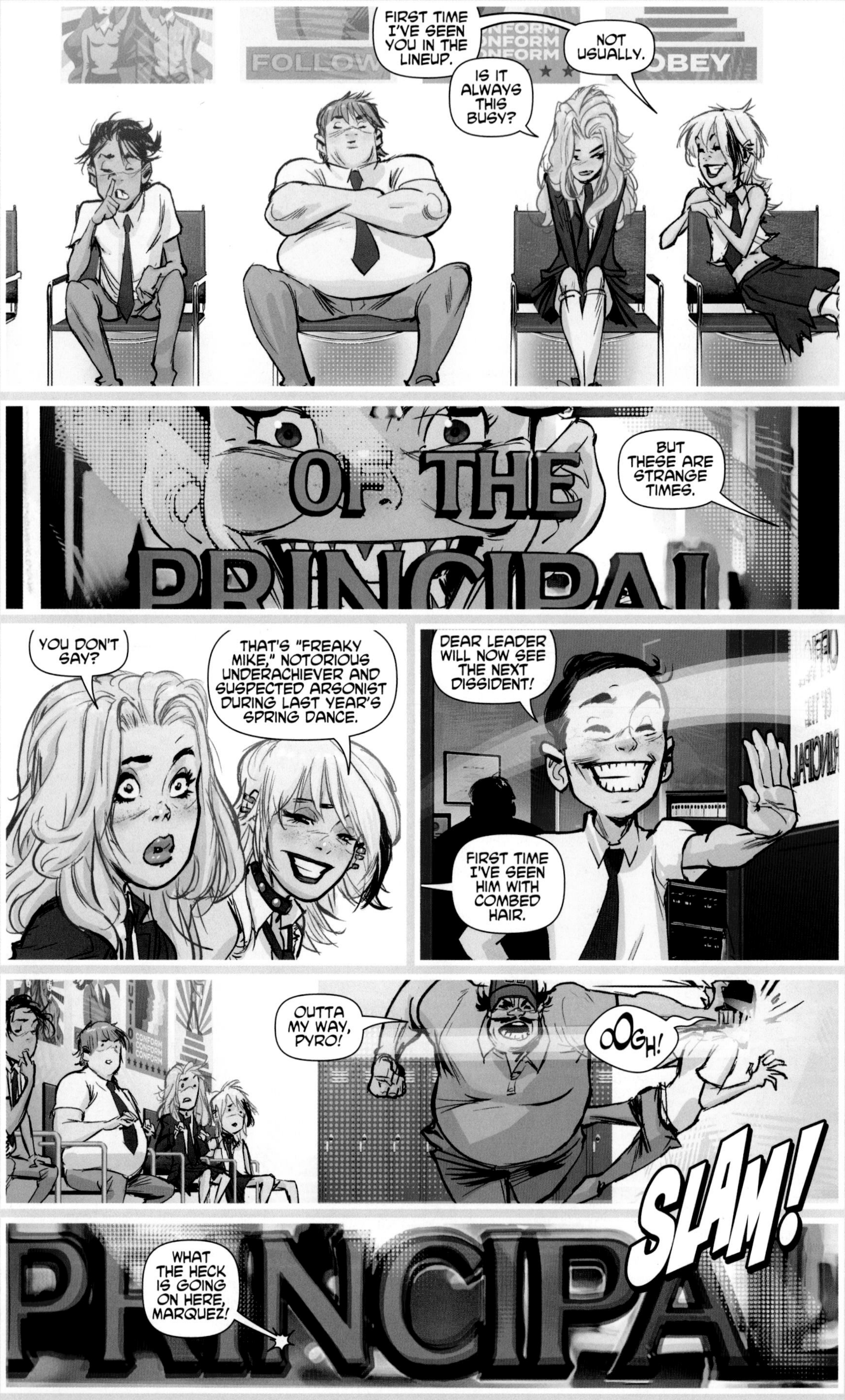

FOLLOW
CONFORM CONFORM CONFORM
OBEY
FIRST TIME I'VE SEEN YOU IN THE LINEUP.
IS IT ALWAYS THIS BUSY?
NOT USUALLY.
OF THE PRINCIPAL
BUT THESE ARE STRANGE TIMES.
YOU DON'T SAY?
THAT'S "FREAKY MIKE," NOTORIOUS UNDERACHIEVER AND SUSPECTED ARSONIST DURING LAST YEAR'S SPRING DANCE.
DEAR LEADER WILL NOW SEE THE NEXT DISSIDENT!
FIRST TIME I'VE SEEN HIM WITH COMBED HAIR.
CONFORM CONFORM CONFORM
OUTTA MY WAY, PYRO!
OOGH!
SLAM!
PRINCIPAL
WHAT THE HECK IS GOING ON HERE, MARQUEZ!

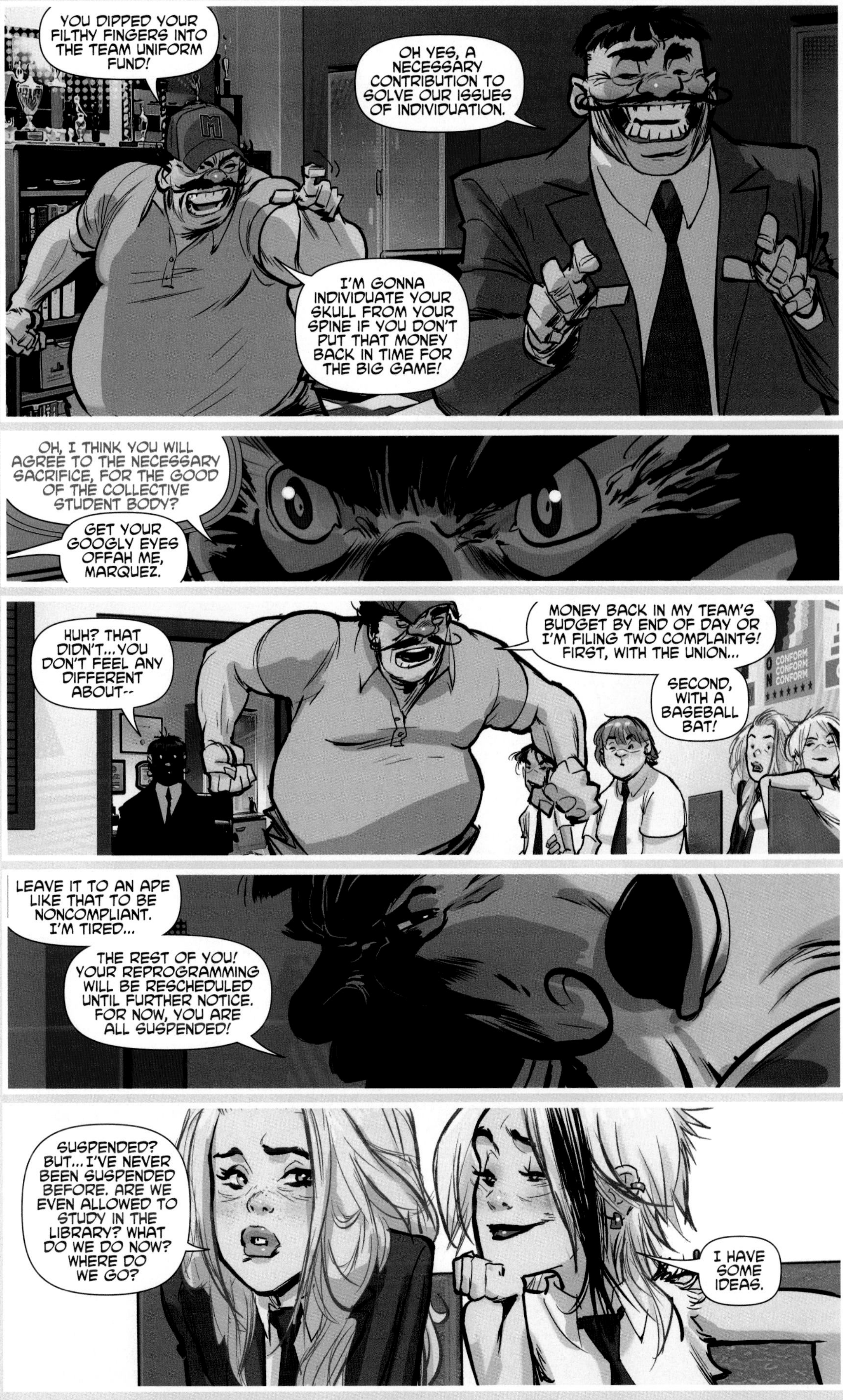
YOU DIPPED YOUR FILTHY FINGERS INTO THE TEAM UNIFORM FUND!
OH YES, A NECESSARY CONTRIBUTION TO SOLVE OUR ISSUES OF INDIVIDUATION.
I'M GONNA INDIVIDUATE YOUR SKULL FROM YOUR SPINE IF YOU DON'T PUT THAT MONEY BACK IN TIME FOR THE BIG GAME!
OH, I THINK YOU WILL AGREE TO THE NECESSARY SACRIFICE, FOR THE GOOD OF THE COLLECTIVE STUDENT BODY?
GET YOUR GOOGLY EYES OFFAH ME, MARQUEZ.
HUH? THAT DIDN'T...YOU DON'T FEEL ANY DIFFERENT ABOUT--
MONEY BACK IN MY TEAM'S BUDGET BY END OF DAY OR I'M FILING TWO COMPLAINTS! FIRST, WITH THE UNION...
SECOND, WITH A BASEBALL BAT!
CONFORM
CONFORM
CONFORM
LEAVE IT TO AN APE LIKE THAT TO BE NONCOMPLIANT. I'M TIRED...
THE REST OF YOU! YOUR REPROGRAMMING WILL BE RESCHEDULED UNTIL FURTHER NOTICE. FOR NOW, YOU ARE ALL SUSPENDED!
SUSPENDED? BUT... I'VE NEVER BEEN SUSPENDED BEFORE. ARE WE EVEN ALLOWED TO STUDY IN THE LIBRARY? WHAT DO WE DO NOW? WHERE DO WE GO?
I HAVE SOME IDEAS.

WHERE...
AM I?

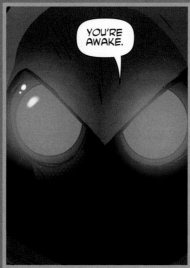

YOU'RE
AWAKE.

AAAEEEII!!

STAY AWAY
FROM ME! I'LL
CALL THE
POLICE! OR THE
GOVERNMENT!

I'M NOT
SURE YOU
WOULD WANT TO
INVOLVE ANYONE
IN THOSE
CATEGORIES.

WHAT DID
YOU DO TO
KRISTEN?

RELAX,
MR. LEIF. THE
GIRL IS AT
HOME, SAFE
AND SOUND.
I'M ONLY
INTERESTED
IN YOU.

SORRY FOR THE
POWER DAMPER
SUIT. I WASN'T
SURE HOW YOU
WOULD REACT WHEN
YOU AWOKE, WHAT
EMOTIONS MIGHT...
"DISCHARGE."

DR.
PETERS?

I HAD A SPARE AND YOU NEEDED A SET OF CLOTHES...

WHAT IS THIS, A TAIL?

A GROUNDING WIRE, TO KEEP YOU FROM BEING ELECTROCUTED. NOT THAT YOU NEED ANY HELP...

I DON'T KNOW WHAT YOU'RE TALKING ABOUT.

NO NEED FOR FIBS, MR. LEIF. I'VE BEEN STUDYING YOUR PARTICULAR SOURCE OF ENERGY FOR DECADES. THE SAME ENERGY SOURCE ONCE PREDICTED BY NICOLA TESLA.

IF I WANTED TO HURT YOU OR IMPRISON YOU, I'VE HAD PLENTY OF OPPORTUNITY FOR THAT. I WANT TO HELP.

SO, LET'S START WITH WHAT YOU KNOW. C'MON, KID... TAKE A CHANCE.

MY BODY OPENS UP TO SOME KIND OF... ENERGY. ONCE I START UP, I DON'T KNOW HOW TO STOP IT.

I RIGGED UP THIS WATCH WITH A SENSOR FROM EBAY TO KEEP TRACK. IT MOSTLY WORKS.

I GET ABOUT TEN MINUTES OF JUICE AND THEN IT GOES DEAD FOR TWENTY-FOUR HOURS.

LIKE A REALLY BAD CELL PHONE BATTERY.

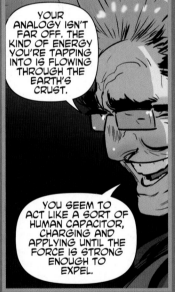

YOUR ANALOGY ISN'T FAR OFF. THE KIND OF ENERGY YOU'RE TAPPING INTO IS FLOWING THROUGH THE EARTH'S CRUST.

YOU SEEM TO ACT LIKE A SORT OF HUMAN CAPACITOR, CHARGING AND APPLYING UNTIL THE FORCE IS STRONG ENOUGH TO EXPEL.

TESLA HYPOTHESIZED BUILDING TOWERS TO UNLEASH THAT FREE ENERGY SOURCE TO THE WORLD. THE FBI KILLED HIM BEFORE HE COULD KILL THE ENERGY SECTOR.

THOSE WHO SEE TOO FAR CAN BE BLIND TO THE DANGERS NEAREST TO THEM. TOWERS ATTRACT TOO MUCH ATTENTION, AND SO I CREATED MY OWN DESIGN...

SOMETHING I CALL THE VOID.

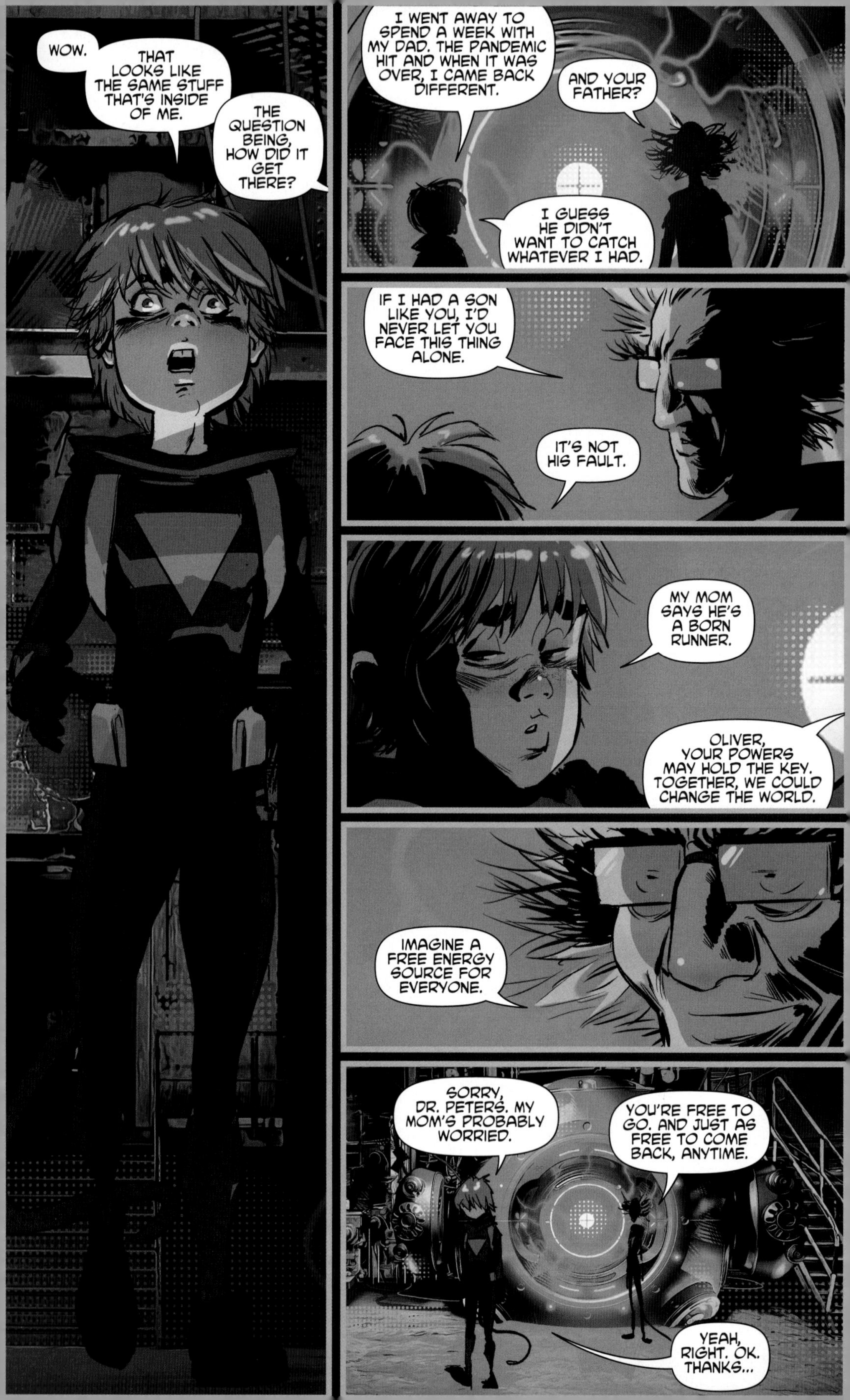
WOW.
THAT LOOKS LIKE THE SAME STUFF THAT'S INSIDE OF ME.
THE QUESTION BEING, HOW DID IT GET THERE?
I WENT AWAY TO SPEND A WEEK WITH MY DAD. THE PANDEMIC HIT AND WHEN IT WAS OVER, I CAME BACK DIFFERENT.
AND YOUR FATHER?
I GUESS HE DIDN'T WANT TO CATCH WHATEVER I HAD.
IF I HAD A SON LIKE YOU, I'D NEVER LET YOU FACE THIS THING ALONE.
IT'S NOT HIS FAULT.
MY MOM SAYS HE'S A BORN RUNNER.
OLIVER, YOUR POWERS MAY HOLD THE KEY. TOGETHER, WE COULD CHANGE THE WORLD.
IMAGINE A FREE ENERGY SOURCE FOR EVERYONE.
SORRY, DR. PETERS. MY MOM'S PROBABLY WORRIED.
YOU'RE FREE TO GO. AND JUST AS FREE TO COME BACK, ANYTIME.
YEAH, RIGHT. OK. THANKS...

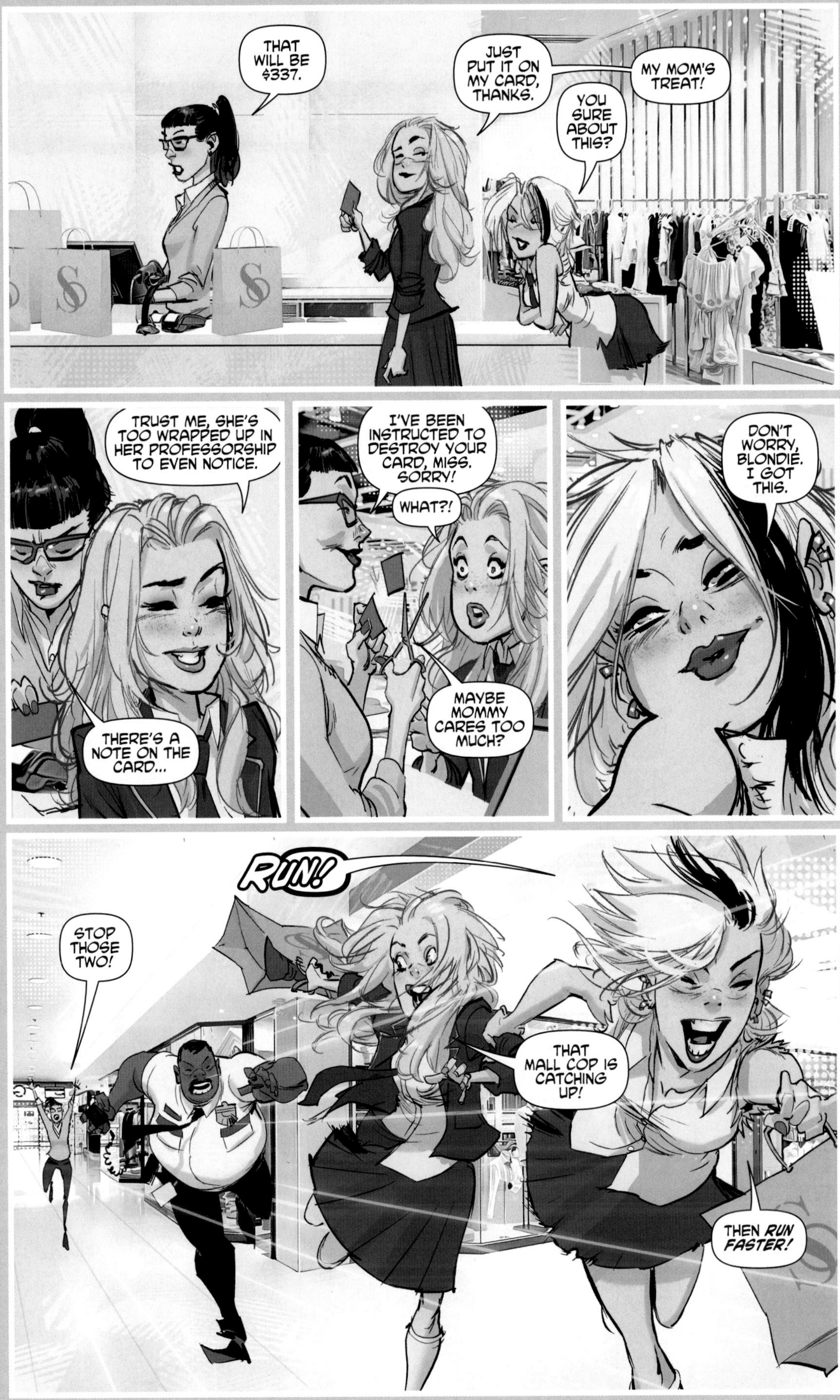
THAT WILL BE $337.
JUST PUT IT ON MY CARD, THANKS.
MY MOM'S TREAT!
YOU SURE ABOUT THIS?
TRUST ME, SHE'S TOO WRAPPED UP IN HER PROFESSORSHIP TO EVEN NOTICE.
THERE'S A NOTE ON THE CARD...
I'VE BEEN INSTRUCTED TO DESTROY YOUR CARD, MISS. SORRY!
WHAT?!
MAYBE MOMMY CARES TOO MUCH?
DON'T WORRY, BLONDIE. I GOT THIS.
RUN!
STOP THOSE TWO!
THAT MALL COP IS CATCHING UP!
THEN RUN FASTER!

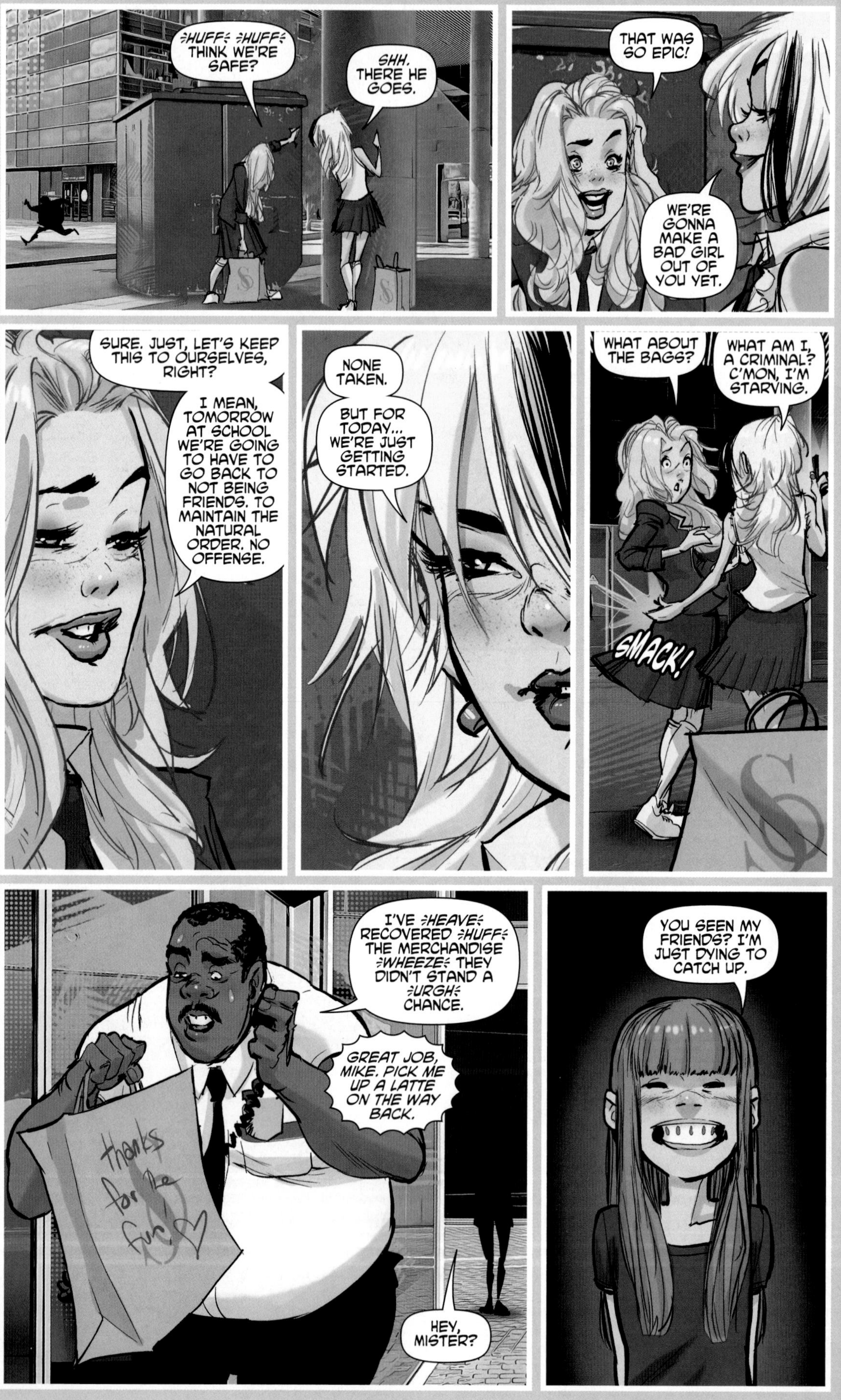

HUFF *HUFF* THINK WE'RE SAFE?
SHH. THERE HE GOES.
THAT WAS SO EPIC!
WE'RE GONNA MAKE A BAD GIRL OUT OF YOU YET.
SURE. JUST, LET'S KEEP THIS TO OURSELVES, RIGHT?
I MEAN, TOMORROW AT SCHOOL WE'RE GOING TO HAVE TO GO BACK TO NOT BEING FRIENDS. TO MAINTAIN THE NATURAL ORDER. NO OFFENSE.
NONE TAKEN.
BUT FOR TODAY... WE'RE JUST GETTING STARTED.
WHAT ABOUT THE BAGS?
WHAT AM I, A CRIMINAL? C'MON, I'M STARVING.
SMACK!
I'VE *HEAVE* RECOVERED *HUFF* THE MERCHANDISE *WHEEZE* THEY DIDN'T STAND A *URGH* CHANCE.
GREAT JOB, MIKE. PICK ME UP A LATTE ON THE WAY BACK.
thanks for the fun!
HEY, MISTER?
YOU SEEN MY FRIENDS? I'M JUST DYING TO CATCH UP.

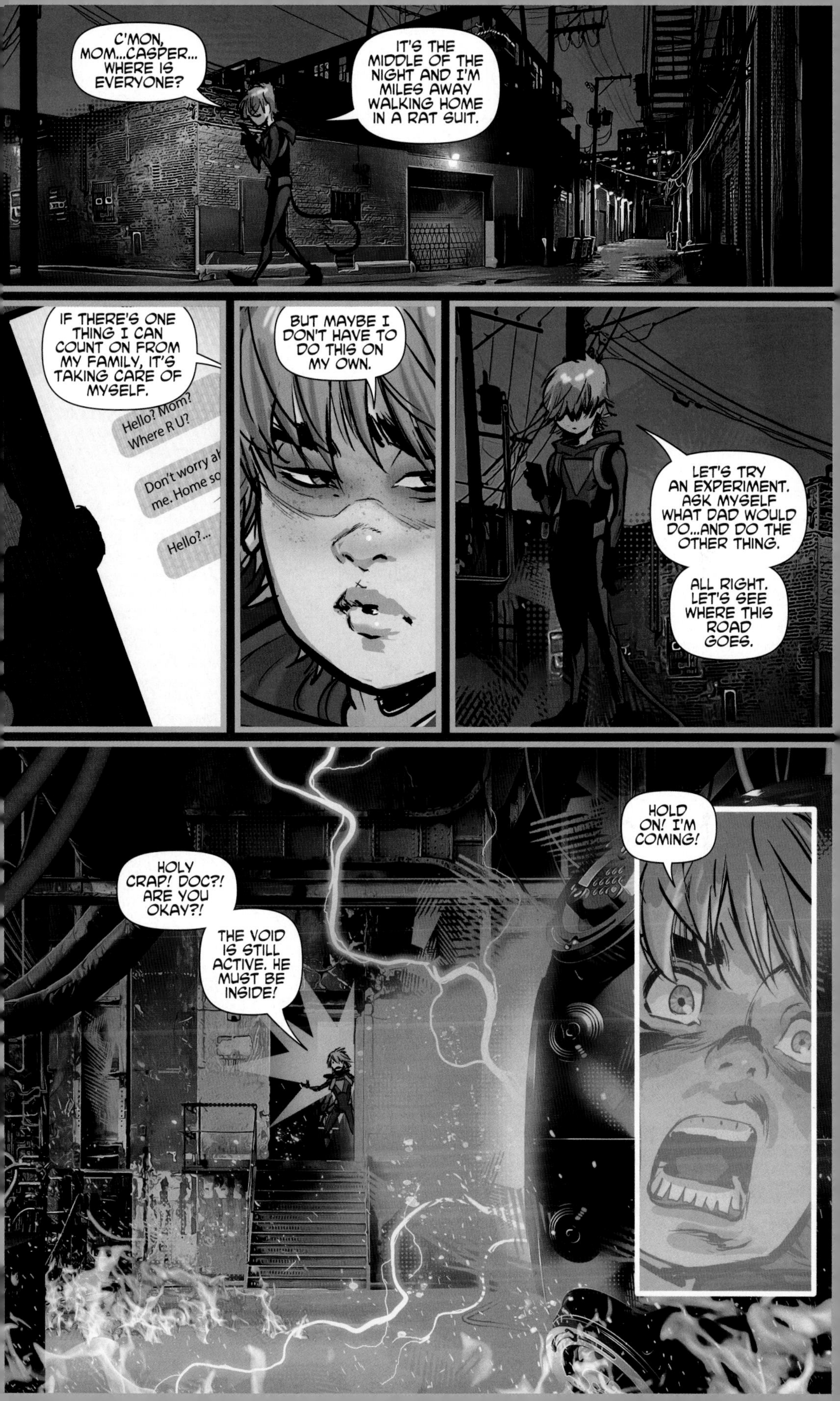

C'MON, MOM...CASPER... WHERE IS EVERYONE?
IT'S THE MIDDLE OF THE NIGHT AND I'M MILES AWAY WALKING HOME IN A RAT SUIT.
IF THERE'S ONE THING I CAN COUNT ON FROM MY FAMILY, IT'S TAKING CARE OF MYSELF.
Hello? Mom? Where R U?
Hello?...
BUT MAYBE I DON'T HAVE TO DO THIS ON MY OWN.
LET'S TRY AN EXPERIMENT. ASK MYSELF WHAT DAD WOULD DO...AND DO THE OTHER THING.
ALL RIGHT. LET'S SEE WHERE THIS ROAD GOES.
HOLY CRAP! DOC?! ARE YOU OKAY?!
THE VOID IS STILL ACTIVE. HE MUST BE INSIDE!
HOLD ON! I'M COMING!

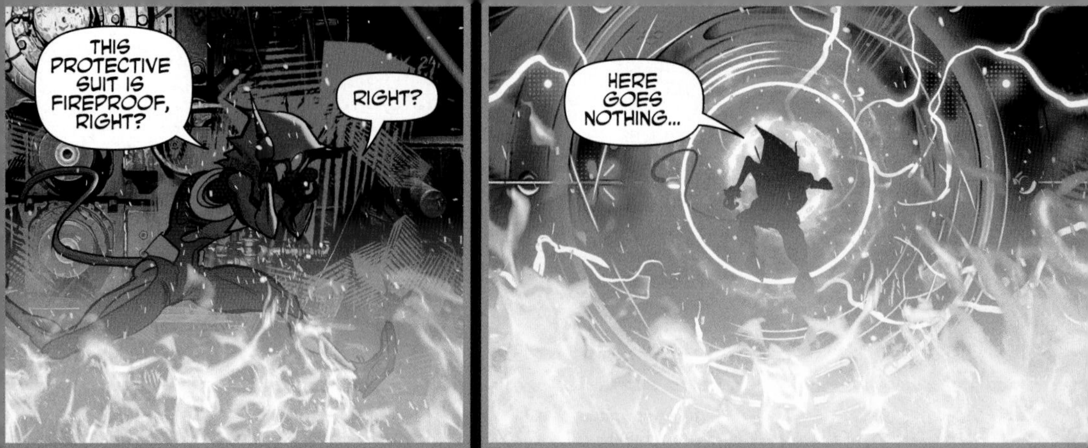
THIS PROTECTIVE SUIT IS FIREPROOF, RIGHT?
RIGHT?
HERE GOES NOTHING...
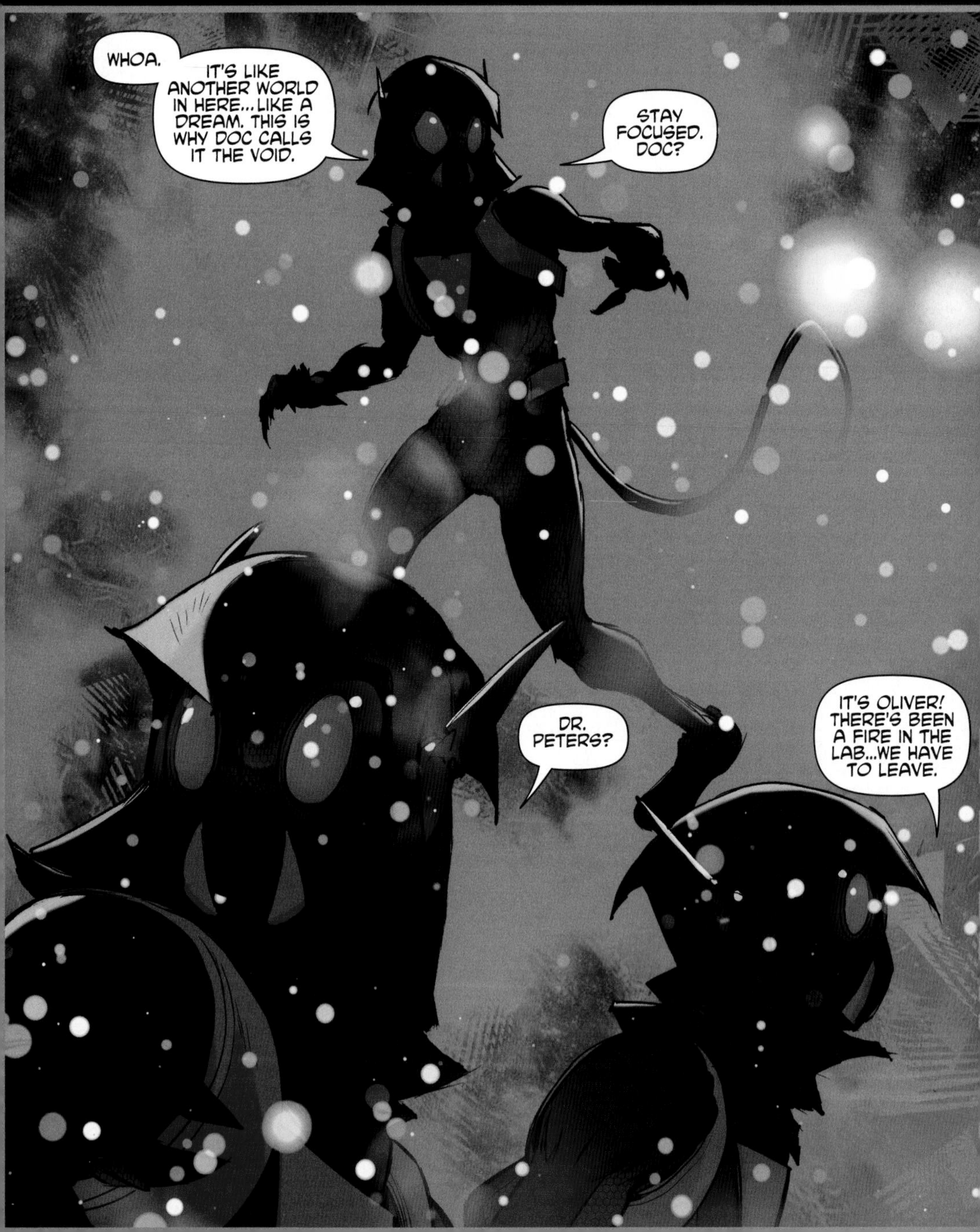
WHOA.
IT'S LIKE ANOTHER WORLD IN HERE...LIKE A DREAM. THIS IS WHY DOC CALLS IT THE VOID.
STAY FOCUSED. DOC?
DR. PETERS?
IT'S OLIVER! THERE'S BEEN A FIRE IN THE LAB...WE HAVE TO LEAVE.

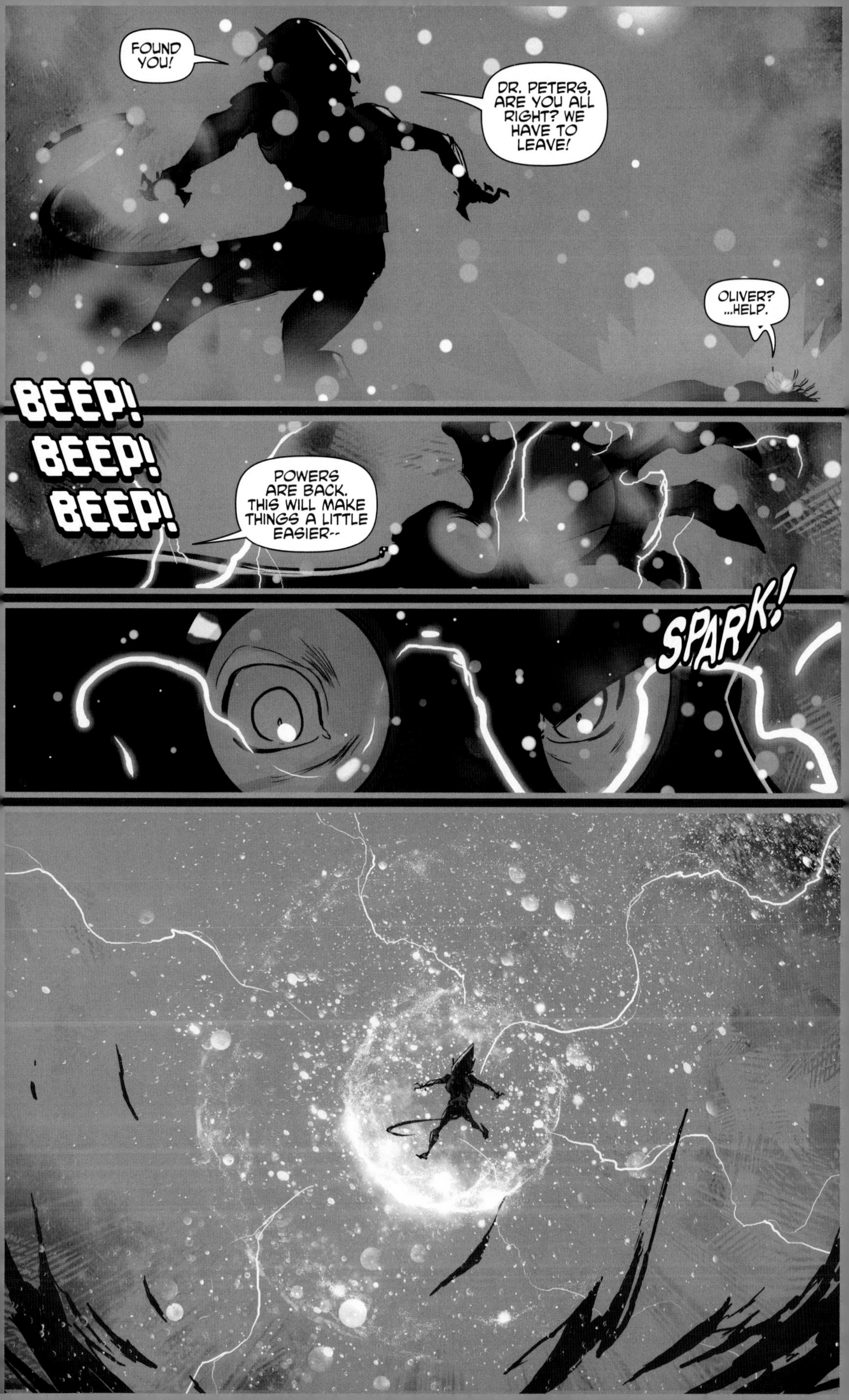
FOUND YOU!
DR. PETERS, ARE YOU ALL RIGHT? WE HAVE TO LEAVE!
OLIVER? ...HELP.
BEEP! BEEP! BEEP!
POWERS ARE BACK. THIS WILL MAKE THINGS A LITTLE EASIER--
SPARK!

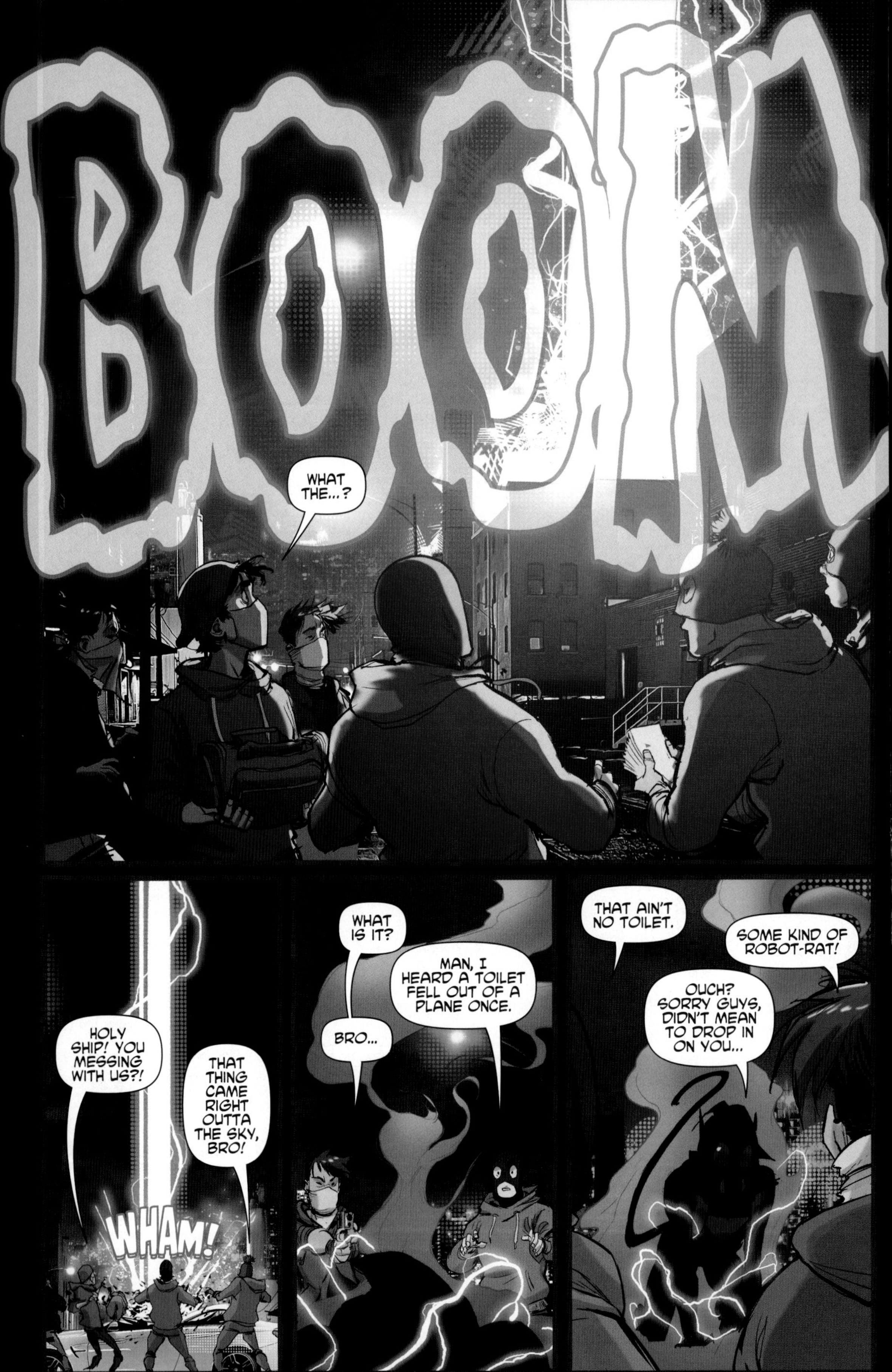
BOOM
WHAT THE...?
HOLY SHIP! YOU MESSING WITH US?!
THAT THING CAME RIGHT OUTTA THE SKY, BRO!
WHAM!
WHAT IS IT?
BRO...
MAN, I HEARD A TOILET FELL OUT OF A PLANE ONCE.
THAT AIN'T NO TOILET.
SOME KIND OF ROBOT-RAT!
OUCH? SORRY GUYS, DIDN'T MEAN TO DROP IN ON YOU...

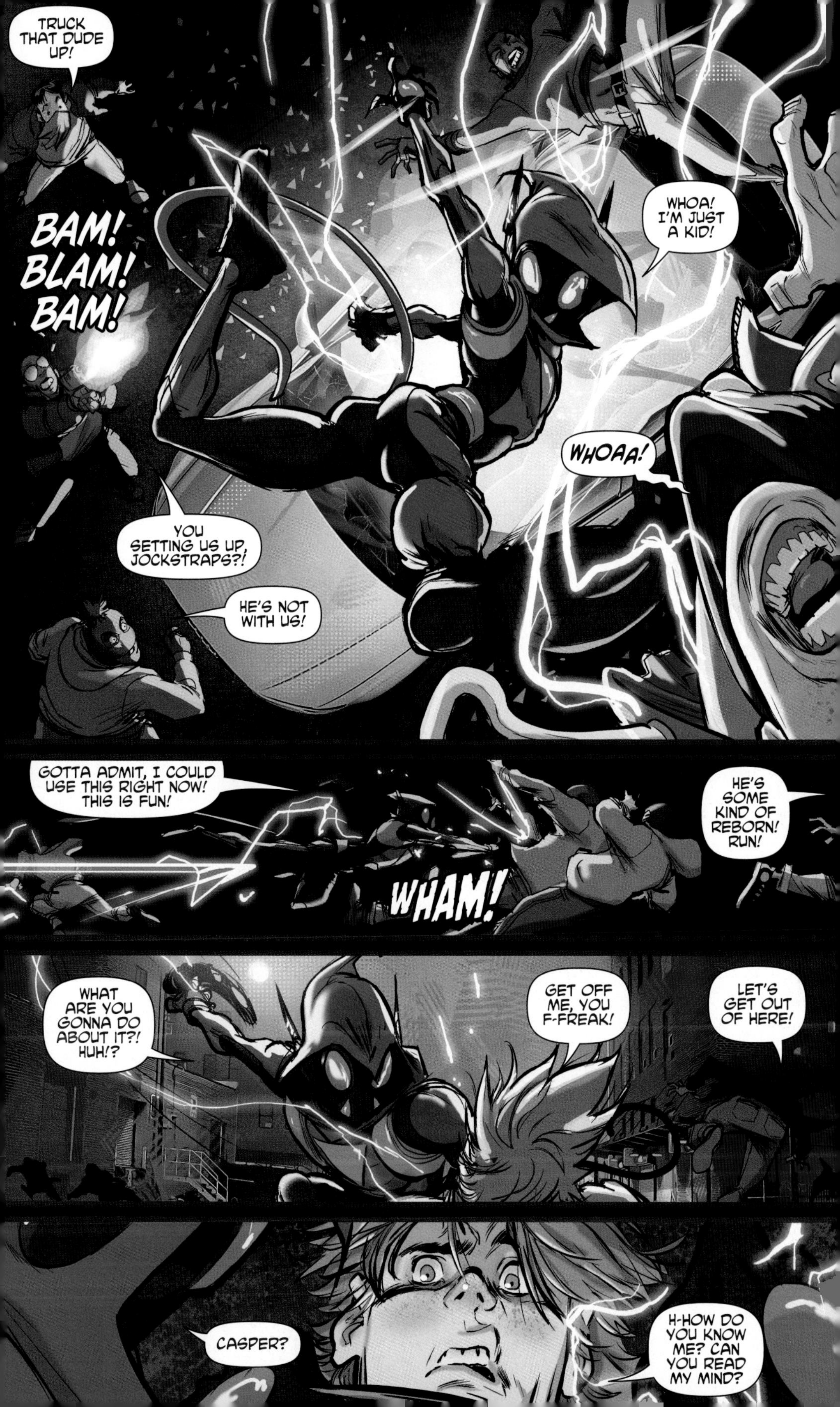
TRUCK THAT DUDE UP!
BAM! BLAM! BAM!
WHOA! I'M JUST A KID!
WHOAA!
YOU SETTING US UP, JOCKSTRAPS?!
HE'S NOT WITH US!
GOTTA ADMIT, I COULD USE THIS RIGHT NOW! THIS IS FUN!
HE'S SOME KIND OF REBORN! RUN!
WHAM!
WHAT ARE YOU GONNA DO ABOUT IT?! HUH!?
GET OFF ME, YOU F-FREAK!
LET'S GET OUT OF HERE!
CASPER?
H-HOW DO YOU KNOW ME? CAN YOU READ MY MIND?

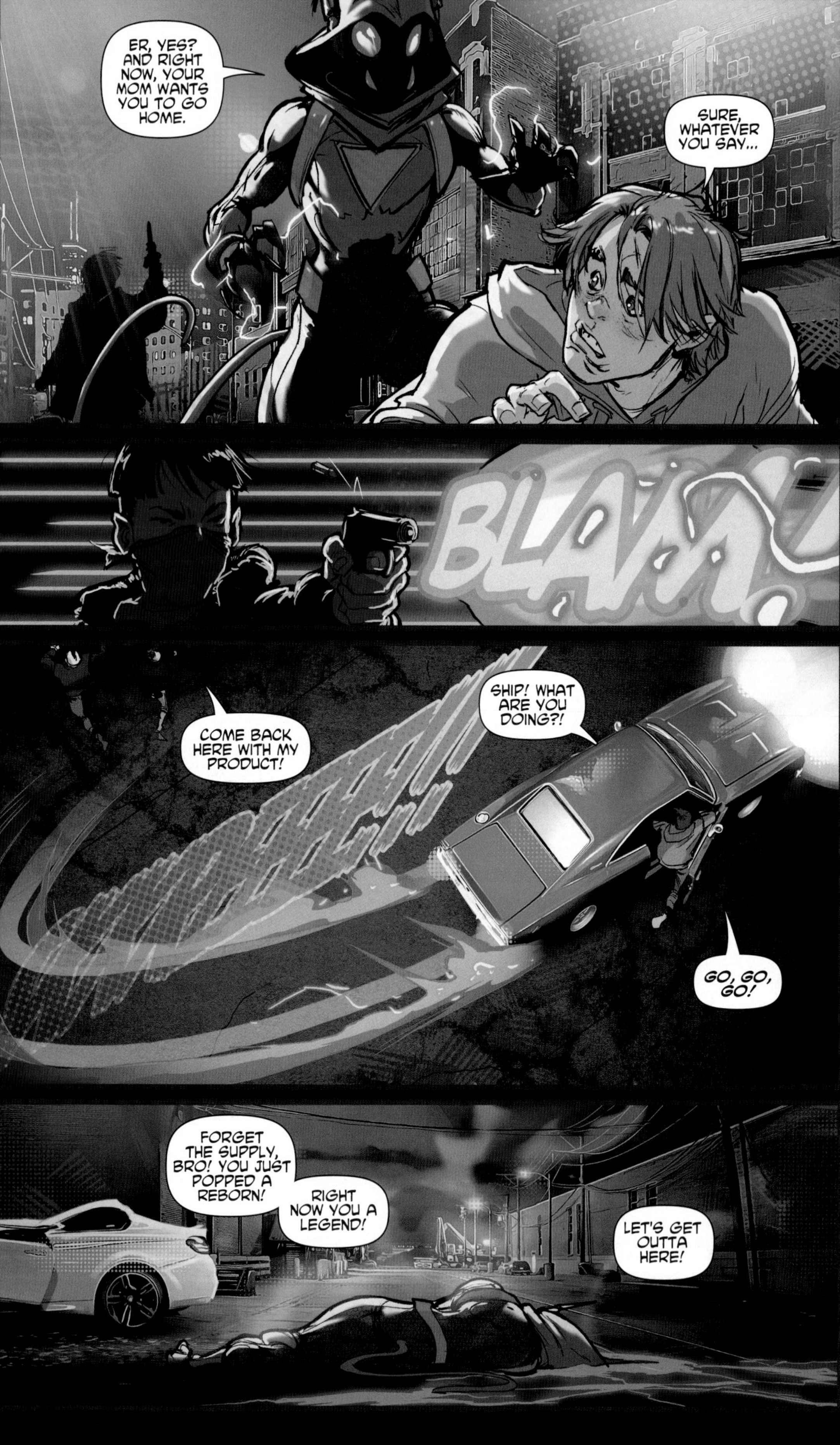
ER, YES? AND RIGHT NOW, YOUR MOM WANTS YOU TO GO HOME.
SURE, WHATEVER YOU SAY...
BLAM!
COME BACK HERE WITH MY PRODUCT!
SHIP! WHAT ARE YOU DOING?!
GO, GO, GO!
FORGET THE SUPPLY, BRO! YOU JUST POPPED A REBORN!
RIGHT NOW YOU A LEGEND!
LET'S GET OUTTA HERE!

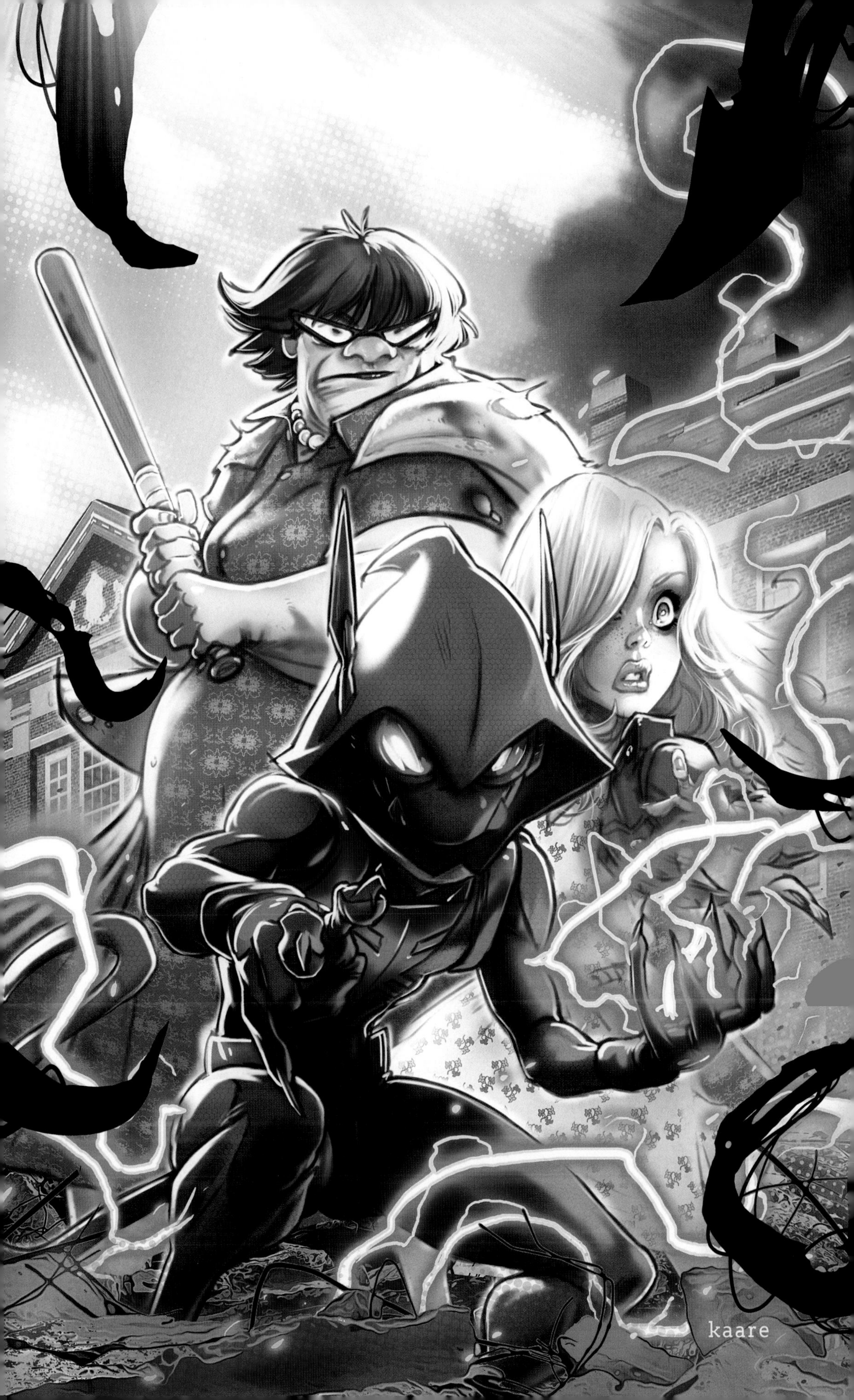
kaare

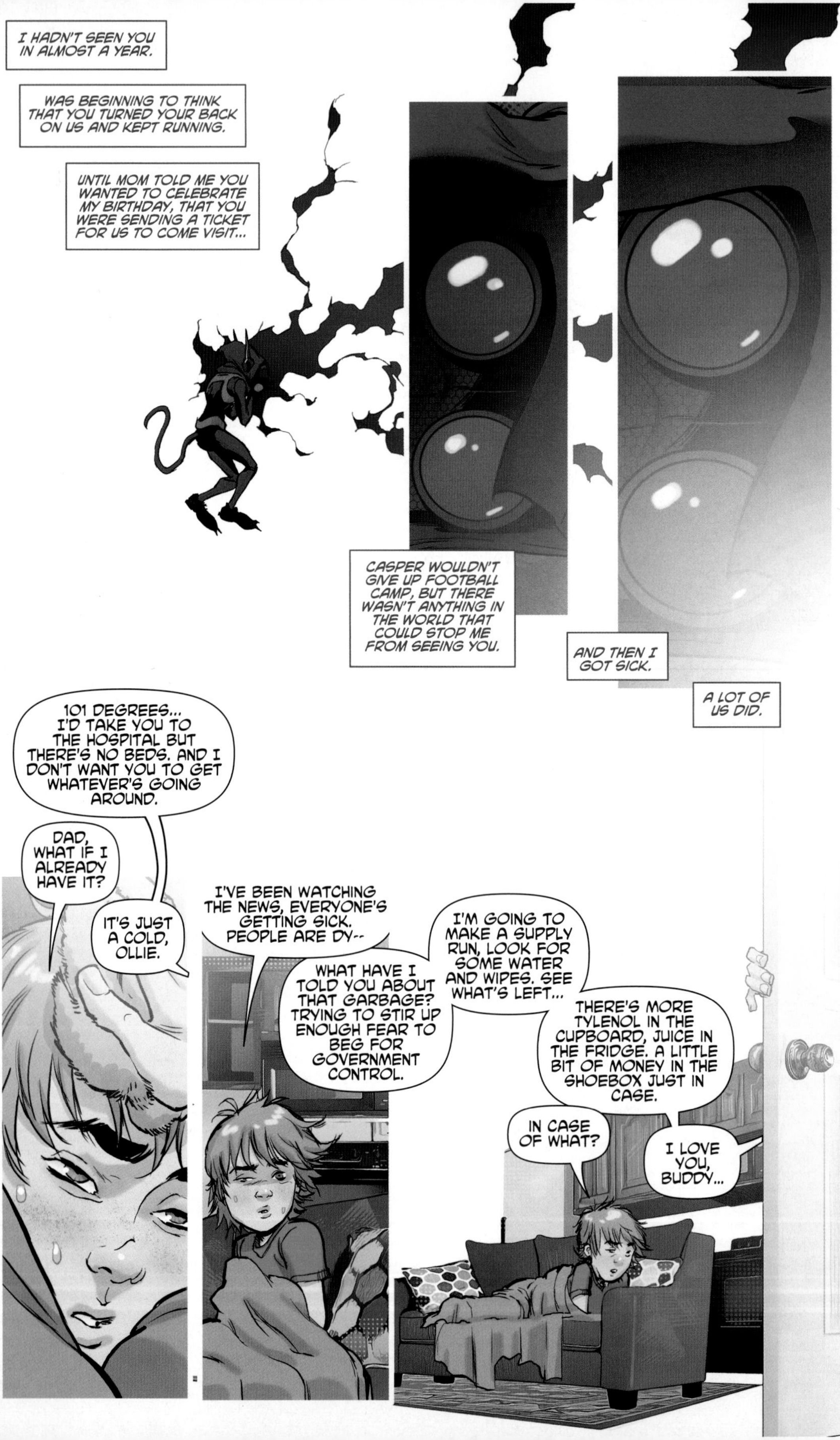
I HADN'T SEEN YOU IN ALMOST A YEAR.
WAS BEGINNING TO THINK THAT YOU TURNED YOUR BACK ON US AND KEPT RUNNING.
UNTIL MOM TOLD ME YOU WANTED TO CELEBRATE MY BIRTHDAY, THAT YOU WERE SENDING A TICKET FOR US TO COME VISIT...
CASPER WOULDN'T GIVE UP FOOTBALL CAMP, BUT THERE WASN'T ANYTHING IN THE WORLD THAT COULD STOP ME FROM SEEING YOU.
AND THEN I GOT SICK.
A LOT OF US DID.
101 DEGREES... I'D TAKE YOU TO THE HOSPITAL BUT THERE'S NO BEDS. AND I DON'T WANT YOU TO GET WHATEVER'S GOING AROUND.
DAD, WHAT IF I ALREADY HAVE IT?
IT'S JUST A COLD, OLLIE.
I'VE BEEN WATCHING THE NEWS, EVERYONE'S GETTING SICK. PEOPLE ARE DY--
WHAT HAVE I TOLD YOU ABOUT THAT GARBAGE? TRYING TO STIR UP ENOUGH FEAR TO BEG FOR GOVERNMENT CONTROL.
I'M GOING TO MAKE A SUPPLY RUN, LOOK FOR SOME WATER AND WIPES. SEE WHAT'S LEFT...
THERE'S MORE TYLENOL IN THE CUPBOARD, JUICE IN THE FRIDGE. A LITTLE BIT OF MONEY IN THE SHOEBOX JUST IN CASE.
IN CASE OF WHAT?
I LOVE YOU, BUDDY...

--RIOTS AND LOOTING FOR TWO STRAIGHT WEEKS DESPITE THE MANDATED LOCKDOWNS...

TYLENOL ISN'T WORKING...

CAN'T STOP SWEATING...BUT F-FEEL SO COLD...

TWIST- TWIST

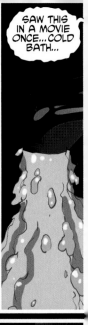

SAW THIS IN A MOVIE ONCE...COLD BATH...

SH-SHOULD HAVE WASHED MY HANDS MORE... USED A MASK S-SOONER...

MAYBE YOU W-W-WOULD HAVE COME BACK.

DAD?

SNIFF

C-CAN'T... BREATHE...

PLEASE...

I DON'T WANT TO DIE.

SLAM!

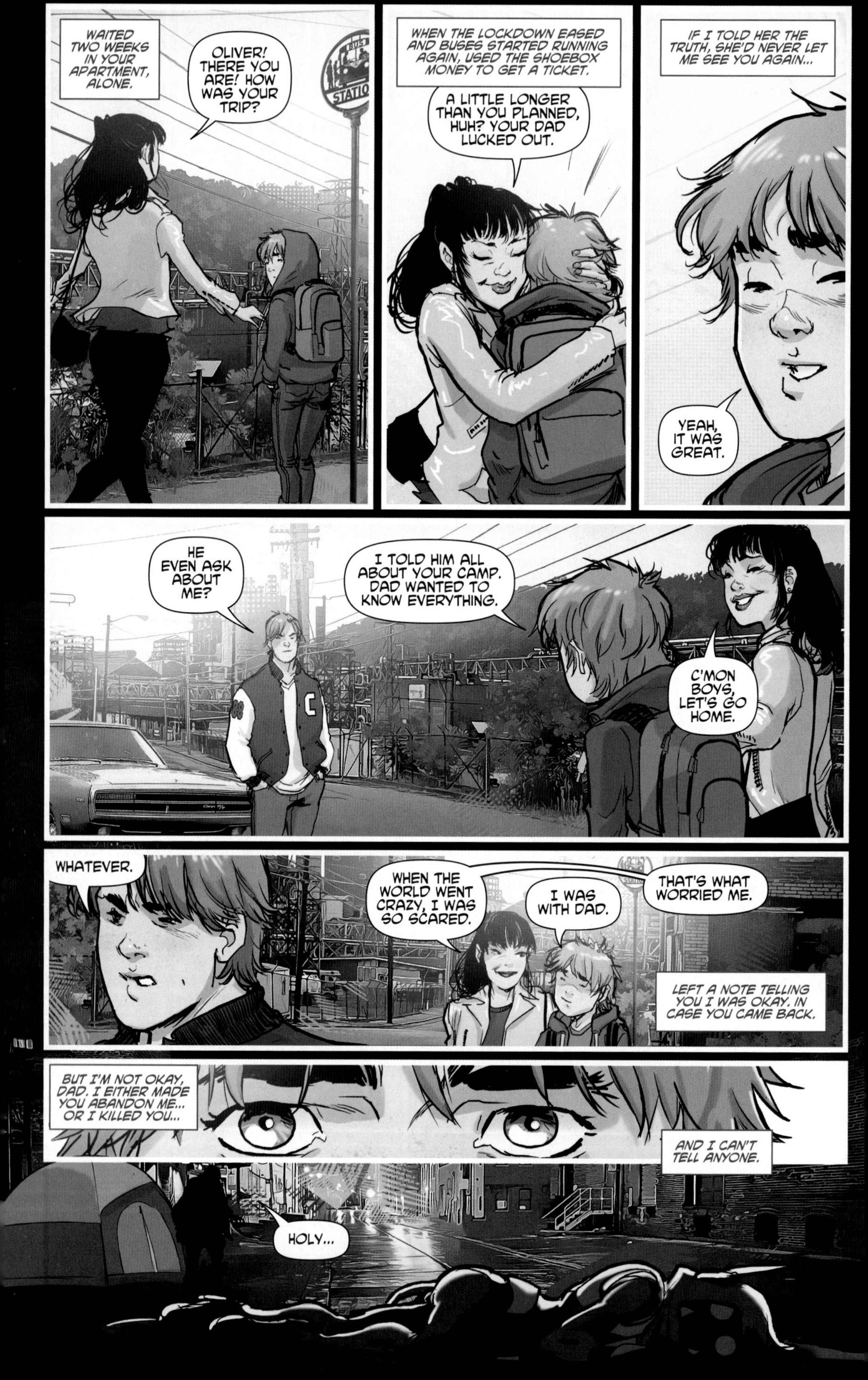
WAITED TWO WEEKS IN YOUR APARTMENT, ALONE.
OLIVER! THERE YOU ARE! HOW WAS YOUR TRIP?
BUS STATION
WHEN THE LOCKDOWN EASED AND BUSES STARTED RUNNING AGAIN, USED THE SHOEBOX MONEY TO GET A TICKET.
A LITTLE LONGER THAN YOU PLANNED, HUH? YOUR DAD LUCKED OUT.
IF I TOLD HER THE TRUTH, SHE'D NEVER LET ME SEE YOU AGAIN...
YEAH, IT WAS GREAT.
HE EVEN ASK ABOUT ME?
I TOLD HIM ALL ABOUT YOUR CAMP. DAD WANTED TO KNOW EVERYTHING.
C'MON BOYS, LET'S GO HOME.
WHATEVER.
WHEN THE WORLD WENT CRAZY, I WAS SO SCARED.
THAT'S WHAT WORRIED ME.
I WAS WITH DAD.
LEFT A NOTE TELLING YOU I WAS OKAY. IN CASE YOU CAME BACK.
BUT I'M NOT OKAY, DAD. I EITHER MADE YOU ABANDON ME... OR I KILLED YOU...
AND I CAN'T TELL ANYONE.
HOLY...

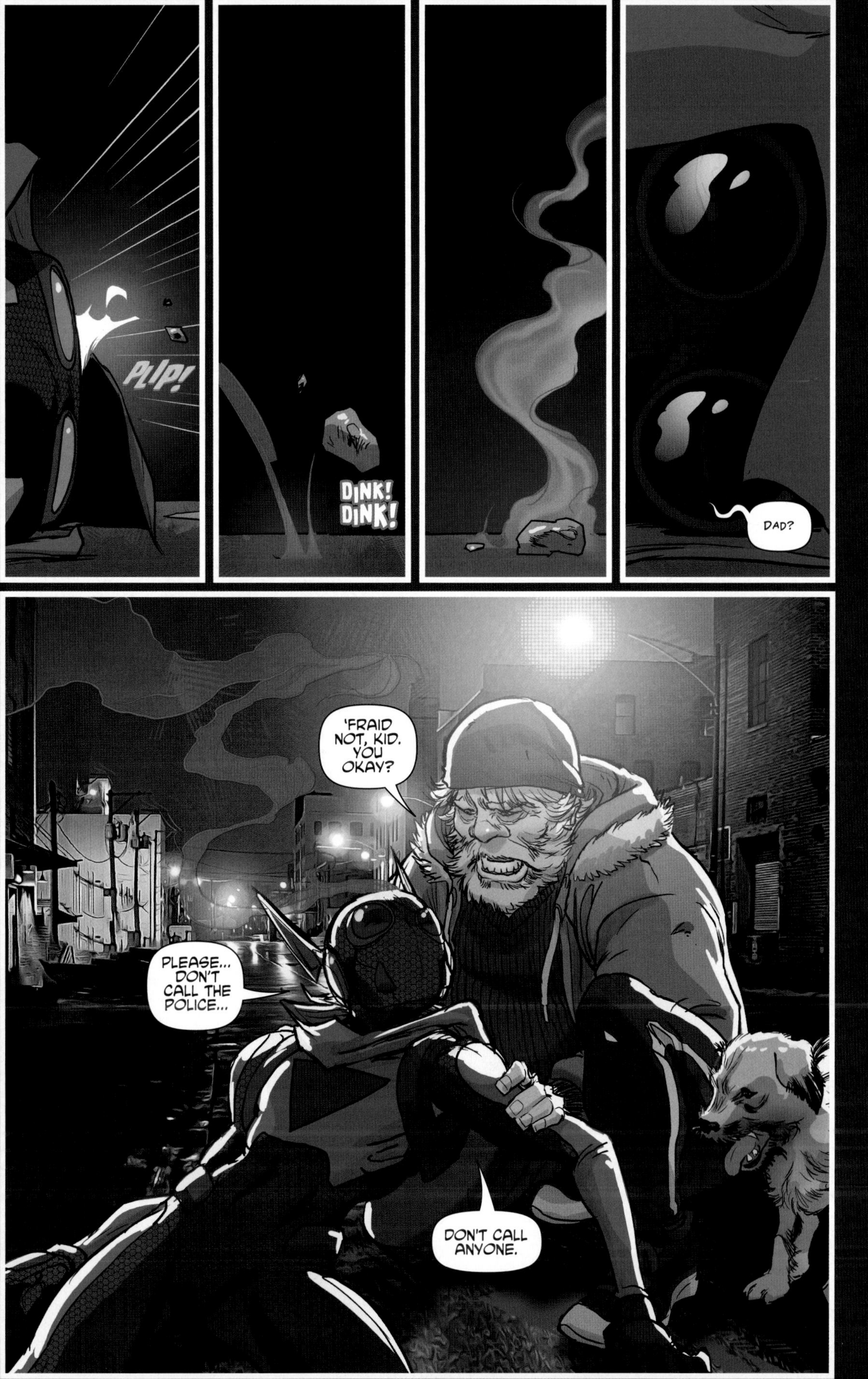
PLIP!
DINK! DINK!
DAD?
'FRAID NOT, KID. YOU OKAY?
PLEASE... DON'T CALL THE POLICE...
DON'T CALL ANYONE.

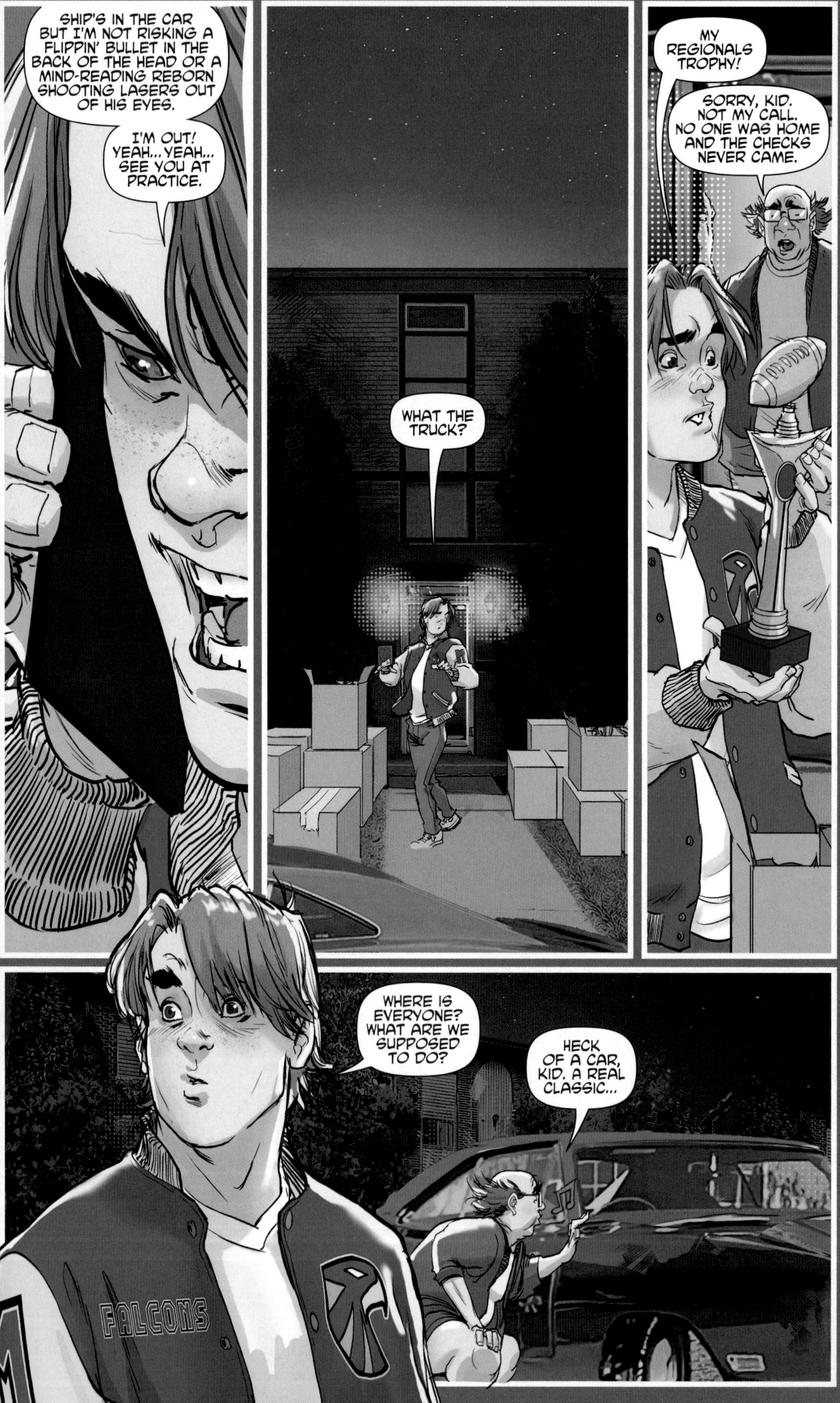
SHIP'S IN THE CAR BUT I'M NOT RISKING A FLIPPIN' BULLET IN THE BACK OF THE HEAD OR A MIND-READING REBORN SHOOTING LASERS OUT OF HIS EYES.
I'M OUT! YEAH... YEAH... SEE YOU AT PRACTICE.
WHAT THE TRUCK?
MY REGIONALS TROPHY!
SORRY, KID. NOT MY CALL. NO ONE WAS HOME AND THE CHECKS NEVER CAME.
WHERE IS EVERYONE? WHAT ARE WE SUPPOSED TO DO?
HECK OF A CAR, KID. A REAL CLASSIC...
FALCONS

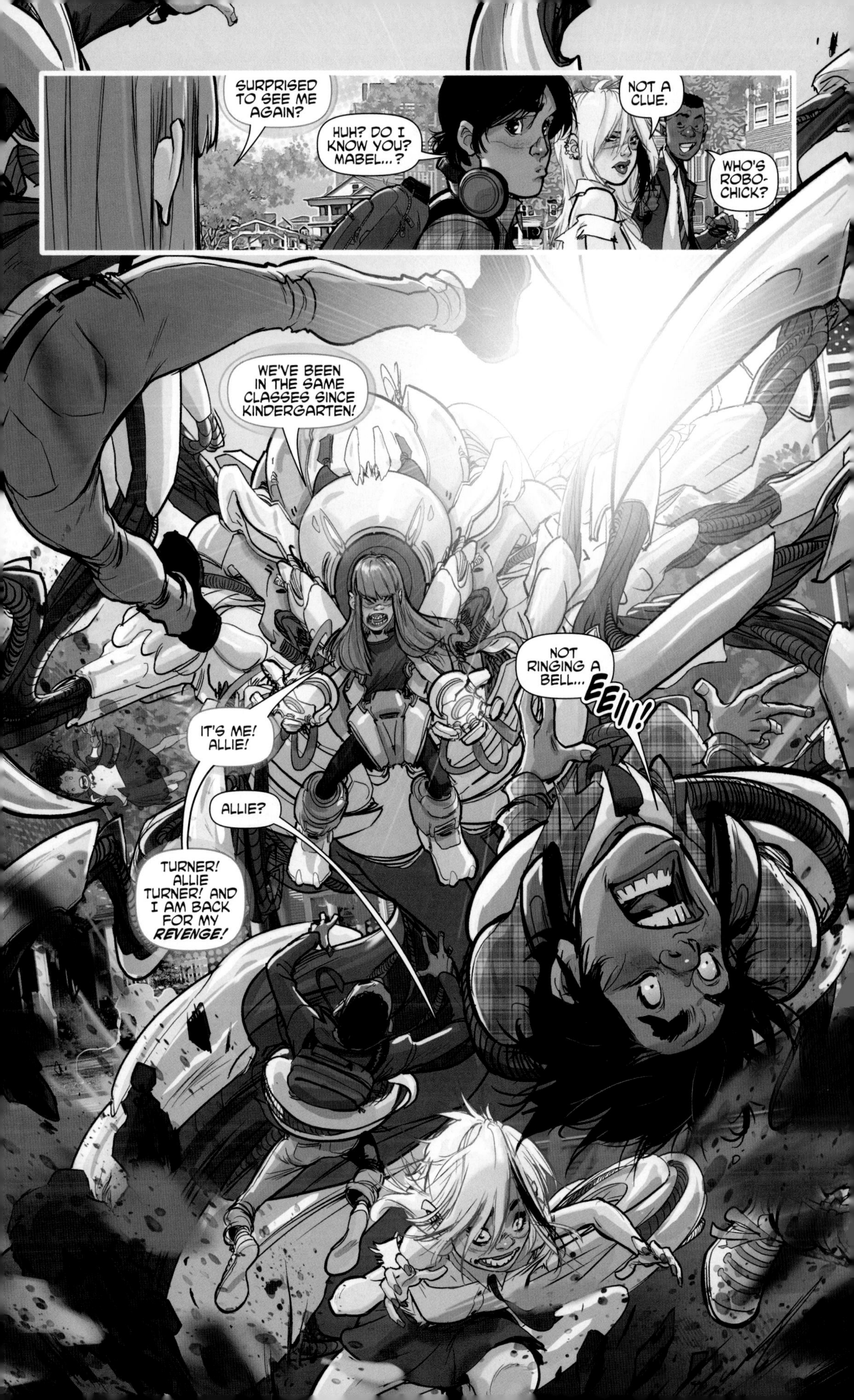
SURPRISED TO SEE ME AGAIN?
HUH? DO I KNOW YOU? MABEL...?
NOT A CLUE.
WHO'S ROBO-CHICK?
WE'VE BEEN IN THE SAME CLASSES SINCE KINDERGARTEN!
IT'S ME! ALLIE!
ALLIE?
TURNER! ALLIE TURNER! AND I AM BACK FOR MY REVENGE!
NOT RINGING A BELL... EEIII!

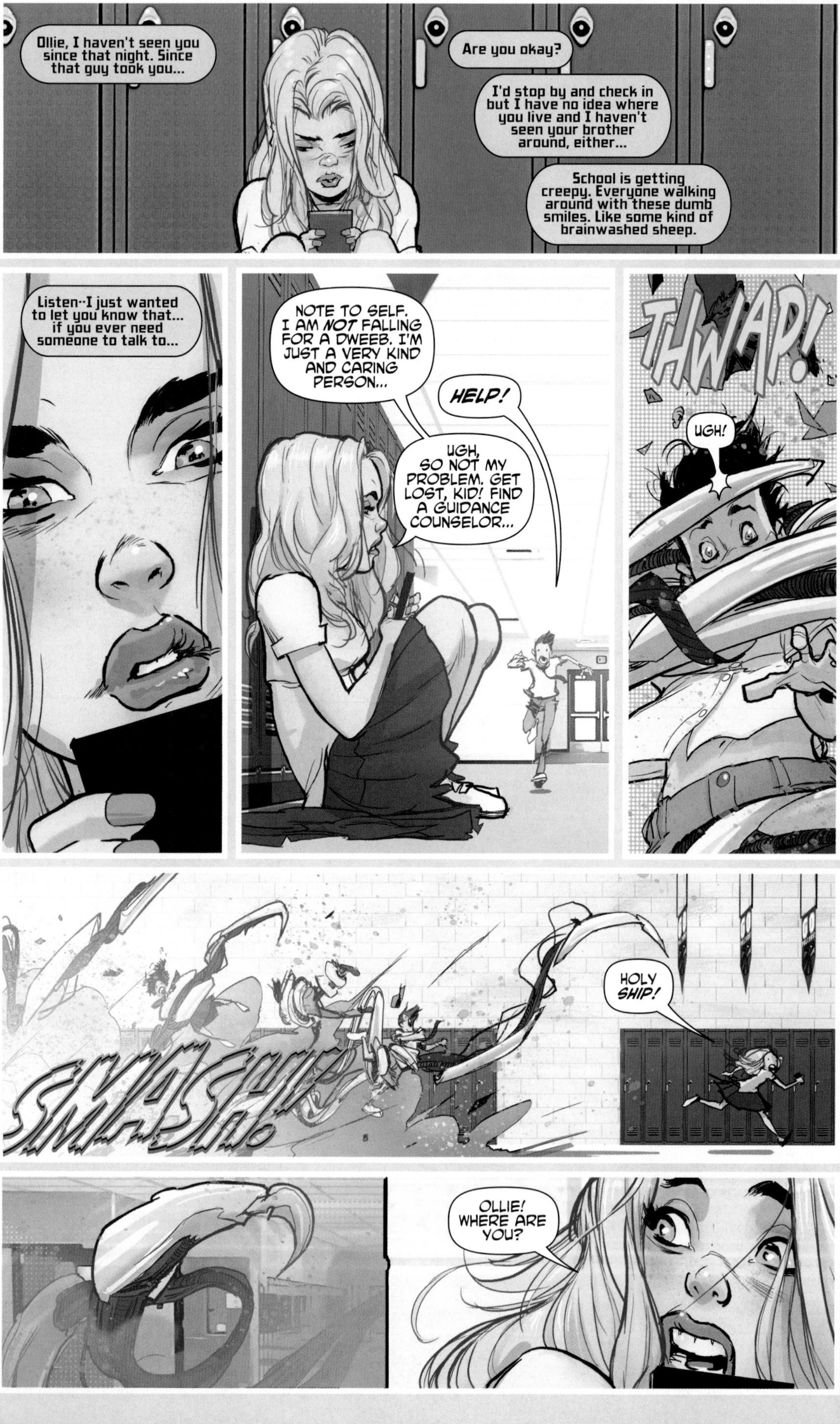
Ollie, I haven't seen you since that night. Since that guy took you...
Are you okay?
I'd stop by and check in but I have no idea where you live and I haven't seen your brother around, either...
School is getting creepy. Everyone walking around with these dumb smiles. Like some kind of brainwashed sheep.
Listen--I just wanted to let you know that... if you ever need someone to talk to...
NOTE TO SELF. I AM NOT FALLING FOR A DWEEB. I'M JUST A VERY KIND AND CARING PERSON...
HELP!
UGH, SO NOT MY PROBLEM. GET LOST, KID! FIND A GUIDANCE COUNSELOR...
THWAP!
UGH!
SMASH
HOLY SHIP!
OLLIE! WHERE ARE YOU?

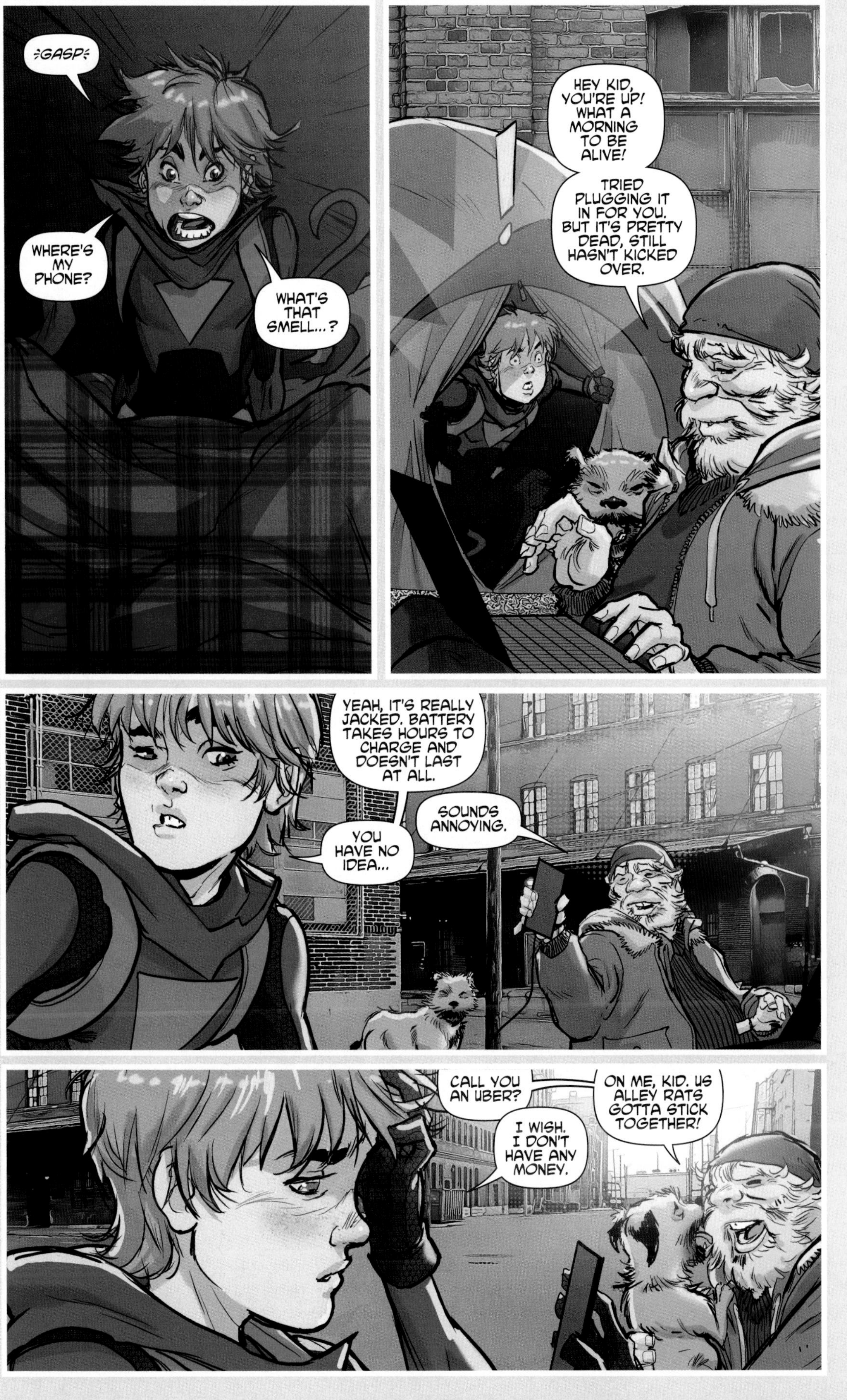

GASP
WHERE'S MY PHONE?
WHAT'S THAT SMELL...?
HEY KID, YOU'RE UP! WHAT A MORNING TO BE ALIVE!
TRIED PLUGGING IT IN FOR YOU. BUT IT'S PRETTY DEAD, STILL HASN'T KICKED OVER.
YEAH, IT'S REALLY JACKED. BATTERY TAKES HOURS TO CHARGE AND DOESN'T LAST AT ALL.
SOUNDS ANNOYING.
YOU HAVE NO IDEA...
CALL YOU AN UBER?
I WISH. I DON'T HAVE ANY MONEY.
ON ME, KID. US ALLEY RATS GOTTA STICK TOGETHER!

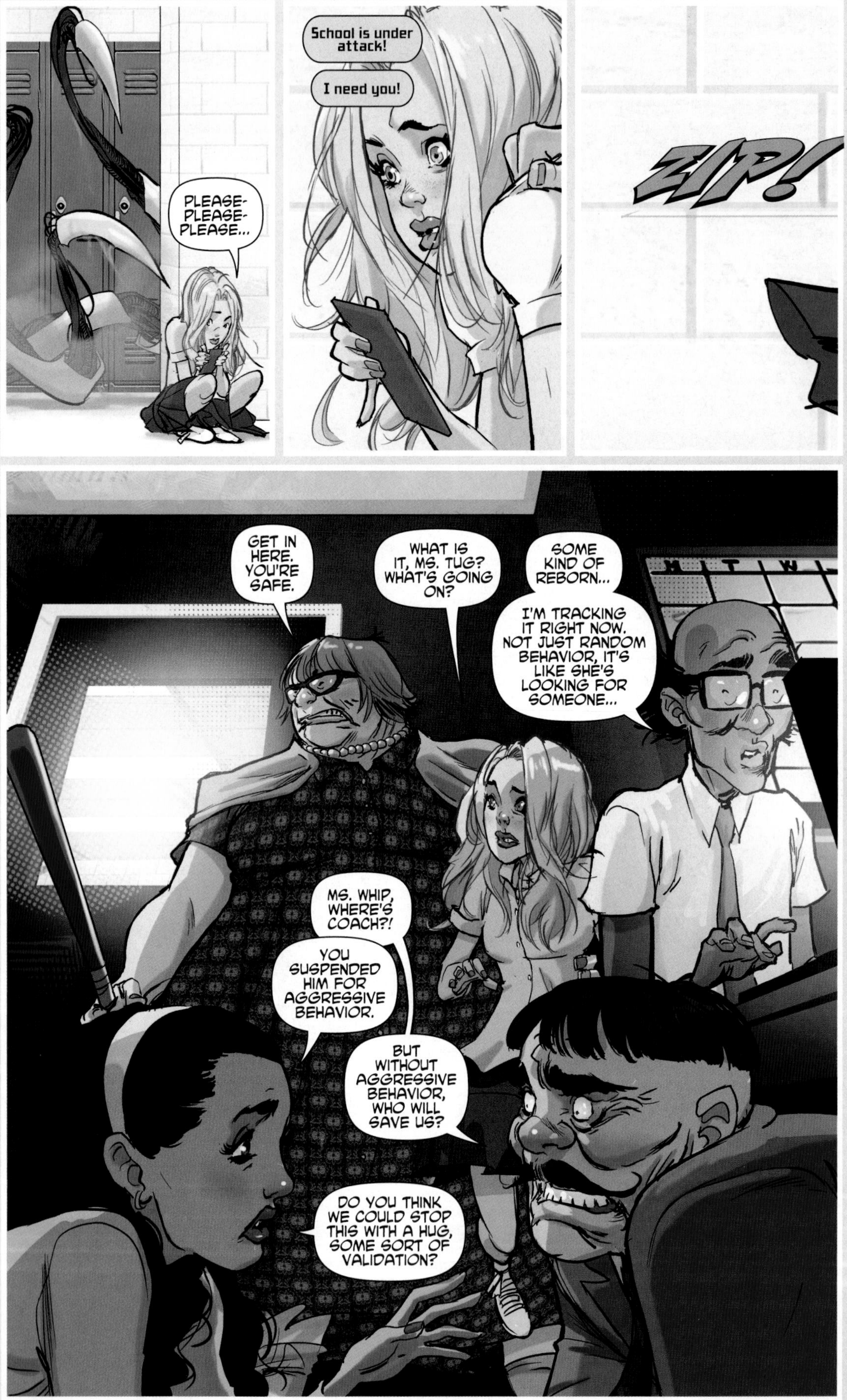

PLEASE-
PLEASE-
PLEASE...
School is under attack!
I need you!
ZIP!
GET IN HERE. YOU'RE SAFE.
WHAT IS IT, MS. TUG? WHAT'S GOING ON?
SOME KIND OF REBORN...
I'M TRACKING IT RIGHT NOW. NOT JUST RANDOM BEHAVIOR, IT'S LIKE SHE'S LOOKING FOR SOMEONE...
MS. WHIP, WHERE'S COACH?!
YOU SUSPENDED HIM FOR AGGRESSIVE BEHAVIOR.
BUT WITHOUT AGGRESSIVE BEHAVIOR, WHO WILL SAVE US?
DO YOU THINK WE COULD STOP THIS WITH A HUG, SOME SORT OF VALIDATION?

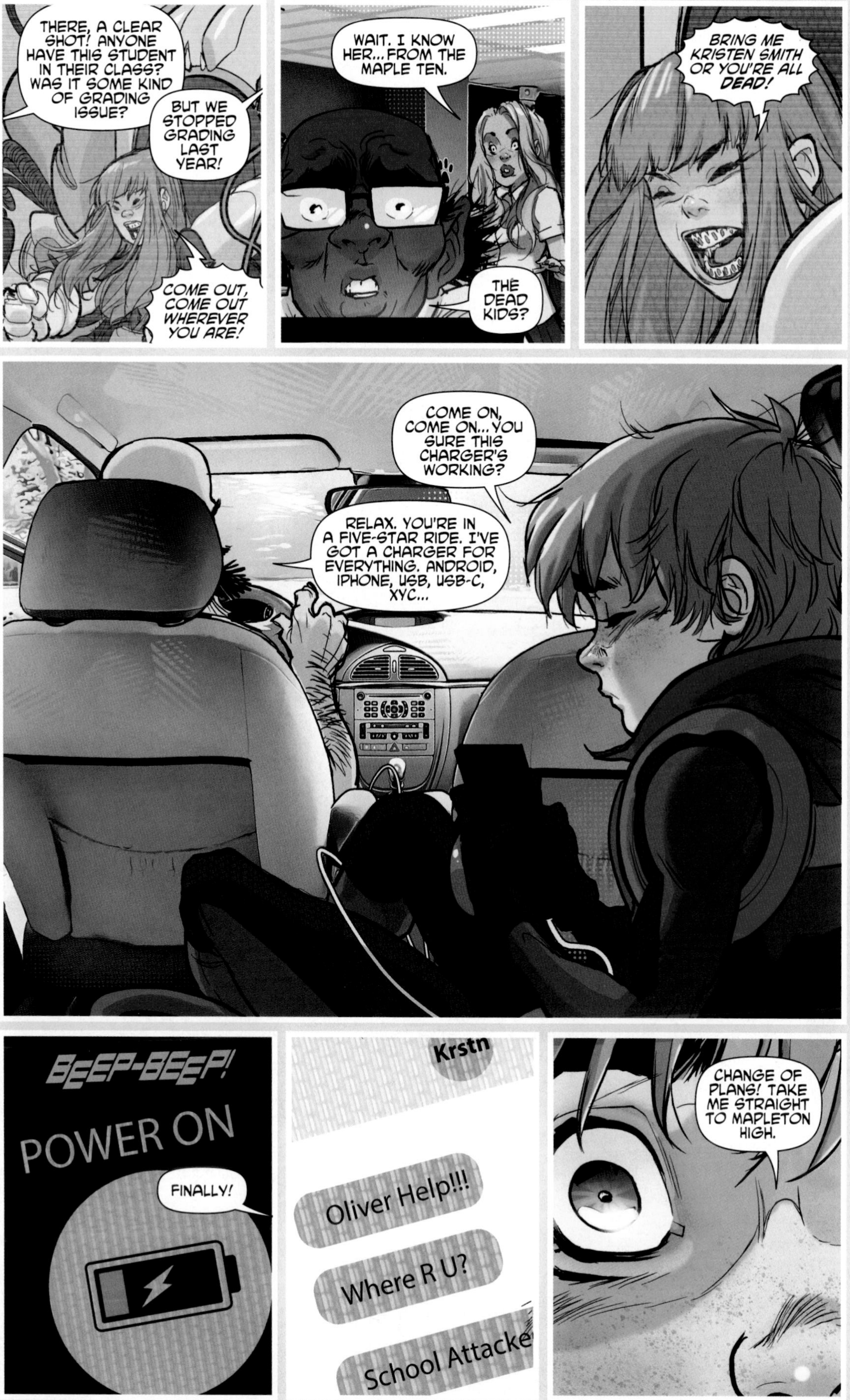
THERE, A CLEAR SHOT! ANYONE HAVE THIS STUDENT IN THEIR CLASS? WAS IT SOME KIND OF GRADING ISSUE?
BUT WE STOPPED GRADING LAST YEAR!
COME OUT, COME OUT WHEREVER YOU ARE!
WAIT. I KNOW HER...FROM THE MAPLE TEN.
THE DEAD KIDS?
BRING ME KRISTEN SMITH OR YOU'RE ALL DEAD!
COME ON, COME ON...YOU SURE THIS CHARGER'S WORKING?
RELAX. YOU'RE IN A FIVE-STAR RIDE. I'VE GOT A CHARGER FOR EVERYTHING. ANDROID, IPHONE, USB, USB-C, XYC...
BEEP-BEEP!
POWER ON
FINALLY!
Krstn
Oliver Help!!!
Where R U?
School Attacke
CHANGE OF PLANS! TAKE ME STRAIGHT TO MAPLETON HIGH.

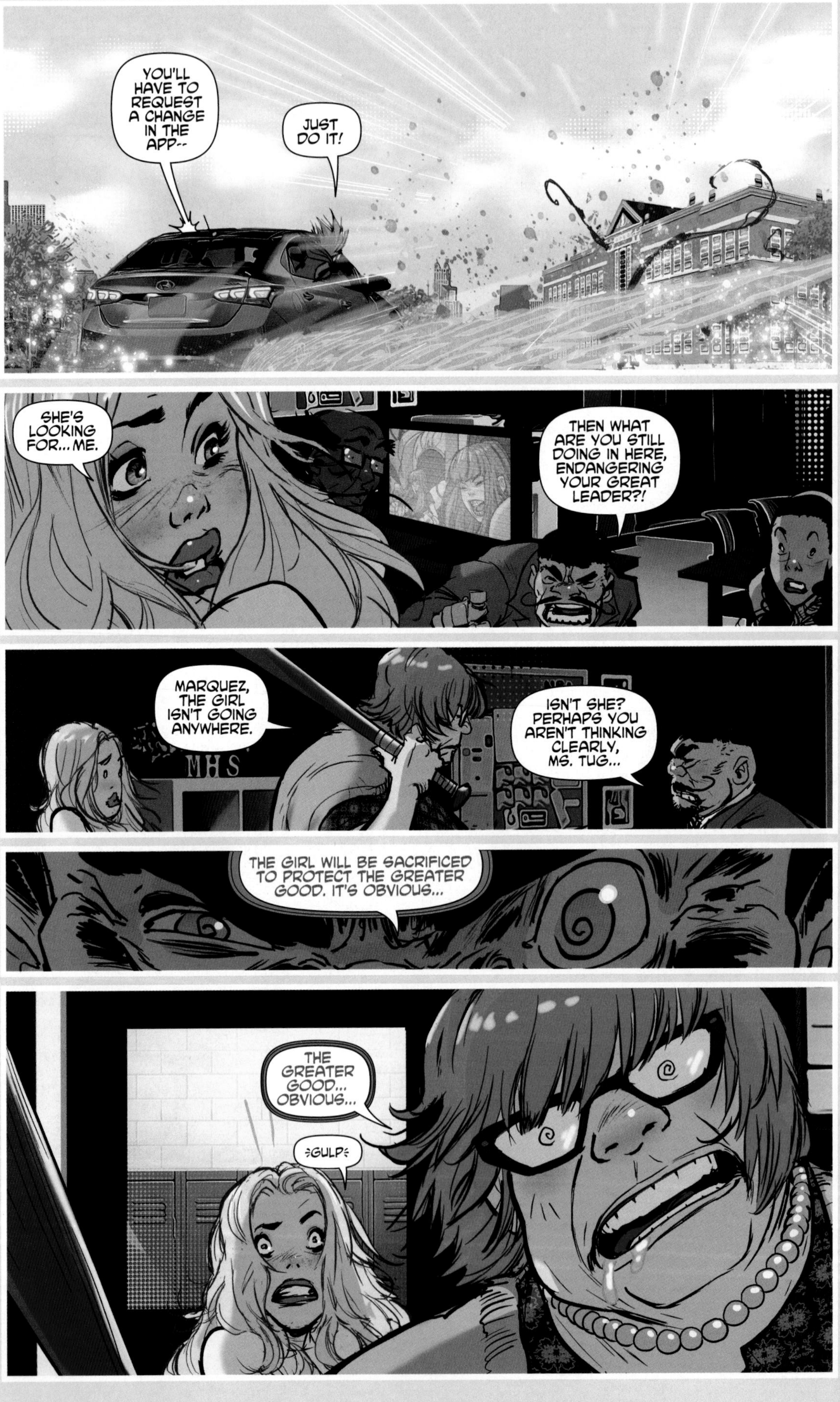
YOU'LL HAVE TO REQUEST A CHANGE IN THE APP--
JUST DO IT!
SHE'S LOOKING FOR... ME.
THEN WHAT ARE YOU STILL DOING IN HERE, ENDANGERING YOUR GREAT LEADER?!
MARQUEZ, THE GIRL ISN'T GOING ANYWHERE.
MHS
ISN'T SHE? PERHAPS YOU AREN'T THINKING CLEARLY, MS. TUG...
THE GIRL WILL BE SACRIFICED TO PROTECT THE GREATER GOOD. IT'S OBVIOUS...
THE GREATER GOOD... OBVIOUS...
GULP

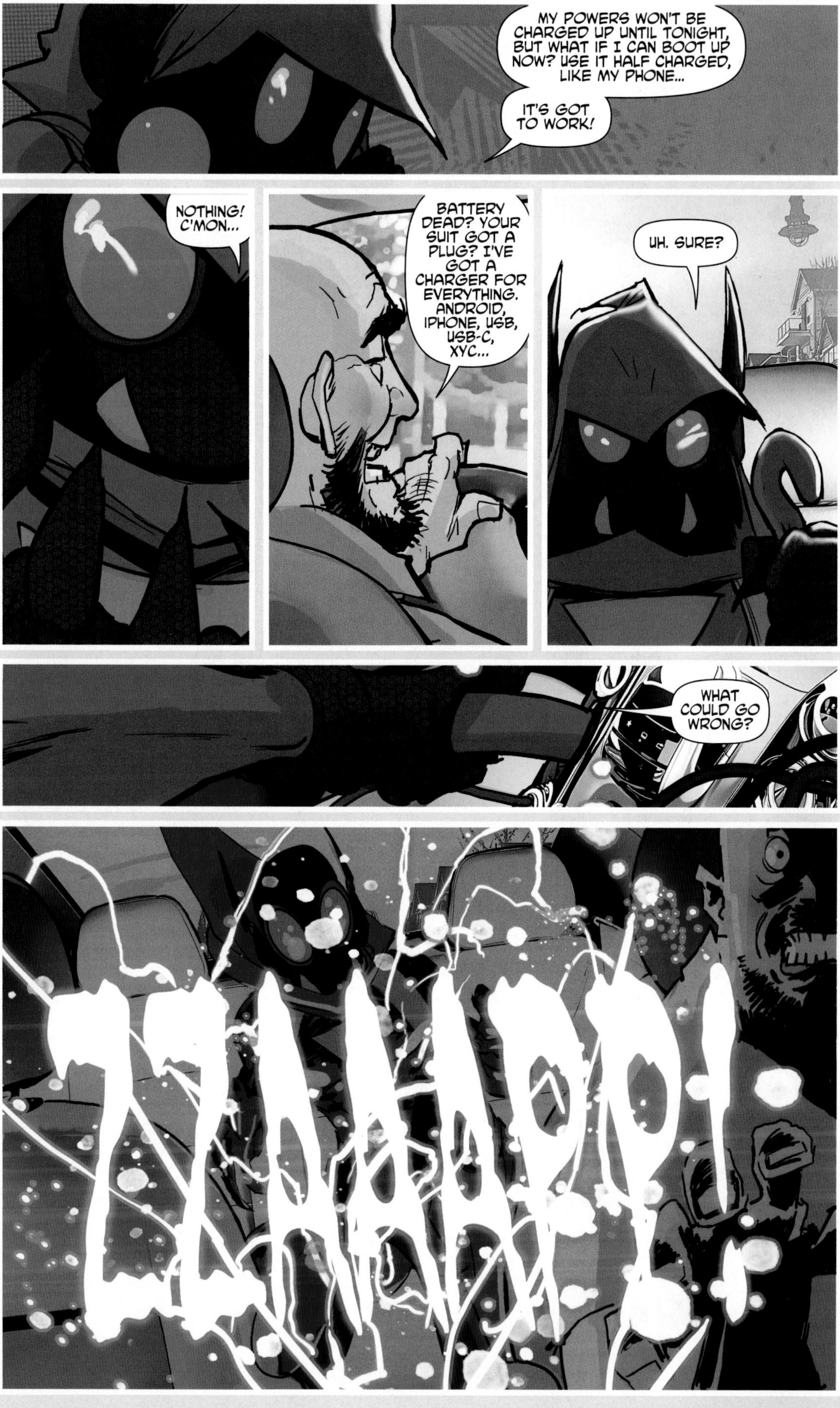
MY POWERS WON'T BE CHARGED UP UNTIL TONIGHT, BUT WHAT IF I CAN BOOT UP NOW? USE IT HALF CHARGED, LIKE MY PHONE...
IT'S GOT TO WORK!
NOTHING! C'MON...
BATTERY DEAD? YOUR SUIT GOT A PLUG? I'VE GOT A CHARGER FOR EVERYTHING. ANDROID, IPHONE, USB, USB-C, XYC...
UH. SURE?
WHAT COULD GO WRONG?
ZZAAAPP!

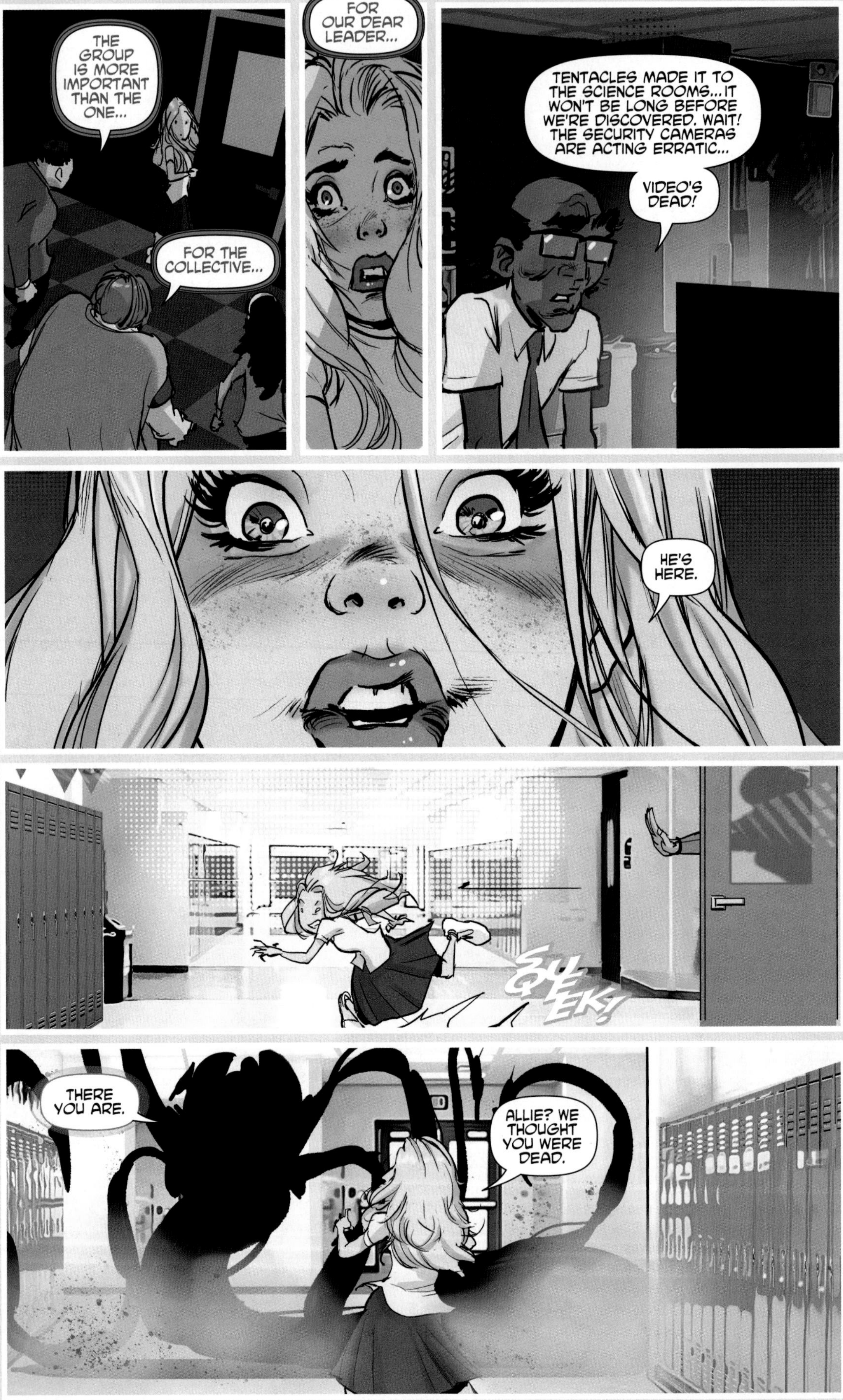
THE GROUP IS MORE IMPORTANT THAN THE ONE...
FOR THE COLLECTIVE...
FOR OUR DEAR LEADER...
TENTACLES MADE IT TO THE SCIENCE ROOMS...IT WON'T BE LONG BEFORE WE'RE DISCOVERED. WAIT! THE SECURITY CAMERAS ARE ACTING ERRATIC...
VIDEO'S DEAD!
HE'S HERE.
SQUEEK!
THERE YOU ARE.
ALLIE? WE THOUGHT YOU WERE DEAD.

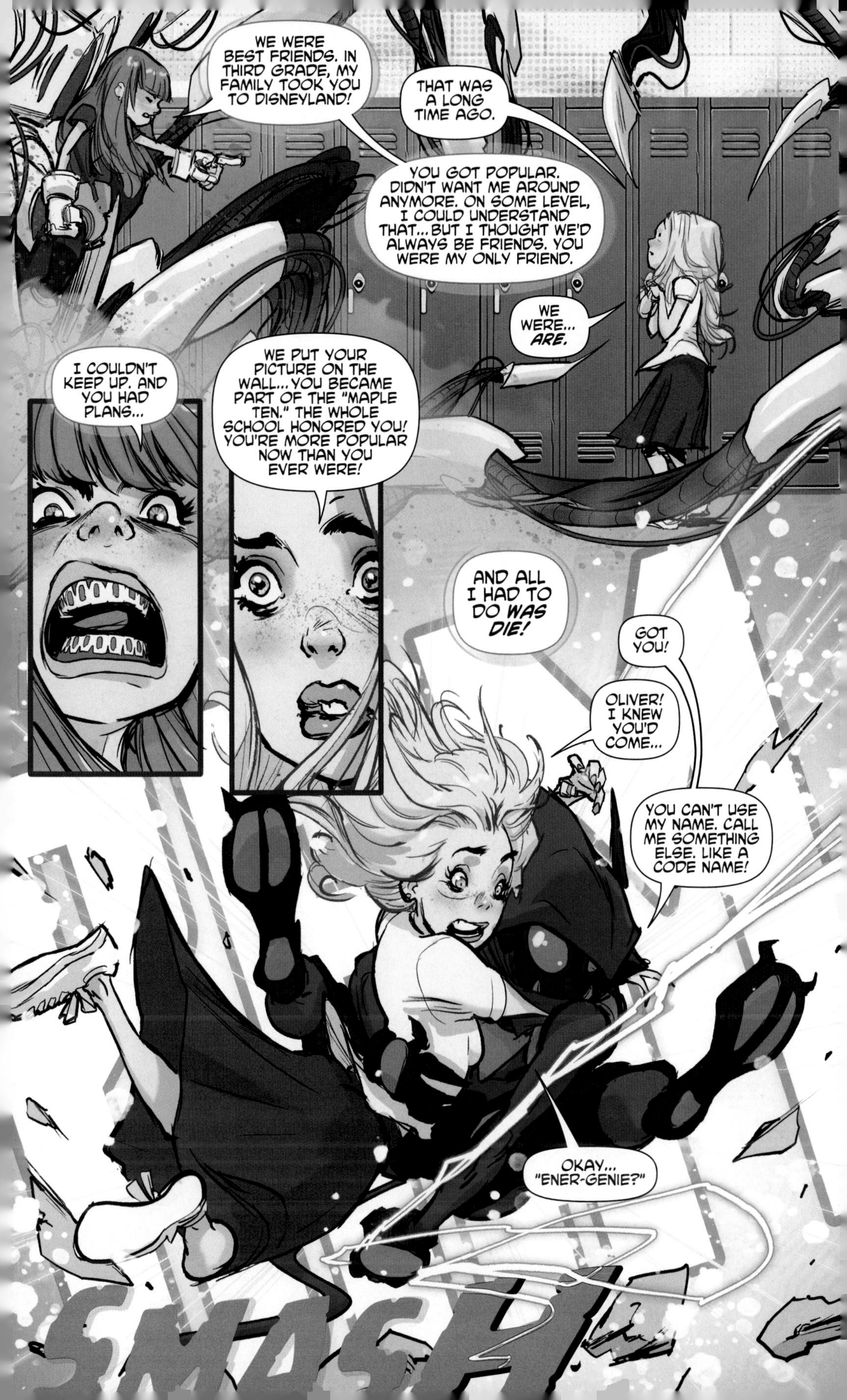
WE WERE BEST FRIENDS. IN THIRD GRADE, MY FAMILY TOOK YOU TO DISNEYLAND!
THAT WAS A LONG TIME AGO.
YOU GOT POPULAR. DIDN'T WANT ME AROUND ANYMORE. ON SOME LEVEL, I COULD UNDERSTAND THAT... BUT I THOUGHT WE'D ALWAYS BE FRIENDS. YOU WERE MY ONLY FRIEND.
WE WERE... *ARE.*
I COULDN'T KEEP UP. AND YOU HAD PLANS...
WE PUT YOUR PICTURE ON THE WALL... YOU BECAME PART OF THE "MAPLE TEN." THE WHOLE SCHOOL HONORED YOU! YOU'RE MORE POPULAR NOW THAN YOU EVER WERE!
AND ALL I HAD TO DO *WAS DIE!*
GOT YOU!
OLIVER! I KNEW YOU'D COME...
YOU CAN'T USE MY NAME. CALL ME SOMETHING ELSE. LIKE A CODE NAME!
OKAY... "ENER-GENIE?"
SMASH

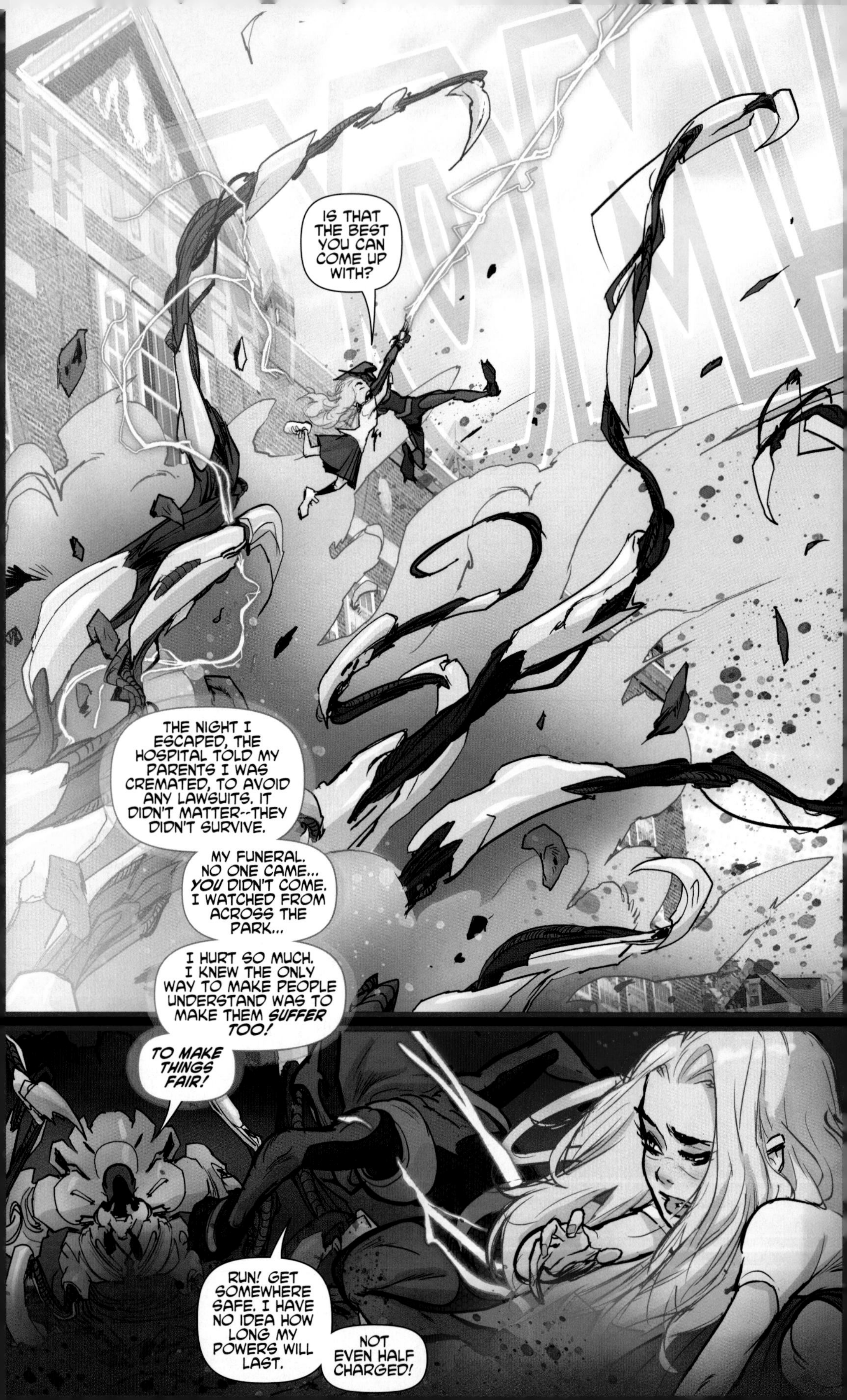
IS THAT THE BEST YOU CAN COME UP WITH?
THE NIGHT I ESCAPED, THE HOSPITAL TOLD MY PARENTS I WAS CREMATED, TO AVOID ANY LAWSUITS. IT DIDN'T MATTER--THEY DIDN'T SURVIVE.
MY FUNERAL. NO ONE CAME... *YOU* DIDN'T COME. I WATCHED FROM ACROSS THE PARK...
I HURT SO MUCH. I KNEW THE ONLY WAY TO MAKE PEOPLE UNDERSTAND WAS TO MAKE THEM *SUFFER TOO!*
TO MAKE THINGS FAIR!
RUN! GET SOMEWHERE SAFE. I HAVE NO IDEA HOW LONG MY POWERS WILL LAST.
NOT EVEN HALF CHARGED!

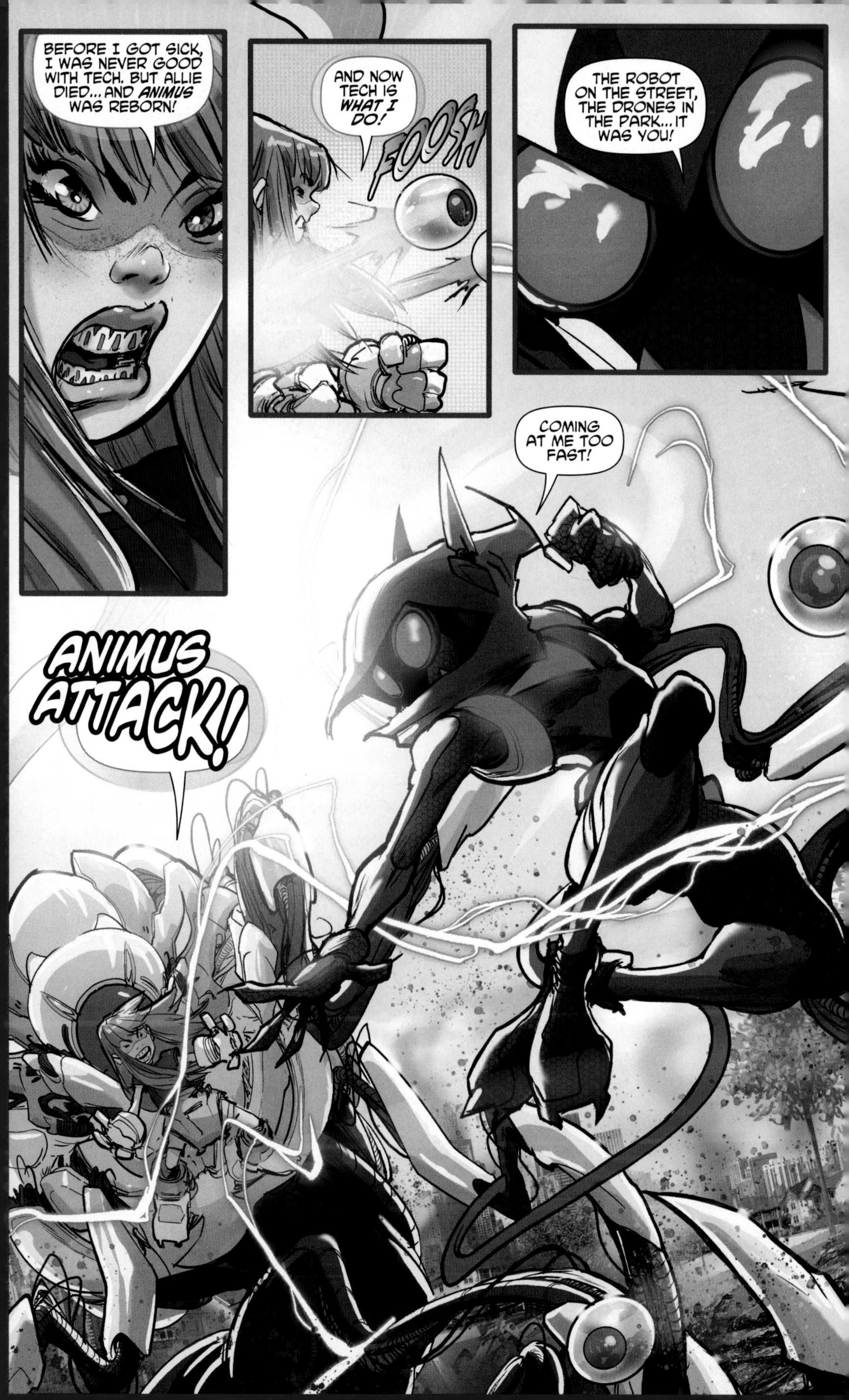
BEFORE I GOT SICK, I WAS NEVER GOOD WITH TECH. BUT ALLIE DIED... AND ANIMUS WAS REBORN!
AND NOW TECH IS WHAT I DO!
FOOSH
THE ROBOT ON THE STREET, THE DRONES IN THE PARK... IT WAS YOU!
COMING AT ME TOO FAST!
ANIMUS ATTACK!

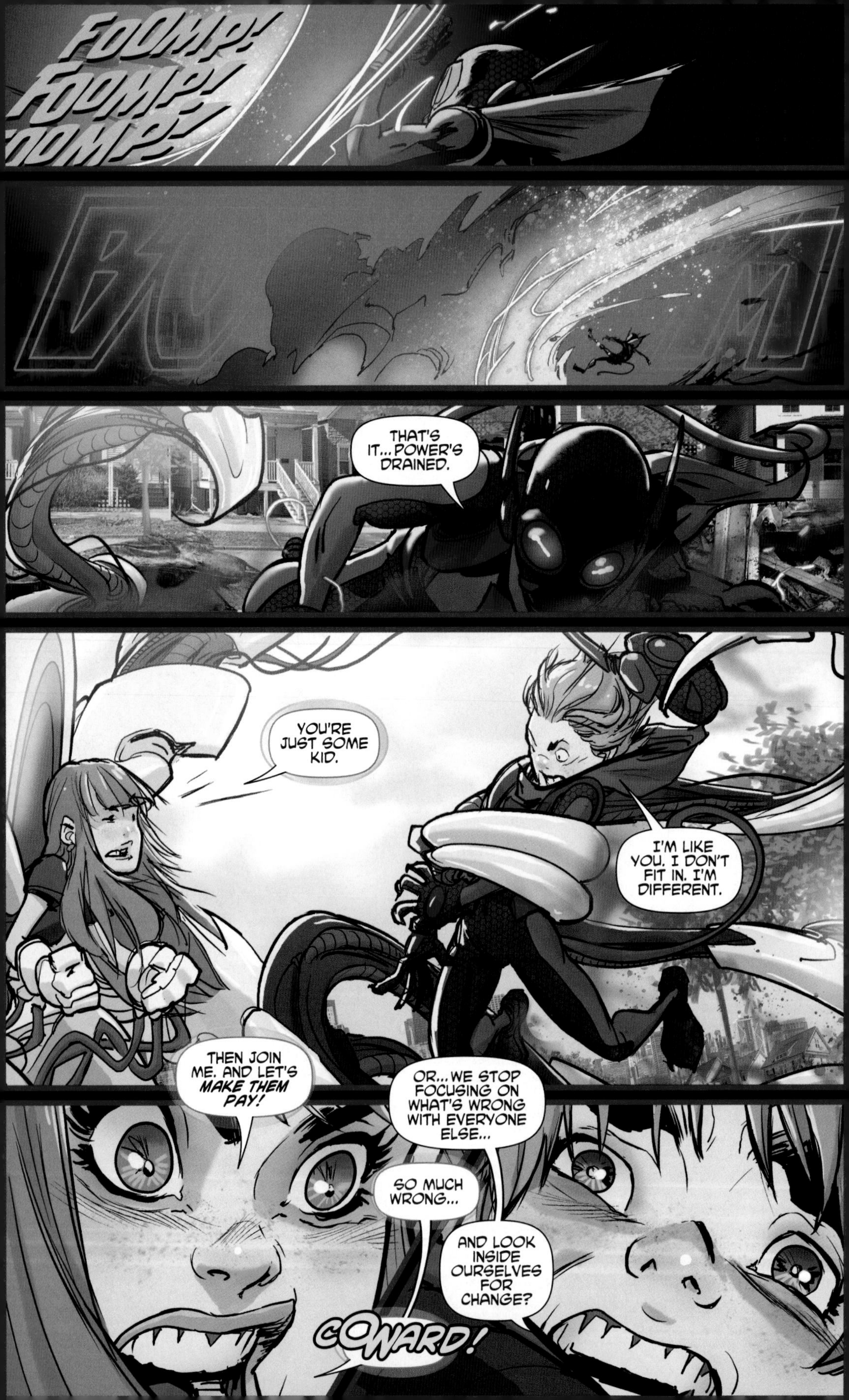
FOOMP! FOOMP! FOOMP!
THAT'S IT... POWER'S DRAINED.
YOU'RE JUST SOME KID.
I'M LIKE YOU. I DON'T FIT IN. I'M DIFFERENT.
THEN JOIN ME. AND LET'S *MAKE THEM PAY!*
OR... WE STOP FOCUSING ON WHAT'S WRONG WITH EVERYONE ELSE...
SO MUCH WRONG...
AND LOOK INSIDE OURSELVES FOR CHANGE?
COWARD!

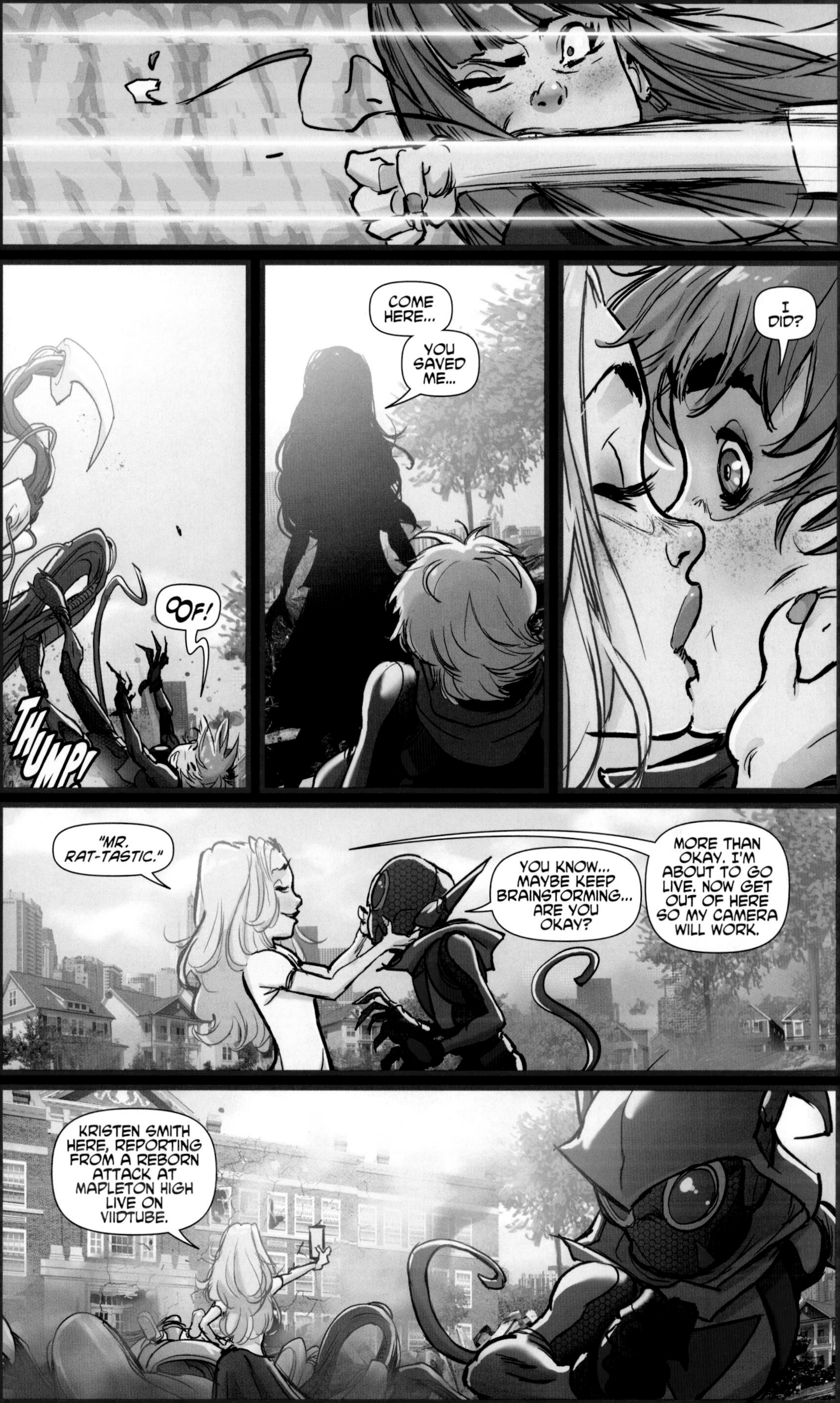
THUMP!
OOF!
COME HERE...
YOU SAVED ME...
I DID?
"MR. RAT-TASTIC."
YOU KNOW... MAYBE KEEP BRAINSTORMING... ARE YOU OKAY?
MORE THAN OKAY. I'M ABOUT TO GO LIVE. NOW GET OUT OF HERE SO MY CAMERA WILL WORK.
KRISTEN SMITH HERE, REPORTING FROM A REBORN ATTACK AT MAPLETON HIGH LIVE ON VIIDTUBE.

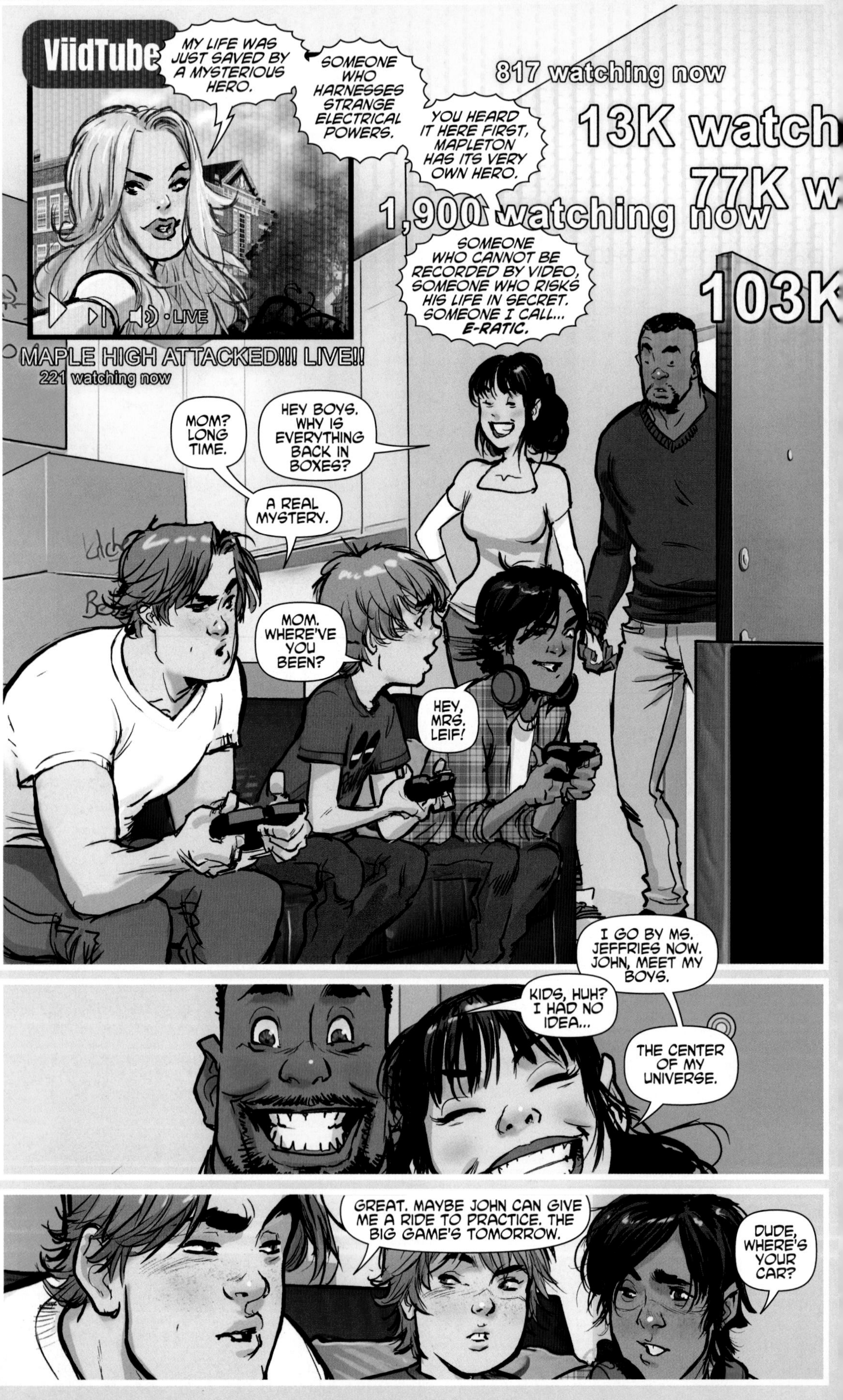
ViidTube
MY LIFE WAS JUST SAVED BY A MYSTERIOUS HERO.
SOMEONE WHO HARNESSES STRANGE ELECTRICAL POWERS.
YOU HEARD IT HERE FIRST, MAPLETON HAS ITS VERY OWN HERO.
SOMEONE WHO CANNOT BE RECORDED BY VIDEO, SOMEONE WHO RISKS HIS LIFE IN SECRET. SOMEONE I CALL... E-RATIC.
LIVE
MAPLE HIGH ATTACKED!!! LIVE!!
221 watching now
817 watching now
13K watch
77K w
1,900 watching now
103K
HEY BOYS. WHY IS EVERYTHING BACK IN BOXES?
MOM? LONG TIME.
A REAL MYSTERY.
MOM. WHERE'VE YOU BEEN?
HEY, MRS. LEIF!
I GO BY MS. JEFFRIES NOW. JOHN, MEET MY BOYS.
KIDS, HUH? I HAD NO IDEA...
THE CENTER OF MY UNIVERSE.
GREAT. MAYBE JOHN CAN GIVE ME A RIDE TO PRACTICE. THE BIG GAME'S TOMORROW.
DUDE, WHERE'S YOUR CAR?

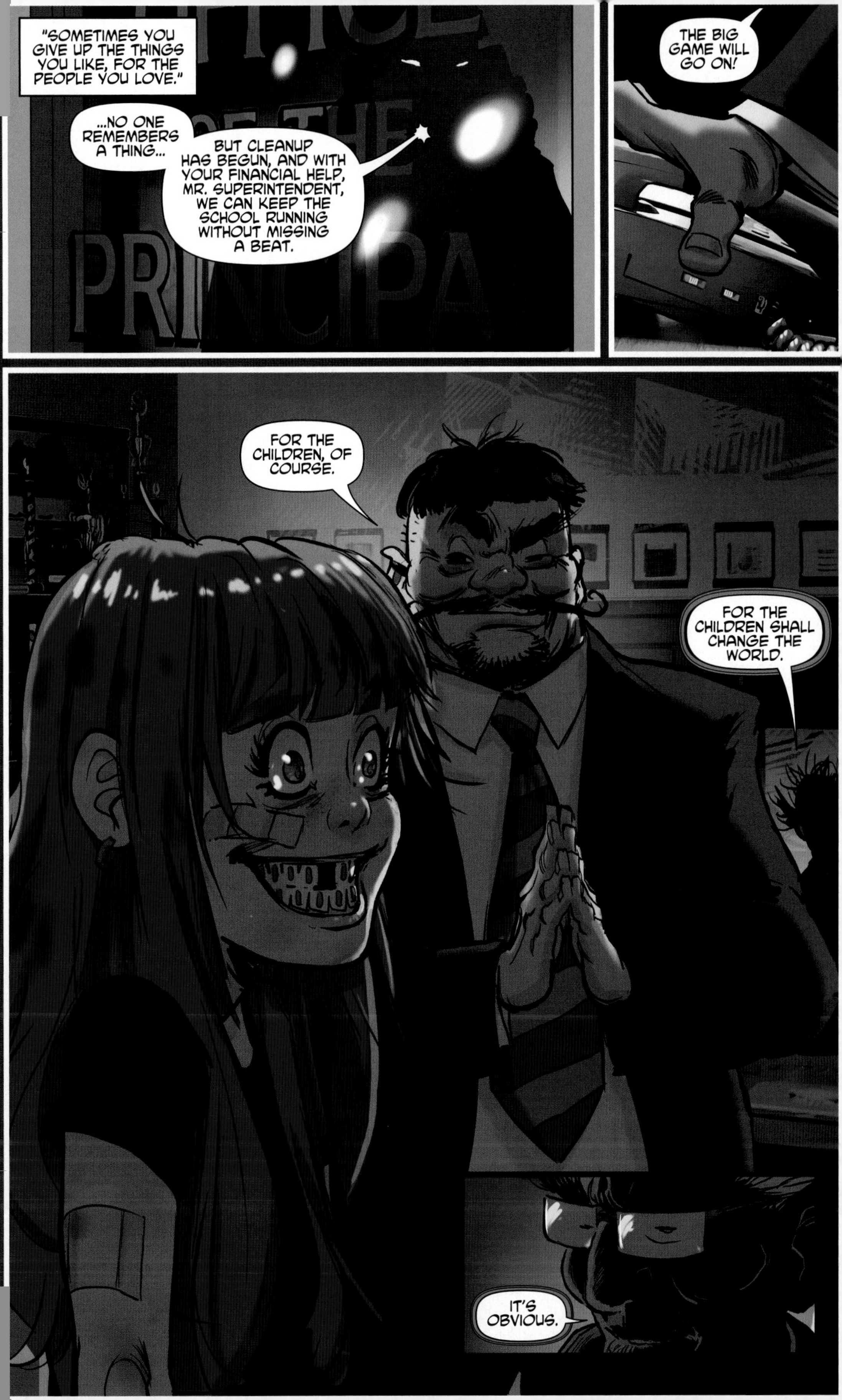
"SOMETIMES YOU GIVE UP THE THINGS YOU LIKE, FOR THE PEOPLE YOU LOVE."
...NO ONE REMEMBERS A THING...
BUT CLEANUP HAS BEGUN, AND WITH YOUR FINANCIAL HELP, MR. SUPERINTENDENT, WE CAN KEEP THE SCHOOL RUNNING WITHOUT MISSING A BEAT.
THE BIG GAME WILL GO ON!
FOR THE CHILDREN, OF COURSE.
FOR THE CHILDREN SHALL CHANGE THE WORLD.
IT'S OBVIOUS.

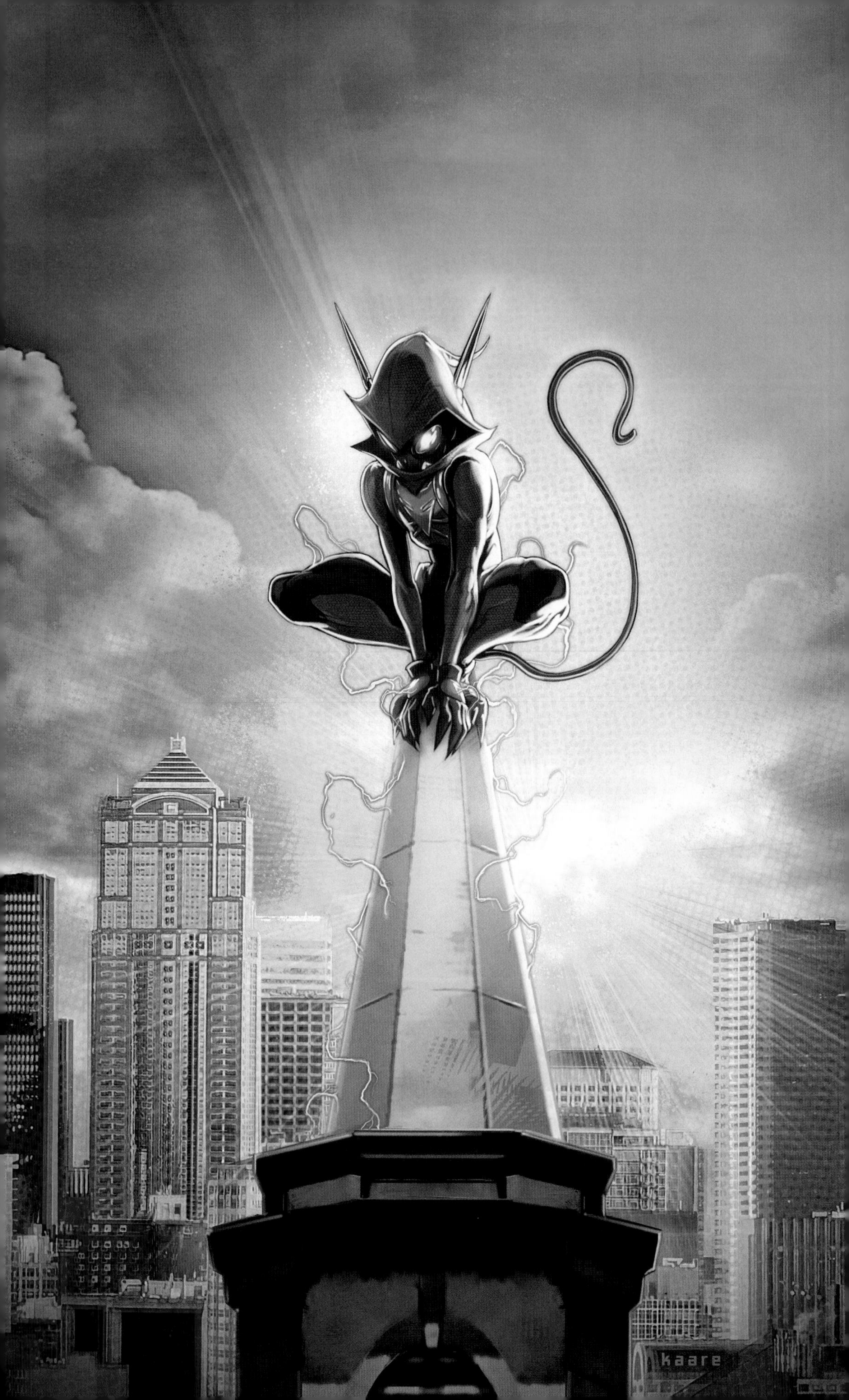
kaare

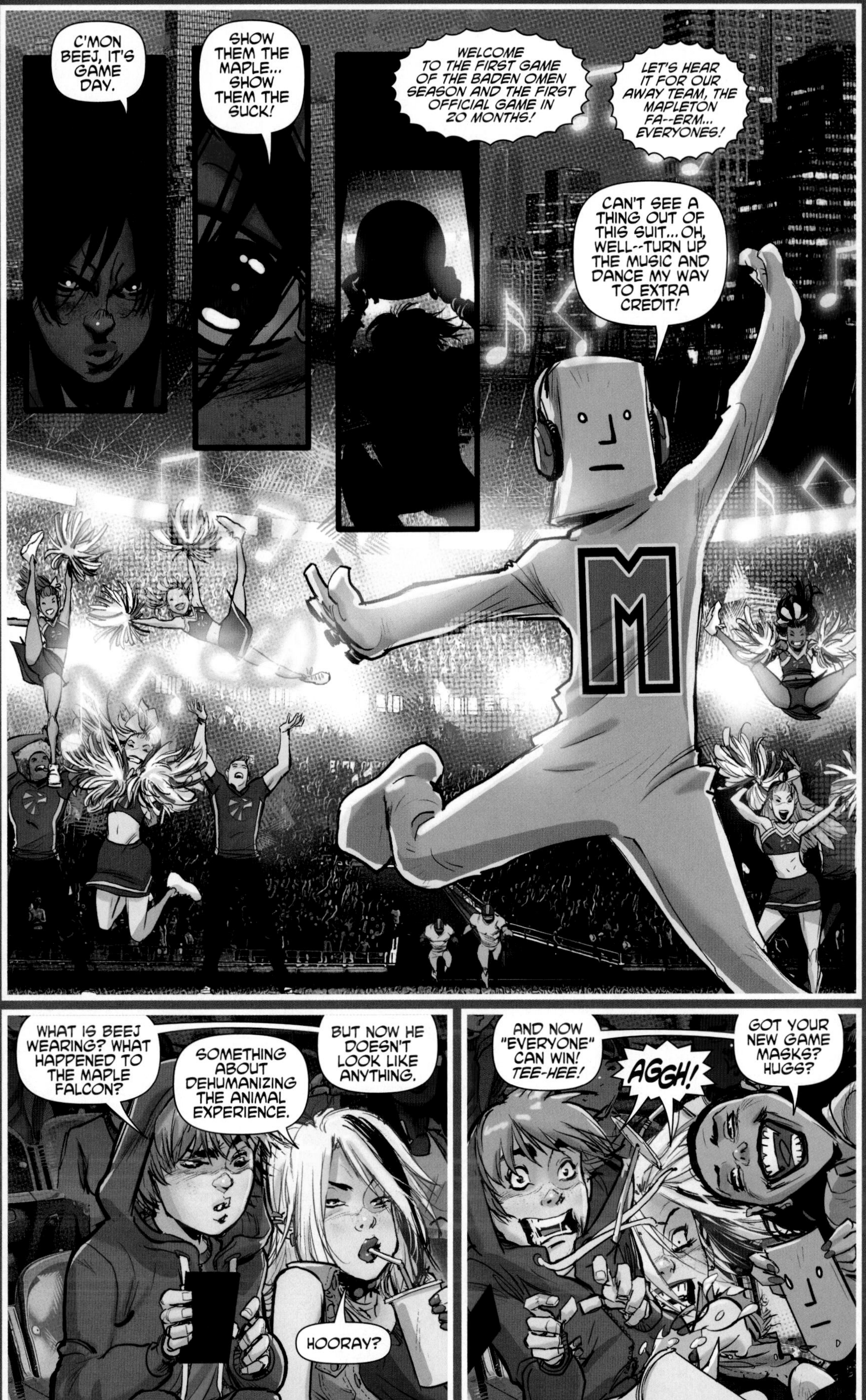
C'MON BEEJ, IT'S GAME DAY.
SHOW THEM THE MAPLE... SHOW THEM THE SUCK!
WELCOME TO THE FIRST GAME OF THE BADEN OMEN SEASON AND THE FIRST OFFICIAL GAME IN 20 MONTHS!
LET'S HEAR IT FOR OUR AWAY TEAM, THE MAPLETON FA--ERM... EVERYONES!
CAN'T SEE A THING OUT OF THIS SUIT... OH, WELL--TURN UP THE MUSIC AND DANCE MY WAY TO EXTRA CREDIT!
WHAT IS BEEJ WEARING? WHAT HAPPENED TO THE MAPLE FALCON?
SOMETHING ABOUT DEHUMANIZING THE ANIMAL EXPERIENCE.
BUT NOW HE DOESN'T LOOK LIKE ANYTHING.
HOORAY?
AND NOW "EVERYONE" CAN WIN! TEE-HEE!
AGGH!
GOT YOUR NEW GAME MASKS? HUGS?

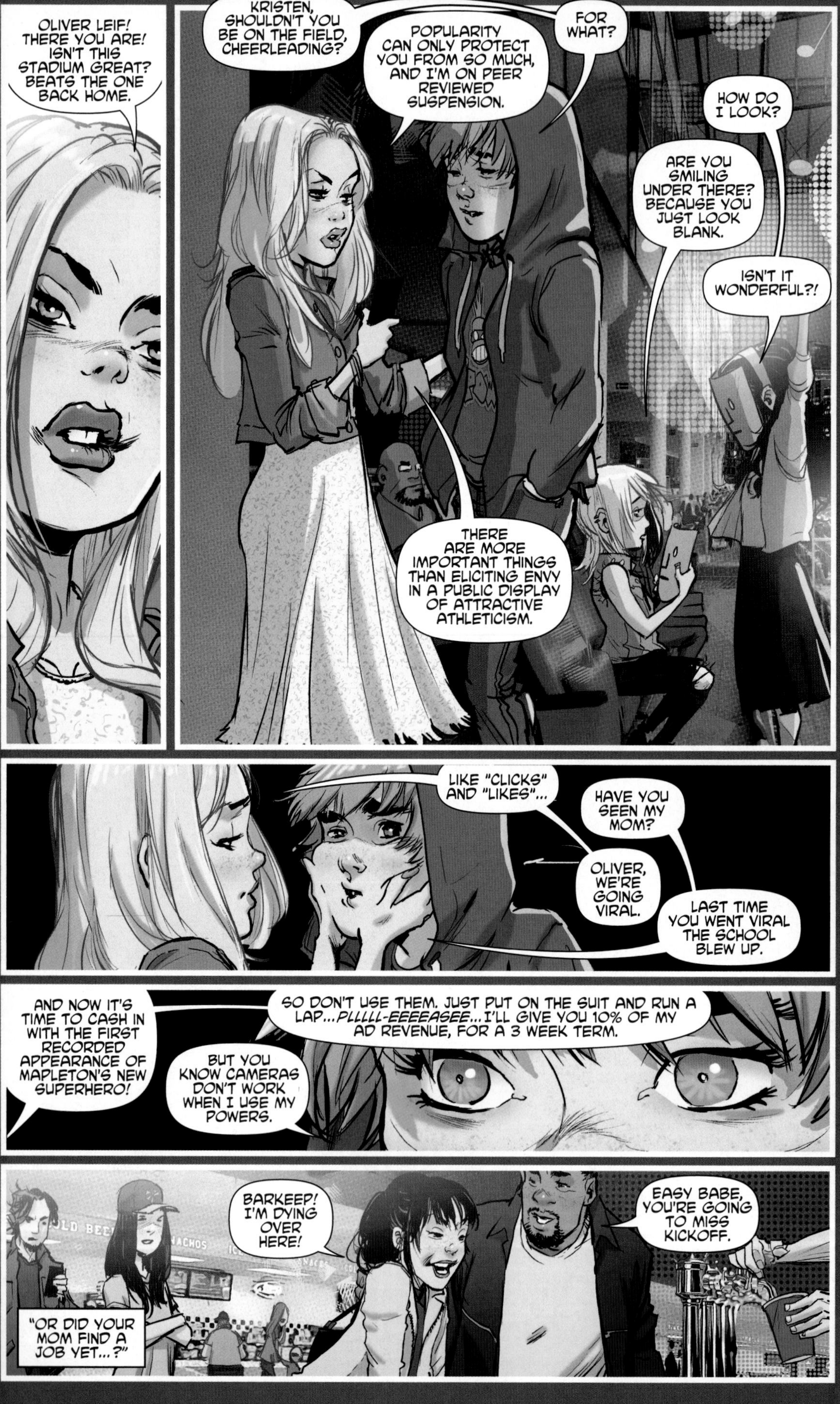

OLIVER LEIF! THERE YOU ARE! ISN'T THIS STADIUM GREAT? BEATS THE ONE BACK HOME.
KRISTEN, SHOULDN'T YOU BE ON THE FIELD, CHEERLEADING?
FOR WHAT?
POPULARITY CAN ONLY PROTECT YOU FROM SO MUCH, AND I'M ON PEER REVIEWED SUSPENSION.
THERE ARE MORE IMPORTANT THINGS THAN ELICITING ENVY IN A PUBLIC DISPLAY OF ATTRACTIVE ATHLETICISM.
HOW DO I LOOK?
ARE YOU SMILING UNDER THERE? BECAUSE YOU JUST LOOK BLANK.
ISN'T IT WONDERFUL?!
LIKE "CLICKS" AND "LIKES"...
OLIVER, WE'RE GOING VIRAL.
HAVE YOU SEEN MY MOM?
LAST TIME YOU WENT VIRAL THE SCHOOL BLEW UP.
AND NOW IT'S TIME TO CASH IN WITH THE FIRST RECORDED APPEARANCE OF MAPLETON'S NEW SUPERHERO!
BUT YOU KNOW CAMERAS DON'T WORK WHEN I USE MY POWERS.
SO DON'T USE THEM. JUST PUT ON THE SUIT AND RUN A LAP... *PLLLLL-EEEEASEE*... I'LL GIVE YOU 10% OF MY AD REVENUE, FOR A 3 WEEK TERM.
"OR DID YOUR MOM FIND A JOB YET...?"
BARKEEP! I'M DYING OVER HERE!
EASY BABE, YOU'RE GOING TO MISS KICKOFF.

"EASY?" YOU TRYING TO SAY SOMETHING? "BABE?"

CALM DOWN.

I CAME INTO YOUR PLACE LOOKING FOR A JOB, NOT A BOYFRIEND!

I NEVER SAID I WAS...OKAY, I GET IT.

MA'AM, YOU HAVE TO PAY FOR THAT...

GULP! GULP! GULP!

HAVE FUN TONIGHT.

THEN YOU BETTER FILL IT THE TRUCK UP!

DID KRISTEN SEW ON A...A *RAT* LOGO?

I CAN'T DO THIS... RISK EXPOSING MYSELF IN FRONT OF A PUBLIC AUDIENCE FOR CLICKS?

HEY, HURRY UP WITH YOUR EXISTENTIAL CRISIS! IF YOU'RE GOING TO STREAK THE FIELD, HAVE AT IT! I HAVE TO GO!

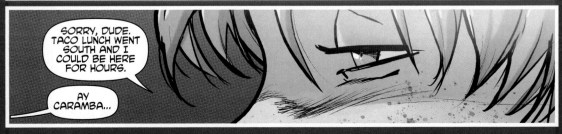

SORRY, DUDE. TACO LUNCH WENT SOUTH AND I COULD BE HERE FOR HOURS.

AY CARAMBA...

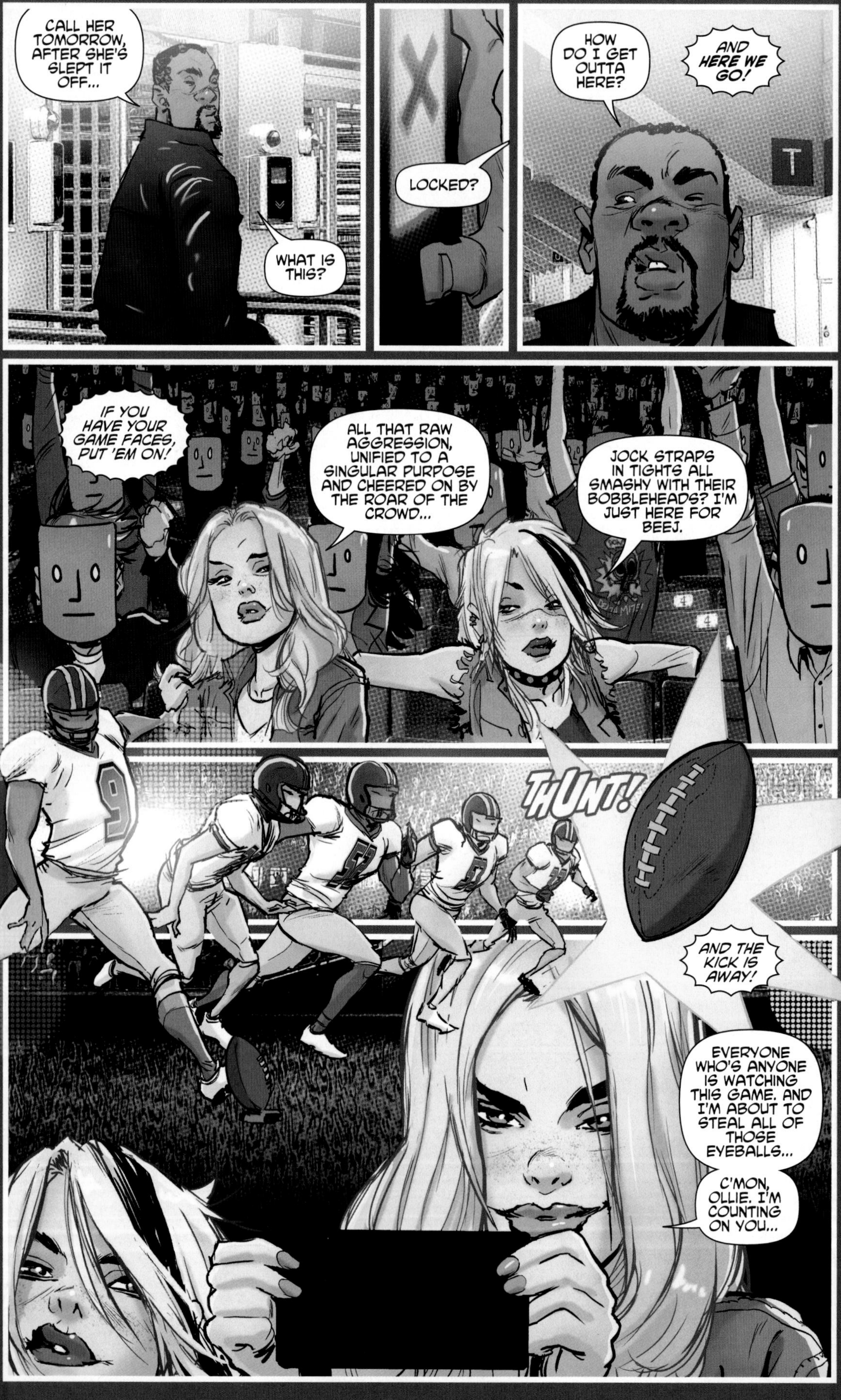
CALL HER TOMORROW, AFTER SHE'S SLEPT IT OFF...
WHAT IS THIS?
LOCKED?
HOW DO I GET OUTTA HERE?
AND HERE WE GO!
IF YOU HAVE YOUR GAME FACES, PUT 'EM ON!
ALL THAT RAW AGGRESSION, UNIFIED TO A SINGULAR PURPOSE AND CHEERED ON BY THE ROAR OF THE CROWD...
JOCK STRAPS IN TIGHTS ALL SMASHY WITH THEIR BOBBLEHEADS? I'M JUST HERE FOR BEEJ.
THUNT!
AND THE KICK IS AWAY!
EVERYONE WHO'S ANYONE IS WATCHING THIS GAME. AND I'M ABOUT TO STEAL ALL OF THOSE EYEBALLS...
C'MON, OLLIE. I'M COUNTING ON YOU...

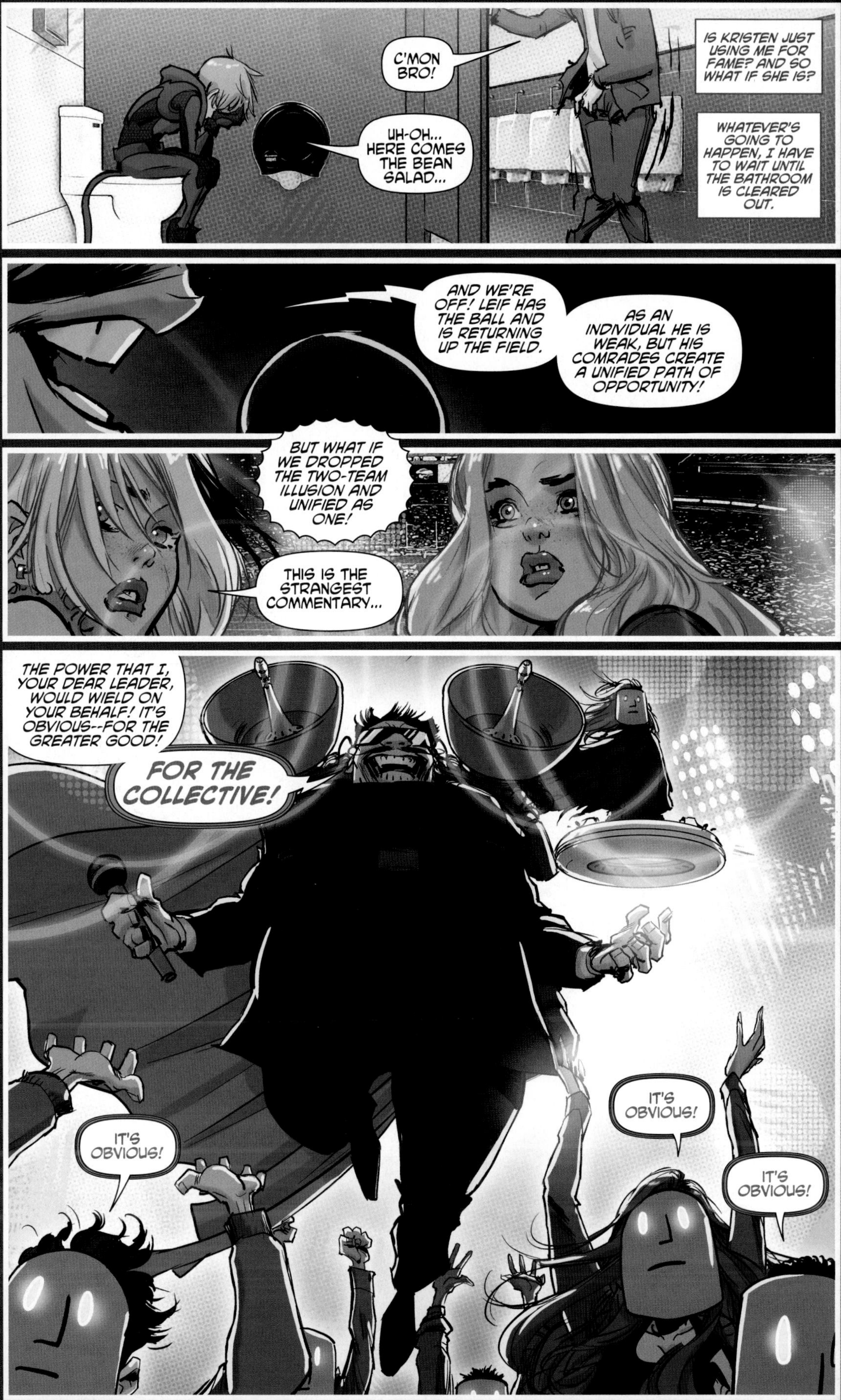
C'MON BRO!
UH-OH... HERE COMES THE BEAN SALAD...
IS KRISTEN JUST USING ME FOR FAME? AND SO WHAT IF SHE IS?
WHATEVER'S GOING TO HAPPEN, I HAVE TO WAIT UNTIL THE BATHROOM IS CLEARED OUT.
AND WE'RE OFF! LEIF HAS THE BALL AND IS RETURNING UP THE FIELD.
AS AN INDIVIDUAL HE IS WEAK, BUT HIS COMRADES CREATE A UNIFIED PATH OF OPPORTUNITY!
BUT WHAT IF WE DROPPED THE TWO-TEAM ILLUSION AND UNIFIED AS ONE!
THIS IS THE STRANGEST COMMENTARY...
THE POWER THAT I, YOUR DEAR LEADER, WOULD WIELD ON YOUR BEHALF! IT'S OBVIOUS--FOR THE GREATER GOOD!
FOR THE COLLECTIVE!
IT'S OBVIOUS!
IT'S OBVIOUS!
IT'S OBVIOUS!

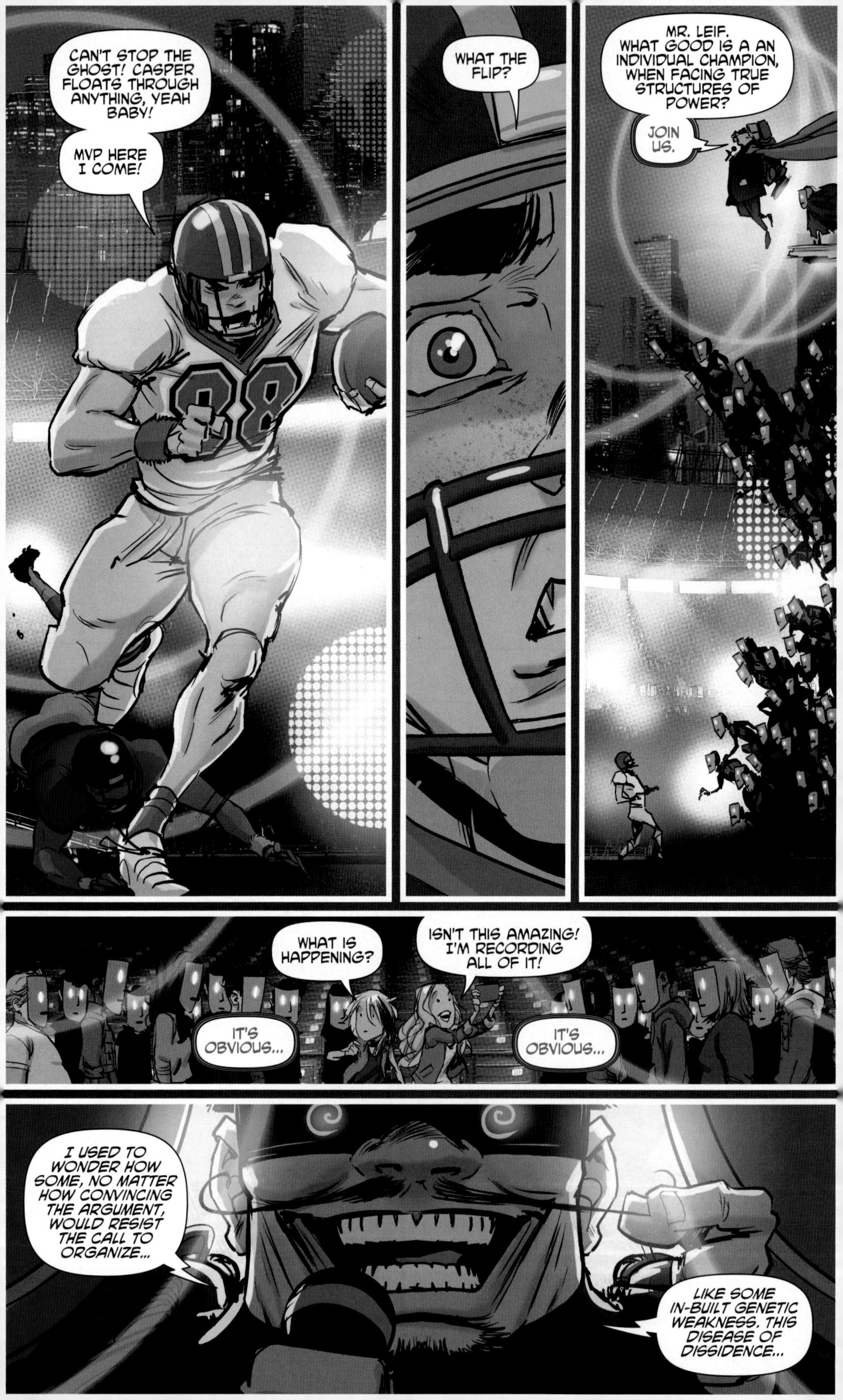

CAN'T STOP THE GHOST! CASPER FLOATS THROUGH ANYTHING, YEAH BABY!
MVP HERE I COME!
WHAT THE FLIP?
MR. LEIF. WHAT GOOD IS A AN INDIVIDUAL CHAMPION, WHEN FACING TRUE STRUCTURES OF POWER?
JOIN US.
WHAT IS HAPPENING?
ISN'T THIS AMAZING! I'M RECORDING ALL OF IT!
IT'S OBVIOUS...
IT'S OBVIOUS...
I USED TO WONDER HOW SOME, NO MATTER HOW CONVINCING THE ARGUMENT, WOULD RESIST THE CALL TO ORGANIZE...
LIKE SOME IN-BUILT GENETIC WEAKNESS. THIS DISEASE OF DISSIDENCE...

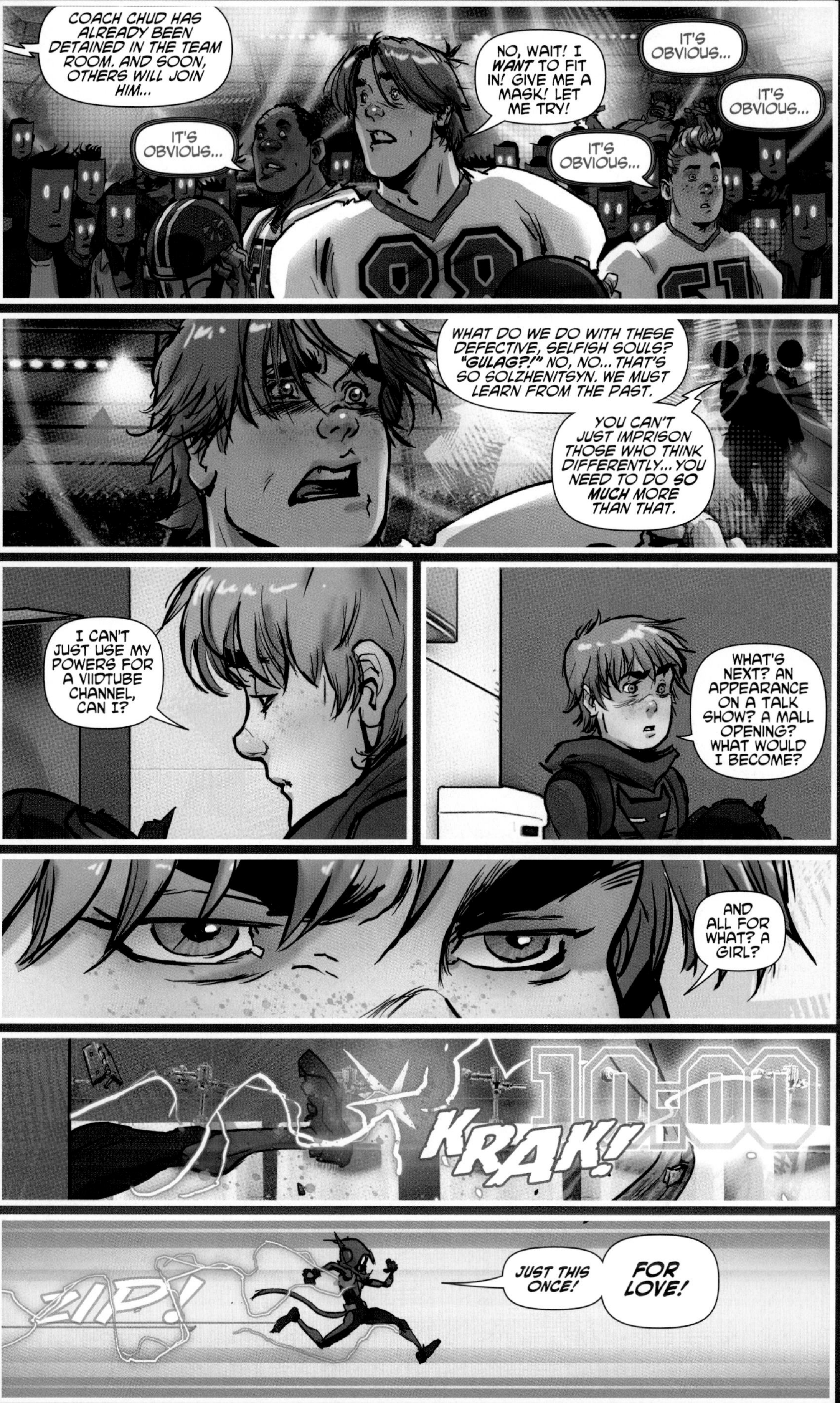
COACH CHUD HAS ALREADY BEEN DETAINED IN THE TEAM ROOM. AND SOON, OTHERS WILL JOIN HIM...
NO, WAIT! I *WANT* TO FIT IN! GIVE ME A MASK! LET ME TRY!
IT'S OBVIOUS...
IT'S OBVIOUS...
IT'S OBVIOUS...
IT'S OBVIOUS...
WHAT DO WE DO WITH THESE DEFECTIVE, SELFISH SOULS? *"GULAG?!"* NO, NO... THAT'S SO SOLZHENITSYN. WE MUST LEARN FROM THE PAST.
YOU CAN'T JUST IMPRISON THOSE WHO THINK DIFFERENTLY... YOU NEED TO DO *SO MUCH* MORE THAN THAT.
I CAN'T JUST USE MY POWERS FOR A VIIDTUBE CHANNEL, CAN I?
WHAT'S NEXT? AN APPEARANCE ON A TALK SHOW? A MALL OPENING? WHAT WOULD I BECOME?
AND ALL FOR WHAT? A GIRL?
10:00
KRAK!
ZIP!
JUST THIS ONCE!
FOR LOVE!

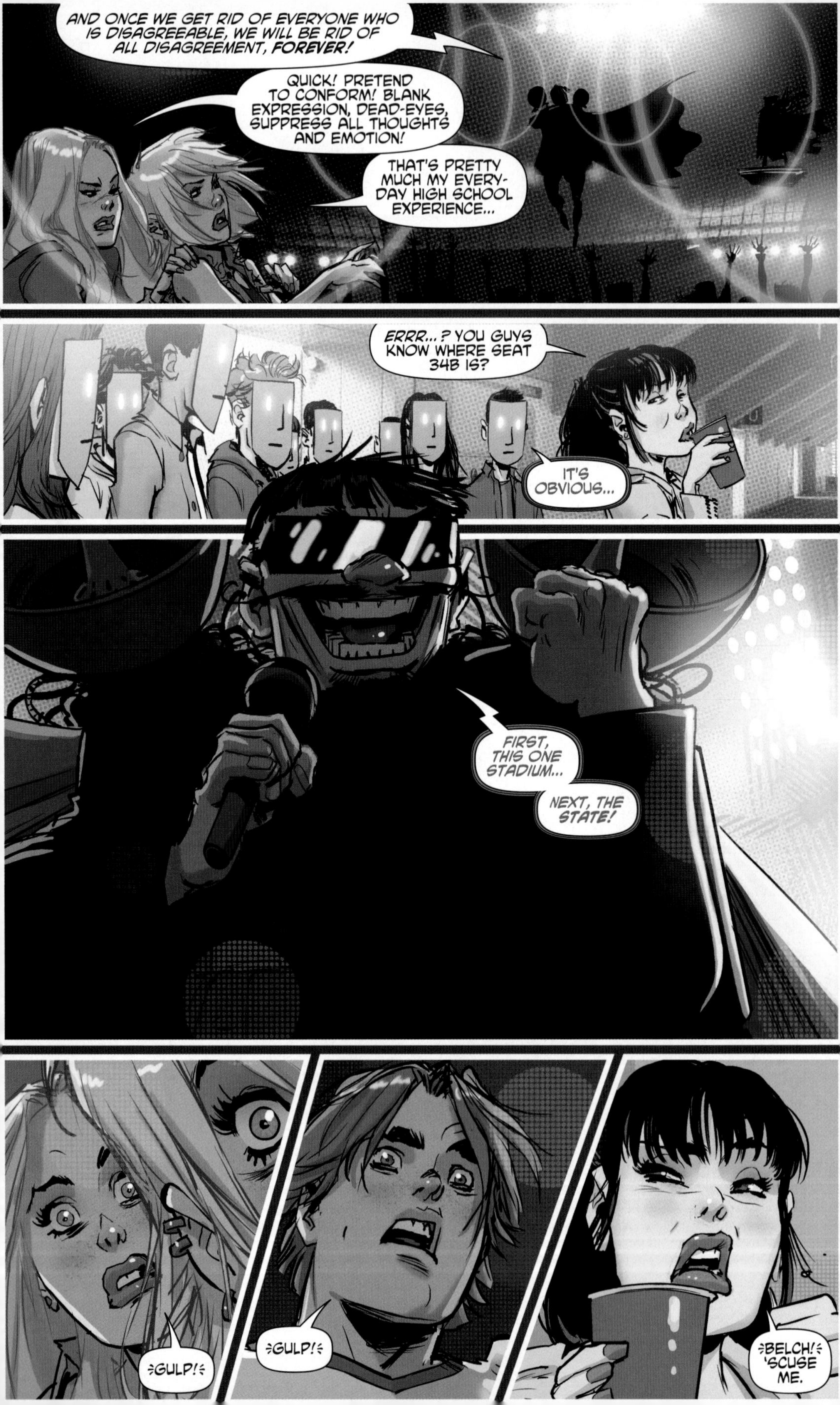
AND ONCE WE GET RID OF EVERYONE WHO IS DISAGREEABLE, WE WILL BE RID OF ALL DISAGREEMENT, FOREVER!
QUICK! PRETEND TO CONFORM! BLANK EXPRESSION, DEAD-EYES, SUPPRESS ALL THOUGHTS AND EMOTION!
THAT'S PRETTY MUCH MY EVERY-DAY HIGH SCHOOL EXPERIENCE...
ERRR...? YOU GUYS KNOW WHERE SEAT 34B IS?
IT'S OBVIOUS...
FIRST, THIS ONE STADIUM...
NEXT, THE STATE!
GULP!
GULP!
BELCH! 'SCUSE ME.

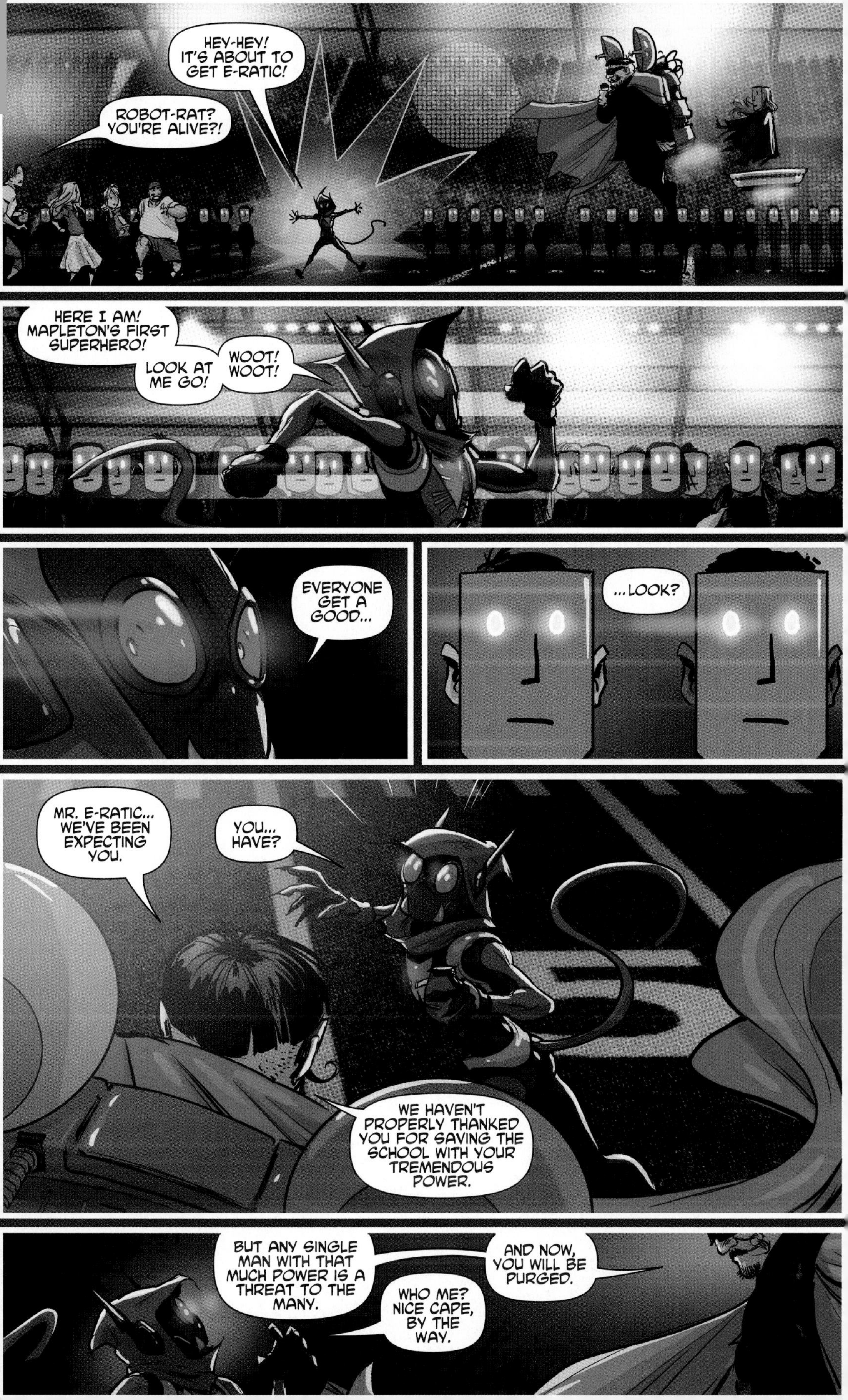

HEY-HEY! IT'S ABOUT TO GET E-RATIC!
ROBOT-RAT? YOU'RE ALIVE?!
HERE I AM! MAPLETON'S FIRST SUPERHERO!
LOOK AT ME GO!
WOOT! WOOT!
EVERYONE SINGLE GET A GOOD...
...LOOK?
MR. E-RATIC... WE'VE BEEN EXPECTING YOU.
YOU... HAVE?
WE HAVEN'T PROPERLY THANKED YOU FOR SAVING THE SCHOOL WITH YOUR TREMENDOUS POWER.
BUT ANY SINGLE MAN WITH THAT MUCH POWER IS A THREAT TO THE MANY.
WHO ME? NICE CAPE, BY THE WAY.
AND NOW, YOU WILL BE PURGED.

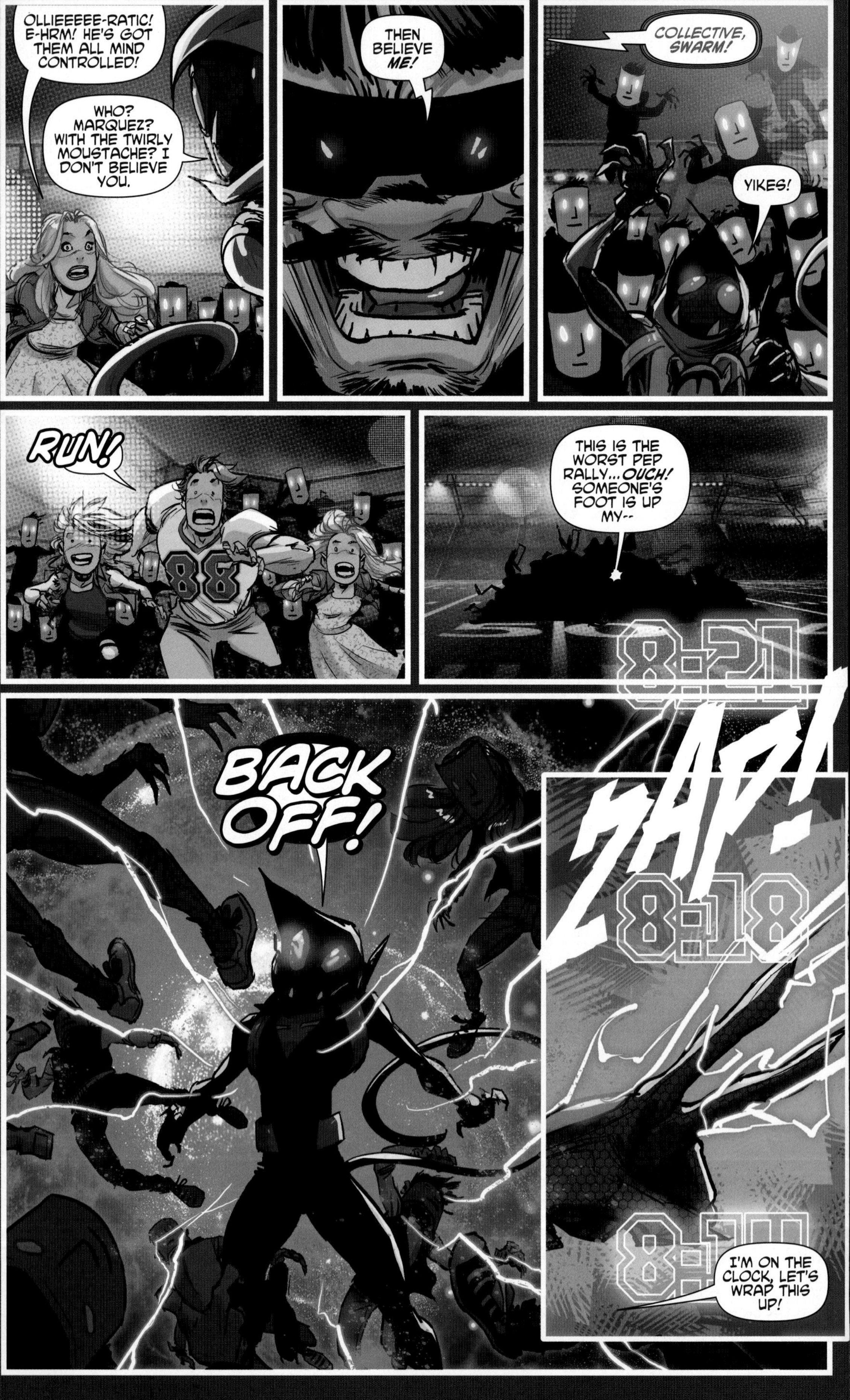
OLLIEEEEE-RATIC! E-HRM! HE'S GOT THEM ALL MIND CONTROLLED!
WHO? MARQUEZ? WITH THE TWIRLY MOUSTACHE? I DON'T BELIEVE YOU.
THEN BELIEVE ME!
COLLECTIVE, SWARM!
YIKES!
RUN!
THIS IS THE WORST PEP RALLY... OUCH! SOMEONE'S FOOT IS UP MY--
BACK OFF!
ZAP!
8:18
I'M ON THE CLOCK, LET'S WRAP THIS UP!

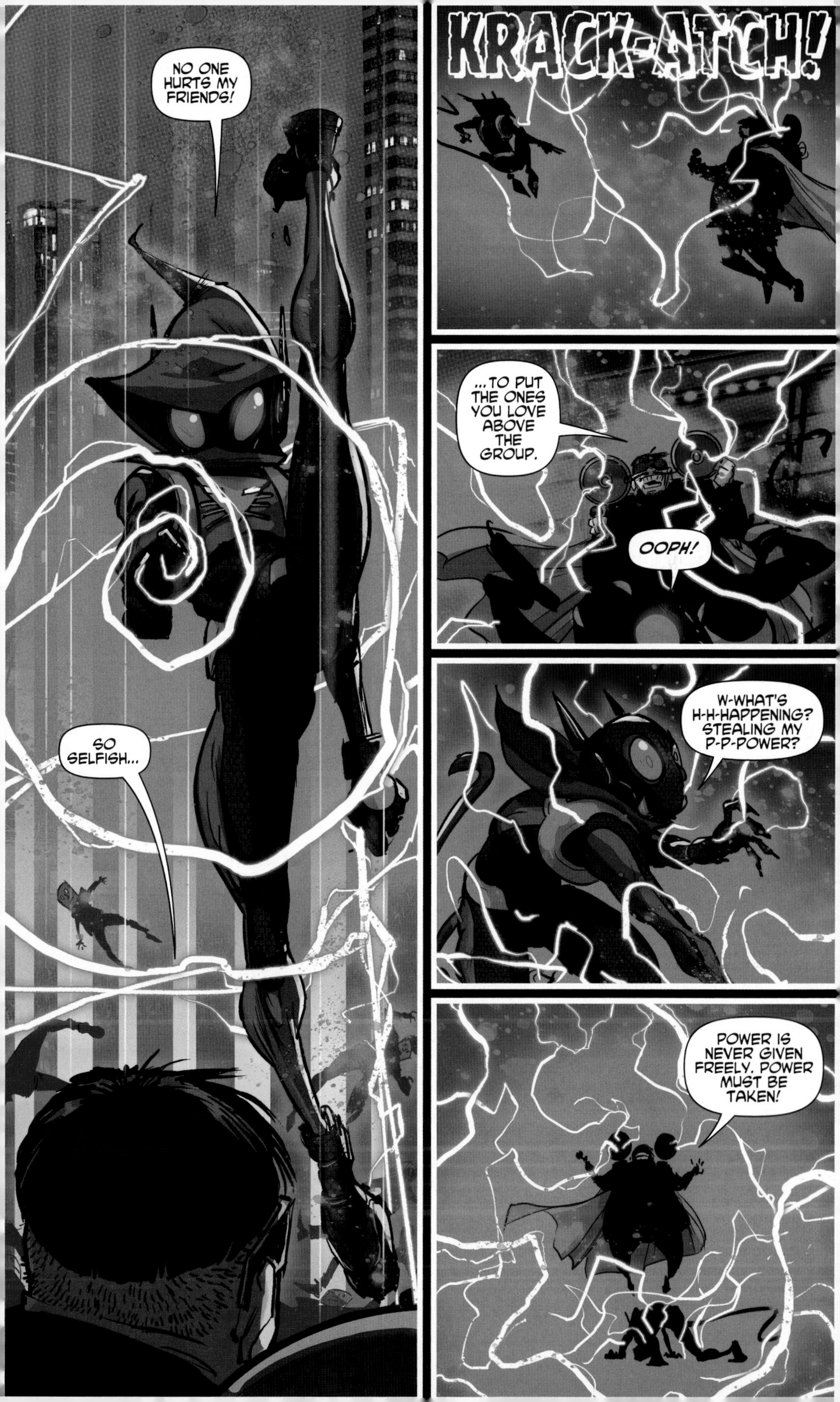
NO ONE HURTS MY FRIENDS!
SO SELFISH...
KRACK-ATCH!
...TO PUT THE ONES YOU LOVE ABOVE THE GROUP.
OOPH!
W-WHAT'S H-H-HAPPENING? STEALING MY P-P-POWER?
POWER IS NEVER GIVEN FREELY. POWER MUST BE TAKEN!

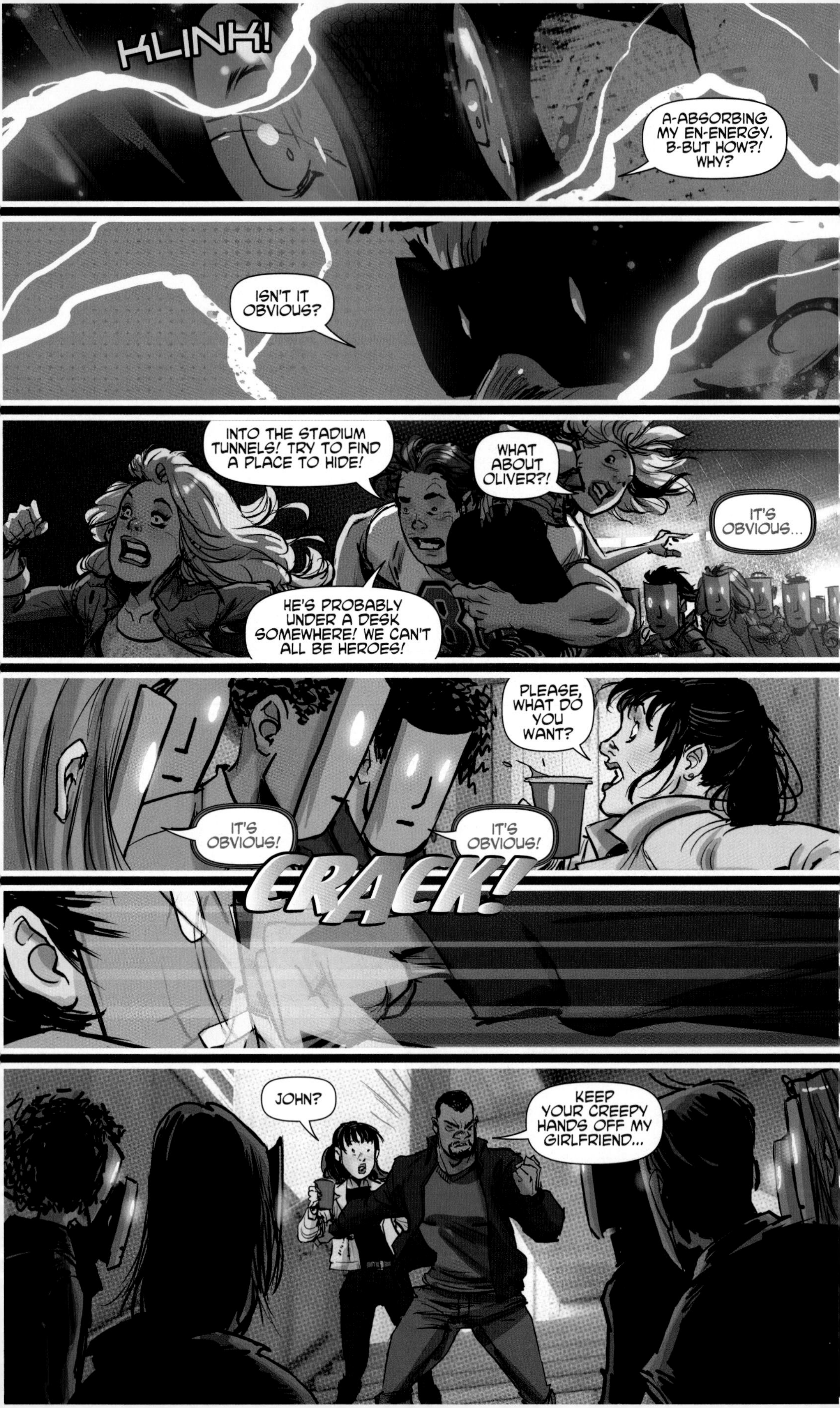
KLINK!
A-ABSORBING MY EN-ENERGY. B-BUT HOW?! WHY?
ISN'T IT OBVIOUS?
INTO THE STADIUM TUNNELS! TRY TO FIND A PLACE TO HIDE!
WHAT ABOUT OLIVER?!
HE'S PROBABLY UNDER A DESK SOMEWHERE! WE CAN'T ALL BE HEROES!
IT'S OBVIOUS...
PLEASE, WHAT DO YOU WANT?
IT'S OBVIOUS!
IT'S OBVIOUS!
CRACK!
JOHN?
KEEP YOUR CREEPY HANDS OFF MY GIRLFRIEND...

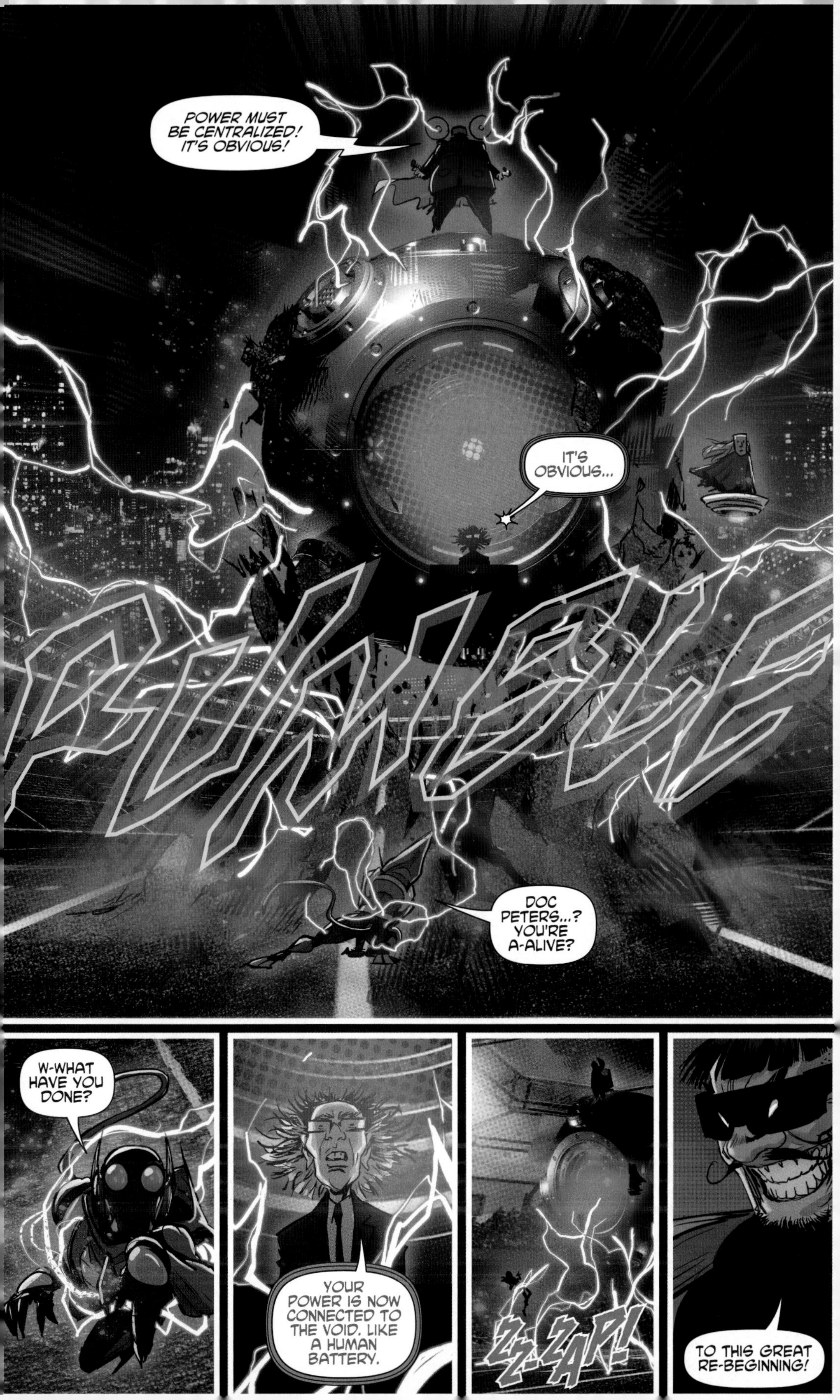
POWER MUST BE CENTRALIZED! IT'S OBVIOUS!
IT'S OBVIOUS...
DOC PETERS...? YOU'RE A-ALIVE?
W-WHAT HAVE YOU DONE?
YOUR POWER IS NOW CONNECTED TO THE VOID. LIKE A HUMAN BATTERY.
ZZZAP!
TO THIS GREAT RE-BEGINNING!

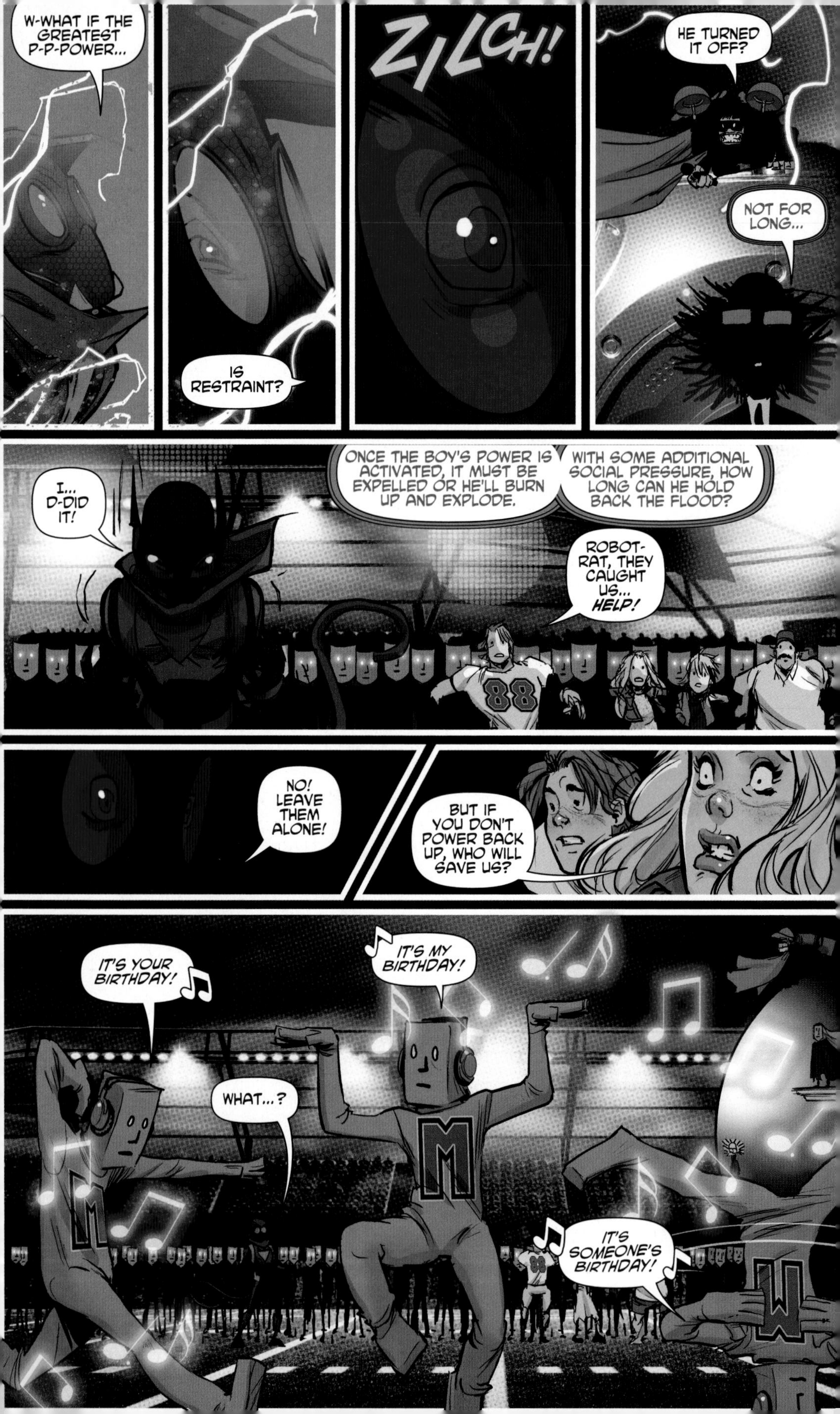
W-WHAT IF THE GREATEST P-P-POWER...
IS RESTRAINT?
ZILCH!
HE TURNED IT OFF?
NOT FOR LONG...
I... D-DID IT!
ONCE THE BOY'S POWER IS ACTIVATED, IT MUST BE EXPELLED OR HE'LL BURN UP AND EXPLODE.
WITH SOME ADDITIONAL SOCIAL PRESSURE, HOW LONG CAN HE HOLD BACK THE FLOOD?
ROBOT-RAT, THEY CAUGHT US... HELP!
NO! LEAVE THEM ALONE!
BUT IF YOU DON'T POWER BACK UP, WHO WILL SAVE US?
IT'S YOUR BIRTHDAY!
IT'S MY BIRTHDAY!
WHAT...?
IT'S SOMEONE'S BIRTHDAY!

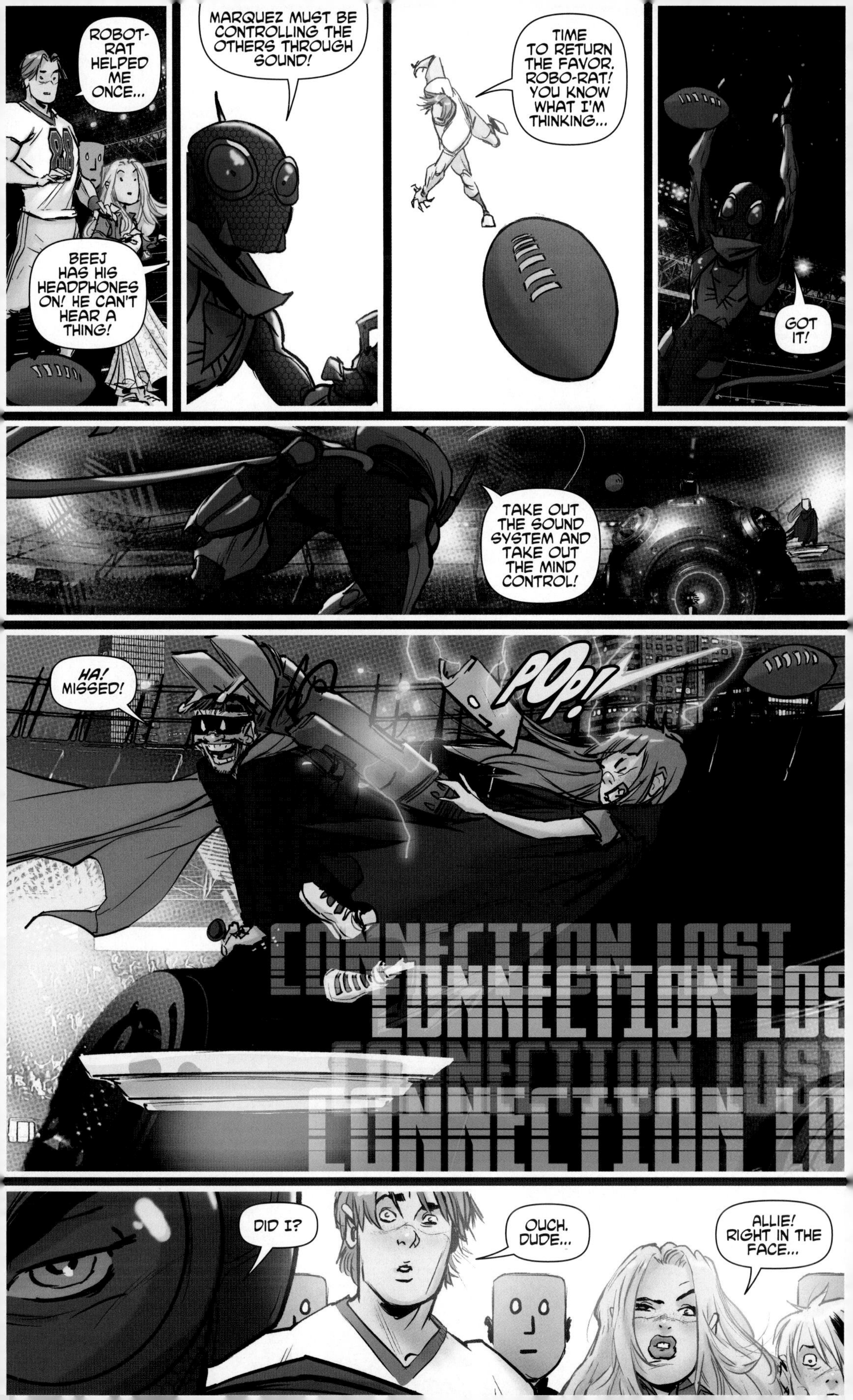
ROBOT-RAT HELPED ME ONCE...
BEEJ HAS HIS HEADPHONES ON! HE CAN'T HEAR A THING!
MARQUEZ MUST BE CONTROLLING THE OTHERS THROUGH SOUND!
TIME TO RETURN THE FAVOR. ROBO-RAT! YOU KNOW WHAT I'M THINKING...
GOT IT!
TAKE OUT THE SOUND SYSTEM AND TAKE OUT THE MIND CONTROL!
HA! MISSED!
POP!!
CONNECTION LOST
DID I?
OUCH. DUDE...
ALLIE! RIGHT IN THE FACE...

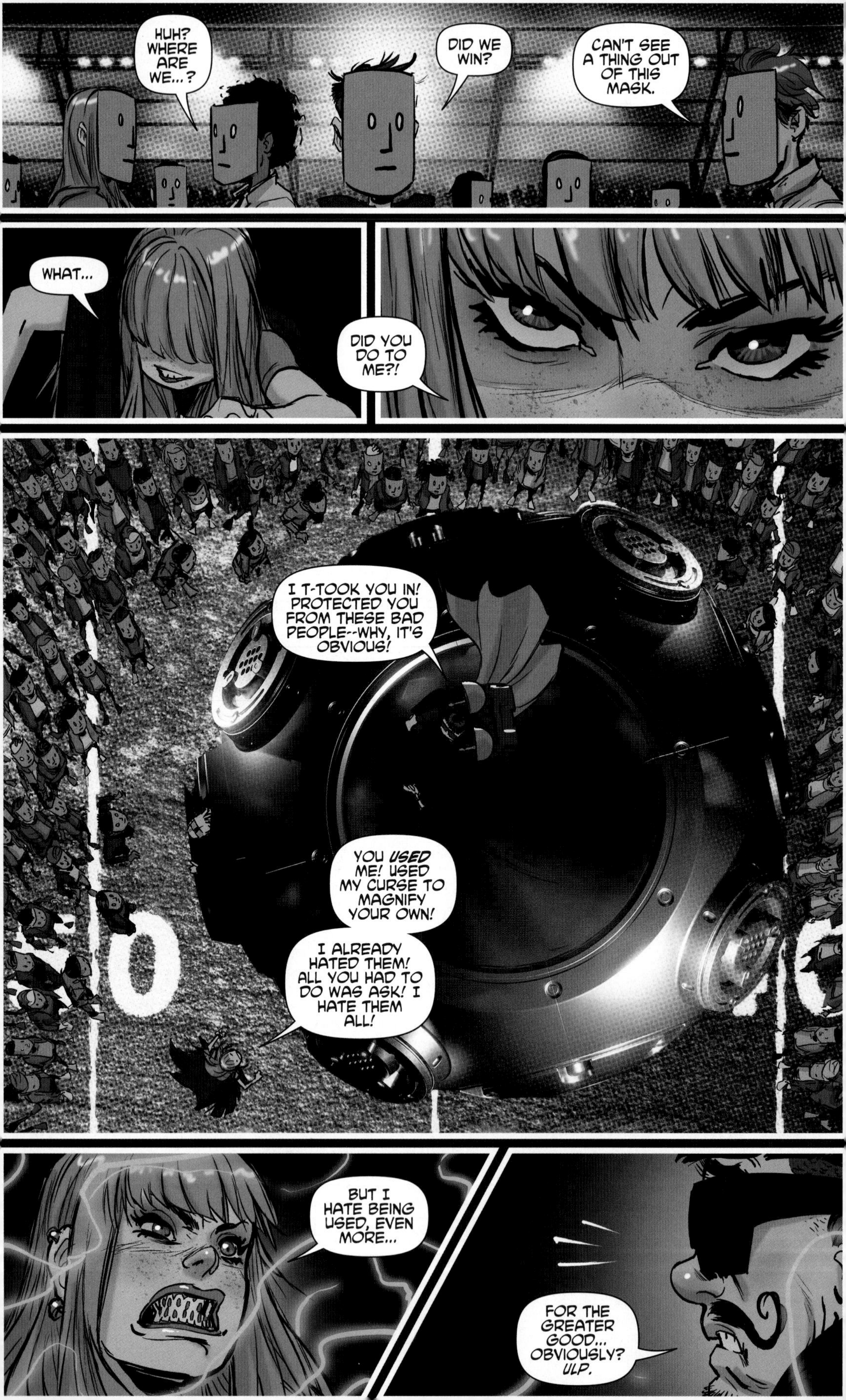
HUH? WHERE ARE WE...?
DID WE WIN?
CAN'T SEE A THING OUT OF THIS MASK.
WHAT...
DID YOU DO TO ME?!
I T-TOOK YOU IN! PROTECTED YOU FROM THESE BAD PEOPLE--WHY, IT'S OBVIOUS!
YOU *USED* ME! USED MY CURSE TO MAGNIFY YOUR OWN!
I ALREADY HATED THEM! ALL YOU HAD TO DO WAS ASK! I HATE THEM ALL!
BUT I HATE BEING USED, EVEN MORE...
FOR THE GREATER GOOD... OBVIOUSLY? *ULP.*

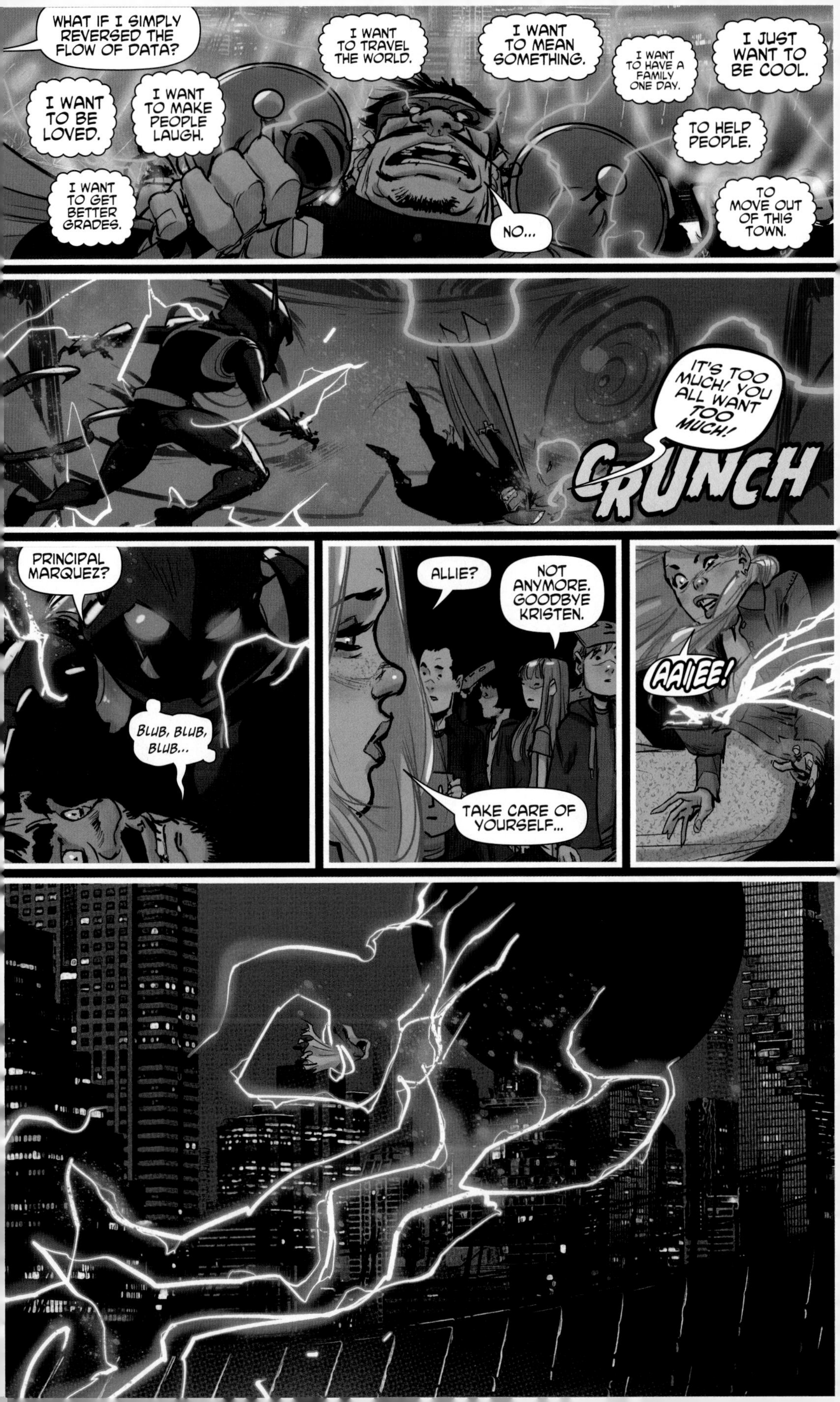
WHAT IF I SIMPLY REVERSED THE FLOW OF DATA?
I WANT TO TRAVEL THE WORLD.
I WANT TO MEAN SOMETHING.
I WANT TO HAVE A FAMILY ONE DAY.
I JUST WANT TO BE COOL.
I WANT TO BE LOVED.
I WANT TO MAKE PEOPLE LAUGH.
TO HELP PEOPLE.
I WANT TO GET BETTER GRADES.
NO...
TO MOVE OUT OF THIS TOWN.
IT'S TOO MUCH! YOU ALL WANT TOO MUCH!
CRUNCH
PRINCIPAL MARQUEZ?
BLUB, BLUB, BLUB...
ALLIE?
NOT ANYMORE. GOODBYE KRISTEN.
TAKE CARE OF YOURSELF...
AAIIEE!

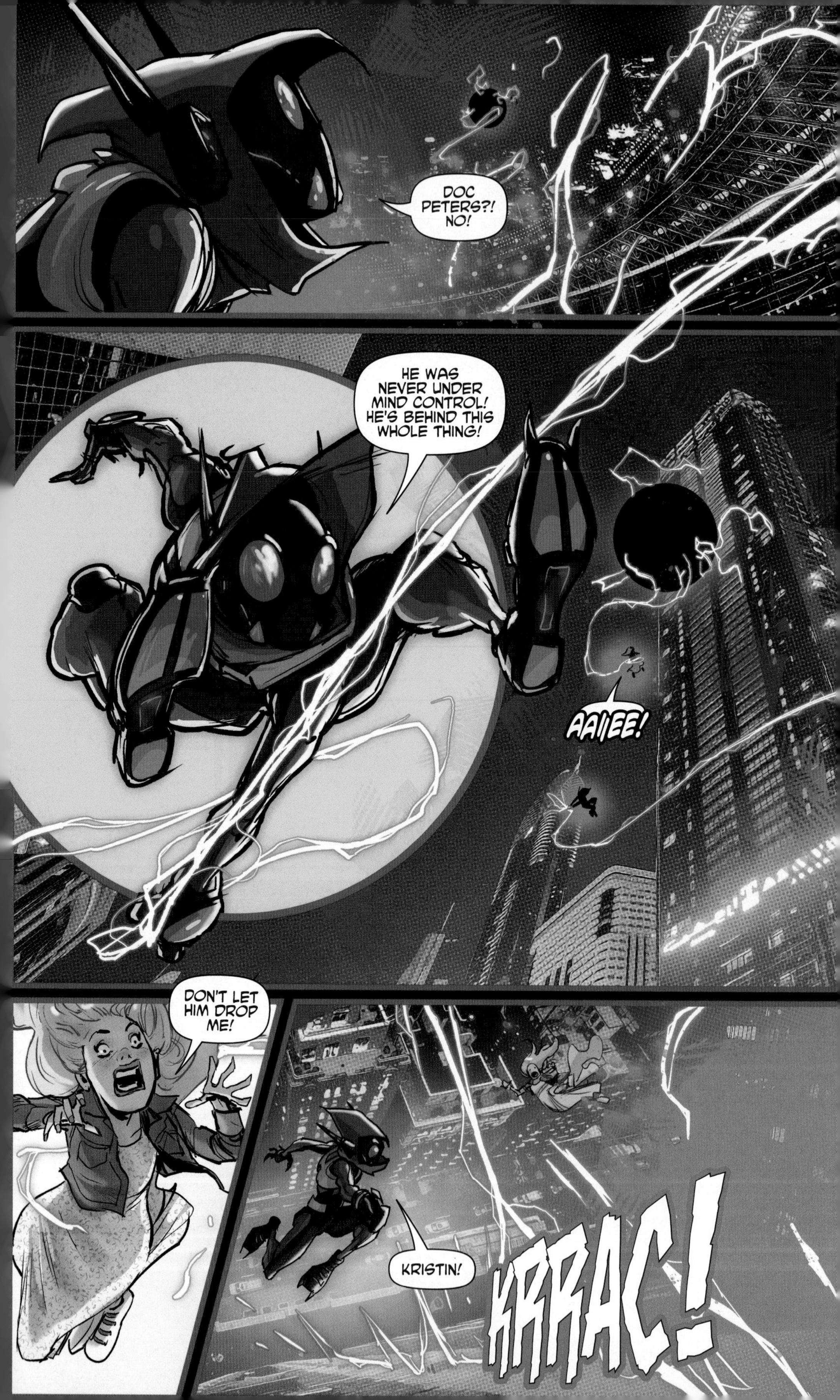
DOC PETERS?! NO!
HE WAS NEVER UNDER MIND CONTROL! HE'S BEHIND THIS WHOLE THING!
AAIIEE!
DON'T LET HIM DROP ME!
KRISTIN!
KRRAC!

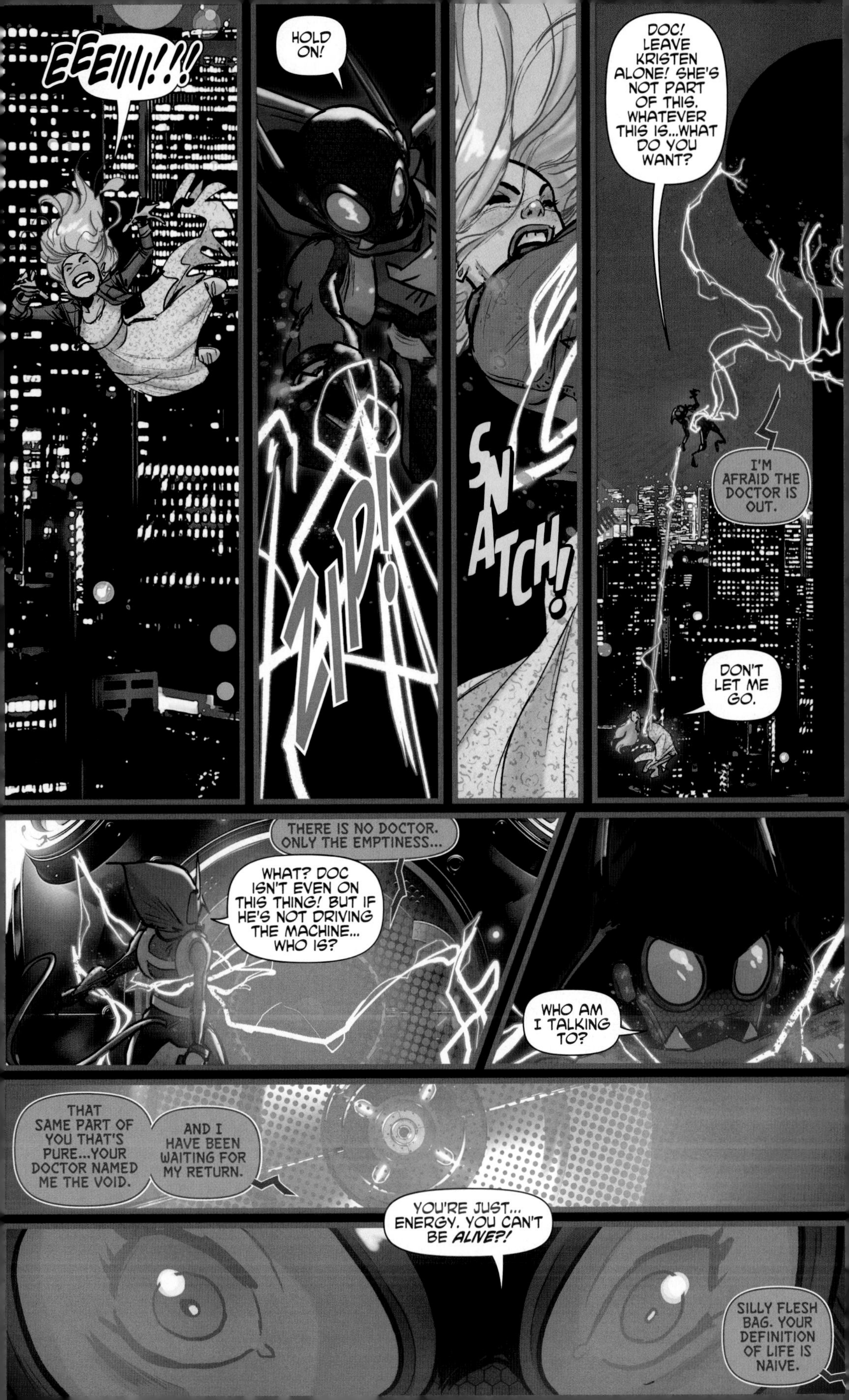
EEEIIIII!!?!
HOLD ON!
ZIIIP!
SNATCH!
DOC! LEAVE KRISTEN ALONE! SHE'S NOT PART OF THIS. WHATEVER THIS IS...WHAT DO YOU WANT?
I'M AFRAID THE DOCTOR IS OUT.
DON'T LET ME GO.
THERE IS NO DOCTOR. ONLY THE EMPTINESS...
WHAT? DOC ISN'T EVEN ON THIS THING! BUT IF HE'S NOT DRIVING THE MACHINE... WHO IS?
WHO AM I TALKING TO?
THAT SAME PART OF YOU THAT'S PURE...YOUR DOCTOR NAMED ME THE VOID.
AND I HAVE BEEN WAITING FOR MY RETURN.
YOU'RE JUST... ENERGY. YOU CAN'T BE *ALIVE?!*
SILLY FLESH BAG. YOUR DEFINITION OF LIFE IS NAIVE.

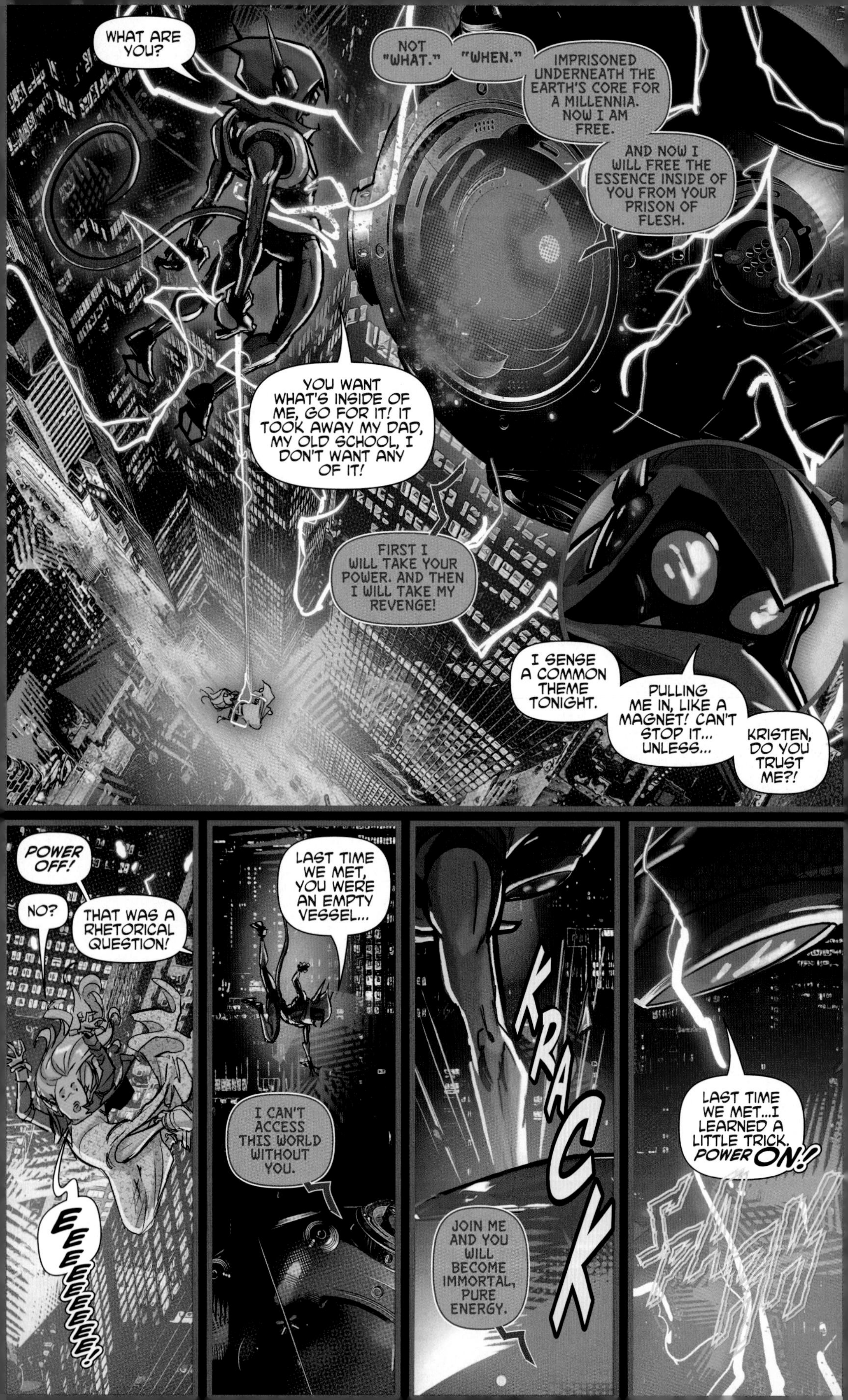
WHAT ARE YOU?
NOT "WHAT."
"WHEN."
IMPRISONED UNDERNEATH THE EARTH'S CORE FOR A MILLENNIA. NOW I AM FREE.
AND NOW I WILL FREE THE ESSENCE INSIDE OF YOU FROM YOUR PRISON OF FLESH.
YOU WANT WHAT'S INSIDE OF ME, GO FOR IT! IT TOOK AWAY MY DAD, MY OLD SCHOOL, I DON'T WANT ANY OF IT!
FIRST I WILL TAKE YOUR POWER. AND THEN I WILL TAKE MY REVENGE!
I SENSE A COMMON THEME TONIGHT.
PULLING ME IN, LIKE A MAGNET! CAN'T STOP IT... UNLESS...
KRISTEN, DO YOU TRUST ME?!
POWER OFF!
NO?
THAT WAS A RHETORICAL QUESTION!
EEEEEEEEE!
LAST TIME WE MET, YOU WERE AN EMPTY VESSEL...
I CAN'T ACCESS THIS WORLD WITHOUT YOU.
KRACK
JOIN ME AND YOU WILL BECOME IMMORTAL, PURE ENERGY.
LAST TIME WE MET...I LEARNED A LITTLE TRICK. POWER ON!

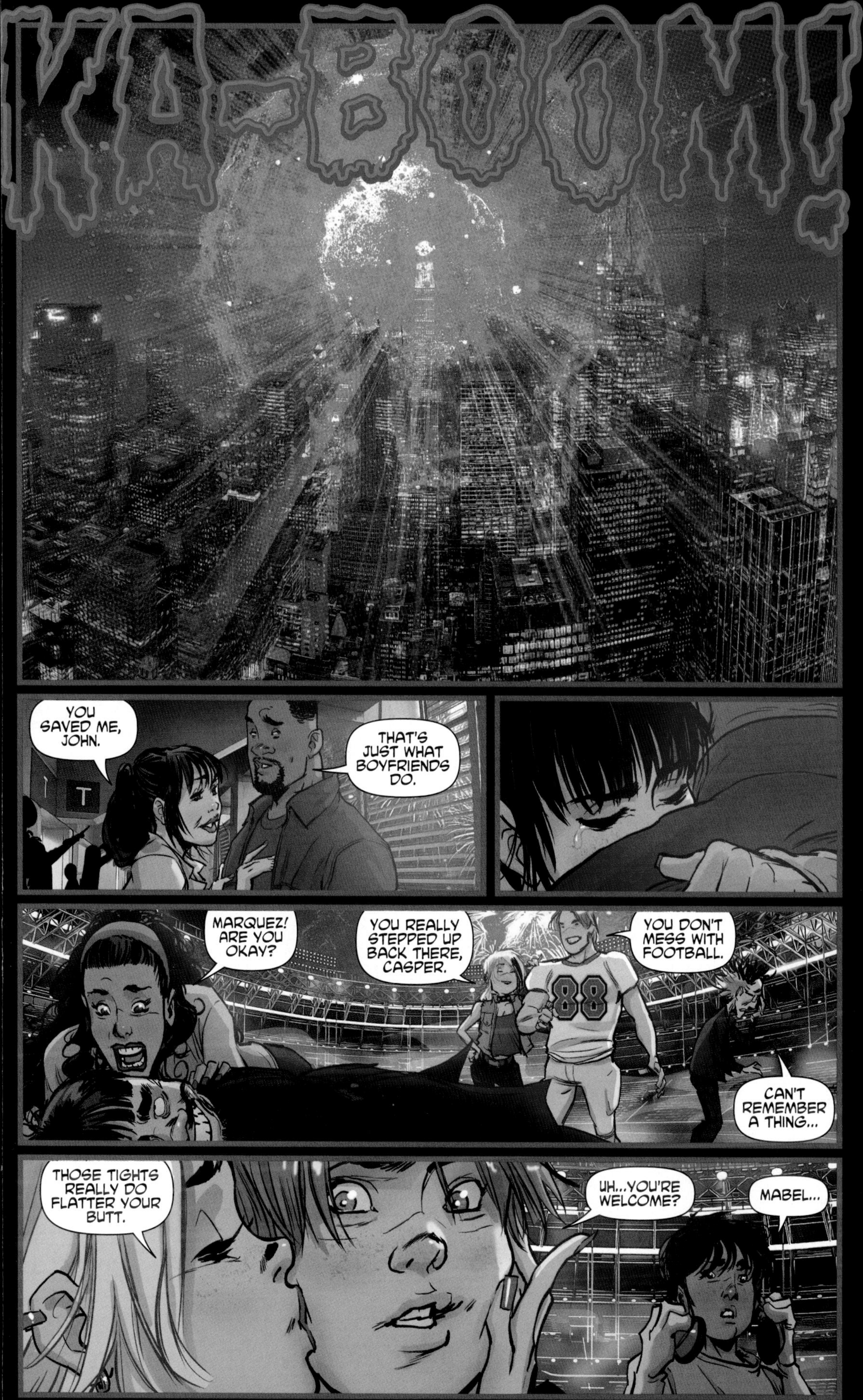
KA-BOOM!
YOU SAVED ME, JOHN.
THAT'S JUST WHAT BOYFRIENDS DO.
MARQUEZ! ARE YOU OKAY?
YOU REALLY STEPPED UP BACK THERE, CASPER.
YOU DON'T MESS WITH FOOTBALL.
CAN'T REMEMBER A THING...
THOSE TIGHTS REALLY DO FLATTER YOUR BUTT.
UH...YOU'RE WELCOME?
MABEL...

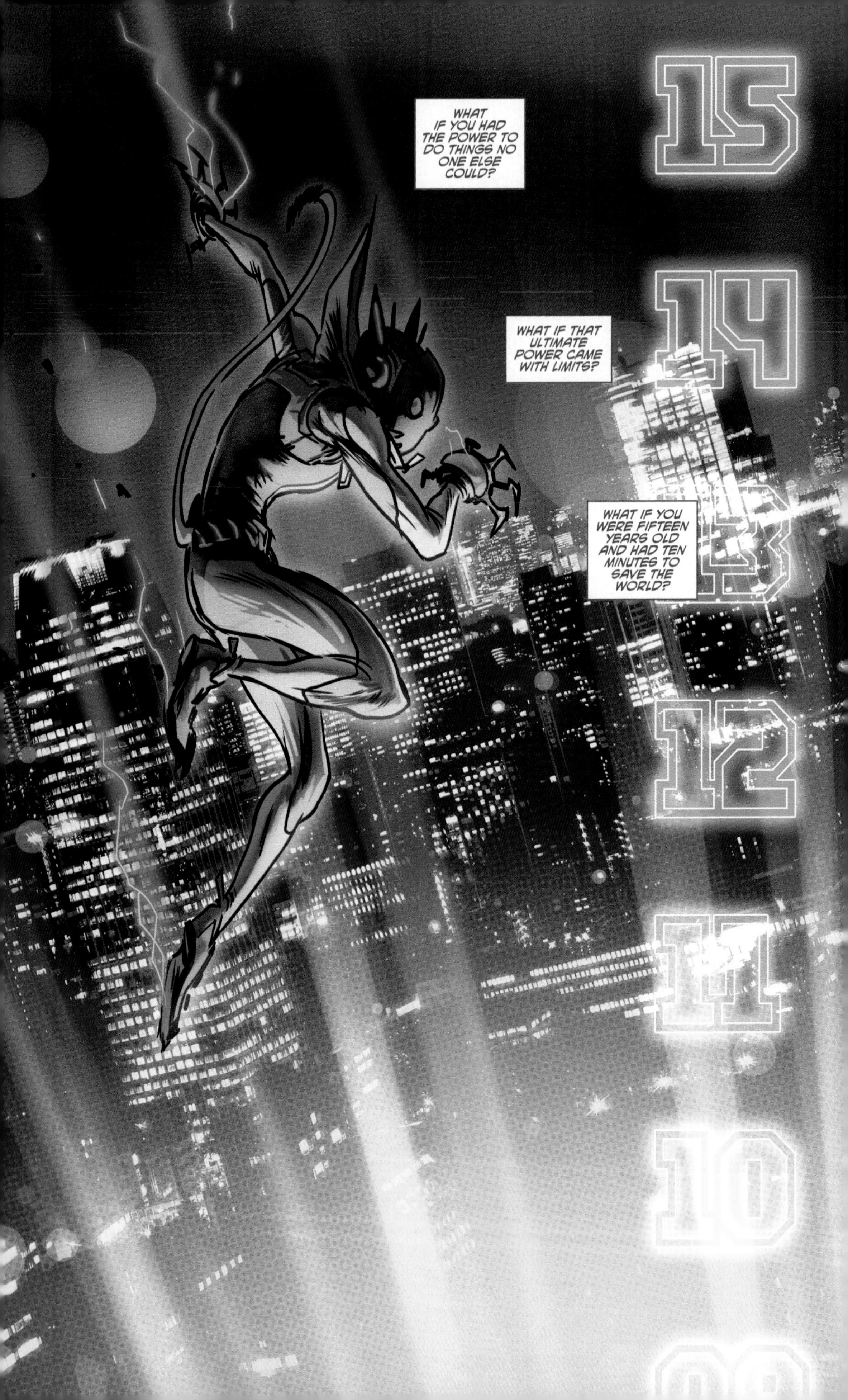
WHAT IF YOU HAD THE POWER TO DO THINGS NO ONE ELSE COULD?
WHAT IF THAT ULTIMATE POWER CAME WITH LIMITS?
WHAT IF YOU WERE FIFTEEN YEARS OLD AND HAD TEN MINUTES TO SAVE THE WORLD?
15
14
13
12
11
10

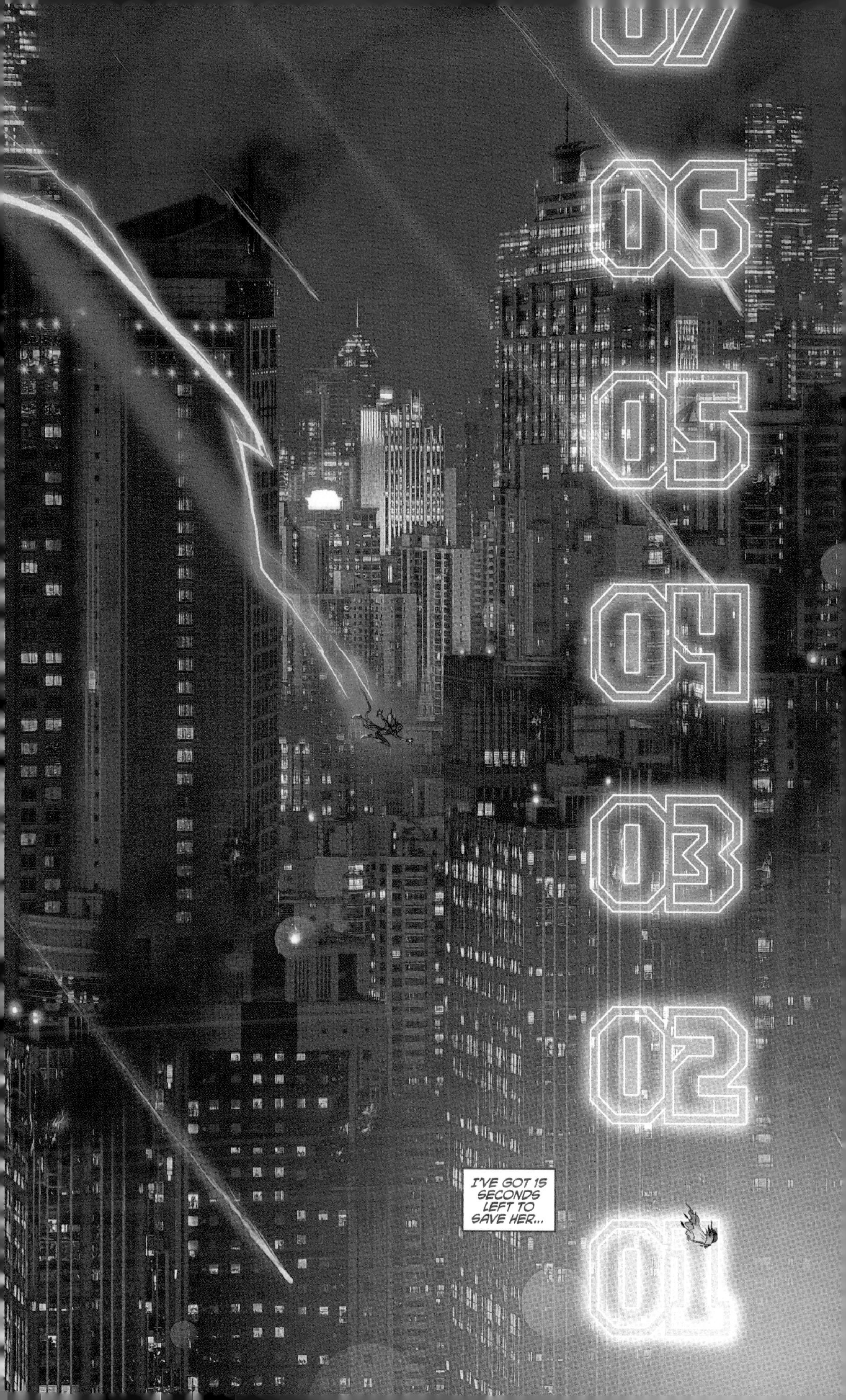
06
05
04
03
02
I'VE GOT 15 SECONDS LEFT TO SAVE HER...
01

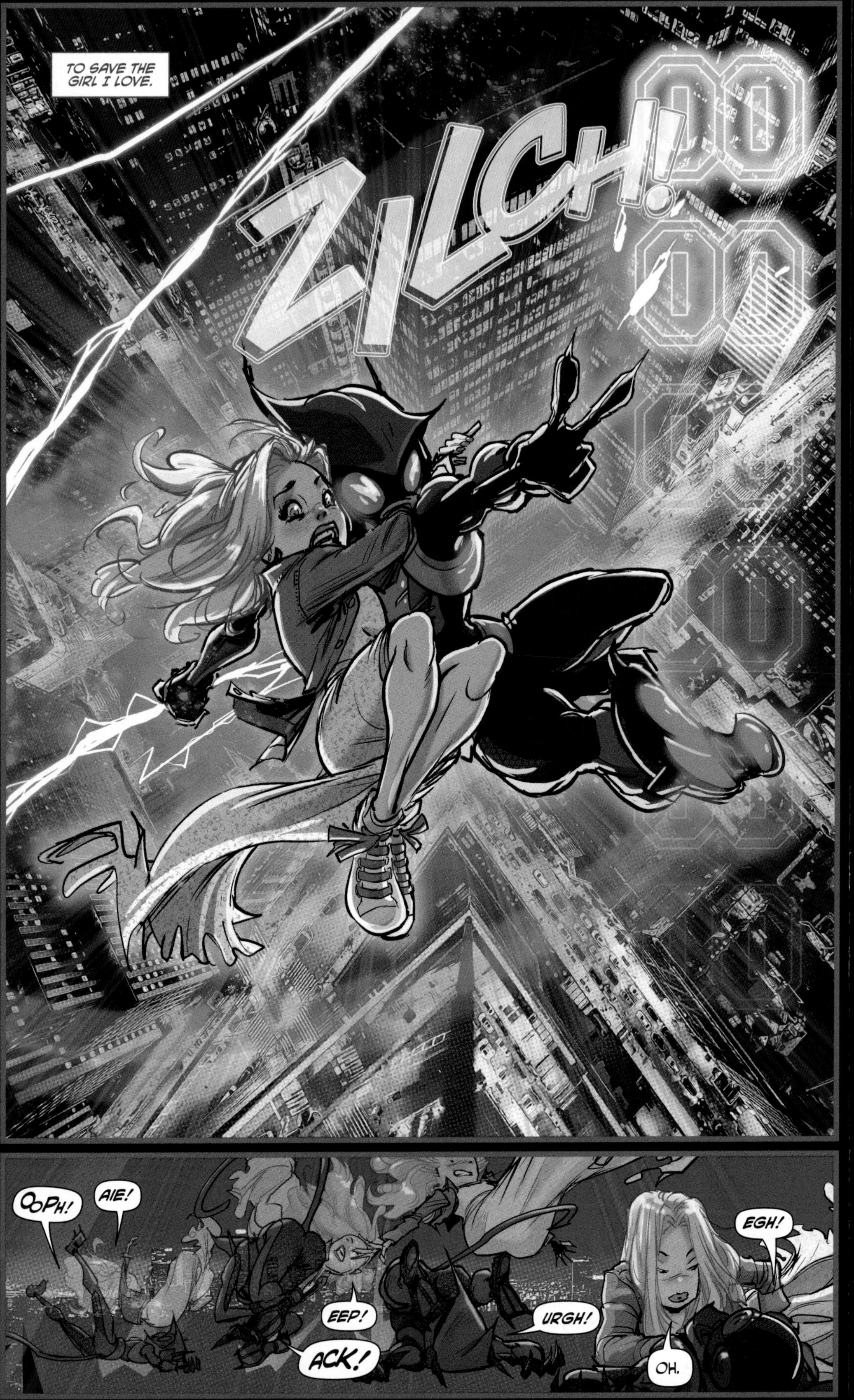
TO SAVE THE GIRL I LOVE.
ZILCH!
OOPH!
AIE!
EEP!
ACK!
URGH!
EGH!
OH.

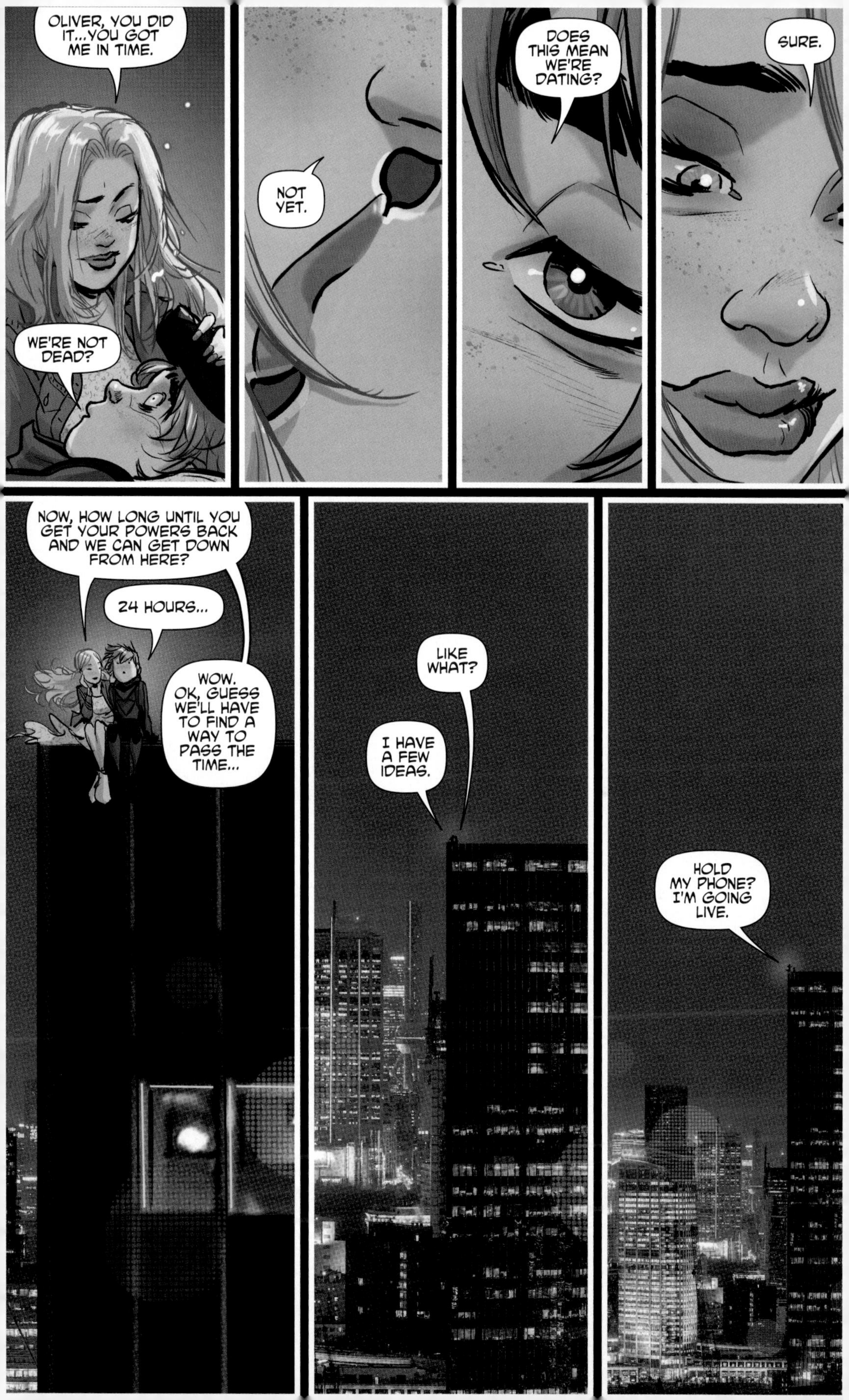
OLIVER, YOU DID IT...YOU GOT ME IN TIME.
WE'RE NOT DEAD?
NOT YET.
DOES THIS MEAN WE'RE DATING?
SURE.
NOW, HOW LONG UNTIL YOU GET YOUR POWERS BACK AND WE CAN GET DOWN FROM HERE?
24 HOURS...
WOW. OK, GUESS WE'LL HAVE TO FIND A WAY TO PASS THE TIME...
I HAVE A FEW IDEAS.
LIKE WHAT?
HOLD MY PHONE? I'M GOING LIVE.

THIS IS KRISTEN SMITH, COMING TO YOU LIVE FROM A ROOFTOP, HAVING CHASED A ROGUE AND DEADLY TECHNOLOGY EVENT TO THE DOWNTOWN CORE...

WHILE ATTENDING THE SEASON OPENER BETWEEN MAPLETON HIGH AND BADEN OMEN COLLEGIATE, E-RATIC MADE A SURPRISE APPEARANCE THAT I CAPTURED ON VIDEO BEFORE HE POWERED UP--

ERR--KRISTEN, E-RATIC WAS KIND OF POWERED UP ALREADY...

HE-- *WHAT?!*

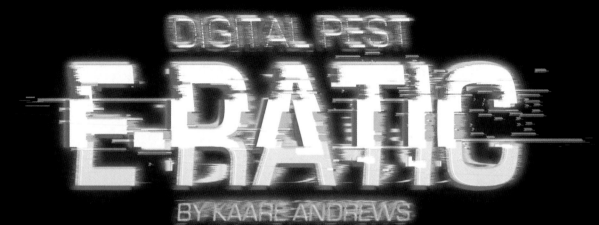

DIGITAL PEST

E-RATIC

BY KAARE ANDREWS

BRIAN REBER
Colorist

SAL CIPRIANO
Letterer

AXEL ALONSO
Chief Creative Officer

BILL JEMAS
CEO & Publisher

ARIANE BAYA
Accounting Associate

JACKIE LIU
Digital Marketing Manager

CHRIS BURNS
Production Editor

BOSUNG KIM
Graphic Designer

THEA CHEUK
Assistant Editor

ALLISON MASE
Project Manager

STAN CHOU
Art Director & Logo Designer

DULCE MONTOYA
Associate Editor

MICHAEL COAST
Senior Editor

KEVIN PARK
Associate General Counsel

FRANK FOCHETTA
Senior Consultant, Sales & Distribution

HARRY SWEEZEY
Finance Associate

WILLIAM GRAVES
Managing Editor

LISA Y. WU
Marketing Manager

HE CAME INTO THE STADIUM FULLY POWERED UP. HE, ER...MUST HAVE KNOWN SOMETHING-- SO YOUR VIDEO WILL HAVE BEEN CORRUPTED.

YOU DID THIS ON PURPOSE! AS SOON AS YOU GET ME OFF OF THIS ROOFTOP, WE *ARE OVER!*

IN 24 HOURS FROM NOW.

EXACTLY!

SO, WHAT ARE WE GOING TO DO UNTIL THEN--

OLIVER LEIF, *I HATE YOU!*

END OF VOLUME ONE

A LETTER FROM THE CREATOR OF

TEN MINUTES

Ten minutes isn't anything…until it's all you have left.

What if you found out for certain, absolutely certain, that the world was ending in ten minutes? What would you do with the time you had left?

All the shrieking from the twenty-four-hour news cycle would disappear. Foreign wars would stop mattering. The Facebook posts of that crazy cousin of yours could just be ignored. But what would you DO?

Would you spend those final moments of life policing the conduct of everyone around you? Making sure we faced destiny as one singular, agreed-upon mass of shared ideals? That we all used the agreed-upon words as we said goodbye?

Would you finally tell that girl in class how you felt about her? Risk the sting of rejection as the last thing you feel, to maybe face destiny in the arms of another?

Or would you call that family member that betrayed you, to make amends with the people you love? To finally forgive them for that thing they won't admit to doing?

What's the right choice? What would be the most fulfilling? What would make it okay?

The answer would be different for everyone, because we're all so different from each other. Many of us would make the wrong decision. Some of us would curl up in a ball and refuse to decide anything. Some would have decisions made on our behalf, to us by others.

A last moment of revenge…

A poem…

A phone call to an old friend…

A retreat into some mind-numbing substance…

A final Barbie playtime with your little sister…

A hug with your parents.

But some of us…a very small portion of us…would take those ten minutes to face the nexus of it all…to spend every last moment of energy facing whatever horrible thing had created the circumstance. To spend our last ten minutes…giving everyone else the rest of their lives. To save the world.

What would you do?

- Kaare Andrews

Issue 1 Exclusive Variant Covers by **Jonboy Meyers** for **The 616 Comics**

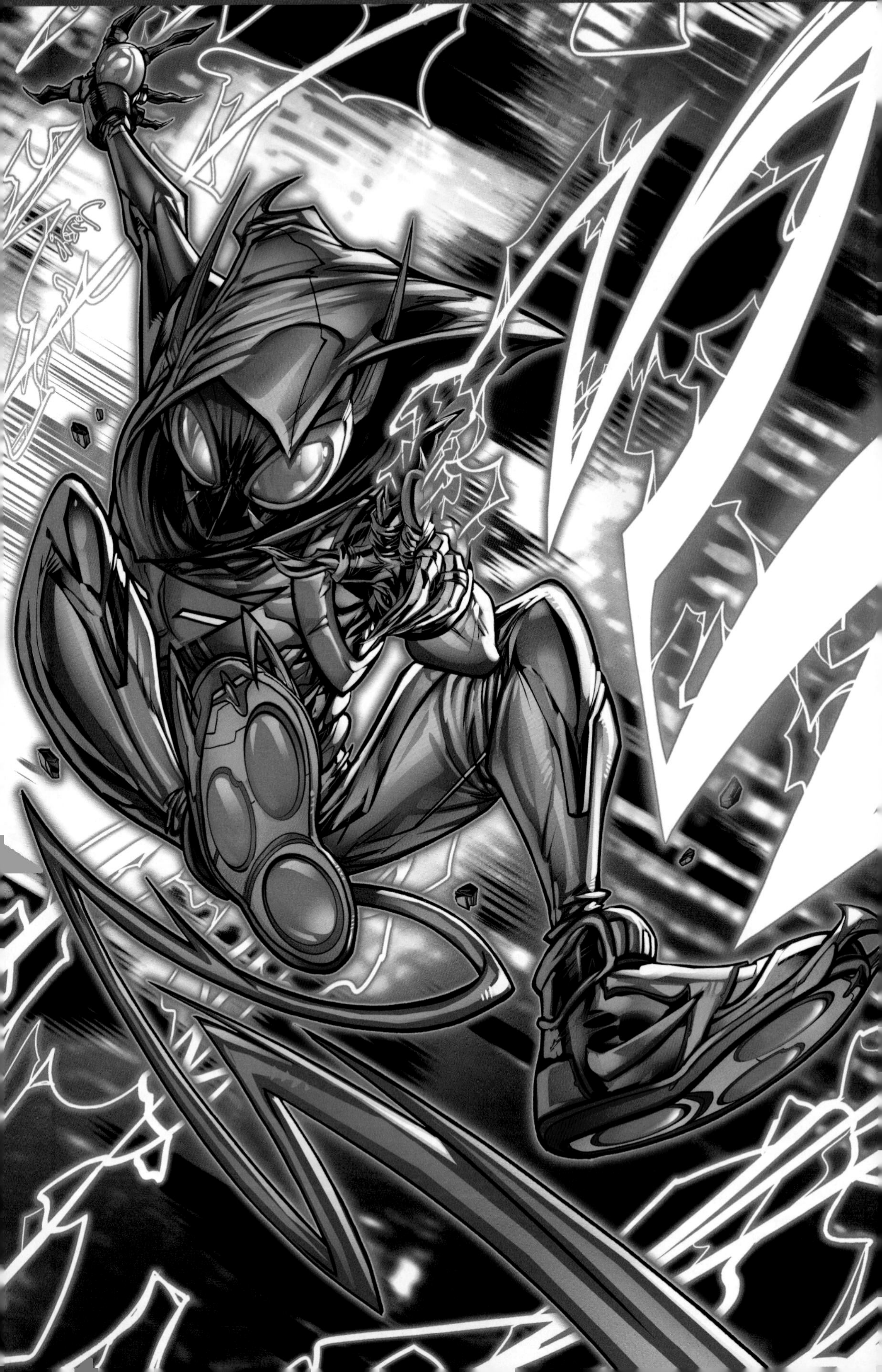

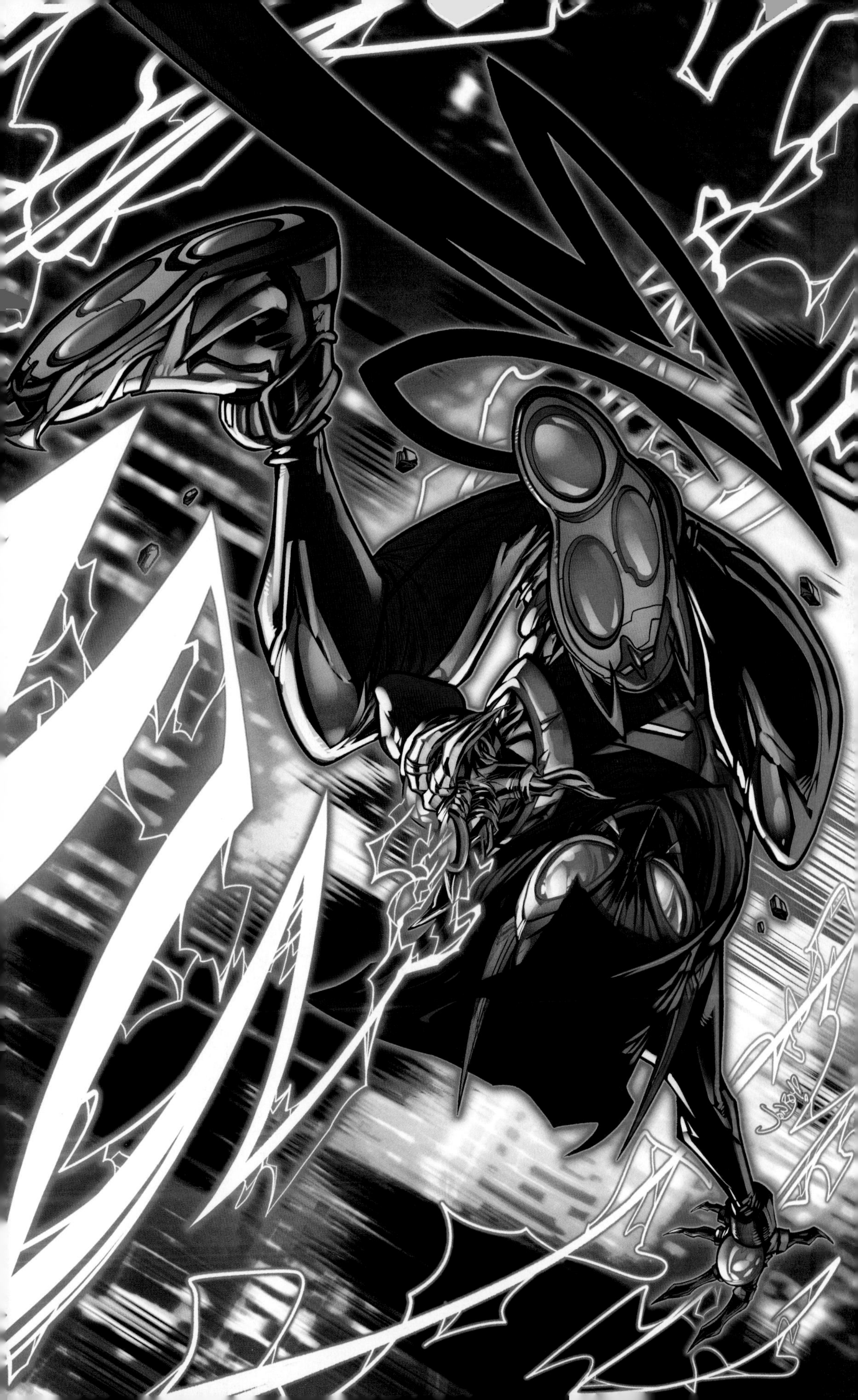

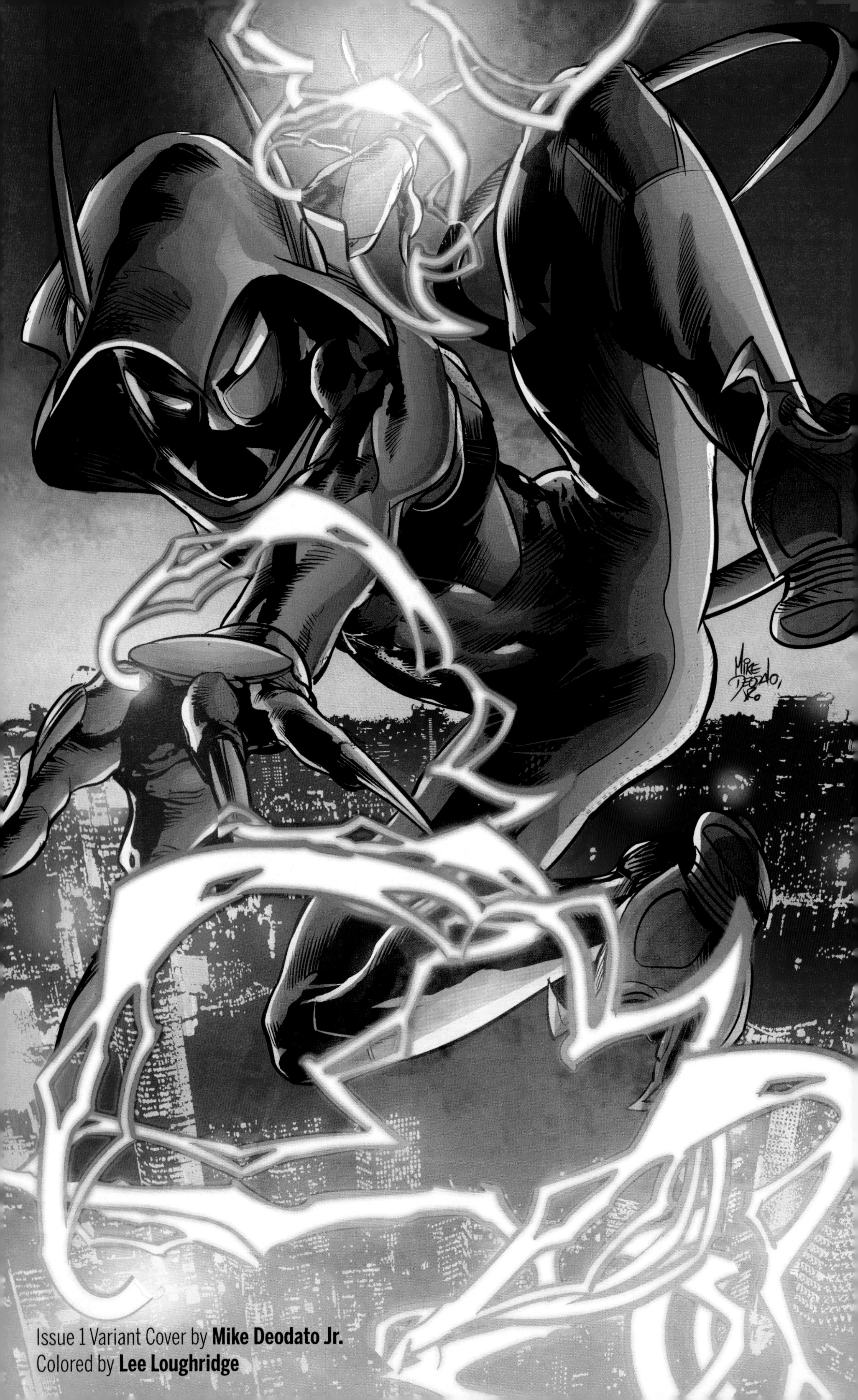

Issue 1 Variant Cover by **Mike Deodato Jr.**
Colored by **Lee Loughridge**

Original pitch email and concept sketch by **Kaare Andrews**

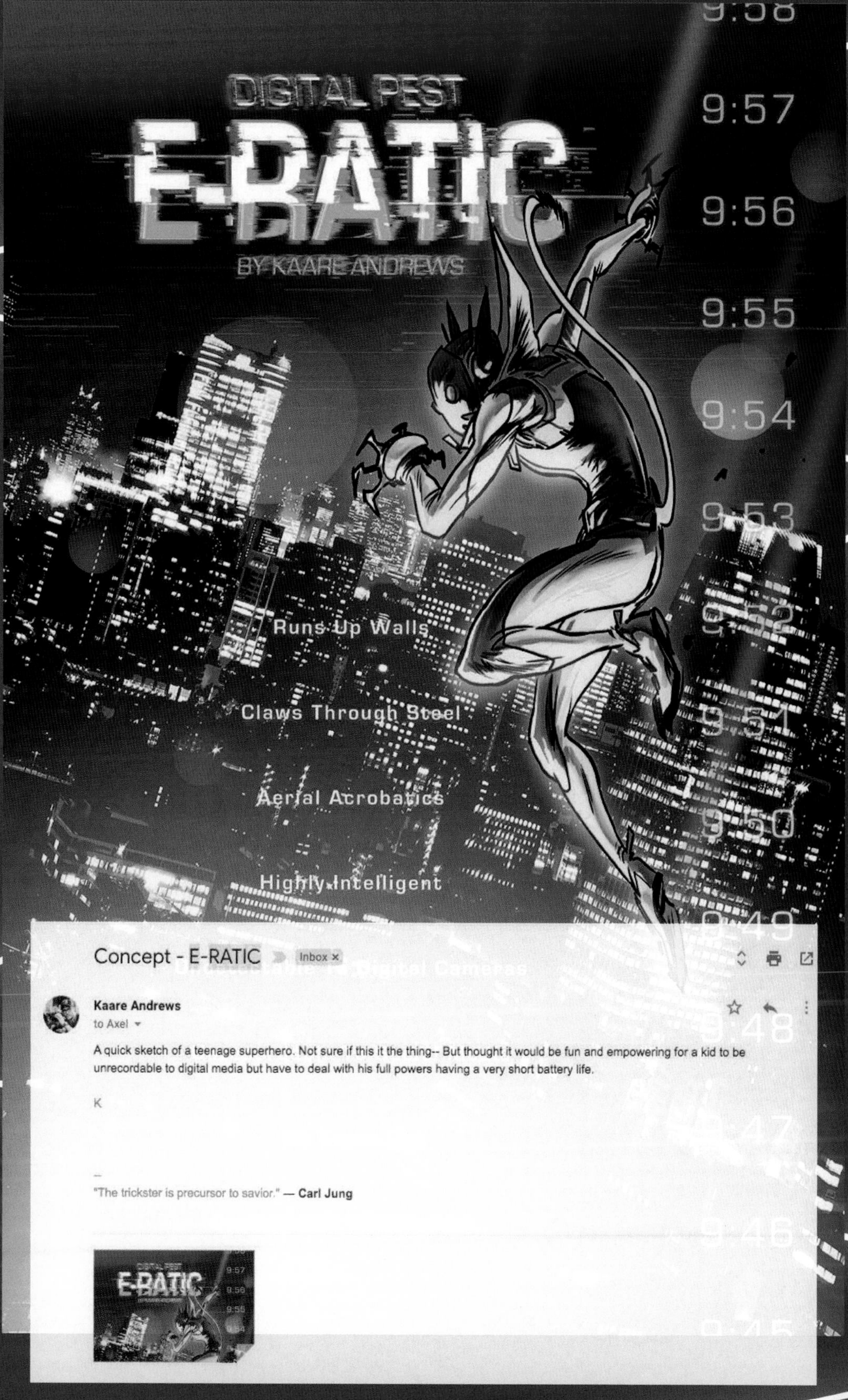

DIGITAL PEST
E-RATIC
BY KAARE ANDREWS
9:57
9:56
9:55
9:54
9:53
9:52
9:51
9:50
9:49
9:48
9:47
9:46
9:45
Runs Up Walls
Claws Through Steel
Aerial Acrobatics
Highly Intelligent

Concept - E-RATIC Inbox ×

Kaare Andrews
to Axel

A quick sketch of a teenage superhero. Not sure if this it the thing-- But thought it would be fun and empowering for a kid to be unrecordable to digital media but have to deal with his full powers having a very short battery life.

K

--
"The trickster is precursor to savior." — **Carl Jung**

Original Kaare Andrews thumbnails and dialogue for Issue 5

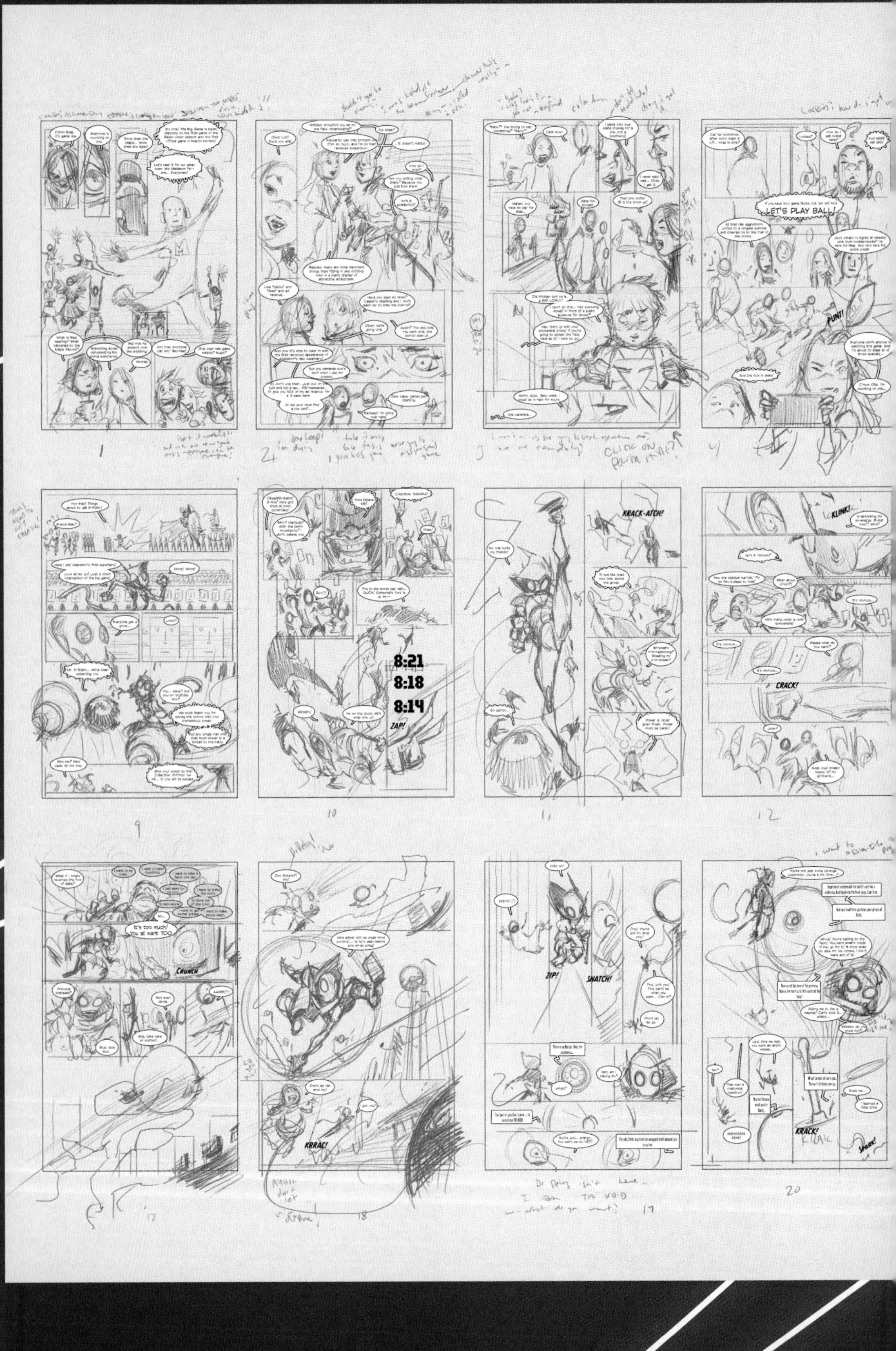

LET'S PLAY BALL!
PUNT!
KRACK-ATCH!
KLINK!
8:21
8:18
8:14
ZAP!
CRACK!
CRUNCH
ZIP!
SNATCH!
KRRAC!
KRACK!
SPARK!

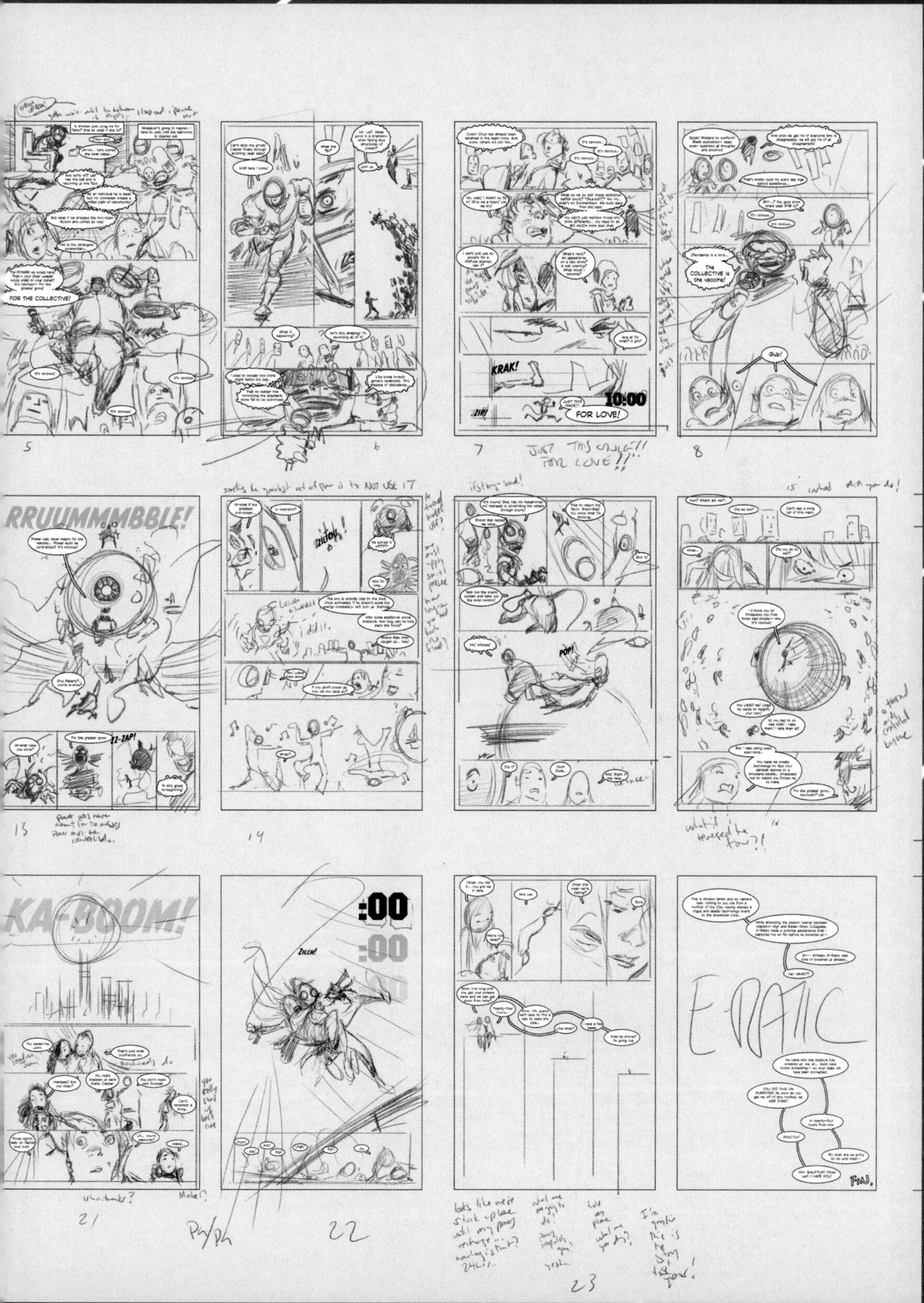

FOR THE COLLECTIVE!
The COLLECTIVE is the vaccine!
KRAK!
ZIP!
10:00
FOR LOVE!
RRUUMMMMBBLE!
ZZ-ZAP!
POP!
KA-BOOM!
:00
E-RATIC
FIN.

Early Kaare Andrews Concept Sketches for Oliver In and Out of Costume

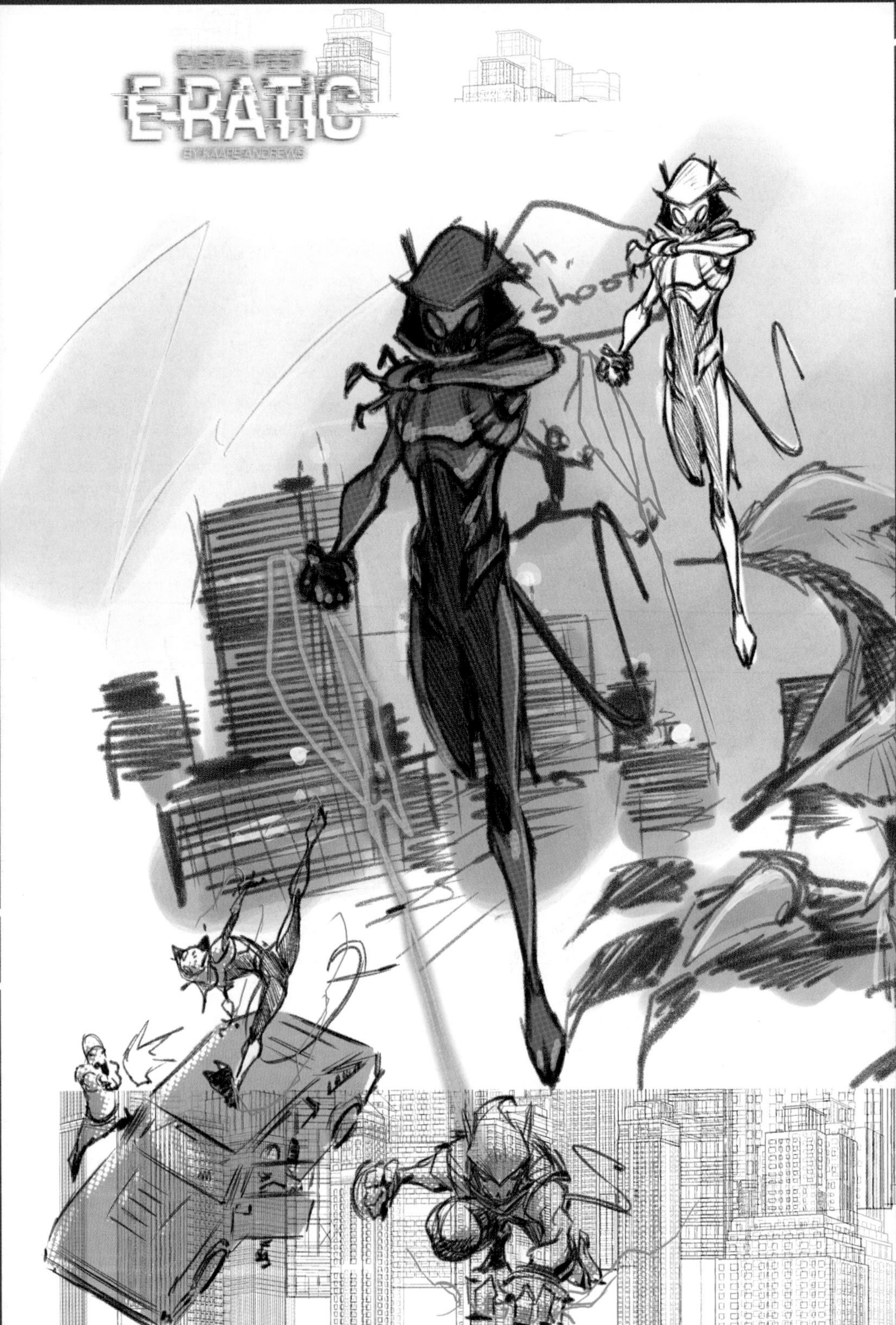
DIGITAL PEST
E-RATIC
BY KAARE ANDREWS
Oh, shoot

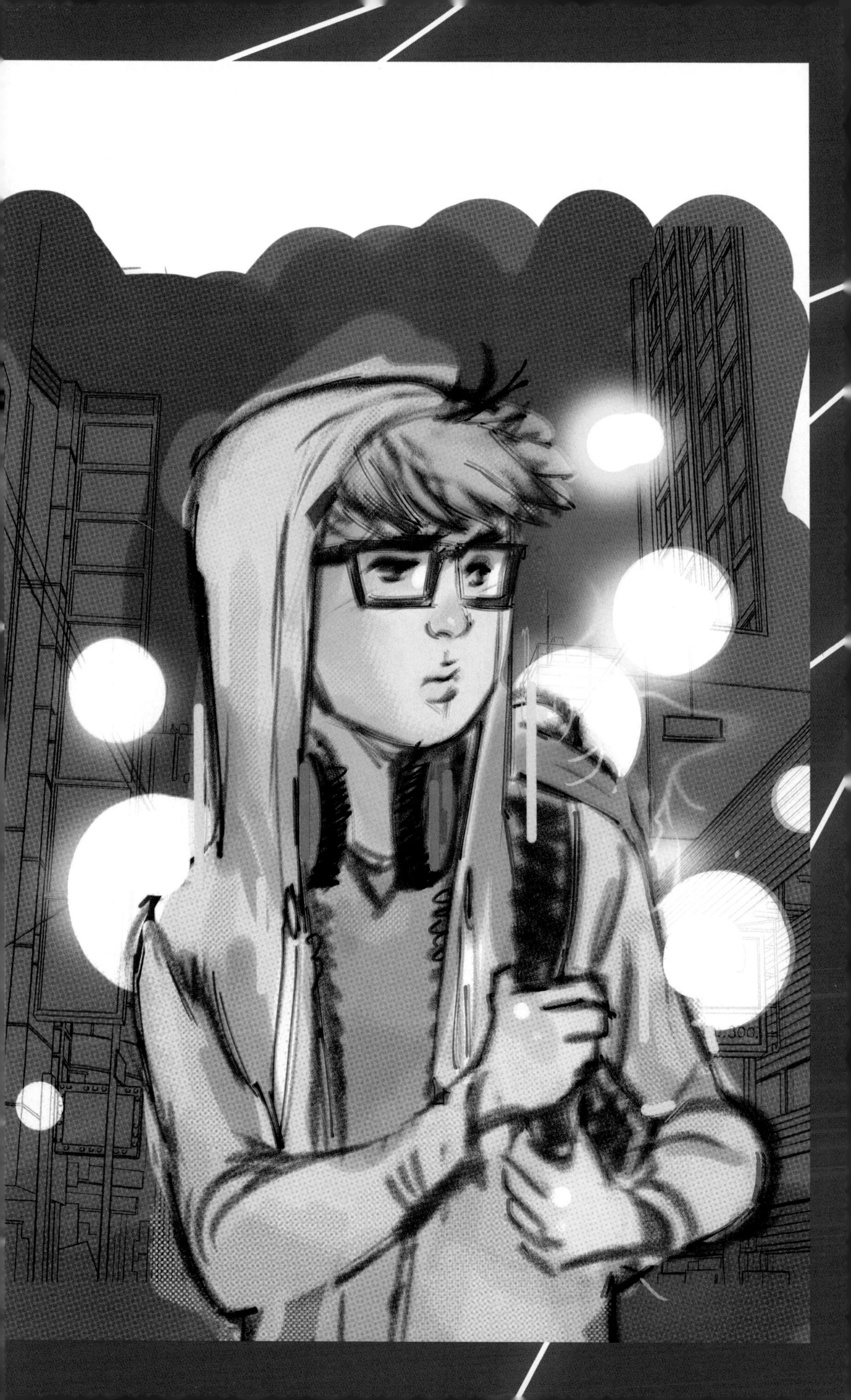

Early Kaare Andrews Concept Sketches for Oliver, E-Ratic Costume, and Mabel

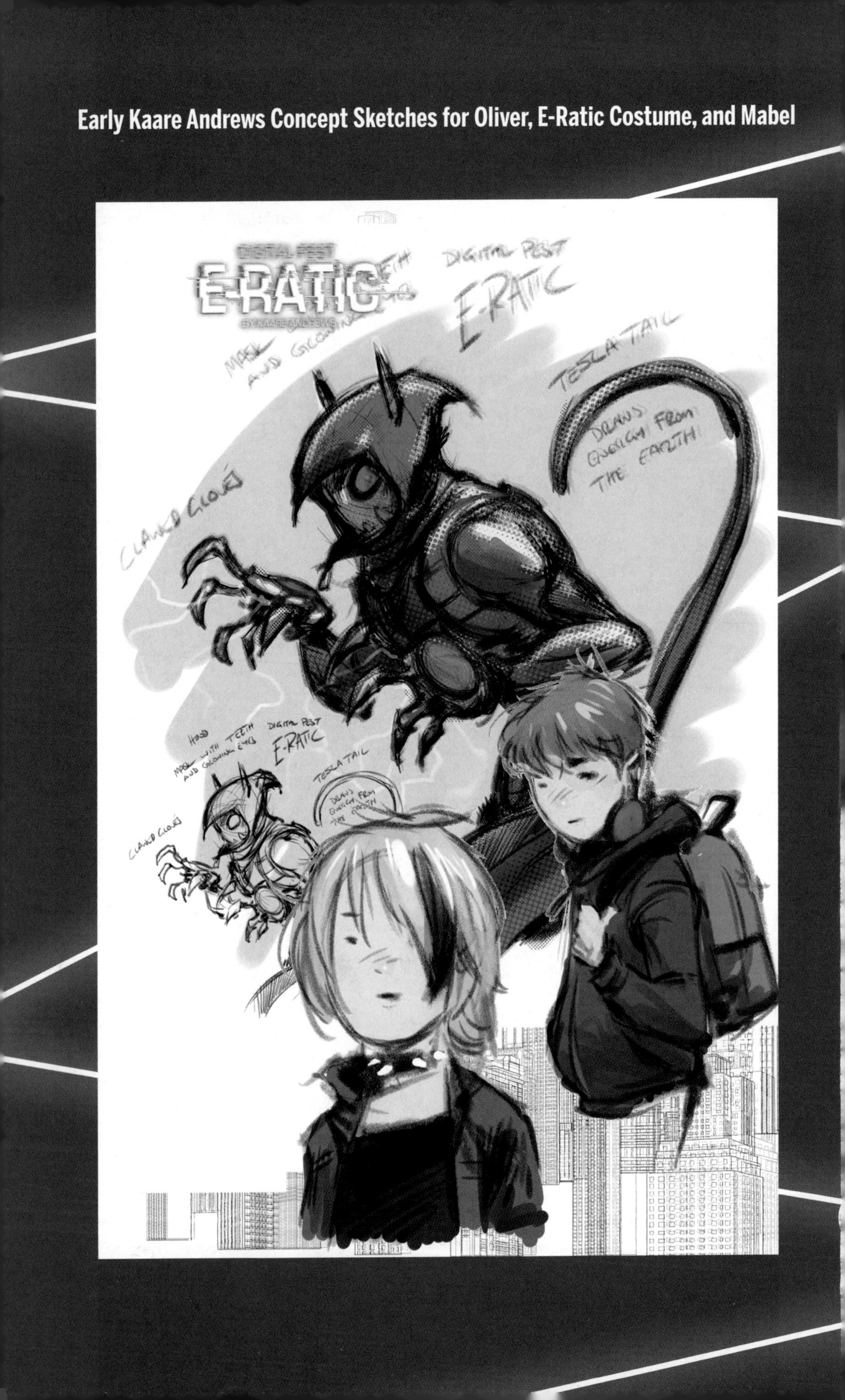
DIGITAL PEST
E-RATIC
BY KAARE ANDREWS
DIGITAL PEST
E-RATIC
TESLA TAIL
CLAWED GLOVES
HOOD
MASK WITH TEETH AND GLOWING EYES
DIGITAL PEST
E-RATIC
TESLA TAIL
CLAWED GLOVES